KU-760-946

EXPOSURE

Also by Evelyn Anthony

ALBATROSS
THE ASSASSIN
THE AVENUE OF THE DEAD
THE COMPANY OF SAINTS
THE DEFECTOR
THE GRAVE OF TRUTH
THE HOUSE OF VANDEKAR
THE LEGEND
MALASPIGA EXIT
NO ENEMY BUT TIME
THE OCCUPYING POWER
THE PERSIAN RANSOM
THE TAMARIND SEED
THE POELLENBERG INHERITANCE
THE RENDEZVOUS
THE RETURN
THE SILVER FALCON
VOICES ON THE WIND
THE SCARLET THREAD
THE RELIC
THE DOLL'S HOUSE

EVELYN ANTHONY

EXPOSURE

BANTAM PRESS

LONDON · NEW YORK · TORONTO · SYDNEY · AUCKLAND

Exposure is a work of fiction: names, characters, places and incidents either are the product of the author's imagination or are used entirely fictitiously. Any resemblance to actual persons, living or dead, is purely coincidental.

TRANSWORLD PUBLISHERS LTD
61-63 Uxbridge Road, London W5 5SA

TRANSWORLD PUBLISHERS (AUSTRALIA) PTY LTD
15-25 Helles Avenue, Moorebank, NSW 2170

TRANSWORLD PUBLISHERS (NZ) LTD
3 William Pickering Drive,
Albany, Auckland

Published 1993 by Bantam Press
a division of Transworld Publishers Ltd
Copyright ©Anthony Enterprises Ltd 1993

The right of Evelyn Anthony to be identified
as the author of this work has been asserted in accordance
with sections 77 and 78 of the Copyright Designs and Patents
Act 1988.

A catalogue record for this book is available from the British Library

ISBN 0593 024176

This book is sold subject to the
Standard Conditions of Sale of Net Books
and may not be re-sold in the UK below the net price
fixed by the publishers for the book.

All rights reserved. No part of this publication may
be reproduced, stored in a retrieval system, or
transmitted in any form or by any means,
electronic, mechanical, photocopying, recording,
or otherwise, without the prior permission of
the publishers.

Typeset in 11½/13pt Sabon by
Chippendale Type Ltd, Otley, West Yorkshire.
Printed in Great Britain by
Mackays of Chatham PLC, Chatham, Kent.

For my very dear friend
Annie Cleland,
with love

I

Julia Hamilton had dodged the private detectives watching her. She had booked her seat on the morning flight to Jersey using another name and travelled to Heathrow by Underground. Timing had been vital; she had to arrive at the terminal at the last minute, check in and speed through to the departure lounge.

Once airborne, she couldn't be followed. The flight was bumpy but Julia didn't mind. She was never airsick and loved flying.

The skies were grey and heavy with rain; as they began their descent, she leaned to look out of the window. Below, the sun was shining through a break in the bank of cloud. The land below was green and the sea dashed against the craggy shoreline, whipped by a sharp wind.

Janey had been waiting to meet her at the airport.

It had been so easy to manipulate her cousins; they were kind, straightforward people. When she said she needed a few days' holiday, they responded with a warm invitation. Julia refused to feel guilty; what she had come to find out was more important than a mild deception. Richard Watson was on that island, and she had come to find him. Richard Watson, she was certain, held some of the missing pieces in a jigsaw of betrayal and death.

It had been easy to gain the introduction. Her cousin Janey Peterson was thrilled to have such a celebrity to show off to her friends.

Julia Hamilton, the Fleet Street megastar, author of a famous book on the Rhys child murders, now head of the *Sunday Herald*'s much publicized new feature, 'Exposure'. Everyone, Janey had enthused, would be dying to meet her.

Including their friend, Richard Watson. A telephone call had secured an invitation to dinner. And there she was, sitting at Richard Watson's right hand, the guest of honour. There were six people round the table that night; Watson and herself, David and Janey Peterson, and a couple called Thomas. He had a booming voice and an avuncular manner. His wife was small, spoke just above a whisper, and was, as Julia had discovered during the pre-dinner drinks, quite waspish.

Julia knew that Richard Watson was observing her. It was the price of a high profile. She was used to paying it, able to deal with men who felt the need to be aggressive, and women jealous of her success. And her good looks. She had enough scars not to be conceited about either.

'We're all such fans of yours,' Bob Thomas said. 'You must tell us what "Exposure" has up its sleeves . . . Rumour has it you're going after a politician?'

Julia said gently,'You never want to listen to rumours. I'm afraid you'll have to wait till the paper comes out.' She gave him a charming smile. He grinned.

'Well, it was worth a try, anyway. So what brings you to our little island – hot on the trail of some juicy scandal?' Julia shook her head.

'Afraid not. I'm having a lovely pre-Christmas break staying with David and Janey. Just relaxing and being spoiled.' She smiled at them as she said it. They were so generous and hospitable. So genuinely proud of her.

So different from the ruthless, grasping denizens of her professional world. Fiona, the waspish little wife of Bob Thomas, leaned across and said to her, 'You wrote that book, didn't you – the one about the Rhys murders – a few years ago? I can't remember the name, but it was so much better than Truman Capote's book . . . I can't remember the name of that, either . . . '

Julia said, '*The Colour of Blood.*'

'That's right,' Thomas bellowed. 'I thought yours was wonderful, brilliant analysis.'

'Thank you,' Julia said. 'I'm glad you liked it.'

'Well,' his wife whispered, 'I wouldn't say I exactly liked it because of the subject. Horrifying, actually. Dreadful having to deal with child murders like that. Didn't it bother you? You must have been very young?'

Julia said, 'Yes, putting it mildly, it bothered me a great deal. I felt afterwards I had to write in depth about what happened and why. It was the only way I could get it out of my mind.'

Then her host, Richard Watson, joined in. 'I'll admit I didn't read your book,' he said. 'I found the reporting harrowing enough, even though it was brilliant. You've never followed up with another one?'

'No, I just haven't the time. My publishers have given up nagging me. I'm really a journalist, that's what I love doing. The book was a catharsis. I don't think I'll ever do another.'

'I envy you,' Bob Thomas said. 'I wish I could write a book. Couldn't put anything down to save my life.'

'I've talked enough about myself,' Julia said, turning to Richard Watson. 'Tell me about you. How did you come to live here?'

Not rich, her cousin Janey Peterson had said. But very comfortable. Retired from a senior job in industry. Widower, rather a self-contained man, although everybody liked him. He lived in a fantastic house, part of Jersey's past in its way, and he entertained beautifully. Julia was sure to like him. He'd often talked to them about her articles in the *Sunday Herald*. He said she was the main reason he bought the newspaper.

'Well,' he leaned back and looked at her. He was a good-looking man, with remarkably blue eyes that were warm and friendly. Also shrewd. 'My wife died and I took early retirement. We had no children, you see, and I'd nobody to worry about but myself. We'd spent holidays here and made friends, so I decided to live here. You didn't have to be a millionaire in those days, or I assure you I wouldn't have qualified. And what clinched it was seeing this house for sale.'

'Oh yes,' the small-voiced woman called Fiona Thomas whispered from her place on his left, leaning across him to make herself clear to Julia. 'Do tell Miss Hamilton all about that.'

Julia leaned towards her. 'Call me Julia,' she said. 'Please.'

Fiona smiled and sat back. 'Julia,' she murmured. 'How sweet of you . . . '

'This house is rather an oddity. But I was absolutely bowled over by the site and the views. It was very run down when I saw it; the garden was a wilderness, and it was very bleak – pouring with rain, I remember. I was intrigued by it, and, let me say, even more intrigued by the price. It had belonged to someone called Hunter – long before your time, my dear,' he said to Julia. 'She'd married a succession of rich men, and the last husband was one of the richest. She was very beautiful, and apparently very good fun. But in the end, she drank like a fish and became quite impossible. The equivalent of our tabloids absolutely adored her. She was always saying or doing something outrageous, and she was always in the news.'

'I remember,' Janey said. ' "Mink is too hot to sit on," – wasn't that her?'

Richard Watson laughed. 'It certainly was. She had a new motor car with gold-plated fittings, doorhandles, ashtray, and the seats were covered in leopardskin. She'd have been lynched by the anti-fur people today. When the Press asked her why leopardskin, that's what she said. "Because mink is too hot to sit on." It made headlines all over the world. She really knew how to get herself into the papers.'

'She certainly did if she came up with quotes like that,' Julia said. 'I love it, I really love it. Mink is too hot to sit on . . . ' She laughed. 'So what happened to her?'

'It all ended sadly,' Watson said. 'They had this big yacht, *Paradiso* I think it was called, and her antics got her husband kicked off the board of his family business, so they spent their lives cruising from one tax haven to another. She used this house as a *pied-à-terre* when they berthed here. It was a forties time warp when I bought it. My drawing room was fitted up as a private cinema, screen, projector – everything left just as it was. Apparently one day she got bored, or had a row with the Jersey authorities – she was always rowing with people – it was drink, unfortunately. They just left, didn't even bother to put the house on the market. When she died, her executors put it up for sale. And I bought it.'

Someone said, 'You've done wonders with it, Dick. You ought to see the garden he's made. And all that clever lighting at night.'

'Dawn and sunset are the best times,' he said. 'Not that I'm up in time for the sunrises these days. But I've had a lot of fun getting it the way I wanted it. Sheila, that was her name. Sheila Hunter. Such a shame she went to pieces like that.'

'I must read up on her,' Julia said. 'She sounds interesting.'

'Very small beer compared to the scandals we get these days,' Thomas boomed cheerfully. 'Hardly rate a mention in the *Sun*, would she?'

'Now that could be a subject for a book for you,' his wife suggested to Julia. 'I don't think there's been a biography. Of course, nobody dared when she was alive. She was a great one for suing. She had some famous black pearls. They became very fashionable.'

Julia let Richard refill her glass. The food and wine were as well chosen as the candles and winter-flower arrangements on the table. He was a man of taste and style. She liked him. She felt he liked her. She refused to feel guilty because she had come to his house under false pretences to make use of him.

As she was using her nice cousins, Janey and David Peterson, who'd been so delighted to see her. So welcoming. She withdrew from the conversation, adopting the role of a listener.

'The definition of age,' Richard Watson was saying, 'is a desire to talk about the past. I find myself doing it more and more. I spent a few nights in London with my nephew . . . the solicitor, you met him, Janey, he came over for a sailing holiday last summer—'

'Yes, I remember him, charming young man,' Janey said brightly.

Richard Watson grinned. 'Not particularly, he's rather bumptious and pleased with himself, but at least he's kin, so I keep in touch. He took me out to dinner at his smart club – excellent food, much better than restaurants – I found myself talking about the time I spent as a prisoner of war. I don't think I'd thought about it, let alone talked about, for years! And there I was in full flood, banging on about being captured and spending three years in a camp in Germany. I suddenly realized he was bored stiff, poor chap. So I cut it short and changed the subject. I felt what a boring old fool I'd become.'

'That's the trouble,' Bob Thomas snorted. 'The young think they know it all.'

Richard Watson said gently, 'Didn't we? I know I never listened to a word my father said after the age of eighteen. Sad thing was, you know, when I did come back from the POW camp, we couldn't communicate at all. Of course, they were delighted to see me – my mother cried and rushed off to make tea; my old father managed to put his arm round me and then hurried upstairs with my bag. He just didn't know what to say.'

Julia judged the moment had come. 'Did it affect you badly? It must have been awful trying to adjust.'

'It wasn't easy,' he admitted. 'I'd come back home a stranger. To myself as much as to them. I didn't realize what the loss of freedom had done to me. I couldn't make my mind up about anything. I'd lost the habit of taking decisions. If someone had told me what socks to put on in the morning, I'd have done it.'

'How long did that last?' Julia leaned close, engaging his full attention.

'Couple of years. I tried several jobs, couldn't settle to anything; it was quite a common manifestation of POW fatigue. Then I was taken on by ICI as a trainee, and I got interested. Absorbed, actually. And it all started to come right after that.'

Julia took a breath. *Now.*

'I read your book,' she said. 'I have a friend who's mad on the last war and he gave it to me to read. I really enjoyed it. Did you map it out while you were in the prison camp?'

'Yes,' Richard Watson said. 'I did. It was so desperately boring and miserable, and so damned cold in the winter . . . We were always hungry, too. Most of the chaps spent their time talking about escape or playing chess, or bridge. I worked on my insignificant wartime memoirs. I can't believe you found them interesting, but I must admit I'm flattered.'

He smiled at her.

Bob Thomas boomed out, 'Book? What's all this, Dick – been keeping secrets from us?'

'It was years ago – long before I came over here,' Richard Watson protested. 'I had some copies privately printed. I didn't know there were any circulating anywhere. I just wanted to get it off my chest, I suppose.'

'Hidden talents,' Bob Thomas had their attention. 'Better watch out, Julia, or you'll have a rival in Dick here . . . I'd like to read it some time. I bet you've got a copy of the great work stashed away. The Army was the best time of my life. I often regretted not making a career of it. Too young to get into the actual war, but I enjoyed my National Service.'

He looked around for approbation.

Julia said quietly, 'Did you feel like that, Richard? Your book didn't read like that.'

He turned to look at her, and then, suddenly, he turned away.

'I hated the Army,' he said. 'I hated everything about it. And I wasn't a good soldier. The idea of killing someone absolutely appalled me. I had no blood lust.'

'Did you ever kill anyone?'

He hesitated for a moment. Then he said, 'No. But I did save a man's life.'

Julia had borrowed Janey's little Ford run-about to get to the dinner party. She was determined to meet Richard Watson before anyone else arrived.

As they got into the two cars, Janey complained.

'What a pity you made such a fuss about being on time. We could have driven back together and had a lovely *post mortem* on the evening.'

'Knowing you, darling,' her husband retorted, 'we'll have one as soon as we get inside the front door. Do you know, Julia, she really enjoys talking about the party afterwards more than the party itself. I warn you, you'll be in for a long session unless you're firm. Janey, you'd better drive.'

'I should think so,' his wife giggled, 'after the size of that last brandy. Julia, you can follow us, all right?'

Julia started the car, and set out after them, keeping the rear light in view. In spite of the cold wind blowing in off the sea, she opened the window and breathed in the salty air. She couldn't believe it. She went over Richard Watson's story in her mind; he had made it so real, so vivid. No-one had spoken a word till he'd finished.

And then, as if some high tension had been released, everyone changed the subject and took refuge in banter and small talk. The last hour after dinner was the longest Julia could remember. Coffee was followed by an exodus of the women from the dining room, leaving Richard Watson and his male guests to port and cigars. The only other man Julia knew who continued the archaic practice of separating the sexes was William Western. But then he was a law unto himself, and he said so. He was also Julia's boss . . . She remembered a Saturday night spent at the mansion in Hampshire, when her dinner companion had announced that this was the part of the evening he enjoyed most, as she got up to leave.

She had ignored him when he tried to talk to her afterwards.

When finally the men rejoined them in the big drawing room with its spectacular sea views, everyone moved round and she found herself sitting beside her cousin, David. Liqueurs were brought for what the booming Mr Thomas called 'the girls'. Julia refused anything.

'This is nice,' David said, sinking deeper into his chair, cradling a half-full balloon of brandy. 'At last I've got a chance to talk to you. My darling wife's monopolized you from the moment you arrived. Tell me, how are Hugh and May? We must look them up when we come over next time.'

Julia assured him that her parents were well and would love to see them both.

'And tell me about the job,' he went on, lighting a cigar and bent on enjoying himself. 'What's it like working for Western?'

Julia checked her screaming impatience to get out of there and get to a telephone. She said, 'Impossible, most of the time. He's impossible as a person. Totally demanding and absolutely ruthless. He's also a genius, if that excuses it. I'm not sure it does. Just don't ask me if I like him, will you!'

'I don't have to, after that. But then you love the rat race, don't you, Julia, and look what a success you've made. Top job, big salary. You're a public figure. And the really nice thing about you is it hasn't made you the least big-headed. You're just as sweet as you ever were.' He stretched over and patted her knee. Julia judged he'd had a little too much of Richard Watson's brandy.

'I've no reason to be big-headed,' she said. 'I've had all the lucky breaks, David. Starting with Western picking me out. Otherwise I'd be still plugging away on a provincial newspaper with nothing more in my sights than editing the women's page. David—'

He grinned at her. 'Yes? You're fidgeting, aren't you? Sorry. Here, I'll move and let Bob Thomas come and talk to you. Watch out for your ear drums, though. He's a nice fellow, but my God he's got a voice like a bloody foghorn—'

'No,' she said quickly. 'No, don't. I was really thinking of the time.'

'You in a hurry to get home? Tired?' He peered at her.

'No, I'm not tired. But I did want to call someone . . . '

'Oh,' he said. 'Oh, I see. Janey said you had a special boyfriend. Is that it?'

'Yes,' she said eagerly. 'It's nearly a quarter to one. I promised I'd ring him, but I don't want to make it too late. He gets up at the crack every morning.'

'Right,' he put out the cigar, and heaved himself to his feet.

'Dick,' he announced, 'you've wined and dined us all too well. And I've got an early appointment in the morning. So we should be on our way.'

Julia whispered, 'Thanks, David,' as she moved to shake hands with Richard Watson and say goodbye.

She didn't want to go into the kitchen and drink coffee with them when they arrived back at the Petersons' house. But Janey insisted. She ushered them inside, and started putting coffee into mugs and filling the kettle.

'How did you enjoy it?' she asked Julia. 'Interesting, isn't he? And what an extraordinary story – I suppose it's true. What do you think, darling?' Julia gave her cousin a pleading look.

'I think,' he said, 'that it was absolutely true. And what's also true is that Julia wants to ring the love of her life and you and I are going to bed. Switch the kettle off, and come on. Night, Julia. Don't forget to put the lights out when you come up. And I do have an early stint tomorrow. Bless you.'

Julia waited till they had gone upstairs. She went into the passage and listened till she heard their bedroom door shut. Then she went into the sitting room and closed the door after her. She picked up the phone and dialled London. He wouldn't be asleep, she knew he sat up till all hours, reading, watching late-night TV. And there was nobody there to nag him about going to bed. He would be awake and waiting.

Waiting for her call.

It only rang three times before he answered.

'Ben,' she said. 'Ben, it's me. I'm fine . . . fine . . . ' He was already interrupting. She cut in on him. 'Just listen, will you? It came right out of the blue tonight. At the dinner . . . yes. Yes . . . Ben.' She took a deep breath. 'You're not going to believe this, but I think we've found our man.'

At ten-thirty next morning, Ben made the call as they'd arranged; there were two days of her visit left, and she had to get back to London. She came in and said to Janey, 'That was the office – I've got to go back early. I'm so sorry to cut it short like this – I've had such a lovely time.'

Janey drove her to Jersey airport. 'I'll miss you,' she said. 'You made such a hit with everyone, you'll have to come back.'

'I will, I promise,' Julia said. 'And thank you for giving me such a lovely holiday. Bless you.' She kissed her and went off to the departure lounge.

What an incredible coincidence. She let her mind roam during the short flight. Just when she was losing hope, luck smiled on her.

A dinner party in Jersey with a retired business executive had provided the missing clue. A clue so carefully concealed that every lead after Germany and the interview in a Sussex village had ended in nothing. For want of a nail the battle was lost in the end, as the old doggerel ran. She had found the nail.

So many things depended on trifles, a snap judgement, a decision taken without any inkling of the ultimate consequences. And it had all started with an invitation and a distant dream.

The letter had been signed by a secretary to Lord Western of Western International Newspapers. He would like her to come down to his house in Hampshire for a personal vetting, with a view to offering her a job.

Julia had thought it was a practical joke till she telephoned the number. But it was no leg-pull by a colleague. It was real. The invitation was to come down for dinner, stay the night and leave after breakfast. Black tie, the brisk voice told her.

She, the voice, would send her a map of how to get there. She, Julia, should reply to Lady Western direct. She nearly lost her nerve and backed away from it. Her father was a country solicitor, her background middle class. Life peers with country mansions issuing one-night invitations were not part of her experience. She'd worked for five years on provincial papers starting at sub-NUJ rates on a small weekly till she got her job as junior reporter with the *Yorkshire Post*. When her news editor wanted to entertain his staff, he took a room in the local pub.

It had been a daunting experience; her old Renault looked like a battered beetle as it turned into the sweep of drive and drew up before the façade of Hollowood Park. A butler took her suitcase, and she followed him up the steps and into the hall.

A woman came forward to meet her. Julia never forgot her first sight of Evelyn Western. She was astonishingly beautiful, with white hair and a delicate face that was still lovely in old age.

She came up and shook hands with Julia and smiled down at her; she was nearly six feet tall and straight as a rod.

'Miss Hamilton – how nice of you to come. I'm Evelyn Western. Now, would you like a drink before you go up to change?' She didn't wait for an answer. 'Of course you would, after that long drive. Come along, you're the first to arrive. I do admire people who are punctual. I'm hopeless myself.'

Julia got an impression of nice pictures and comfortable furniture in a big panelled room, but she was too nervous to observe her surroundings in detail.

She asked for a glass of sherry, which was not what she wanted. Evelyn Western sat down next to her.

'You're very young,' she said. 'Twenty-six?'

'Twenty-seven,' Julia answered.

'My husband believes in young talent. He's had his eye on you for some time – did you know that?'

'No, I didn't. I just got the letter mentioning a job with the *Herald* and I couldn't believe it. It's like a dream come true.'

'What a nice thing to say,' the older woman remarked. 'I shall tell William. He reads the good provincials; he's always on the look out for new people with fresh ideas. He spotted you quite early on. I remember him saying to me one morning, "There's a girl here, Evie, Julia Hamilton. *Yorkshire Post*. I like what she writes. She might do for us one day." ' Julia hadn't known what to say. She sipped the sherry. There was a pause and Evelyn Western said, 'I'm telling you this so you won't be frightened of my husband when you meet him. He'll grill you to see what you're made of, but stand up to him and you'll be all right. He knows I'm going to say this because I always do when someone comes here for the first time. Some of the young men don't like it, but I feel you won't mind.'

Julia looked at her. She had very blue eyes, cleverly made-up to emphasize their colour.

'I don't mind, Lady Western. I'm very grateful to you. I was so nervous coming here I nearly turned round and went home. But I won't forget what you've said. Thank you.'

'Not at all. Now, I think you should go up and change. We'll gather in the drawing room at a quarter to eight. Baker will take you up. See you then.'

Much of what followed was indistinct in her memory when she tried to describe it to her parents. Her mother wanted to know what the bedroom was like, avid for details, but Julia couldn't supply them. It was full of chintz and bright colours, and a handsome bathroom with an enormous round bath. She'd been too frightened of being late to try it before dinner. Afterwards, when she came up and it was all over, she slipped into the bath and thought about the evening. There were twelve for dinner, three couples, another girl, two single men and herself, and the Westerns. Evelyn Western introduced her to the other guests and then steered her towards her husband. Julia knew the face; it was well publicized, but she was shocked to see how slight he was. His wife stood over him like an elegant giraffe. Julia was somewhere around five foot eight, she'd never bothered to find out exactly, and she was at eye level with William Chancellor Western. He had greying hair, a fresh unlined complexion, and pale grey eyes like ice chips.

He repeated his wife's greeting. 'How nice of you to come. I shall call you Julia. Did you have a good journey? I hope the directions were clear—'

'Perfectly clear, thank you, Lord Western. It's very kind of you to have me. What a wonderful house –' It wasn't mere politeness. She'd never seen a more beautiful drawing room in any coffee-table book of Great Houses. The plaster work was exquisite, the ceiling soared above a massive chandelier lit with real candles. The pictures . . . Julia had studied history of art among her degree subjects, and she recognized works by the great English portrait painters, from a massive Vandyke group to a lovely joyous Raeburn of a mother and two children playing with a spaniel. Western saw her looking round.

'You like pictures?' he asked, without waiting for more than a nod. 'Know anything about them?'

'A little,' Julia answered. His manner was disconcerting. He asked a question and then followed on without bothering about an answer.

'You studied history of art, I remember,' he said. She was amazed that he should know such a detail.

'I make it my business to research anyone thoroughly before I offer them a job. A lot of people can write a good newspaper piece. It takes intelligence and intuition to be a good reporter.

'You're seated next to Leo Derwent, over there. Foxy-faced young man, very pushing. He's a politician. See what you think of him, and tell me about it after dinner.' Then he had moved on and left her standing, staring after him.

Julia felt her face burn at the peremptory manner and the rude way she'd been abandoned in a room full of strangers. Don't be afraid of him, his wife had said.

Well I bloody well won't be intimidated, Julia decided. He's not going to walk over me just because of a job. She finished the glass of champagne which had been handed to her by the butler and walked straight across to the man so aptly described as foxy-faced.

'I think we're sitting next to each other,' she said. 'We were introduced but I never catch anyone's name. I'm Julia Hamilton,' and she gave him her most charming smile.

Leo Derwent had never heard of her, neither the name nor the face registered in his personal computer of people worth cultivating, but it was a very pretty face, with fiery red hair standing out like a halo. And big dark eyes. Unusual.

A very sexy little piece, he decided, and wondered whether that cunning shit Western was offering him a titbit. He had a way of putting politicians in his pocket. No doubt he knew Leo's weakness for sexy girls who enjoyed playing games. He looked down the front of Julia's dress and said in a careful accent. 'Aren't I lucky? Leo Derwent – your glass is empty. So's mine. Let's see if we can catch the Admirable Crichton's eye—' He was a dreadful specimen; with his phoney vowel sounds and his self-promotion.

It would have been easy to dismiss him as shallow and pretentious. But under the veneer, so painfully acquired, of manners and attitudes that were not natural to him, Julia sensed there lurked a predator as cunning and ruthless as the animal he unfortunately looked like. He monopolized her during dinner, setting out to impress her with his achievements.

'I really think,' she whispered at last, 'I'd better say something to the man on my left – I don't want to be rude – you've been so interesting.'

And she escaped him, leaving him uncertain whether she had snubbed him or she knew something about social customs at smart dinner parties that he hadn't picked up for himself. The dining room was as spectacular as the drawing room. The table was laden with early silver, the food and wine were superb. When dinner was over Evelyn Western stood up. 'We'll have coffee in the drawing room, and don't be too long, Billy, please!' After a quarter of an hour she said to Julia, 'I won't have them sitting for hours in the dining room. Why should we have to wait, twiddling our thumbs, till they've finished the port. Ah, here they are – come along, go and sit down next to William. Over there on that sofa. And remember,' her voice lowered, 'don't let him bully you.' For a moment she touched Julia on the arm. 'He likes you, I can always tell.'

He turned those slate-coloured eyes on her. 'Good dinner, wasn't it?'

'Delicious,' Julia answered.

'I love food,' he announced, 'it's one of life's great pleasures. I hate women who diet. My wife never had to bother, she's always been thin. You didn't pick, I noticed.'

Julia took a deep breath. He was doing his damnedest to disconcert her. If she gushed, he'd despise her.

'I was starving,' she said. 'I hadn't had any lunch.'

To her surprise he laughed. 'Neither had I. Didn't have time. I saw you getting on well with Leo. What did you think of him?' Again without waiting for an answer, 'Clever fellow, come up by his boot straps. Could be Prime Minister one day, only I won't see it.'

Julia said coolly, 'Well I hope I don't. I wouldn't buy a *new* car from him, never mind a second-hand one.'

'I see,' he said. 'Not afraid to speak your mind, are you? Good. And you're right. He's a sharp little crook and one day he'll be caught out. Ever done a profile?'

'Not the kind you'd publish, Lord Western,' she answered. 'The papers I worked for wanted nice cosy articles about local people. Head of the Hospital Management Committee, Councillor Bloggs at home with his family. That sort of thing.'

'Well, I want you to do a piece on Leo Derwent,' he said. 'Not for publication – you're not going to run before you can walk – but just to show me what you *might* be able to do. Send it up to my office by Wednesday. You'll be starting under Harris; he's been News Editor for ten years and he's a very good man. But he's jealous of new blood. He won't take you seriously, he doesn't rate women beyond fashion and features, so do what he says, smile sweetly and be patient. Are you patient? Not with that hair, I bet. Never mind. You'll have to learn.'

'I'll try,' Julia promised. 'Can I say something?'

'In a minute, I haven't finished. You aren't patient, are you?' He laughed again. 'Get the feel of the paper, and don't mind the boys; they'll all have one thing on their minds, but I expect you're used to that. What's your own situation – regular boyfriend? Don't blush, I like to know everything about my protégés. You're a protégée; I think you've got promise.'

'Thank you,' Julia said. 'I wasn't blushing. I didn't think you had a right to ask, that's all.'

'I have all the rights,' he said firmly. 'You'll have to accept that. Now – you wanted to say something?'

He paused, and they looked at each other. He had a hard, cold stare and she hated being transfixed like that. She mustered her courage and stared back. 'I just wanted to say that this is the opportunity of my life and thank you for giving it to me. I won't let you down.'

He did something that made her jump. He patted her hand. 'I'm sure you won't. And make no mistake, Julia, you'll be fired if you do. Now I can see my dear wife looking bored, so I must go and rescue her.'

He stood up. He moved on without glancing back at her. One of the women moved across and sat beside her. Her husband had been on Julia's left at the dinner table. She was in her forties, beautifully dressed but there wasn't a line or a laughter crease on the smooth surface of her skin. 'I hear you're going to work for William,' she said. 'How exciting!'

'Yes,' Julia said. 'Yes, I'm sure it's going to be. If I can stand the pace.'

What a long time ago, she thought, buckling her seat-belt as they came in to land.

Five years had passed since the naïve country reporter had come face to face with the great man, and gone away determined to prove herself. Now she recognized the technique. He liked putting people on their mettle; if they failed to measure up they were no use to him. She remembered sitting up for two nights, reference books and *Hansard* by her elbow, writing and rewriting the profile of Leo Derwent. Western hadn't even acknowledged it. She remembered crying in the lavatory because she was sure she hadn't got the job, but a week later she got a letter telling her to report to Harris. Slowly she settled into the routine of the news room, and made her best effort to get on with Harris.

The first day she had introduced herself, she felt so nervous that she stammered slightly. The man pushed thick horn-rimmed glasses off his nose and looked at her without interest.

'Mr Harris? I'm Julia Hamilton,' she said. 'I . . . er, I've come to start . . . ' He didn't help her. He was somewhere in his early forties, greying hair and an unwelcoming manner.

'Yes, I know. Your spot's over there. Find your own way round. Davis'll give you something to do.' Then the glasses came down and he went back to reading a print-out. Julia didn't see him glance up when she turned away and watch her go across to the bank of WPs and screens and find the vacant place he had indicated. He saw Davis, who was next to her, grin and offer a hand. Davis would be nice to her; Davis was always nice to women – the secretaries, the messenger girls, even the odd cleaner if they were attractive. Harris wondered how the pretty redhead, blushing to her ears with first-day nerves, would cope with Davis. He shrugged mentally. Not that he cared. The old man liked to foist someone on him from time to time. Like all tyrants, he enjoyed springing surprises. There'd been a number of Young Turks brought in from outside, potential rivals for his job. Ben Harris had seen them all off. He had nothing to worry about with a girl. She was the first girl Western had introduced, which must signify something, he supposed. Some whim, some mischievous quirk had prompted Western to single her out and land her in Harris's lap.

She wouldn't last; he didn't think he had to make it difficult for her, though he was ready to do so; she'd cut her teeth in the news room and if she was ambitious, and sensible, get herself into the Women's Feature where she would have a future.

Ben Harris had come up via the provinces, working as a teenager on freebie news sheets, on to the weekly newspapers, running errands, at the end of everyone's boot. But he had talent; he could write and he could angle a story for maximum news impact. He worked and pushed himself upward, ending on a quality Midlands newspaper, where he became news editor. And then the offer came to move to London, to the Mecca of the Western Group. He was married by then, with two children.

His wife hadn't wanted to move. She liked her home in Birmingham; she had friends, the children were doing well at school. The marriage started to break up when they moved down to London. They'd been divorced for many years. Ben Harris lived for his job. Sometimes, with a few too many drinks inside him, he boasted he'd sucked printer's ink instead of mother's milk. He was tough, he had no friends, only colleagues in the office, and potential rivals. He had one motto and it was the only thing he believed in. Watch your back. He wouldn't have to watch it with J. Hamilton.

She'd been there a month when he told Davis to give her a few minor stories to cover. He noticed that she had seen Davis off, without making an enemy; nobody else had got closer to her than a drink in the pub after work.

He gave her grudging credit for that. Everything she produced was cut to pieces by the sub-editor. Most of it went into the shredder and was never used. Ben Harris waited for her to whinge. Most people would have complained, not to him – he didn't waste time with the minnows on his staff – but he'd have heard about it. He knew everything that went on.

But J. Hamilton, as he called her, disdaining a Christian name, got on with the next assignment, and said nothing. He began to think of her as a pro; quiet, dedicated and adaptable. One morning he asked to see her copy. She'd been covering a protest over a stretch of dangerous road near a school. It was a bottom of the page, half-inch stuff, not important enough to rate a photograph. Just a group of parents parading with placards. Routine, dull . . . He read the piece. He called the sub who murdered Julia's work as part of his job. Ben Harris said, 'This is good. Don't fuck about with it. Don't say I said so.'

He watched her progress; it was steady, and it showed decided flair. She had taken the tough period of initiation with dignity and guts. She was popular with the rest of the staff who'd begun to accept her as a colleague. They'd stopped making bets on who would get to lay her first. Incredibly, as Harris realized, she had become one of them. She went out on her stories – often with a photographer now – she stood her round in the pub after work, she asked no favours of anyone because she was a woman. He called her in one day.

She had matured; she was confident now. She called him Ben, because he'd snapped at her once, 'Drop the Mr Harris for Christ's sake – I'm not a bloody shop walker!'

'How's it going J?' he asked her.

He never smiled, Julia noticed. When he said something complimentary it was with a scowl. 'Fine, I think. I'm getting a lot of stuff in these days. I hope you're happy with me.'

'You'd know if I wasn't,' he said. He dropped his heavy glasses on his table. 'I didn't think you'd last,' he said flatly.

'I know,' Julia answered quietly. 'That made me all the more determined.' He glanced at her quickly, and then said, as if the words were chewed-up glass, 'You're doing all right. Don't try and run before you can walk, that's all.'

Julia smiled. 'I won't, because you won't let me.'

'Too right,' he agreed. 'Now I'm busy, even if you're not.'

Julia had been on the staff for nine months when William Western exploded his bombshell. A big news story had just broken. The mutilated and abused bodies of two five-year-old twin girls had been discovered in a wood outside a Welsh village on the border.

It was shaping up to be one of the most gruesome sex murders of children since the Moors killings thirty years ago.

When the directive came down to Ben Harris he couldn't believe it. *I want Julia Hamilton to cover this. Let's see what she's made of. Western.* Ben slammed the note down on his desk and shouted an obscenity. He didn't care who heard him. Send an inexperienced young woman up to cover a horrendous child murder like this – Western must be off his trolley.

He opened his office door and yelled into the bedlam of the news room. 'Tell J. Hamilton to come in here!' Then he banged the door shut. Davis, who had become a good friend to Julia, raised his eyebrows in a comic grimace. 'He's yelling his head off for you. Stand up to him, Julia – it's the only way. If he fires you, we'll all come out on strike!'

'Like hell you will,' she managed to smile at him. 'I can't think what I've done . . . '

When she came into his office, Ben Harris looked up and glared. 'I've just had this come down from the top floor,' he said. 'You can read it, but you're not bloody going.'

Julia scanned it quickly.

She said quietly, 'I've got to go. I haven't any choice.'

'Sit down a minute,' he told her. 'Just listen to me. You're a good reporter. You're doing well. I like your stuff and I'm bloody difficult to please. But this isn't on. This is the biggest murder story we've had for decades, and it's going to be one of the worst. Those kids were tortured and raped. Whoever did it, mutilated them while they were still alive. I wouldn't send a woman to cover this story in any circumstances. And you've never touched a murder story, have you?

'This isn't going to be just human interest, grief-stricken parents, shock horror in the community, all that crap – this means inquests, police-incident rooms, autopsies, the lot! It's no job for you. If you foul up on this, you're finished. That's the way he works.'

'If I refuse the job I'm finished,' Julia said. 'That's why he picked me. He said it, let's see what she's made of – I've got to go, Ben, or I might as well resign now.'

He looked up at her. She was pale, he realized, shocked by the prospect. But she was right. Western would write her off if she refused.

'You know, it might be better if you did just that,' he said slowly. 'I've seen tough men gutted by something like this. Don't do it. Call the old bastard's bluff. I'll back you.'

'I know you will,' she answered. 'But it's not the point. I can't walk away from it, or I'm not fit to be in the job. I'll go, Ben, and I'll show him what I'm made of. Now, will you back me up?'

He stood up. 'I'll back you, J. Hamilton,' he said. He looked angry. 'But only so long as you don't screw up.'

'Thanks,' she said. 'I'll try not to.'

The double murder was a sensation. The tabloids shrieked with gory headlines, the quality papers reported with restraint and sobriety; the *Sunday Herald* gained plaudits from all sides for the concise unsentimental coverage under the byline J. Hamilton. The reports were a masterly analysis of the horror that had engulfed a family and a small community in a Nonconformist village. There was no sensationalism, just clear prose of depth and integrity, exploring the personal and social elements in the sexual perversion of the crime.

No-one suspected that the writer was a woman.

When the arrests were made, Julia was called back to London. A local man, married with children, was charged with the double murders. They were close neighbours of the twins' family.

On her first day in the office, she was fêted and congratulated. The grinning Davis smacked a kiss on her cheek. A personal note of commendation was sent down from Western. That evening she was borne off to the pub to celebrate. Ben Harris came up to her.

'It's about time I bought you a drink,' he said. 'You deserve it. Come and sit down over here.' He seldom socialized with his staff. He kept himself remote, immersed in his job. Nobody else liked to join them.

'You look completely gutted,' he said. 'Take a few days off.'

'I'd rather work,' Julia answered. 'I cope better if I keep going.'

'I told you what it would be like,' he said. 'You wouldn't listen. But it's marked you, and it shows. Drink that up and have another. I don't often stand drinks, so make the most of it.' A rare smile softened his face. He pushed his thick, grey-streaked hair back, and said, 'You did bloody well. I was amazed; and you got better and better.'

'Thanks,' she smiled back at him. 'It's heady stuff, coming from you. Thanks, Ben.'

'Excuse me for butting in—' He looked up sharply. A young man was standing by their table. 'I just wanted to say what a great job you did on those Rhys murders. I'd no idea it was a woman when I read them. My name's Felix Sutton.' He held out a large hand and Julia shook it. 'I'm on the political desk. I hope you don't mind me crashing your party. I just wanted to say it was great stuff.'

He had a friendly, self-confident grin. 'Mind if I sit down?'

'Of course not,' Julia answered. Ben Harris pushed his chair back. She realized that he looked at the intruder with hostility. He gave the young man his well-known scowl. 'I'll be off then,' he said.

Felix suggested they went to a trattoria in Covent Garden. He didn't argue when she said of course she'd pay her half. Sitting opposite him, Julia realized how attractive he was. He wasn't conventionally handsome; he looked like a boxer, with a broken nose and a boxer's body. He was certainly younger than she was, but it didn't seem to matter.

'Before we order,' he said, 'do you want to talk about the case, or have you had enough blood and guts for tonight?'

Julia winced. 'Don't,' she said. 'It was a nightmare. I just had to shut off any feelings or I couldn't have done those interviews or gone to the inquest. All I could do was hang in there to see whoever did it got caught. It kept me sane. Now I've got to put it out of my mind. Or try to. I haven't slept a night through since I went up there,' she admitted.

'I'm not surprised. Let's start with a bottle of wine. The talk round the office is you're marked for stardom. They're all buying drinks and chatting you up now, but some people aren't going to like it. Ben Harris for one,' he said.

'But I've only just started,' Julia protested. 'I couldn't be a threat to him in a million years.'

'That's not how he sees it,' he countered. 'I'll bet he stabbed a few backs on his way up, why shouldn't you? Especially with the old man behind you. Have you been down to the house yet?'

'I went before I started working. He wanted to have a look at me. He said he'd noticed my stuff on the *Post*.'

'I've heard that's how it goes. But only if it's someone he's picked out specially. I wish I'd get a chance to meet him.'

'Maybe you will.' She was careful not to discuss William Western. He didn't pursue it; he talked about himself without bombast, but without modesty either. He'd come to the newspaper as a junior reporter straight from Keele University. He had a first-class degree in Modern History. He had done some amateur boxing, he touched his nose and grinned, reached the all-England semi-finals, but that was just a hobby. He liked keeping fit and worked out at a gym on the weekends. 'What I really want,' he said, as the second bottle of wine was opened, 'is to get to the top. One day I'm going to be sitting in old Warburton's office.' Clive Warburton was chief political correspondent, and a powerful pundit on the Westminster scene.

'You *are* ambitious,' Julia remarked. 'But you've got plenty of time, anyway.'

'No, lady, that's where you're wrong.' He was quite serious, the cheery grin had changed to a look of steely purpose. 'Anyone who thinks they've got plenty of time isn't going to get there. I'm the original young man in a hurry. I want it all and I want it yesterday.'

Suddenly he laughed. 'As you can see I'm an ambitious bastard. Changing the subject, I love your hair. Is it for real?'

'Of course it is,' Julia protested. He smiled at her and it was a naked sexual invitation. 'I suppose I have to take your word for it—'

'You do,' she said firmly. 'It's late and I'm shattered. Let's get the bill.' She paid her share and he took it.

'This was great, let's do it again?'

They were in the street and he was looking down at her.

Julia had ended an affair when she left Yorkshire. There'd been no man in her life since then. 'Why not? I liked it too.'

'Can you lift me back to Islington?'

'Yes, of course.' He squeezed himself into the little car; he was too tall and too big to fit into the front seat comfortably.

'Mine's on the bloody blink,' he explained. 'We had a little argument with a lorry coming up the A10 and the lorry won. Just here, number twenty-eight. It's not as grotty as it looks outside. Quite nice. Want to come in for a drink?'

'Not tonight,' Julia said. 'I'm on my knees I'm so tired. I hope to God I sleep.'

'You would if you came up with me,' he said coolly.

'You're very sure of yourself, aren't you?' She felt suddenly angry. Angry with herself too, because she was tempted.

He grinned and, bending down, aimed a light kiss on her cheek.

'No harm in trying,' he said. 'I hope you'll say yes, next time. See you, Julia.' He got out and ran up the stairs and let himself in. He didn't look back as she drove off.

That was five years ago, and his prophecy had come true. She was the brightest young star in the Fleet Street firmament, with her own byline, and a book analysing the Rhys murders published to general acclaim. And she and Felix had moved into a flat together.

Felix had planned a weekend at the pub on the Avon. He liked fishing and he waved her objections away by saying he'd teach her. 'It's a nice place, not fancy, but they hire out rods and a boat.' Julia had been looking forward to it; London was hot and she'd just come back from a hectic trip to the Midlands to write up on a prominent industrialist who had committed suicide before he could be arrested for fraud.

His company was in receivership. He'd walked out of his Queen Anne house near Melton Mowbray and blown half his head off with a shotgun. A couple of days lazing on a river and making love to Felix would take her mind off his wife and two teenage children.

But on Thursday afternoon the call came through. Western's personal secretary. The same smooth voice, well known to Julia now.

'Lord and Lady Western would like you to dine with them on Saturday and stay the night.'

'This Saturday?'

'It is rather short notice, but they're sure you'll understand.'

There'd been several invitations since that nerve-racking initiation. Julia knew the formula: down for dinner, a smart gathering of politicians, diplomats, people Western wanted to make use of, or who hoped to make use of him. Then leave promptly after breakfast. He called it 'Dine and Sleep', mocking the Royal protocol at Windsor Castle.

'I had something planned,' Julia protested.

'I know they're counting on you,' the voice said. 'Surely you can rearrange it, Miss Hamilton. When can you let me know?'

It wasn't an invitation, it was an order. As the voice was well aware.

'I'll change my plan,' Julia conceded. In a necessary show of independence, she added, 'But you're right, it *is* short notice. I suppose someone else dropped out.'

'Not to my knowledge. Arrive at six-thirty, black tie as usual. I'll let Lady Western know.'

She'd put through a call to Felix. He had been promoted to Clive Warburton's 'Gofer'. Go for this and go for that. But it was a start, and he was making himself very useful.

'Darling,' she said, 'I've got to cancel our weekend. The old man's asked me for a D and S on Saturday. I'm so sorry, but I've got to go.'

'Of course you have,' he answered. 'Might be something in it for you.'

'I was looking forward to going with you,' she insisted. 'I tried to get out of it, but it was impossible.'

'Don't get your knickers in a twist,' he said cheerfully. 'We'll do it another time. The Warbler wants me to go to the all-night debate tonight, so I won't be home. He's out to dinner, lucky old fart. See you.'

Julia put the phone down. He didn't mind about cancelling the weekend. Of course, it was easier for her that he wasn't jealous or possessive.

He took life as it came. Their personal life, she corrected herself. He had tunnel vision when it concerned his career. He expected her to feel the same. They had fun together; they had mutual friends, though most of them tended to be Felix's age and with his interests. But he was good about escorting her to anything important. He could be charming and well mannered when he chose. You catch more flies with honey than you do with vinegar, he quoted. They had a very open, civilized relationship and it suited them both. She just wished he had been as disappointed about losing their weekend as she was.

The flat they shared was a long way from the basement in Pimlico where she lived when she first came to London, and from the shabby chaos of Felix's Islington pad. It was a smart conversion in Chelsea Square, and it belonged to Julia. The furniture belonged to her, and the modern pictures, picked up from local art galleries. Felix said they looked like a lot of daubs to him; he didn't contribute anything but a sophisticated stereo and record player that cost nearly as much as Julia's pictures. She was a star and earning a star's salary.

He didn't resent the disparity; it didn't worry him that she carried three-quarters of their living costs. He was still comparatively low paid, but he had everything to play for. He had Clive Warburton in his sights. His break would come. And when it did, he announced to Julia, then he'd pick up the bills and keep her! And laughed in his carefree way. Sometimes he reminded her of a great casual child, convinced that the world and everyone in it owed him something just because he was there. But he made no personal demands. He lived his life and he expected her to live hers.

She came into the sitting room and put down her overnight case. It was dark-blue leather with her initials stamped on the side.

'I'd better be off now,' she said. 'I hope to God the traffic's not too bad.' She'd heard him come in while she was showering; he'd called out and settled himself to watch the England v. Germany football match. He was mad on all sports and nothing was allowed to interfere with his gym sessions and football.

She might keep him, in actuality, but she was never going to own him. He had made that plain from the start. His nickname in the office was Toy Boy; Julia had heard it and blazed with anger. But he only shrugged and laughed. 'They're jealous I got there first. I don't give a fuck what anyone says.' And he didn't.

He looked up and got to his feet. 'Come and kiss me, beautiful. We've just scored the equalizer.'

He always kissed her hard, using his tongue, and she couldn't help the surge of sexuality when he touched her. He knew it too, and traded on it. 'I have to keep my end up with my megastar,' he liked to tease her, and pull her laughing into bed.

He was a marvellous lover, but on his own terms. He had never said he loved her, even in their closest moments.

'I wonder what the old sod is up to this time?' he said letting her go. 'You won't have a ladder left to climb – I wish I could get a toe on it. Put a word in for me, will you, darling?' He always said it, half in earnest, but not expecting anything. She had never promoted him, she never would. He had his terms for their relationship, and integrity in the job was hers.

'I'll be home on Sunday, lunch-time. Will you be here?'

'Don't know, might go down to the club and get a game of squash. Have a good time, darling, and we'll go fishing another weekend. See you some time Sunday.' As Julia let herself out she heard him exclaim in disappointment. The Germans must have scored another goal.

The second-hand Renault had gone a long time ago. She drove a sleek BMW; the evening dress hanging in its initialled sleeve in the back came from Bruce Oldfield. She had made it early, and she wasn't shy about showing her success in terms of a smart car and good clothes. Appearances counted; Julia had learned that early on.

It was all face value and hype; success was more than talent. She knew she had that and it made sense of the gloss she had applied deliberately to her lifestyle. She had followed Evelyn Western's advice for the second time. 'Spend on yourself; dress well, you mustn't be afraid to stand out. Not that you can help it, Julia. You did that the first time you came down here. Poor child, you looked like the new girl on her first day at school . . .' She had smiled kindly at the memory. 'Now you're a personality, a name people recognize. Make the most of it. And I'll help you if you like. I do know about clothes. But don't let William know; he'd say I was being bossy.'

She had made the introductions, the tactful suggestions, and Julia realized how much Evelyn Western was enjoying herself. There was no hint of patronage. Once she turned to Julia, with her extraordinary blue eyes bright with pleasure, and said, 'You know this is such fun for me. We never had a daughter.'

And with equal tact she bowed out and left Julia to make her own choices and develop her own style.

She knew the route down to Hampshire, the turn off from the motorway and the descent into deep countryside. She eased down at the entrance to the drive, slowed for the speed bumps, and rounded the sweep to the front of the house. The butler had changed since her last visit. Western was a demanding and temperamental employer. He hired and fired in his domestic scene as he did in his business. Or businesses. He controlled a chain of middle-ranking hotels, an investment bank in the City, and mining interests in Brazil and West Africa. And three commercial radio stations and a Midlands TV network.

Her bag and the dress were taken upstairs for her by a maid, and the butler, a Filipino, she noted, said Lord Western was waiting for her in the study. There was no sign of his wife, and Julia was disappointed. Western was her employer, a human iceberg. Evelyn, she felt, was a friend.

William Western was reading when she came in. He looked up, smiled briefly at her and said to the butler, 'Whisky and soda, and vodka on the rocks for Miss Hamilton. Hello, Julia. Good journey down? Saw the smart car driving up scattering my gravel – sit down, over there. How are you? You look well.' She was used to it by now. The questions didn't wait for an answer. She sat opposite him; he even told his guests where to sit. He said, 'I hear you had another engagement.'

'Yes,' she answered. The bloody secretary had passed it on . . .

'Glad you cancelled it and came here instead. I've got something in mind for you. I think you'll like it. Where's that idiot with our drinks? He's been here a week; you'd think he'd know his way round by now. What have I interrupted? Off for the weekend somewhere with Sutton?'

She kept her temper, but it showed, and he seemed amused by it.

'Yes. We were going to fish on the Avon. Felix was going to teach me.'

'About the only thing he could teach you,' he said. 'He's a bloodsucker. Don't waste too much time on him. Ah, at last!' He glared at the Filipino. The man gave a quick nervous glance and offered the drinks. 'The lady first,' Western snapped at him. 'God almighty—' He spoke as if the butler were part of the furniture. 'You wouldn't believe the references – must have written them himself.'

It was shaming, and Julia said thank you, very loudly, to make up for his appalling rudeness, as she took her drink.

'I can't stand stupidity,' he said. 'Drives me mad.'

'Perhaps if you didn't frighten him to death he wouldn't *be* stupid.'

He looked sharply at her. 'Siding with the underdog, are we? Evelyn does the same. She doesn't have to pay the salary. And don't presume to criticize me, I don't allow it. Now, let me tell you who's coming to dinner.' He paused; he liked to play-act sometimes. Julia waited. He was a bully and a tyrant. As a person she disliked him intensely. But she couldn't resist the firecracker mind, the supercharge of energy. It glowed round him like a nimbus.

He took a large swallow of his whisky.

'Nobody,' he said. 'You and Evelyn and me. Almost a family gathering.'

Julia said quietly, 'Lord Western, I'm very flattered.'

'Then don't look disappointed. It'll be worth your while. You can fish with the boyfriend another time. But this could be the most important evening of your life. Now –' He finished his drink, and got up. 'Time to go and change. Evelyn's coming down from London by car, she'll be here in a minute. Seven-thirty. Don't be late.'

'I'm never late,' Julia pointed out. 'You know that.'

'My wife is; hopeless about time. She's fond of you, you know. Thinks you're a nice girl. I think you're a clever one. Much more important.' He left a room so quickly that it made her blink. He never waited for anyone. He left, and that was the end of it, even if someone else was in mid sentence. He was a dreadful, egotistical bulldozer and she hated him, she thought, refusing to gulp down her vodka and hurry after him. But when he said it could be the most important evening of her life, she knew he meant it.

2

Western was walking about stabbing a big cigar to emphasize his words.

Dinner had been tense; she could feel the atmosphere building up, and it wasn't just Western generating drama. His wife was as charming and friendly as always, but there was something wary about her. Anxious. Julia couldn't make it out. And then they gathered in the study.

He spoke abruptly.

'How would you like to head up a new feature?' He saw Julia's expression and said irritably, 'My dear girl – for God's sake you don't think I'm talking about some kind of *Women's* page?'

Julia said, 'Well yes, I did—'

'Don't be stupid,' he snapped. 'I'm talking about a major feature with a new angle. I'm going to call it "Exposure". The *Herald*'s commitment to honesty in public life. Watchdog of the nation. Investigative journalism on the American model.

No holds barred, take on all comers. It'll make *The Sunday Times* "Insight" look like a snoop after the Parish Council!' He stopped. 'Well, what do you think of it? Can you do it?'

Julia shook her head; she saw Evelyn Western watching her. She looked tense. Head up a controversial feature . . .

'I don't know what to say,' she said.

'Well it's the first time since I've known you,' he retorted. 'You're not being modest, I hope. I wouldn't offer you the job if I didn't think you could do it.'

'No,' Julia answered. 'I know you wouldn't. Do you really mean I'd be in charge – not responsible to anyone?'

'Only to me,' he said. 'Directly responsible to me. If you get this right, you could be the *Herald*'s first woman Editor in a few years—'

'Billy, don't overwhelm her,' his wife cut in. Then to Julia, 'It is a wonderful offer.'

'I know,' Julia answered. 'And I'll take it. Lord Western – I really don't know what to say. Thank you sounds so inadequate . . . I can't believe it's going to happen.' She gave a nervous laugh. 'It's incredible.'

Western turned to his wife. For a second longer than usual, they held each other's gaze. Then he said, 'Ring for that half-witted Filipe and tell him to bring some champagne. We've got something to celebrate.'

'To the birth of "Exposure",' he announced, raising his glass.

'And to you, Julia,' Evelyn Western added.

She stood up; reed thin in her straight black crêpe dress; a double row of pearls the size of poppets gleamed in the light. They were the only jewels she wore apart from a very small sapphire surrounded by tiny diamonds on her wedding finger. Given to her before Western had made his first millions. He'd been a small-town accountant when they married. It was an endearing touch of sentiment.

'I know you'll want to get down to details with Julia so I'll go to bed,' she said, 'and leave you to it; try not to stay up all night, will you?' She gave her husband a fond smile, bestowed the last of it on Julia, and was gone. How could she love him? Julia had often wondered. What was there to love in William Western?

And she was such a fundamentally nice woman. Julia gave up. She'd never understand it.

Western finished his champagne. 'I don't really like this stuff,' he remarked, 'but it's supposed to be lucky to christen a new venture. I'm switching to brandy. Like some? No, all right then, stick to your fizzy. But don't drink too much – you're going to need a clear head.

'Now, I suppose you're wondering where to start – well, I've got your first programme mapped out for you. Target would be a better word. I like the sound of it – target. We must work that into the format, it sounds good . . . '

Julia was caught up, enmeshed beyond objective judgement by the speed and energy of the man. Target. Yes, it would catch the reader's eye, whet the public appetite for blood. He knew his public . . .

He had a bumper half-full of brandy in his two hands, leaning towards her. The sheer power of his personality was at full throttle. She felt a rush of exhilaration not too far from the sexual high she got from Felix.

'I want you to go after Harold King,' he said. 'I want that bastard's head on a plate. Money's no object, hire what staff you want – go where you need to – just nail him for me.' He stared hard at her. 'Do it, and you can name your price.'

Julia went to the usual guest room. She'd risen on the Richter scale of Western's approval. It was twice the size of the one she'd occupied that first night five years ago; it had a spectacular view of the lake.

Ideas were spinning like tops in her brain. Harold King. The most controversial figure in the public domain. A genius, a billionaire, a brutal adversary; a power figure that revelled in the spotlight.

There were legends about him, fostered by himself; other rumours spoken in a whisper. Arms dealing, corruption, financial tentacles reaching deep into Eastern Europe.

And friends in very high places who protected him.

'Nail him for me . . . ' Western had said. 'And you can name your price!'

As he promised, it had been the most important evening of her life.

'I can't help feeling guilty,' Evelyn Western said. 'She's still an innocent, Billy. Nobody else would have taken this on.'

'That's why I chose her,' he answered. He was in his dressing room and he came and sat on the bed and took hold of his wife's hand.

'Evie, she's clever, she's ambitious and she's determined. That wasn't a bribe – I meant it. I'll make her the *Herald*'s Editor if she brings this off. And because she's a woman she can get to people and places that won't arouse suspicion.'

'For how long?' his wife countered. 'How long before King realizes she's investigating him? And then what will happen to her? I wish I hadn't encouraged her. She trusts me.'

He squeezed her hand and held it between both of his. He looked tired suddenly, as if a light had been extinguished.

'You did the right thing,' he said. 'I've got to destroy him before he destroys me. And I'll use anyone – anyone – to stop it happening. Now you settle down and take a sleeping pill. I don't want you lying awake fretting. Come on, here's the water, swallow it down . . .'

'Felix,' Julia called out, closing the flat door. 'Felix?' There was no answer. She felt a chill of disappointment.

Why couldn't he have been there to share the excitement with her? Why did he have to go and play his bloody squash when he knew she was coming home?

'Selfish bugger,' she muttered, feeling quelled. 'I'll go home, I'm not sitting here all afternoon till he comes back. I'll ring up and see if they're in for lunch.'

Her parents lived in Surrey. Her father was retired; Julia's brother had taken over the partnership in the family firm of solicitors. He was doing very well and talking of opening an office in London.

He and his wife and two young children lived in the same

suburb of Hampton. They were very close to the parents who doted on their grandchildren. It was not disloyal, Julia admitted, to say that since her career took off, she had drifted apart from the family unit.

Her mother answered the telephone. She sounded surprised and delighted when Julia suggested she drive down.

'That would be lovely; I'll turn down the beef – how long will you be? Oh, don't worry, don't drive too fast – Daddy'll be thrilled to see you.'

It was warm and welcoming. Just what Julia needed. At least brother Tom and his brood of children wouldn't be there monopolizing her parents. She could tell them about the new job. They didn't appreciate the finer points of journalism, and secretly she knew they'd rather she had married a suitable man and settled down, but they were always supportive.

Felix could come back to an empty flat for a change. She jumped into her car and set off. She'd brought him down to Sunday lunch once, and she knew her parents didn't like him. She didn't like him much herself at that moment, and the realization surprised her.

The trouble was, as soon as he put his hands on her, she'd melt like a candle under a match.

It was an excellent lunch. Good plain English food, as her father liked to tell an audience, was the best in the world. He couldn't stand meat mucked up in sauces, and tarted-up vegetables you couldn't get a tooth into. Julia listened with affection. He never changed; he was solid as a rock in his integrity, his political right-wing bias, and his basic decency as a husband, father and professional. A lifetime spent as a solicitor had given him sharp insight into people's characters without making him a cynic. That was remarkable of itself. He beamed across at her.

'You're looking very chipper, Juliette.' He used the pet name from her childhood. 'Anything up?'

They'd cleared away and she'd helped her mother load the dishwasher. They were sitting outside in the garden with their coffee. It was a lovely, spring afternoon. 'Yes,' her mother interposed, 'you look like the cat that's got the cream—'

'Well I have,' Julia answered. 'I've been staying with the boss. I got back this morning. Mum and Dad, he's offered me a tremendous job. My own feature.'

'Oh?' Her mother's bright smile faded a little. Julia realized she'd been hoping for a different kind of cream. A nice man, a possible wedding. Not Felix, who'd behaved like a conceited lout when she introduced him. 'What sort of feature?'

'Well something like "Insight", only much tougher, more aggressive.' Her father was an avid *Sunday Times* reader.

'Good Lord – well that *is* exciting. Are you going to run it?' he asked.

Julia nodded. 'Yes, Dad. It's my baby, I'm the boss; except I'm answerable to Western. And Western wants me to start off by digging up any dirt I can find about Harold King! Isn't it amazing? Big salary, expenses, staff, anything I want—'

Her mother didn't say anything. The phrase about digging up dirt didn't appeal to her. Her father said after a pause, 'Harold King . . . Didn't he ruin a High Court Judge because of some investigation some years ago? Yes, I remember. I'd be a bit careful before you make an enemy of him. He's got a nasty reputation.'

'I know his reputation,' Julia answered. 'And it's pretty obvious that he's cultivated it because he's got plenty to hide and he wants to scare people off. I'm not scared, Dad.'

'I know you're not,' her father said. 'You were always a gutsy girl. But just be careful, won't you? Even in my little backwater practice we heard some very disturbing things about that gentleman and the way he manipulated the law.' And then, because he felt he was damping her enthusiasm, he added, 'But congratulations, darling. We're very proud of you – aren't we, May?'

'Oh yes, very,' her mother responded. And it was true. They were proud of their daughter, even if she had moved into a world they couldn't relate to; her success was visible in the very expensive car, the smart clothes, and the generous presents she gave them at Christmas and on their birthdays. But her lifestyle was alien. They admitted to being old-fashioned, and tried not to judge.

But they felt more at ease with their son and daughter-in-law, a nice sensible girl – and the darling grandchildren. Glamour and high-flying was all very well, but in the end, a woman needed stability.

It would come in time, they assured each other. They were indeed proud to have a daughter who was such a star in her profession.

It was a happy afternoon for Julia. It went past tea-time and she was easily persuaded to stay for supper. It was, inevitably, lunch-time beef served up cold, with a salad and hot potatoes, and it took her back in a rush of nostalgia to her childhood. It had been very happy. No traumas, no teenage upheavals, just stable and predictable, from her earliest memories. She owed them a lot, these elderly parents, caught like the proverbial flies in the amber of their class and upbringing.

With the money she would be making, she had the happy idea of buying her father a new car. And she resolved, on the drive back to Central London, to make more time to go down to Hampton and see them.

When she came into the flat she knew Felix was back, because he'd dropped his racquet and sweatshirt in the hall. He was untidy, and she usually picked up after him to avoid an argument. He didn't mind a bit of a mess, he said; if she did then OK it was up to her to clear it up. He didn't care if *she* left things lying about.

She went into the sitting room. He was sprawled in the chair; for once the TV wasn't on. He was reading the *Observer*. He looked up, grinned at her and threw the paper aside.

'Hi – where've you been?'

'Down to Hampton; I had lunch with Mum and Dad.'

'Oh – good for you. What news, sweetheart? Come on, tell—'

If you'd been here when I got back, you wouldn't have to ask, Julia thought, but didn't say it. They had an independent relationship, mutually agreed. 'I've got a very good offer.' She sat down and said, 'How about a drink for me?'

He brought her a vodka swimming in ice. 'Great. What is it?'

She told him, but without the rush of enthusiasm. She sounded quite cool about it. And for some reason, born of resentment, she didn't mention Harold King, as if she were punishing him by keeping the best part back.

He was very pleased for her. He wasn't jealous – sometimes she thought it was because he was so confident in his own abilities. No trace of a chip on the shoulder with Felix. Thank God.

He got up and stretched, and looked across at her.

'It's late and there's nothing on the telly. How about bed?' She wanted to say, no, you go ahead, I'm not tired, and dent that maddening self-esteem, but she didn't. It wouldn't have worked.

She'd tried that approach once, after a row, and he'd simply shrugged and said, 'Suit yourself.' In the morning she'd capitulated and initiated sex between them.

'You're a clever little piece, aren't you,' he murmured, biting and poking at her ear with his tongue. He used low-grade slang during love making; he called her a bimbo and a piece and she didn't care. He hoisted her on top of him, and for a few seconds Julia thought, I can't go on with this, I've got to stop. And then the flame seared the candle and it began to melt.

Julia's phone rang just before lunch. She'd been making a list of staff she was going to need. Western had offered a suite of offices on the penthouse floor, and she'd taken it, and asked for a private telephone line, not connected to the switchboard. She was glad she hadn't mentioned the name of Harold King to Felix. They'd gone their ways the next morning, and she had felt diminished by the sex they had shared.

It was no longer making love. It was just having sex. It was an unhappy sensation. She put it out of her mind and got down to work. Reflection had convinced her that secrecy was paramount to get the project going. It was one thing to tell her parents, and a phone call bound them to discretion. Very different to set the hare of rumour running through the office, and then through the tight little world of media.

One of the conditions for new staff joining her had to be

secrecy on pain of immediate dismissal. She picked up the phone; 'Julia Hamilton'.

Ben Harris's voice said, 'I've had a private memo from upstairs. Don't come to my office. Meet me at the pub in half an hour.'

He was sitting in a corner when she came in; the lunch-time crowd were gathering. 'Hello, Ben, sorry to keep you waiting. Something came up just before I left.'

'No problem. I haven't wasted good drinking time. Usual for you?'

'Why don't I get it?' she said. 'Scotch for you?'

He nodded. 'I'll get the next lot.'

She sat down beside him. 'Why didn't you want me to come to the office?'

'Because I wanted to talk to you,' he said. He lit a cigarette. He was a heavy smoker. 'I got a memo about you from the old man. About the new job.'

'Yes,' Julia said. 'I knew he was going to tell you himself. I didn't ask for it. I didn't go behind your back.'

'I know you didn't,' he said gruffly. 'You never have. Unlike some. My contract is up in five years. I wouldn't have minded handing over to you, Julia. Never thought I'd bring myself to say that to anyone, but I mean it. You'd make a bloody good Editor.'

'That's a real compliment, coming from you. You're the best.'

He narrowed his eyes against the cigarette smoke and then peered at her.

'Remember the time I told you not to go on the Rhys murders? You wouldn't listen. And you were right. You coped with it, wrote your book, made a name for yourself. But before I say anything else, I want you to know I'm not trying to knock you or cramp your style.

'You're a clever girl and you're not a cow either. Quite an achievement in this game. I like you. So listen to me this time.

'For Christ's sake don't touch this one. Don't go after Harold King!'

Julia set down her drink. 'I didn't know he was going to tell you *that*. Nobody is supposed to know at this stage—'

'He had his reason,' Harris muttered. 'I know about King. He wants me to help you. I said no.'

'Oh God,' Julia exclaimed. Her anxiety was for Harris, not herself. 'You didn't, Ben – you know what he's like. He'll think of an excuse and throw you out on your ear.'

'No he won't,' Harris said sourly. 'Let me tell you a few things about King. No, just listen. I'm not talking about public knowledge. He thrives on that. I'm talking about who and what he really is. He came out of nowhere, and he's covered his tracks so well, no-one's ever been able to find his country of origin or anything about him. Except that he says he's Polish, but even that's a guess.

'He speaks it fluently, without an accent. But he speaks German like a native son. He could be anything. You've heard about the business deals, and the borderline stuff. Anyone opposed him, he wiped them out with lawsuits.

'It's rumoured he has links with the Mafia, contacts with drugs, illegal arms shipments. He's up to his armpits in every dirty deal you can think of – he's bought people with money or blackmail or both.'

'How do you know all this?' she asked him. He stubbed out the little butt of cigarette and fumbled for another.

'Because I started looking into him myself. Ten years ago. Western told me to call it off or lose my job.'

'I don't believe it,' she protested. 'After what he said to me – he made you drop it? Why?'

'King had something on him,' he said, and his voice was very low. 'My guess is, he's about to break it, and that's why Western is going to stick his neck out and strike first. Or stick your neck out. That's the bottom line.'

'What is it?' she asked. 'What could he have on the old man? Why hasn't he used it before? They hate each other, everyone knows that.'

Ben Harris didn't answer her. He pushed back his chair and stood up. 'I'll get us a drink. You want a club sandwich?'

'I'm not hungry and I don't want a drink. I'm working this

afternoon. Ben, you can't just throw out hints like that. Tell me!'

'Are you going to take my advice?' he demanded. He was still on his way to the bar.

'No,' Julia said. 'No, I'm not.'

'Then you might as well get back to your smart new penthouse,' he snarled, and it was the old Ben Harris, jealous, difficult, a man nobody liked.

Julia shook her head. 'You're not getting rid of me,' she said quietly. 'All right, I'll join you. Vodka on the rocks. Make it a small one.'

He came back and sat down. He had a cheese-and-pickle sandwich on a plate. He took a bite out of it. 'Ben,' she said, 'please. Look at it this way. If King is what you say, someone ought to do something about it! Instead of putting me off you ought to help me expose him. '

Ben Harris looked at her. 'Publicity is a funny thing, Julia.' He went on, 'If a man gets himself into the public eye by being a self-confessed shit, but a bit of a character, the great British public takes him to its heart. They say to themselves, He's been a naughty boy, but he's not so bad. Look what he did for those refugee kids from Romania, and didn't he rescue Brighton Soccer Club when the lads went to see him – deep down he's got a kind heart. You know the kind of con trick, and it always seems to work. I don't understand the mentality, but then I wouldn't. I'm Welsh. King has built himself up into an institution. The poor refugee boy picked up from a DP camp by a kind-hearted UNRRA official.

'People have got a sneaking admiration for him. They think, Look where he's got. All that money, all those businesses. Perhaps he has cut a few corners, so who hasn't—?'

'Ben,' Julia said softly, 'why won't you help me?'

He looked at her. She'd never noticed his eyes before. They were as dark as Welsh coal.

'Because I'm scared for you,' he said. 'There were two people rich enough to call King's bluff. Alfred Hayman, the boss of Eros films, and J. D. Lewis, the head of Lewis Publications. Big men, and tough. King wanted their outlets; movies and

TV and a big publishing and magazine network. He went after them in his usual way, buying into the shares, rumour mongering to depress the price – clever articles placed in the financial columns speculating about profits spiralling down – Hayman and Lewis fought him off. They routed the bastard in his takeover bids, and each of them set out to get him.' He looked at her. 'They're dead. Hayman was actually murdered in the Bahamas and Lewis was run off the road one night on his way home to Kent. Nobody was ever charged. King couldn't stop them, so I believe he had them murdered. I travelled to the Bahamas to look into the Hayman killing. I talked to the police. I even got to see the body. It was a contract killing, dressed up to look like robbery. I remember having a drink with the Bahamian copper in charge. He was a smart man, very impressive. He said to me, "This wasn't done by any of our people. They don't shoot a man at point-blank range in the left ear, and then turn his place over for valuables. They use a club or a knife. This killer came from outside on a contract. From the US I'd say." Hayman was fighting King with his own weapons. He'd been buying into King Media Promotions through nominees, and he was gearing up to go public and throw him off the Board.'

'And the other man – Lewis, the boss of the multinational publishers?' Julia asked him. 'Did you look into that too?'

'Yes, on my own time. I'd been told to drop the story after Hayman, but when Lewis was killed, I couldn't leave it alone. It nagged at me. I knew King was involved. I didn't find out anything I could use. Just a hit-and-run accident at night on a wet road. Lewis was driving a Bentley. They're built like bloody tanks. It must have been a hell of a big lorry that hit him, because the car bounced through the barrier and went down an embankment. It was smashed up like a matchbox. If you're going to take on a car like that without getting hurt yourself, you hit them sideways with a three tonner.

'From the tyre marks they reckoned Lewis was going at about eighty miles an hour. As I told you, they never found the lorry or the driver. Case closed. Like Hayman. Now do you still want to mount a personal campaign against Harold

King? I tell you what, go away and think about it. Sit in that plush office with the nice view, and imagine what it would be like to wake up one night and find a man in a hood bending over you with a knife.

'There are contract killers who specialize in sex crimes. It puts the police off if the hit is a woman.'

Julia stood up. 'You've no real proof, Ben,' she said slowly. 'You're just trying to frighten me. And if you really believe it, then you ought to help me stop him. You go back to your office and think about that. Thanks for the drinks.'

Ben Harris watched her leave; several men looked after her, raking the back view. Slim, very neat, elegant legs. And that mane of red hair standing out like a beacon.

She wouldn't listen to him. She was stubborn and she was courageous. And Western had hooked her. Just as years ago, he had hooked him. And then, Harris addressed his remaining inch of whisky, cut him off short and gave him the news editorship as a consolation prize. He wasn't afraid of Western, and he showed it. On the few occasions Western had tried to manipulate a news story, Ben had stood up to him, true to his calling. If his marriage had failed and his grown-up children did their filial duty with a Christmas card, Ben had been true to the job.

He had been jealous and suspicious of all comers because he couldn't bear to face the future without his work; even jealous of Julia Hamilton after the success of her stories on the Rhys murders.

Jealous, but in his professional heart, admiring of a talent and the guts that went with it. She was a nice girl, he couldn't deny that. Success hadn't spoiled her; it hadn't made her conceited. He remembered his remark when she came back from Wales – 'Christ,' he muttered, it seemed like yesterday. She'd looked grey and hollow eyed. Western had thrown her in at the deepest end, sending her on a vile murder of two helpless toddlers. 'It's marked you, and it shows.' He'd been grudging and angry, because he was shocked at what the experience had cost her.

He had a daughter of his own, even if she never bothered to come near him. Julia Hamilton had looked into the darkest pit of human evil, and survived without losing her faith in people. When Ben Harris realized that, he decided to back her. She wasn't out to knife him and get his job; others might like to, but it wasn't her style.

He had been what he termed friendly, until she took up with that bumptious prick Sutton. Then he was irritable, nit-picking and nasty for some time. He had never understood the female mind. So his ex-wife complained, and he didn't argue. He just went off to the pub, or back to the office.

Julia hadn't been scared off the assignment. He knew that. She'd been shaken, he could see, but still determined.

She'd go ahead, and King would soon hear whispers that someone was poking around trying to uncover his past.

He bought himself another Scotch. 'If you really believe it, then you ought to help me stop him. You go back to your office and think about that . . . ' He did think about it. He thought about it when he went in to the big steel and plate-glass Western building and as he finished off his day's work. He thought about it sitting at home with the TV screen flickering in front of him.

He hadn't much to lose. He'd backed off himself once, because Western told him to; was he really going to let a pig-headed young woman take on Harold King, and sit on his hands? He pressed the off button on the remote control. The picture faded to a tiny crimson eye, and that too diminished and was gone. Then he got up and unlocked a cupboard in his bedroom, and took out an unmarked file.

3

'Let's go out to eat tonight,' Julia suggested. Felix looked at her and grinned. 'Good idea. Who's paying? I bought a new suit and some shirts this afternoon – I'm skint.'

'I'm paying,' Julia said. 'And you'd better put on the new suit. We're going to Mario's.'

'We are?' he stared at her. 'Sweetheart, you *are* paying – it's ten quid for an orange juice . . . Are we celebrating something?'

'No,' Julia answered. 'It's down to expenses. I just want to go there and see the place. I've booked a table for nine o'clock. I'm going to change.'

The head waiter at Mario's was a friend of Ben Harris. Julia was discovering that there were unexpected facets to his character. He knew a lot of unlikely people, and he could call in favours when he needed information. Like which evening this week Harold King was dining at Mario's with his family. He always took his wife and daughter out to dinner at Mario's; it was a weekly ritual. He had a special table which was always reserved in case he called up at the last minute, and Harris said he always ordered the same menu. Foie Gras, followed by Steak Diane, ending with a *bombe surprise*. His wife and daughter would drink claret at a hundred and twenty pounds a bottle, Ch. Haut Brion '82, and a vintage Krug to go with the pudding. King never touched alcohol. He was a life-long teetotaller.

Julie dressed in a short, black skirt and a sequinned tank top, with long fake diamond earrings that swung like waterfalls against the blazing hair – Felix whistled when she came in and said, 'You look good; you ought to take me out more often. How do you like the suit? Nice, conservative House of Commons uniform?'

'Very smart,' Julia said. 'You look good, too. Let's go, we can have a drink in the bar and see who's there.'

They took Julia's car, and on the way he said to her casually, 'What are you up to? You're not going to the most expensive watering hole in London on expenses just to have a look at the décor. Who are you interested in?'

She made it sound unexciting. 'Harold King. I've heard he's angling for a Life Peerage. Have you heard any buzz about it? Might be an interesting profile.'

He frowned. 'No. And I don't believe it. He's a bloody crook, he'd never get an honour. It may be a stupid, lousy system, but nobody'd stand for *him* going to the Lords. You going to do a profile on him?'

'No,' she said. 'It's just an idea at the moment. We might be taking a look at the Honours system.'

'Oh, I see,' he settled back in his seat. ' "Exposure" on the trail of corruption, selling honours – great stuff, Julia. So long as you don't expect to get a DBE yourself one day . . . They've got long memories.'

'Hey,' Felix said, looking round, as they took a seat in the upstairs room. 'This is rather smart. I think I could get used to this lifestyle, don't you?'

It was a long room, panelled in eighteenth-century pine; there were big comfortable sofas and occasional armchairs, fine sporting pictures on the walls, fresh flowers and piles of newspapers on the centre table. It was a pastiche of the English country house, and in clever contrast to the chic Italian décor of the restaurant below. There was no bar in sight; orders were taken and drinks brought to the customers.

Julia saw them sitting in a corner. Harold King, with his wife and his daughter. He was familiar enough from TV and photographs, but the reality was different. He was much taller than she expected, with a shock of pure white hair that framed a semi-circle of bald scalp. The eyebrows were white, too, and they bushed out over heavy-lidded pale eyes. It was a powerful, ugly face, the flesh sagged in a dewlap onto his collar. He had a powerful body with heavy shoulders. His skin was coarse and tanned a deep brown, whether from sun or artifice, she couldn't tell. He was sitting in a big chair, and he seemed to sprawl over it, legs spread, feet planted on the carpet, his hands moving constantly as he spoke. To his right a very thin dark woman listened and smiled and occasionally nodded. She was beautifully dressed, and wearing a massive ruby-and-diamond brooch on the neck of her black dress. When she gestured, a diamond as big as a pebble flashed blue fire. The wife of thirty-two years. Marilyn; ex-model, ex-bit-part actress. Incredibly, the delicate creature with her birdlike frame and little painted face was the mother of the hulking blonde girl on the other side of King. Gloria King, a cruel misnomer, for a female version of her father. White-blonde hair, the same pale eyes with tortoise lids, the coarse features and heavy limbs; she wore a suite of gold and diamond jewellery like fetters round her neck and wrists. She never looked away from her father's face. Her eyes were fixed on him in adoration.

Julia murmured to Felix, 'There's King, over there, with the wife and daughter.'

Felix stared openly. 'Jesus,' he said, grinning. 'She's going to need a bloody big cash settlement. I suppose if you thought about the money long enough, you'd get it up . . . Mum looks a better bet. Bit like fucking something out of the Mummy Room in the British Museum. '

'Felix,' Julia hissed at him. 'Keep your voice down.' She

didn't need to warn him because at that moment Harold King began to shout.

'Where the hell's the menu? Where's Phillipe?'

'He's on his way up, sir,' a nervous wine waiter assured him. King scowled at him. His voice rose over the quiet room, so that everyone stopped talking and turned to look at him. 'I want him now – go and tell him to hurry up!'

The head waiter was already hurrying across the room. King waited till he reached the table.

'I want another bottle of Perrier and the menu – what the hell's going on here? You call this service?'

Phillipe was a man of international reputation and part-owner of the restaurant. He held out the leather-covered menu.

'I have it here, Mr King.'

'Take it away; you know perfectly well what we always have.'

He dismissed the man with an angry wave. Phillipe gave a slight bow and said smoothly, 'Of course. Your Perrier will be here immediately.'

'My God,' Julia said. 'Did you see that? What a pig!'

Felix shrugged, 'He was playing games, drawing attention to himself. It's part of the act. I bet he gives Philippe What's-his-name a socking great tip when he leaves and the oily little bugger will take it and bow low. Put the moral indignation away, darling, and let's enjoy ourselves.'

Julia said angrily, 'Nothing bothers you, does it, Felix? How could you excuse behaviour like that?'

'Because I don't sit in judgement like you do,' he said quickly. 'You're the crusading journalist, not me. After all, if I'm going to spend my life with politicians, I can't afford to side with the underdog. There's just no future in it.'

Julia said quietly, 'Then you'll never get to the top, Felix. You make fun of Warburton, but he's got real standards and integrity. That's why he's trusted. Let's go to our table.' She got up and he followed her with a slight shrug. She was in a touchy mood, and he was irritated because he wanted to enjoy himself. He didn't want a moral lecture, he decided, he wanted lobster quenelles.

Harold King noticed the redheaded woman when he passed them on the way to the table specially reserved for him. It was in the middle of the room, giving him a vantage point where he could see everyone and everyone could see him. He noticed her because he hated that colour hair. He had never considered any woman cursed with it to be attractive. One day he'd seen a secretary in the main office with red hair, and ordered her to dye it or be sacked.

With the temper typical of the colouring, she'd told him to stuff his job and stormed out in tears. He had told personnel not to give her a reference.

But this one was familiar. He recognized Western's star protégée, the reporter who'd covered the Welsh child murders and written a serious psychological study of the murders afterwards. Julia Hamilton.

He read every word in Western's newspapers, London and provincial. He noted his staff, his main advertisers, his political stances, his attitude to social, economic and world issues. King always studied his targets in depth while he was preparing to attack them.

This girl was outstanding; he watched her narrowly, dismissing the companion as some young hanger-on. She'd be a good catch for him when the time came. If the bribe was big enough in terms of money and power. Every human being had a price. It would gratify him to rub Western's nose in the shit by employing Julia Hamilton.

For a moment their glances met. King was extraordinarily sensitive; the coarse bullying persona he presented concealed a deeply intuitive understanding of people. It had given him power over them precisely because he knew what made them tick.

Her contempt and hostility were tangible in those few seconds of eye contact. He registered her reaction to him, and stared her down. He also registered that it took quite a long time before she turned her head away. There was contempt in that gesture too, not submission.

He swallowed his glass of Perrier and glared round for the waiter. Yes, he decided, I'll employ you. I'll make you an offer you won't refuse, because nobody could. And then I'll break you. As I've broken other fools who tried to stand against me. And I'll enjoy doing it.

He gave his attention to the first course and dismissed Julia Hamilton from his mind.

His wife was talking trivialities about some charity committee. He didn't bother to listen. She had social ambitions, and he despised her for it. He knew, if she didn't, that all the high-society ladies wanted out of women like her was fat donations from their husbands. In return they patronized them. Money was the key; he didn't mind if Marilyn indulged her silly fantasies. It kept her out of mischief. What he wouldn't allow was his daughter to be dragged into the charade. Luckily she wasn't interested in female time wasting. He looked at her with affection. She was his clone; she looked like him and she wanted only one thing in the world. To be like him. She was his compensation for the son he never fathered. Better than a son. He realized that. A son would have competed. Gloria worshipped at his shrine. 'How's the foie gras?' he asked her. She smiled up at him. 'Delicious, Daddy.' He went on; he was needled by that other woman's refusal to be overborne and he felt spiteful. 'Enjoying yourself, darling?' 'I'm having a wonderful time,' his daughter answered. 'I always love coming out with you.' He reached across and patted her hand. 'You're my girl,' he said. He turned to his wife. 'Isn't she my girl?' The pretty doll nodded obediently. 'Yes, Harry darling.' He knew she had given up competing against her daughter long ago. He also knew that she and Gloria hated each other.

A son, he often reminded himself, might have sided with his mother.

'Good dinner,' Felix remarked. Julia had hardly spoken through the meal. His irritation was growing. Excellent food, exceptional wine – he'd insisted on choosing from the list and he hadn't spared the cost. Why not – Western was paying. And he knew it annoyed Julia.

Why the hell did she have to be so sour? Working herself up into a froth of righteous indignation because Harold King had been rude to some greasy waiter . . . He always shouted the odds in public, it was part of the image. He was surprised she couldn't see it in perspective.

Julia said, 'Let's have coffee and I'll get the bill.'

'I'd like a brandy,' Felix announced. 'Or are you getting into a moral dilemma about the expense account?'

'Order what you like,' she said curtly. She knew him in this provocative mood. Like a spoilt child.

'OK – let's see – Armagnac,' he scanned the wine list. 'The '68 should be nice. I'll have that.'

'And for madame?' the wine waiter enquired.

'Nothing, thank you.' Julia wanted to finish her coffee and go. She had hated the whole evening, and it wasn't just because of Harold King. Felix returned to the attack.

'My old man was a wine merchant,' he announced. 'He knew a lot about wine, but not a lot about business. All the old bugger left me was a champagne taste on a beer income. Julia, what the hell's the matter with you?' He leaned towards her. 'You've been so fucking sour the whole evening. What's the matter?'

She stirred her coffee and then put the spoon carefully into the saucer. She looked up at him. 'You are, Felix. I don't think I like you very much.'

Red seeped up his neck and into his face. He said, 'What is this – some kind of message?'

'I don't know,' Julia admitted. 'Look, don't let's argue about it. I'll get the bill.'

'I haven't finished my drink,' he said loudly. 'Anyway, I think I'd like another one.'

'Please yourself,' she said quietly. 'If you want another you can pay for it.' She signed the bill and pushed back her chair. 'I'll see you later,' she said.

'You'll be lucky,' Felix snapped. 'Thanks for a lousy evening.'

The head waiter came up to her. He had noticed the little scene of friction and the young man scowling at the table as she walked away.

'I hope you enjoyed your dinner,' he said.

'Very much, thank you,' Julia answered.

'May I order you a taxi?'

'I have a car.' Her wrap was brought and she draped it round her shoulders. Felix hadn't followed her. Phillipe saw her to the door.

'Give my regards to Mr Harris,' he said. 'I hope he will come and see us soon.'

'I'll tell him,' Julia promised. She couldn't imagine Ben Harris in a restaurant like Mario's. Perhaps because she knew so little about him. She didn't drive home directly. She detoured round Hyde Park and on an impulse headed towards the Embankment. She loved the river at night. Unfortunately, it wasn't safe to park the car and get out and walk. She didn't want to go back to the flat. She wanted a little time to think.

The relationship was changing; it had been happy in the beginning, deeply sexual on both sides, carefree and without ties. Like a passionate friendship. The few years age difference hadn't seemed significant. Even the disparity in money terms was glossed over. He thought it was a joke to be called her Toy Boy. And she realized, in that pause for introspection, that she had begun indulging him like the spoilt child she chided him for being. But he wasn't a child, he was an ambitious, selfish, unscrupulous man with a talent for sex.

Suddenly, foolishly, Julia's eyes filled up with tears. It couldn't go on. It was demeaning to both of them. She didn't love him, she admitted that. But the truth was worse. She didn't like him any more, and she'd been goaded into saying so that night. It was time to put an end to it. She wiped her wet cheeks and started the engine. When she opened her front door the flat was in darkness. He had gone off somewhere, spending the night with a friend. In the morning he'd turn up and expect her to take him into bed and pretend nothing had happened. It wasn't the first time he'd taken off. But it would be the last.

Inside, she kicked off her shoes. She was glad Felix wasn't there. On an impulse, checking her watch for the first time, she dialled Ben Harris's number.

'It's me,' she said. 'I hope I'm not interrupting anything.'

'Only a bloody boring programme on ITV,' was the answer. 'How did you get on?'

'He was having dinner with his wife and daughter. He actually gave me the hard stare.'

'I bet you gave it back,' Ben said.

'I did, but it wasn't easy. He's horribly intimidating.'

There was a slight pause.

'It hasn't made you change your mind?'

'No,' she said firmly. 'Quite the opposite. You're right, Ben, he's bad news all right. It was a good idea of yours; I'm glad I've seen him. I couldn't see that file of yours tonight, could I?' Again there was a pause.

'I could drop it round in half an hour. Where's lover boy?'

'He's not here,' Julia admitted. 'We had a row.'

'Glad to hear it,' Harris sounded laconic. 'He's a sponging little prick. Take my advice and don't have him back.'

She said slowly, 'I'm not going to. Can you really drop the file over? I don't think I'll sleep much tonight, anyway. I'd like to get started.'

'See you,' he said, and hung up.

She opened the flat door to him. 'Thanks for coming over,' she said. 'It's very good of you.'

'No problem.' He looked round the sitting room. 'Nice place. Do you collect the pictures?'

'Yes; I'd like to get one or two abstracts one day, but they're just too expensive. Sit down, I've made some fresh coffee.'

'I couldn't have tea, could I?'

'Of course you can. Won't be a minute. Tea bag do?'

'Never have anything else,' he called after her.

It was an attractive room. He liked the pictures; they gave colour and originality, a reflection of their owner. He opened the file and leafed through it. She came back with two mugs. He liked her for that. 'Before I give you this,' he said, 'I'm going to ask you one more time – are you still going ahead with this investigation?'

'One more time,' she said, 'yes I am. And I'm going to ask you something. You are going to help me, aren't you?'

'I wouldn't be giving you this if I wasn't,' he said. 'Against my better judgement and all my instincts, I'm going into it with you. But on one condition, and it's not subject to argument.' He looked at her obstinately. She knew the expression. This was his sticking point, whatever it was. 'Name it,' she suggested.

'That you pull back when I tell you to, and leave it to me,' he said. 'Otherwise, J, no file, no deal. And don't promise anything you don't mean.'

Julia hesitated. 'Why should I have to pull out?'

'You won't,' he answered, 'unless I think it's getting dangerous. Which I think is certain, especially if we come up with something. Do you want to think it over?' He had closed the file and put it under his arm. He meant what he said.

'No. You have a head start. I need the file and I need you, Ben. We have a deal. Western won't like it, but he doesn't have to know.'

'The less anybody knows from now on, the better,' he said. He finished his tea. 'Are you getting rid of Sutton? You won't be talked round?' She shook her head. 'No,' she said. 'It's not good for either of us any more. Don't be too hard on him, Ben. It's not really his fault.'

'You're too much for him,' Ben Harris remarked. 'Too bright, too successful, too much of everything. You haven't talked to him about this, have you?'

'No. I just said we might be doing a feature on the Honours system. He doesn't know anything else.'

'Good. I'll be off now, J. Read this through and we'll get our heads together tomorrow. After office hours. Thanks for the tea. I'll see myself out.'

The file started in 1949 with the release of a displaced person from the UNRRA rehabilitation centre in Nessenberg. There were ten thousand men, women and children in that particular camp, human flotsam thrown up by the tidal wave of war. People without papers, identities or proven nationalities. The young man who called himself Hans Koenig was typical of the victims of national chaos and breakdown. He had no papers, claimed he was brought as slave labour from the Polish borders in 1939, but couldn't remember his name or place of birth, or what had happened to his family. He thought they'd been shot. He'd been beaten and traumatized. He remembered nothing.

The history was quite common. Teenagers and children were seized, transported, Germanicized if they were Aryan types, or worked as slaves in factories or on the farms. Girls were sold into domestic service. Hans Koenig insisted he didn't know who he was or where he came from. He had been found in a refugee column fleeing the Allied advance. The medical records said he was suffering from acute emotional trauma. He had been in the camp for four years.

Hans Koenig was just one more statistic in the register of human misery that the officials of UNRRA, the military, and the civilian authorities in the British Section were trying to shift through and sort out.

There were guilty hiding among the innocent; deserters from the German army, SS masquerading as civilians, minor war criminals from the Ukraine and the Balkan States hoping to evade punishment. The SS were easier to identify because of the number tattooed under the armpit, but most had burned or scarred themselves to avoid detection. There was no evidence of guilt in Koenig's medical record. He was a stateless person, without a past and with no future. Julia read slowly through the photostats of those early reports. Suddenly the aftermath of that dreadful war seemed real to her. The grainy newsreels and staccato broadcasting style of documentaries had meant little to someone who hadn't been born at the time. Past misery, hopelessness and human evil spoke to her with a clear voice as she read of the only known origins of the man she had seen in the smart restaurant that night. The coffee was cold beside her. Her watch said it was two forty-five in the morning.

'Nobody even knows his real nationality. He says he's Polish . . . but he speaks German like a native son . . . He could be anything.'

She remembered Ben's description of Harold King. He'd anglicized the name he'd given himself in the camp. Koenig. King. Some subtle indication of the man he would become perhaps, or a mere fancy on her part, looking for motives . . . She started to read again. He had been released into the care of an UNRRA official who stood surety for him and obtained a set of temporary papers from the British Control Commission in the Munich area. The copy of the document showed faded signatures: the Control Commission Officer in charge of refugees, a Major Grant, and the UNRRA official, Phyllis Lowe. A woman had got Hans Koenig out of the camp. The rest was Ben's work, the result of his detailed and careful investigation into what happened after that. Phyllis Lowe had continued to work with the United Nations organization among the refugees for another six months. She had lived in requisitioned accommodation in Nessenberg itself, and the young man had stayed with her. She had employed one of the many destitute German civilians to teach him English. The man had been a schoolteacher, and exempt from the Army because of a club foot.

At the end of the six months, Phyllis Lowe had resigned her job and returned to England, taking Hans Koenig with her.

And there, like a line drawn across the page, Ben had come to a dead end. There were no official records, nothing. Nobody in Nessenberg knew Phyllis Lowe or remembered the young man. The schoolteacher had died in 1953 and his family had left the district. The work of UNRRA went on for several more years before it was disbanded.

Phyllis Lowe went to England with her protégé. Dead stop. Everything known about Harold King from the fifties onward, came from one source. Himself. Harris had included the relevant chapters on King's early life from the biography he had had printed by one of his own publishing companies. The hack wrote movingly of his time in the camp, and of the English lady who had rescued him. She came across as a kind-hearted spinster who treated him as a substitute son, and died tragically of cancer a few months after bringing him to England with her. She had bought him a few hundred pounds of savings certificates, and with this he had founded his fortune.

It was the standard story, part tear-jerker, part eulogy. With his benefactor's small legacy, King, as he now called himself, bought a stock of remaindered books and an old van. He sensed that people needed escapism. They were sick of war and hungry for entertainment.

Everyone wanted books, and books was what King gave them. He travelled the country, selling from his van, buying up books wherever he found them, renting a small shop that became a chain of retail book shops, then a printing business and in the early sixties he had enough money to acquire a small publishing company that had gone broke publishing quality books and unknown authors. King had pulped the whole stock. The hack made the act of vandalism sound like an instance of his genius. King recruited his own new authors, and King Publishing was born. 'I sold dreams to people,' was the famous quote, 'because I had a dream myself. And I made it come true.'

Ben Harris added his own footnote to the story.

King's stable of writers specialized in crime novellas. Cheap to produce, cheap to sell. Lurid mass-market trash that peddled violence and sex in tune with the new fashion for permissiveness. They made a fortune for him. This was well known; he boasted of it, sneered at his critics and branched out into soft-porn magazines.

Nothing new there. But Harris had ferreted out a less well-known detail of how he founded his publishing empire. He had lent money to the philanthropic owner of that early publishing house, promising to maintain its literary standards, and then called in the loan without warning.

The man had lost his business and died penniless a few years later. No-one had bothered to ask what had happened to him.

It was a technique King had perfected over the years. He had a sixth sense; he could smell a business in trouble as a predator smells blood. He bought into them, usually under nominees, then took them over and turned them into profitable enterprises that he either sold on or enlarged for his own purposes. Within twenty-five years he had acquired a major publishing house, two quality London monthly magazines, and a substantial stake in Midlands Independent Television. Besides property interests, and a construction company engaged in building work in the Middle East.

It was common knowledge, and he announced it regularly, that his next project was to run his own national newspaper.

At forty he had got married to a beautiful model, who had done a stint as an actress, and told the world that from now on he was going to be a family man. The string of mistresses he ran with maximum publicity were sent packing. There were no more photographs of King at functions and first nights with 'friends' hanging on his arm.

There hadn't been a whisper of a woman since. King was presented as the devoted husband and father of his little Gloria. And it had all begun with a kind-hearted English lady in a camp full of refugees in ravaged Germany after the war. Hans Koenig, the nameless, hopeless young man, traumatized by his experiences, had touched her heart. And when she died, leaving him friendless in England, he swore to justify her faith in him. There was another famous quote. 'She believed in me. I wasn't going to let her down. I owed it to her to get out and make a success.'

It was an incredible story. A sharp dealer, a tough business opponent, a genius without mercy for those less able than himself – a man without morals or scruples who didn't give a damn for his reputation. The sentimentalist beating his breast about his benefactress. The faithful husband and doting father. The impulsive philanthropist who helped orphaned children in Romania, and saved a football club because the players came to see him.

The man whose most dangerous adversaries had met violent deaths. Julia closed the file. Incredible was the right word.

She was in the kitchen eating breakfast when she heard Felix come in. She had managed to sleep for a few hours; it had been fitful and troubled by dreams related to what she had read. She felt a little jump of anxiety as the kitchen door opened.

'Hi,' he said. 'I'm back.' He came in and closed the door. He looked puffy eyed and unshaven. Julia looked at him and thought that wherever he'd spent the night, there hadn't been a razor.

'Hello,' she said. She spread marmalade over her slice of toast.

'Any breakfast for me?'

'Yes, if you make it,' she answered.

'Oh. Still hating my guts, are we? Any use saying I'm sorry? I behaved like a stupid shit last night.' Julia had never heard an apology from him before. And with painful insight she knew why. He'd been with a woman. He was feeling guilty because he'd slept with someone else. She sighed.

'There's plenty of coffee. Sit down, Felix. Don't worry. I'm not hating anyone this morning. I think it's time we had a talk.'

'I meant it,' he said. 'I was bloody to you. I'll make it up to you.' He reached over and caught her wrist. 'Kiss and make up,' he suggested. He brought her hand up to his mouth and licked her palm.

Julia pulled sharply away. 'That won't work any more, Felix.'

He shrugged. 'OK, if you're still humpy with me—' He picked up a mug and poured coffee. 'What do you want to talk about? Got any aspirin? I shouldn't have had that second Armagnac.' He tried a grin, making a joke of it. It had always worked with her before. The cheeky-boy act followed by a good session on the mattress. She shook her head. 'I meant what I said last night. That's why I don't want to sleep with you this morning. I don't want to go on living with you any more. It's not working for either of us. Is it – truthfully?'

'It's working all right with me,' he said. 'I don't make demands on you, Julia, you do your thing and I do mine.'

'You did your thing last night, didn't you?' she said it calmly and he reddened. 'I don't want to hear about it – it doesn't matter. It just proves what I'm saying. We don't love each other, and now we're not even friends any more.'

He sipped his coffee. 'We never were,' he said, surprising her. 'All we ever really had was sex. I loved it with you and you couldn't get enough of it with me. But we didn't have a lot in common. Ambition maybe. I always felt you wanted something more, some kind of emotional hook. I wasn't ready for it. I'm still not. Sorry.'

'I'm sorry too,' Julia said. 'But we did have some happy times, so don't let's forget that. I know I won't. You'll find someone else, Felix. If you haven't already.'

He looked at her honestly. 'I haven't,' he said. 'I've had the odd bonk here and there. Like last night. But it didn't mean anything. I think a lot of you Julia. I mean it. You're bright, I admire that. You'll go far up the old ladder. And one day I'll be up there too. What do you want me to do – move out?'

'Yes,' she said slowly. She chided herself for being so tired that she felt very near to tears. Not enough sleep, that was all. She'd be too busy to be lonely. 'Yes, but I don't want to rush you. You've got to find somewhere else that suits you. We can – well, keep out of each other's way till you do. I've got to go, Felix, or I'll be late.'

'I've got to shower and shave,' he agreed. 'Or I will have the Warbler giving me black looks. I'll see what I can fix up. And do me a favour, will you? Don't cry. We'll always be friends.' He sat on at the table when she hurried out. It was a pity. He felt depressed. She was a great girl. But she was right. He'd started cheating on her in the last year.

His afternoons weren't always spent at the squash court or the gym. It was time to move on. Time to get out from under her shadow. Spread his wings on his own account. Some of his friends had been telling him that for a while now. She was just that bit older and she had the status and the money. Deep down he felt belittled and he was beginning to resent it. So he cheated on her. Which didn't enhance his self-image. He got up, dropped the mug in the sink and went out to get ready for work. He heard the front door close and knew that Julia had gone.

'Well?' Ben Harris asked. 'Where are you going to start?'

Julia said, 'Right at the beginning. Page one, line one. How do we know Phyllis Lowe is dead?'

He looked up sharply, scowling. 'What do you mean?'

'Did you check? Has anybody seen a death certificate? No, they haven't. Everyone took King's word for it. So I sent someone down to St Catherine's House first thing this morning to look up every Phyllis Lowe who died between April and June in 1949. Those are the dates given in that load of rubbish he had written about himself. Cancer was diagnosed in April, just as the daffodils came out, and she died as the roses bloomed in their back garden. No-one called Phyllis Lowe died in the London area in that year during that period. In fact – ' she put the list in front of him, ' – the only single women of that name who died of cancer in the whole of London during that year were all fifteen to twenty years too old to be her! See for yourself.'

Ben scanned the list.

'Christ,' he muttered. 'You're right. But let's say he gave all that crap to his author, about the date and time of year – just to make it sound good – it doesn't mean she didn't die—'

'But not when or where he said,' Julia pointed out. 'Ben, this could be a wild guess, but I'm going to follow it up.'

He said, 'What's the wild guess?'

'I think she may still be alive. And if she is, I want to talk to her. Now, let's work out where we start looking.'

'UNRRA had records of all their personnel. They must be somewhere, and they'd give her family personal details – home address, next of kin, that sort of stuff. But, J, it's forty years ago—'

'I know,' she agreed. 'But didn't people have ration books, identity cards? Listen, they've traced medical records back to the First World War just recently. They'd been lying about in local hospitals and nobody had bothered to throw them out. I've got a good team of researchers.'

Ben Harris said, 'How about the area where King says he was living with her – it's in that book – the house with the fucking roses in the back garden. Tell them to try the local doctors. Some of these practices keep medical records for years – even after the patient's dead – nobody bothers to chuck them away—'

'And,' Julia interrupted, 'if they moved on, their records were forwarded to the new doctor. Tell me,' she changed the subject suddenly, 'why do you think King lied about her? It wasn't just to make a good sob story. Why not tell the truth instead of inventing a whole scenario?'

'Because the truth wasn't quite as pretty as the lie,' Ben Harris said.

'Then we've got to find it out,' Julia told him.

She tapped the file with one finger.

'Everything else came to a dead end. You went to Germany, you went to Nessenberg; there was a record of a Hans Koenig among the ten thousand DPs who were there in forty-nine. We know this woman got him out and took him in to live with her. Then she says she's going to England and that's the last anyone hears of her. He could have entered this country illegally and made up the whole story.'

Ben Harris had a rare smile. She saw it then.

'I'd love that,' he said. 'I'd really love to prove something like that. Just for starters. How many people can you put on to this?'

'You tell me,' Julia answered. He considered. 'Three pairs. A pair works better in this kind of job; one sees something the other one's missed. Two to work through the Hammersmith medical centres, ask around the neighbourhood where this Phyllis Lowe had a house – if she did – two to track down any former British employees of UNRRA, and another couple to go back to Nessenberg and do a better job than I did. UNRRA worked very closely with the military authorities, but also with the German civil administration.'

He'd pushed his glasses up onto his forehead, his eyes narrowed in concentration. 'I may have missed something, but what?'

'There's only one way to find out,' Julia answered. 'How's your German, Ben?'

He looked up. 'Pretty good – why?'

'Because I think we should go to Nessenberg. Can you take a few days off?'

'I haven't been away from the office in God knows how long. I've plenty of time owing to me. Brennan would love warming my seat for a bit.' Brennan was one of his assistants, and Ben suspected him, as he suspected everyone, of eyeing his job.

'Then that's settled,' she said. 'Wednesday suit you?'

'Wednesday's fine,' he agreed. 'You don't take long making up your mind, do you, J?'

'What's the point of waiting – anyway, it would help if I

was out of my flat for a bit. Felix is looking for somewhere else to live. It'll give him time.'

He said, 'It's none of my business, but I'm glad you didn't chicken out. It's about time he got off his butt and looked after himself.'

'Don't be too hard on him,' she said. 'He took it very well; I don't want to be unkind. We did have some very happy times together.'

'Glad to hear it,' he sounded snappish. 'You'd better book the flight and the hotel – the Nessenberghof is a good one, or it was when I was there. May have changed now; ten years is a long time. We'll need to hire a car.'

'I'll get that organized,' Julia promised.

'Right,' he stood up. 'How long do you reckon to stay?'

'As long as it takes. I can't help it, Ben. I just have this gut feeling. It all starts with Phyllis Lowe.'

'It ends with her, that's the trouble,' he answered. 'I'll be off now.' He had reached the door, when she said, 'I'm off, too. Why don't we stop off and have a drink on the way home. I could do with one.'

Ben took his glasses off and stuffed them into his breast pocket.

'Well, I've no pressing engagements for this evening. Why don't we make it dinner?'

'I don't see what they hope to find out in Germany,' Evelyn Western pointed out. 'All that's been gone over and over and nobody got anywhere.'

She was driving to London with her husband. The glass partition was shut, so the chauffeur couldn't hear their conversation.

'That's exactly what I said to Julia,' he answered. 'But she's got some idea in her head about the woman who brought the bastard to England. There's no record of her dying when King's biographer says she did. She's following up on that. I don't believe it matters. He's lied about himself so often, one more lie doesn't make much difference. Good thing is she persuaded Harris to work on it with her. He said no to me. I told you.'

'You can't blame him after last time,' his wife said.

'I hadn't any choice,' Western insisted. 'They'd found Richard Watson. I had to back off.'

'I know,' she placed her hand over his, comforting him.

'It might have been a bluff, but I couldn't risk it. The honours list was up for confirmation, we were going at full throttle with the TV franchise – I *had* to pull Harris off the story.'

'We should have gone to see him,' she said slowly. 'I said so at the time. But you wouldn't listen to me, Billy.'

'I knew him, you didn't,' he retorted. 'He wasn't the sort to be bought off. That's all King needed – proof that I'd been to see Watson or made some attempt to bribe him. Then he'd have crucified me.'

'He's going to do that now,' Evelyn answered. 'It's just a matter of time.'

'Time is what it's all about,' he said. 'He wants the *Herald*, and he's waiting for the right moment before he pulls the rug out on me. But I'm going to get there first, Evie. I'm going to show him up as a liar and a crook, and nothing he says will be believed after that.'

'And you really believe that Julia can do it?'

'With Harris to help her – yes. I have to believe it. I have to.'

Evelyn Western looked out of the window. It was raining and the glass was blurred and opaque in the failing light.

'I wish he was dead,' she said.

Western didn't answer. He had thought that often enough. It was the last desperate option. But he didn't say so to his wife.

4

Harold King swivelled his chair so he could look out of the enormous plate-glass window. It offered a magnificent panoramic view of London, with the silver sweep of the Thames so far below it looked like a ribbon. In the distance he could see the pointed towers of Westminster and the House of Commons. Once, when he had made his first million, he joined the Liberal Party; he liked the idea of becoming an MP. He had stood during the next by-election and been roundly defeated by the Labour candidate. Since then he had conducted a merciless campaign against the MP in particular and the Party in general. The defeat had wounded his pride, and he never forgave anyone or anything that touched his self-esteem. Beyond the Commons lay his ultimate goal. The Lords.

But that was some way in the future. That would be his next target after he had increased his power and sphere of influence by the acquisition of the *Sunday Herald*. And with it the political journalists that had made the newspaper famous, and the financial section that was so well respected that it had inside information from the Treasury and the Chancellor's office. Western had built himself a power house in that newspaper.

He had recruited the best people, paid them the top salaries and got himself a life peerage. He was the friend of ministers in the Government and courted by the Opposition. He was everything that Harold King intended to be at the apex of his own career. And his train of thought, sunny and optimistic on that morning, like the weather outside his window, switched to something his daughter Gloria had said on their way home from dinner at Mario's. He listened to Gloria. She had his sharp eye for people, his jungle instincts.

'Did you know that woman, Daddy – the one with the red hair?' He'd felt his wife's eyes on him, knew that she tensed against some discovery of a fresh liaison, which Gloria would have enjoyed bringing into the open. Gloria didn't care if he slept with women. She knew she was the only one that counted.

'No, why? I know who she is – she's a journalist on the *Herald*. Why, Gloria?'

'Because she was looking at you, Daddy. The way you look when you hate somebody.' His wife made a mistake, partly from relief.

'Don't be silly, why should some stranger look at your father like that?'

'Shut up,' he said curtly. 'Gloria notices things. I got the same feeling. Funny you felt it too, sweetheart. Maybe I should run a check on her.'

He hadn't done anything about it until now, when one thought led from the *Herald* to its staff members.

He reached into a silver box and brought out a cigar. He smoked, and he ate what he pleased. He had the blood pressure of an eighteen year old. He enjoyed flaunting it in the face of his doctors, proving that the rules for lesser men did not apply to him. And he was as potent as ever. Joe took care of that side of his life. Joe took care of a lot of things.

Julia Hamilton. He'd follow Gloria's instinct. Joe could nose around and see what he could pick up on her.

He dialled an outside number. A woman on the other end said that Joe was in the sauna.

'Tell him I'll boil his ass if he doesn't get out of there. Now.' He didn't have to hold more than a couple of minutes.

'Mr King – sorry you had to wait.'

'Tell that stupid cow not to fob me off when I call,' King snapped. 'I want you up here right away. I've got something for you.'

'Give me fifteen minutes,' the man called Joe said.

'Ten,' King commanded and hung up.

On the other end of the line, the man standing soaked in sweat, with a towel wrapped round his middle, turned to the coloured girl.

'Next time my boss calls, you just say hold on and get me – you understand?'

She had big, frightened dark eyes. 'I'm sorry, Joe – I'm sorry.'

'Next time,' he said, 'you will be. Now get my fucking clothes.'

Nessenberg was much smaller than Julia had expected. It curled up like a cat, snug, neat and prosperous. It was unaffected by the turmoil of reunification and the problem of refugees from the war-ravaged Balkans. The Nessenberghof was still there. Harris remarked that it looked exactly the same as it did ten years ago.

It was comfortable and conservative. Their rooms were pleasant with views over the garden at the rear.

'It feels strange,' she said. 'I've never been to Germany and it's not what I expected. Everyone smiles and seems so friendly.'

'And so they are – the south isn't like Prussia; the southerners are famous for their charm, and for being the cradle of the bloody Nazis. I've found it easier to deal with the easterners. The Berliners are something else again. A race on their own. You'd like them. They enjoy life, and they stuck out after the war with that bloody Wall running through the middle of them. You must go there one day.'

'How do you know it so well?' she asked him.

'My wife is German,' he said. 'We used to come over for holidays. I got to know the country and to like it.'

'I didn't know you were married.'

He brushed it aside. 'I'm not; we got divorced fifteen years ago.'

'Do you have children?' Julia asked him. They were drinking coffee after a snack lunch in one of the cheerful cafés in the main street.

'Two. Son and daughter. I don't see much of them. I don't see them at all,' he remarked, and there was a bitter note in his voice.

'I'm sorry,' she said awkwardly. 'It must be hard for you.'

'They took their mother's part. That was it. I didn't try to argue the case. They were old enough to make up their own minds.'

It must have been a bad divorce; she didn't like to pry any further. To her surprise he started to talk. He drank his coffee and leaned back in his seat and said, 'I met Helga when she came to stay with my parents as an exchange student. My kid brother went over to her family to learn German and she came to us to learn English. She was very pretty. Blonde, blue eyes, real *Herrenvolk* type. Nice girl, too. I fell like the proverbial ton of bloody bricks and married her. I was a reporter on the *Birmingham Advertiser*. We lived in a rented flat and she went out to work as a mother's help. We hadn't any money, but we were pretty happy. Shame it all went wrong.'

Julia leaned a little towards him. It still hurt, she could see that. No wonder he said his German was good.

'What went wrong?'

'I moved to the *Herald*,' he said flatly. 'We'd been in Birmingham for twelve years. We owned a nice little house in the suburbs by then, she had a lot of friends, local bridge club, golf twice a week – solid middle-class lifestyle. The kids were at school and doing well. I was News Editor of the *Birmingham Post* by then, and it was a good job. But I wanted more challenge, J. I didn't want to stand still. And a job on the *Herald* was the big opportunity. So I took it and moved them all down to London. Long and short of it was, Helga hated it, the kids hated it, and I escaped into my work. We rowed, I stayed out more and more – it's not difficult in our job, you know that – and in the end she left me. Moved back to Birmingham, got a job, met another man and remarried. End of story. Want some more coffee, or shouldn't we try and make a start?'

He'd said all there was and he wanted to close the topic. Julia said, 'Yes, but thanks for telling me about it. Where do we start, Ben?'

'No harm in retracing my steps. We start with the Bauhaus. The Town Hall and the records office. They weren't very helpful last time, but now we're all one happy European family, it may be easier.'

'May I ask the reason for your request?' The clerk at the enquiries was a woman in her middle thirties; she wore the disdainful and suspicious look common to civil servants the world over. What, it conveyed, did these foreigners want, asking to see the old records of the late nineteen forties . . .?

Ben answered. 'We're trying to trace a missing relative.'

'You've left it rather late, haven't you? A German national?'

'No—' Julia interrupted. They were speaking in English. 'My uncle. He had no nationality; he was in the DP camp.'

The woman raised her thin eyebrows. 'Then we would have no records of anyone like that. I don't know who would; it's so long ago. I'm sorry.'

She had turned away in dismissal when Ben said, 'But you would have records from the British Control Commission. I saw them here some years ago. And I found some documentation. My friend's uncle was discharged into the surety of an English woman working among the refugees. This was sanctioned and approved by the military authorities and he was allowed to live here with her.'

Julia took it up again. She felt that Ben had antagonized the woman. She tried a soft approach. 'If we could just look and see if there is anything connecting her with him afterwards. It means so much to my mother, and she's in poor health. There might be some clues we could go on. Please?'

There was a hesitation, then with a slight shrug of resignation, the woman did her good deed for the day.

'You can look through what we have,' she said. 'But I don't see what you hope to find. Unless you missed something last time.' She spoke curtly to Ben.

'That's why we need to look again,' Julia headed him off. 'Just to make sure. I'm very grateful to you.'

'Sign this form please. I'll get someone to take you down when it's been authorized. Sit over there; I don't know how long it will be.'

It was a full half-hour before a girl came with the form duly signed and countersigned. Ben murmured to Julia, 'I think she's a dyke. I wasn't getting anywhere.'

'You should try turning on the charm,' she whispered back.

'Haven't any.' He followed her down the stairs into the lower floor.

There was the musty smell of disuse and slight damp, and the artificial light emphasized the bare and ugly room with its stacked files and the metal table with a single hard chair.

The girl spoke in German. 'The file for the Control Commission on refugees in 1949 is no. 17203. I can leave you. You have two hours before we close. There's a bell by the door. Please ring when you have finished.'

'I will,' Harris said. He gave her a big smile, and said to Julia, 'Was that better?'

'Not much. She thought you were going to bite her. Leave the soft soap to me, Ben. It's not your style. Now – I'm in your hands.'

'Nothing!' Ben Harris exclaimed. The air was dusty and cold; their time was almost up. 'Same stuff. No clue. Phyllis Lowe got him out of the camp, we know where they lived – I tried that and it wasn't even the same house any more. Official notification she was leaving for England. Nothing –' he repeated. 'Come on, J, we're wasting our time here.'

Julia leant on the table; her elbows hurt from the hard surface. There was dust in her throat from the old paperwork and her hands were dirty. 'It can't be right,' she said. 'It can't just stop like that. It doesn't read right. Ben – if we can come in here and be left alone with this stuff, what's to stop someone else coming and taking something out?'

'What? You suggesting King's been here?'

'I think someone has. Look, don't you realize that there isn't any address or reference given for Phyllis Lowe apart from the bare details of her position with UNRRA. They wouldn't have accepted her guarantee for a displaced person without knowing she was a respectable, responsible person. She'd have had to make an official application to start with. There's no copy of that. No copy of the officer dealing with it replying, or giving his recommendation. Just that one release document. Let me have another look at it. Let's see the page numbers.'

He turned the file backwards.'There,' he said. 'No luck. No page number. Nothing else was attached. But you're right. There would have been correspondence, references, all that sort of cross-checking. Why the hell didn't I see it before?'

'Because you weren't looking,' she said. 'What you saw was what's been left for anyone to find. Proof that she got King out and then applied to leave the country with him. You didn't look because you weren't looking for Phyllis Lowe. You were looking for something about King. Wait a minute – this signature – Major Grant.' She stood up quickly.

'Ben, if we can track him down, we'll get the information.'

'If he's alive,' Harris said slowly. 'There were some very young Majors at the end of the war. He could be in his seventies. You're pretty bright. Major A. B. Grant, liaison officer UNRRA. Right there, under the signature. Let's go. We can get someone working on it right away.'

She shivered; the temperature had dropped and the room with its dusty archives was dank and cold. The files had been doctored. Which meant that they were on the right track. Harold King had built up Phyllis Lowe into a surrogate mother. But he didn't want the world to know any more about her.

Harris rang the bell, and after a few minutes the same girl came in. She was obviously anxious to get rid of them. It was time to close the offices. 'You are satisfied?' she asked.

'Yes, thank you. We found some useful information,' Ben answered.

'Sign here please.' She put a release form in front of them; it was an undertaking that file no. 17203 had been examined and returned and that nothing had been altered or removed. 'Both signatures, please,' she said.

Ben pushed the form across to Julia with his pen.

'You must have a lot of these,' he remarked. 'Do you keep them all?'

'There's not so many,' the girl told him. 'Not for such a long time ago. We have everything up to date on computer now. But this old stuff – ' she raised her shoulders slightly. ' – it just lies here getting dusty. One day someone will clear it out. We could use the space.'

'I'm sure,' Ben agreed. 'How long have you worked here?'

'Three years. Thank you, Fräulein,' she took the form from Julia.

'Where will you keep this form?' he asked her. She moved to the door, urging them out. 'We don't keep it. It goes on computer. Excuse me, but we must hurry. I'll take you upstairs.' She locked the filing room behind her, and their steps clattered on the stone floors and up the stairs to the main office. They stepped outside into the late-afternoon sunshine.

He called out, '*Danke schön*,' and the girl said, '*Bitte*,' and shut the door.

Julia and he began to walk to the hired car.

From the ground-floor window, the girl watched them go. Then she went into the receptionist's office and called out 'Frau Walter?' No answer. She had gone on the tick of the clock, as she always did. Other members of the staff were talking and getting their coats on as they prepared to leave. The old porter-cum-caretaker would lock all the doors and check the windows before he too left.

The girl picked up the telephone in the office and punched a number. It was an answering machine at the other end of the line. She spoke quickly, but clearly. 'This is Minna. An English couple came here, poking round the exchange commission file – 1949. I'll take a note of their names.' She hung up, looked round to make sure nobody had seen her make the call. Then she joined the trickle of secretaries and local officials leaving the Bauhaus.

'I've got a friend,' Ben said, 'he's got contacts in the War Office. He might be able to check on the records.'

'You've got friends everywhere,' Julia remarked.

'Part of my job,' he answered. 'Contacts are 80 per cent of getting a story first. I did this guy a favour a few years ago. A well-known General was caught buggering rent boys in some gay club. He was retired on the usual grounds, ill-health. He'd been a good soldier and he had friends. They didn't want to see him crucified. I killed the story.' He looked at her. 'I'm old-fashioned, J. I don't believe in character assassination just for the fun of it. Even though it sells newspapers. They'll find Major A. B. Grant if he's still alive.' He checked his watch. 'Too late to call up now. I'll get on to him in the morning. I know a nice little restaurant where we could have dinner, if you like – if it's not closed down.'

'Why not? I'll meet you in the bar at eight.'

'Seven,' Ben corrected. 'This is provincial Germany. They eat early.'

Felix had found a one-bedroomed studio in Pimlico. The girl he had casual sex with noticed a 'to rent' sign in the window of the converted house and rang him to suggest he looked at it. He knew that it was close to where she lived, but shrugged that off.

She was a fun girl, but he wasn't going to get involved. He had packed up his clothes and the stereo and his CDs; it was lucky Julia was going to be away. Meeting, however briefly, in the flat would be awkward for both of them. He had arranged to sleep out for the two nights before she left. He felt no animosity towards her.

He was surprised to feel relieved that the relationship was over. He had never admitted to himself until then that, in spite of his determination to be independent and live his own life, he had found the last year increasingly oppressive. He owed Julia, and he didn't feel comfortable. That discomfort had made him more selfish and wayward to offset the obligation. I'm a free man, was what he was saying to her and to himself, but it hadn't been true. Toy Boy had stung her to indignation. Typically he had shrugged it off, but he recognized that it was just bravado. The jeers had rankled, and he had punished Julia by being extra macho in his attitude. His dominance was sexual, and he used it to subdue her, and even inflict little humiliations. He looked round the flat they'd shared together, at those bloody awful pictures she was so pleased with, and heaved a huge sigh of relief that it was over. And because the burden was lifted, he left her a note. *Hope I haven't left too much of a mess. Thanks for some great times. I'm at 832 8474, if you feel like a drink some time. Felix.* That made him feel better still, and he went out with his belongings with a light heart and put the keys back through the letter-box. The retired detective keeping watch from a parked car on the opposite side of the street saw him go. He'd been one of a forty-eight-hour watch on the place, ever since Joe said he wanted it staked out. The woman had driven off with luggage, and now the boyfriend had moved out. It was clear for them to get into the flat.

Joseph Patrick was a fixer. He'd learned to manipulate from his childhood in a Dublin orphanage. They'd given him the surname Patrick because he'd been dumped on the doorstep on St Patrick's day. He was a small, weedy child, who had to use his wits to survive the bullying of bigger boys and the pitiless Christian discipline of the Brothers who were in charge of human refuse like himself. Bastards, slum children, abandoned through shame or cruel economic necessity. Children from respectable families who were smitten by death or debts or the curse of alcoholism. The orphanage opened its doors to them all. Few left unscathed when they reached adulthood. Joe Patrick learned two lessons in survival very quickly. Make yourself useful to the people with the power, that applied equally to the bully boys who ruled inside the dormitories and the members of staff who ruled the whole community, and never, ever, give trouble or support anyone who did.

He knew no loyalty except to himself. He conformed to the rigid religious routine without absorbing any moral sense. He became known as someone who would run errands, spy on troublesome fellows, accommodate homosexual demands if they were made upon him. He left the orphanage with a good reference from the Brothers and an introduction to a small shopkeeper who employed youths at their behest. Within three months Joe had opened the back door to a gang that beat the old man unconscious and robbed the till. They knocked Joe on the head for good measure, so he was not suspected.

His entry into the criminal community of the city was on the same pattern as life in the orphanage. He made himself useful and he didn't show a high profile. He knew he was much cleverer than the men who gave him a few quid for doing their dirty work, watching shops or private premises that were targets for burglary.

He went on to scout for girls likely to turn prostitute, hanging around the bars and pubs, looking for runaways or teenagers who wanted drugs. He supplied the drugs, and introduced the users to the pimps who ran them. He had a couple of tarts himself, and he beat them as mercilessly as he had been beaten as a child, if they slacked off or tried to keep some of the money. He was tall and thin, with Irish good looks and bad teeth. He combed his curly dark hair and dressed in trendy clothes, and the police employed him as a snout. It was a dangerous tightrope, even for someone as agile as Joe Patrick. He had a drinking partner, a drunken copper who had more in common with the crooks he spent his time with than the Force. It was time for Joe to get out of Dublin. The word was out for him. Time to get out while he was still on two legs. Joe took the advice. He had some money, a lot of clothes, and an address his pal had given him. He went to London and introduced himself to a small, seedy firm of private detectives.

They hired him as a legman.

And that was how Harold King found him. He'd worked for King for eighteen years, starting with a small surveillance job on a journalist who had written uncomplimentary articles about King Publishing and its pornographic output. Joe was told to dig dirt. He didn't find any so he supplied it. He still ran two or three girls on the side, and he set the journalist up with one of them. He photographed her giving him a blow job in the back of the car. There were no more articles about King's porno magazines. Impulse and curiosity made King ask to see him.

The man had initiative. Nobody had told him to set up the victim. King saw the cheap, flashy man in his mid twenties, with all the cunning of the petty criminal in his sharp eyes. But there was a brain under the mophead of curls. King sized him up and came to a decision.

He could use someone like this gutter rat. And he would always be able to control him. He looked him up and down and drew on his big cigar and said, 'You want to work for me?'

The bad teeth, legacy of poor diet and neglect, fanned out into an ingratiating smile. 'Sure. Sure I do.'

'And you don't mind what you have to do?'

The shoulders lifted under their over-wide pads.

'I'm not partic'lar. Whatever.' He had a thick nasal Dublin whine that offended King. It would amuse him to take this piece of human garbage and remodel it.

'Then see a dentist and get something done about your teeth. If you work for me you look the way I want you to. You talk the way I want and you dress the way I tell you. Understand me?'

Men with power over him had been talking to Joe Patrick in those terms all his life. He had no pride, only a price.

He ran his hand through the curls on his head.

'You're the boss, Mr King. That's great by me.'

As he waved him out of the office, King called him back suddenly.

'And get that nit nest cut off!'

Joe Patrick had been his man ever since. He was barbered and well dressed now, his accent smoothed into phoney American; when he went to the States to sort something out for King he lapsed back into the brogue. He had a smart flat off Hyde Park and he drove a BMW. He was a businessman, with cards printed to prove it. Joseph G. Patrick, export import, and an office address in Covent Garden. He lived with two coloured girls and he had supplied King with women since he married and the 'starlets' and 'models' he liked to be seen with in public were given the shove. No girl who serviced King would have dared talk about it. Joe Patrick had maimed women if they crossed him.

And he paid handsomely because that was King's way. He bought discretion with money, and implicit in everything was the threat of Joe if they stepped off the track.

King wanted this woman Hamilton looked over. Joe had done many similar jobs over the years. They were the bread-and-butter jobs, like providing the right girl. He had done other, more complicated things for King. They put the jam on his daily bread. And they had taken Joe to some interesting places. He knew the States quite well, and parts of Europe.

Responsibility had given him a certain gloss. He had self-confidence and he had learned how to behave with people better educated than the waif beaten into learning by the good Brothers at home.

Joe was a chameleon, he could blend into his surroundings. The flat was empty, but there wasn't much point in waiting. The Hamilton woman could come back at any time. He fixed for an entrance to be made that afternoon.

There was a double mortise on the front door, but it didn't trouble Joe's expert. He picked both locks and stood aside for Joe to enter.

'You stay here,' Joe mouthed at him. They were on the first-floor landing of the Chelsea conversion. The front door had opened on a buzzer from one of the top-floor flats; stupidly the woman pushed to open before she asked the name on the intercom. Joe's man had his answer ready.

'Interflora,' he said. 'I'm delivering to Number Two. Hamilton? No reply so I'll leave the plants outside the door. Thank you.'

And he and Joe were inside the building and up the first flight of stairs. 'Anyone comes, you call me.' Then he was in Julia's flat.

He knew how to search without leaving any signs. He opened drawers, lifted clothes and felt underneath; he shoved his hands under the mattress of the double bed, rifled through the fitted cupboards, opened the one remaining big suitcase and the hat box. He knew where people hid money and jewellery and personal papers. He found nothing, but some gold trinkets and a little spare cash in a drawer. He didn't touch them.

There was an answer machine. He switched it on, listened, made quick notes and reset it. He was looking for business papers, anything connected with her job on the *Herald*. She didn't bring stuff home. The messages were personal. A call from her mother, two from friends asking her and someone called Felix – the boyfriend who'd moved out – to dinner.

And Felix's note with his telephone number. Joe copied it. Then he went through the waste basket in the living room. Among the empty envelopes and a few circulars, he found a screwed-up piece of scrap paper. Someone had jotted down a rough schedule.

8.30 Heathrow. arr. Munich 12.15 C. time check in Ness. approx 1 p.m. Joe put the note in his pocket. He had been in the flat for under ten minutes. He came out. 'OK, close it up.' His man relocked the door and they slipped downstairs and out into the street.

Joe didn't know what he'd found, but he had a number which might come in useful. He knew where the ex-boyfriend could be contacted.

There was no trace of the camp outside Nessenberg. A housing estate had been built on the site. Julia and Ben drove out the next morning.

'It's incredible,' she said, 'seeing how they rebuilt everything after the war. I never realized till I came here.'

'They're a resourceful people,' Ben answered. 'Disciplined and industrious.'

'More than that, surely,' she questioned. 'I've seen newsreels and photographs – the whole country was devastated.'

'They're proud,' he said. 'My wife said to me once, "We were defeated, but we're not going to be beaten." Her family had been bombed out, and two of her uncles were missing in Russia. She came from Hamburg.

'That was really pasted. But they'd rebuilt it by the time we came over. I don't think her father and mother were too pleased she'd married me, but they put a good face on it. They were crazy about the grandchildren.'

'I'm sorry you don't see them' Julia said. 'Maybe you'll get together when they get older.'

'I don't see why,' he said. 'I wasn't a very good father. They're going their own way. Let's talk about something else.'

He looked grim and irritable. She was beginning to understand him better. Bad temper was his cover for feelings. For hurt and, she suspected, for real loneliness. She was beginning to like him as well as understand him. In a good mood he was wonderful company. They had enjoyed an excellent dinner the night before in another restaurant – his old stamping ground had become a grocer's shop. He ordered German food and wine and the conversation was wide-ranging and easy.

He talked about Germany and the resurgence of the neo-Nazis, the problems of reunification for a country which had been split in half ideologically, with a generation brought up with different work and social ethics. He was extremely intelligent and well informed and she was fascinated.

She said so then, as they drove back to the hotel.

'I really enjoyed last night, Ben. I learned a lot from you. I've learned a lot from this trip.'

'I thought I'd been a bloody bore,' he admitted. 'It's just that it was a part of my life because I married Helga. Don't know why I go on about it now. Anyway, we got something out of our trip. Major A. B. Grant.'

Julia said, 'When will your War Office contact let you know?'

'We should get something today,' he answered. 'All they've got to do is track down the records of who was here and whether there's a "deceased" after the name. Everything's on the touch of a computer key.'

'If he's dead,' Julia shook her head, 'we're back to square one. Somehow I don't think he will be.'

He smiled slightly at her. 'You're an optimist, J. I'm a pessimist. I'm the guy who says the bottle's half-empty. You say it's half-full.'

The hotel proprietor was a plump, efficient lady with a friendly smile. She greeted them as they came in.

'Good morning! Herr Harris, there is a message come through on our fax machine for you. I have it here.'

Julia craned over his shoulder. He read the script quickly and turned to her. 'It's better than a half-full bottle,' he said quietly. 'Major Grant married a local girl. He retired to live over here in seventy-four. They've even got the address for us. He draws a disability pension.'

Impulsively Julia grabbed his arm. 'Ben – this is our breakthrough! Where is he?' For a moment his hand came over and gripped hers. Then he released himself. 'At Hintzbach, about twenty kilometres away. I'll call him.'

The owner of the town's biggest supermarket was also head of the local Veterans' association. He had been a panzer sergeant in his twenties and suffered a wound in the Western Desert that saved him from the Russian front. He had ended the war as a civilian stores administrator for the 101st Division which was engaged in fighting the American Sixth Army. He had watched his country overrun, its towns destroyed, its population driven on to the roads in search of shelter from the fighting. He had seen his people starve, and die, and his comrades penned up in POW camps where the rations were so short that thousands perished. He had escaped because he was a civilian with the lower part of his leg removed. But he was a soldier in his heart, and everything he saw in the new Germany convinced him that the defeat of Adolf Hitler was the worst disaster in his country's history. His views had not changed with his prosperity. He and his wife had worked and saved, and the result was his business, a big modern house in its own grounds, and his position as a respected member of the community. He was also the unofficial liaison with old soldiers who needed help.

Help had come from many unexpected quarters. From America, where the members of the old Bundt were still loyal, from South and Central America where sympathizers hadn't forgotten their homeland. The Veterans' Association had used its resources to rehabilitate men still suffering from the war in the early years, and to build homes for the elderly and incapacitated, even providing small pensions for their widows to supplement the State allowance. The branch at Nessenberg had recognized his work by making him its President. He was very proud of that position. More proud than he was of the big modern shop that had grown from his first venture into trade, and the money that came from it.

He could still serve, albeit silently. His three sons were his grief and disappointment. They were liberal-minded, enlightened and quite alien to him. They were shamed by the past; they rejected racism and deplored any militarism or nationalist feelings. They were the new Germans and their father couldn't understand them. Politics were not discussed at home. He hoped that the criminals and layabouts pouring into their country under the guise of refugees, taking State money and jobs from their own people, would teach them how wrong they were. But he said nothing any more. He had his friends and his contacts and they belonged to his past. His answer machine was in his private office and only a few people knew the number. He took note of Minna's message.

Minna was the daughter of a colleague who'd served with SS Panzer Division in the East. He belonged to the fighting unit, not the prison guards and execution squads so emphasized by their enemies. All countries had their undesirables. Atrocities were common in a war. He had erected a mental barrier against history. The camps had existed but they were exaggerated out of all proportion by the Jews. Already the numbers of dead were being called into question. Minna was her father's daughter, imbued with his loyalties and ideals. Years ago – many years ago – he had had a visitor. A fellow soldier from the Western Desert where his lower leg had been torn off by a British mortar. The man said he was acting for other ex-soldiers who had shed their uniforms and taken refuge from the enemy in the DP camps at Nessenberg. The alternative had been to starve as prisoners of war.

The DPs were fed and given medical care. They were the lucky ones in that dreadful period. He was asked to protect those who had bluffed screening officers and UNRRA officials.

Over the years there had been people snooping, looking for someone in the records. He had made sure that anything incriminating was removed, leaving one or two documents as instructed. Now the snoopers were back. They had been looking at the same file, the file for the Control Commission in 1949. He remembered them, those well-fed, sleek British officers, quartered in his town, sifting and questioning, looking for so-called war criminals or deserters. He hated still, remembering them. They were long gone, and the interfering busybodies from the United Nations with them.

From England, these two had come. Minna had noted their names. He decided to pay Minna a call and find out more before he fulfilled his obligation.

And paid back some small part of the handsome donation he'd accepted for the Association's hardship fund.

The road to Hintzbach took them through some pretty Bavarian country and the place where Major Grant and his wife had retired to live was a picture-book village, with clapboard houses and narrow streets. Everything was clean and orderly, and the street cafés and beer halls were full of customers. It was lunch-time and the shops were closed. The house they were looking for was next to the wine store. Window boxes full of bright flowers and an incongruous British name plate painted in garish colours. 'Rooks Nest.'

They left the car in a side street – it was forbidden to park in the main road – and went to the front door. Ben had spoken to the wife. The Major was not very well, but she would ask, and who wanted to see him please? An author, Ben explained, doing some research for a book on the work of the Control Commission with refugees. They promised not to stay too long, but would be grateful for a short interview.

She opened the door to them. Julia saw a slight, dark woman with a little grey in her hair. She was pretty, even in age, and she must have been at least seventy. She wore a flowered apron and a blouse with a crisp frill at the neck.

'I'm Mr Harris,' Ben stepped forward, holding Julia by the elbow, 'and this is Miss Hamilton.'

'Come in please.' The hall was small and dark and smelled of furniture polish. 'My husband is very excited to see you,' she had a charming smile. 'But he does get tired. He's in here. Shall I get you some coffee? Or a glass of beer?'

'Coffee, please,' Julia answered. It was a downstairs room converted into a bedroom. Major Grant was sitting in an armchair with a knitted rug over his knees. A fire was alight in the grate.

Ben went across and shook his hand. Julia did the same. It was cold and skinny, like a bird's claw. He looked frail, with sparse white hair and hollow cheeks. 'It's very good of you to see us, sir,' Ben said.

'It's a pleasure,' the old man smiled at them. 'I don't get visitors from home these days. Do sit down, make yourselves comfortable. My wife will bring us some coffee and some of her cake. She makes marvellous chocolate cake.' They talked about the weather, he asked a few questions about England – he hadn't been back for five years, since then he'd had a minor stroke, and he didn't get about much. Julia felt he had lost touch with his own country. He gave his wife a devoted look when she came back with a tray. 'I'll leave you,' she said. 'I have things to do.' 'No, no,' he protested, 'stay and talk, darling. After all, you were as much a part of that time as I was.' He turned to Julia who was sitting closer to him than Ben Harris. 'Gerda was a DP. That's how we met. She can be a great help; she can tell you what it was like from experience.'

'That,' Ben said gently, 'would be invaluable.'

They had talked for an hour before Julia raised the subject of Phyllis Lowe. 'I'm particularly interested in the English women who came to work for UNRRA; I've contacted many of them who are still around,' she avoided saying 'still alive', 'but I can't find any trace of Phyllis Lowe. I know she befriended a DP, a young man called Koenig.' She looked enquiringly at them. They had left England in seventy-four, King was not then a public figure. The old man looked up and said sharply, 'I knew Phyllis. And I knew Koenig. I tried to warn her about him, but she simply wouldn't listen, would she, Gerda?'

'No,' his wife answered. 'She was completely taken in by him. My nationality had been established by then and I was working for Alfred. Millions of documents were destroyed during the bombing, mine were lost at Frankfurt, but my parents' marriage certificate helped to prove I was who I said. So I was released from the camp. I didn't know Koenig inside – there were thousands of us – but I did know Phyllis Lowe. She was a nice woman—'

'She was a fool,' the Major interrupted. His wife reproved him quietly; they were in a dialogue that excluded Ben and Julia, reliving their own past. 'She was in love with him,' she said. 'Crazy in love, she wouldn't listen to anyone.'

'In love with Koenig?' Julia asked. 'Were they lovers?'

'Of course they were,' Grant said irritably. 'They made a fool of me to start with. She was nearly forty and he must have been around twenty-five – six. She convinced me he was a poor stray with a traumatic past – dragged out of his home when his parents were shot, working as a slave labourer on a farm, hunted like an animal with all the other poor devils when the Russians invaded. She wanted to take him out of the camp, educate him, and give him a chance of a new life. A lot of the DPs settled in Europe if they couldn't get to the States, for example. I believed her.

'She was so damned convincing, and I knew she had a reputation for hard work on behalf of the refugees. She was well liked and respected. So I recommended he be released in her surety. He'd never given any trouble, he seemed a decent lad. Very respectful, rather gauche. I interviewed him several times. He told the same story as Phyllis did. The Fräulein had been so kind, she was like a mother. I remember the swine squeezed out a few tears on one occasion.

'It was put up between them, but I didn't find that out till later. As soon as he left the camp, they were living openly together.'

'Did she educate him – I read somewhere she employed a local man to teach him English?' Ben asked.

'Huh – she did indeed. She spent money like water on him. She got clothes for him, she scrounged and bribed for cigarettes

– she even had the cheek to ask me for Players because he liked them! And didn't he change his spots, eh, Gerda?'

'Yes,' his wife said, 'he did. He was arrogant, greedy, and he even humiliated the poor woman. She seemed to like it. He'd go round the cafés boasting about his rich English mistress and how she did exactly what he wanted. Alfred had a serious talk with her, didn't you, darling – he tried to point out that she was making a complete fool of herself, that the man was exploiting her. And what did she say to you?'

'She said she had never been so happy in her life, and I didn't understand her Hans, as she called him. "He's young and full of life, and whatever you say, he loves me. I know he does." And then she told me she was going to marry him and take him to England.'

He sighed, as if he had exhausted himself, reliving the past. For a moment there was silence, his wife looked at Julia and nodded, as if to say, please, that's enough.

Julia stood up, 'Major Grant, we mustn't keep you any longer. Just one more question. Did she marry him?'

'Yes,' he answered. 'She did. She was a civilian, you see, and we had no jurisdiction, or I could have stopped her. She married him six months after he got out of the camp, resigned from UNRRA and said they were going to England. She did come and say goodbye to me, at least.

' "We're going to be so happy," she said to me. "I'll keep in touch Alfred." But she never did. We never heard of her again.'

'Thank you very much, sir,' Harris shook the thin hand. 'You've been a great help.'

The Major said, 'Are you writing this book together?'

'Collaborating on it,' Ben answered.

'Goodbye, Major Grant, and take care of yourself.' Julia didn't shake hands with him; he looked as if he'd fall asleep as soon as they left. In the hall she turned to his wife.

'I do hope it hasn't been too much for him,' she said. 'He looked so tired.'

Gerda Grant shook her head. 'He's old,' she said. 'We both are. But we have our two sons and grandchildren, and we've had a happy life together. It wasn't easy for Alfred being married to a German. But we loved each other and that's what mattered.'

'What was she like – Phyllis Lowe – to look at?'

'Very handsome. Very smart. I think she was an upper-class English lady – a lot like her came to work for UNRRA. Sophisticated and superior to him in every way. But she was blind, quite blind. I wonder what happened to her, when they got to England.'

'I wonder, too,' Julia said. 'Goodbye and thank you. I hope your husband goes on well.'

They walked to the car in silence. Ben started the engine.

'Well,' he said at last. 'That was a turn up for the book!'

The last person to use that phrase was a betting-mad friend of her father's.

'No wonder we couldn't find a death certificate,' Julia answered. 'We'll get on to that right away. She'd have been Koenig, that's why we drew a blank. Ben, you realize we've sent out teams looking for everything under the name of Lowe – come on, let's get back to the hotel – I can call through to the office.'

'He married her,' Ben muttered, the car picking up speed, 'to get to England. But why lie? What's he got to hide, J?'

'Something more than making a fool of a woman old enough to know better. Very convenient, getting cancer, leaving him a bit of money . . . '

'You think she did die, then?'

'Yes, but I'll be very interested to see that death certificate.' She looked at him and said suddenly, 'They were a sweet old couple, weren't they? You forget there are people around like that.' He didn't answer. Julia felt she had unwittingly touched a sore spot. He put up a tough front, but that failed marriage had left a scar.

The girl called Minna nodded. 'He said it,' she insisted. 'He said they had found something.'

He had gone home at lunch-time, and she had come over from the Bauhaus. His wife had left them together in the sitting room. She never concerned herself with her husband's activities for the Veterans, and she knew Minna's father was an old comrade. She hoped the family wasn't in trouble. If they were, her man would sort it out.

'You've got the names?'

'Here.' She passed him a slip of paper.

'Describe them to me,' he said.

'The man was around forty or so – dark, wore glasses – the woman was younger than him. She had very red hair, she was pretty and she had expensive clothes.'

'Good,' he said. He consulted the scrap of paper. Minna had copied all the details on the form. 'Staying at the Nessenberghof,' he muttered. 'I can make a few enquiries. Leni is a friend of my wife's – I can see the hotel register. Thank you, Minna. Always watchful.'

'Always loyal,' she finished the motto for him. 'I must go, or I'll be late.'

She looked at him silently, a fresh-faced, attractive young woman who had been born twenty years after the war ended. She gave the forbidden salute. Slowly, he returned it. Then the door closed behind her.

Julia put down the telephone. 'They've got to go back over the same ground. One thing did come up, though,' she frowned, looking at her own scribbled shorthand notes. 'There's an elderly couple next door to the house where Phyllis Lowe lived with King. They remember a young man and a much older woman moving there. My team has it all on tape. Ben, I think we should fly back, there's nothing more we can do here.' She stood up and stretched a little. He noticed how full her breasts were as she made the movement.

He said, 'Let's stay tonight. I'll show you Munich. We could fly out in the morning.'

'We could,' Julia agreed. 'All right, let's do that. I'll call through and book the flights.'

'I'll do it,' he said briskly. 'Do you drink beer, J?'

'Not if I can help it,' she laughed at him.

'You can't go to Munich and not go to a *bier keller*,' he said. 'See you downstairs at six.'

* * *

It was a new experience for Julia. The city was beautiful, rebuilt after its travails during the war; there was an atmosphere of gaiety as evening approached. The shops were brightly lit and crammed with goods. The cafés and bars and beer halls were full of Bavarians setting out to enjoy themselves. She was struck by how many of them were dark, far removed from the blond Aryan ideal which had been born in that very place over half a century ago. Ben took her to a *bier keller* as he'd promised. It was hot, smoky and noisy, but the good spirits of the people round them were infectious. A group at a nearby table started to sing, and soon everyone was joining in, steins banging in rhythm on the tables.

'It's crazy,' she said to Ben. 'It's like a Hollywood movie – but don't they know how to enjoy themselves!'

'We came to the Oktoberfest one year with the kids,' he said. 'They loved it. The whole place goes wild, drinking, singing, wearing national costume. You'd never think Nazism started here, would you?'

'No,' she said, brought down to earth suddenly. 'No, you wouldn't.'

He stood up. 'I think you've had enough beer, so let's move on to something more civilized.'

She took his arm as they came out into the street. 'I enjoyed that, I wouldn't have missed it for anything. Where are we going now?'

'To the Bernerhof,' he said, and he looked down at her and smiled. 'From the ridiculous to the sublime, depending how you look at it. The best food and wine in Bavaria.' She didn't let go of his arm as they walked.

They sat in the bar and had drinks while they studied the menu. A pianist was playing sentimental sixties music, the lights were low, the atmosphere relaxed and leisurely.

The women were elegant and the men very different from the boisterous beer drinkers in the *bier keller*. It was low key, luxurious and subtly sensual as if to say, Everything is here for your pleasure. Whatever form that pleasure takes, it's our pleasure to provide it! They dined in a cubicle in the restaurant;

it was intimate and they sat close. She drank more wine than she intended and revelled in the rich food.

When the coffee, frothing with cream, was brought to them, she said to Ben, 'I haven't had a cigarette for ten years. I'm going to have one now.'

'I know the feeling,' he answered. 'That's what this place does to you. You feel you're King of the world, and you can do what you like, and to hell with it. You look very pretty.'

He was not looking at her when he said it. She could feel his body against hers on the cushioned seat.

He hadn't touched her, not even her hand as it lay on the table. He didn't need to; his desire suddenly ignited hers, and she said softly, 'Never mind the cigarette. Why don't we spend the night here?'

He half turned to her, and then put his hand on her face and raised it. He kissed her slowly, not like Felix, with his importunate tongue and greedy technique, but in gentle exploration.

Then he said, 'Are you sure, J? Are you sure it's what you want?' She laid two fingers on his mouth. 'After what you've just done, I'm sure.'

When he undressed her, he said simply, 'You're beautiful. I want to look at you.' She saw their naked reflections in the big gilt mirror on the wall opposite the bed, and turned round for him, pivoting slowly until he caught hold of her and they sprawled on the bed, locked in a frenzy of desire.

It was a long night. They made love and slept and then made love again. She thought hazily, as she drifted into an exhausted, sated sleep, Felix was a boy. I've been with a man.

When she woke in the morning, he was already up. She could hear sounds in the bathroom. He came out wearing a towelling robe.

'I let you sleep,' he said. He sat beside her on the edge of the bed. He took hold of her hands and held them.

'If you're sorry about last night, we can forget about it. No strings.'

'No strings,' Julia agreed. 'You'd already booked the room, hadn't you?'

'Yes,' he admitted. 'Just in case. I've wanted you for years – ever since you walked into that office looking like a scared kid on your first day. I wouldn't admit it to myself. But I mean it. I'll back off if you want me to.'

She took her hands away and leaned back on the pillows. She sighed.

'Oh Ben, you are a bloody fool.' She smiled at him and held out her arms. 'I don't mind missing breakfast, if you don't.'

As the plane began its descent to Heathrow, Julia glanced at him. He had closed his eyes, stowed his glasses away in his breast pocket. I must get him a case to put them in, she thought. Nobody's looked after the details for him for a long time.

She loved flying; she leaned forward to watch the ground coming up to meet them. It exhilarated her to anticipate the touchdown, the force of braking and the smooth transition from hundreds of miles an hour to a gentle taxiing across the runway.

She nudged him gently. 'Ben – wake up. We've landed.'

He opened his eyes. 'I wasn't asleep, just dozing. I'm shagged out, and it's all your fault.' He unbuckled her seat-belt for her.

'You look sensational,' he murmured. 'How is an old man like me going to cope?'

'You don't have any problems,' Julia whispered back. 'Come on, I want to see what's on that tape.'

Ben Harris eased her out into the gangway. 'I think we're going to make a very good team. You're a pro, J. And so am I.'

They set off for the Western building, with Julia driving. As they eased into the reserved parking space, she turned to him.

'Thank you for taking me to see Munich,' she said. 'It was all wonderful.'

'Thank you for coming with me.' He turned her face up to him and gave her a firm, short kiss on the lips.

'Now, let's get to work.'

'Lord Western?' He was conferring with his advertising director when his personal secretary came in. She never interrupted him unless it was important. Even so he scowled at her. The revenue was down on the last quarter and he had been roasting his executives.

'What is it?'

'Miss Hamilton called in; she'd like to see you some time after five, if that's convenient.'

'Am I free?'

'You have two half-hour appointments, then nothing from six o'clock on. Mr Osborne at five and Peggy Beaumont from Features at half past. Shall I say six o'clock to Miss Hamilton? I do have a note that Lady Western is expecting you to go to the Park Lane for drinks with Princess Margaret on that NSPCC appeal—'

Western didn't hesitate. 'Cancel Osborne till nine o'clock tomorrow. Pick a slot for Peggy in late morning. Tell Julia to come up here at five, I can give her an hour and a half clear.'

He went back to bullying his advertising director.

'I've brought the tape,' Julia said. 'I'd like you to hear it when you've looked over what we found out in Nessenberg.' She placed the typed report in front of him. He opened it, skimmed through the pages and then looked up at her.

He said coldly, but with triumph, 'Lying bastard. The saintly spinster lady was a randy forty year old who liked screwing boys.'

He went on, tapping the paper with his fingers. 'He got into England because he was married to a British subject. Then she dies and he gets his hands on her money – this is good stuff. We're just beginning to lift the stone and see the maggots.'

'It gets better,' Julia said. 'Let me play you this tape.' She'd brought a small cassette-player with her. She slipped the tape inside and switched on.

'Louder,' Western commanded. 'I can't hear it.' She turned up the volume. The voices were old, and sometimes they talked through each other.

'Yes,' the woman spoke first. 'Yes, I remember them. She was much older, very tarty looking, used to smoke in the street—'

'Nice looking woman,' the male voice interrupted. 'Too good for that fellow. He was just poncing on her. Never did a day's work, lounging about till all hours. They didn't mix with anyone. They went out a lot at night.' 'And they had awful rows,' his wife spoke up. 'You could hear them shouting. I rang up and complained once, and she was rude to me. She drank a lot.' The researcher's voice. 'How do you know? Did you see her drunk?'

'No, but you heard him, didn't you, Dick, yelling when the window was open. Accusing her of being drunk—'

'I'm sure he hit her,' the man broke in. 'He was just the type. Foreigner, nasty, conceited brute. I'm sure he hit her. Don't blame her for drinking, living with him. They were said to be married. They called themselves Mr and Mrs Koenig.'

'They had a char,' his wife reminded him. 'She said there were bottles all over the place.'

'A char?' The researcher wasn't old enough to recognize the term.

'A cleaner. Charwoman. She worked part time for us, and she gossiped to my wife.'

'How long before Mrs Koenig got ill?'

There was a pause and the question was repeated.

'Ill? She wasn't ill. She had an accident, but she wasn't ill.' They were both talking at once.

'What kind of accident?' Julia was watching Western. He was pale and crouching forward, his body tensed over the little machine.

'She fell, didn't she, Alfred? Fell in the garden and fractured her skull. I expect she'd been drinking.' The note of an old animosity to the tarty but attractive Mrs Koenig sang through the recorded voice.

'Jesus,' Western said, and then checked himself, as the interview went on. 'He called an ambulance, and she was taken off to hospital. He told the char she'd died a few days later. He was crying, she said. I said it was an act.'

'You took her part,' the voice was shrill. It was obvious that the Koenigs were not the only people who had quarrelled all those years ago. 'He wasn't as bad as you made out. You didn't like him because he was a foreigner. He was a Polish refugee, that's what I heard.'

'What happened after that? You're sure I'm not tiring you?' The researchers were trained not to harass anyone or apply pressure to the elderly. And these were very elderly. The preliminary information at the start of the tape placed them by name and gave their ages as eighty-five and eighty-seven. They had been resident in the old people's home for thirteen years. The husband was in a wheelchair, and his wife was partially sighted.

'No, no, we're enjoying talking to you. I can't remember what I had for lunch, and she's worse, but I can remember what happened forty years ago as if it was yesterday. You want to know what?'

'After Mrs Koenig died, did the husband stay on?'

'No. He moved out and the house was sold very quickly. There was a real shortage of houses in those days. Never saw or heard of him again.' Julia leaned forward and switched the tape off.

'I'm getting this transcribed and my girl will go back and get it signed by them both and witnessed by a solicitor.'

'What did she tell them?' Western asked. 'They didn't connect anything with King?'

'She said she was trying to trace Koenig because of a legacy. She had to edit the tape because they talked their heads off. She was rather sorry for them. They were shut in together all day, bickering and nagging at each other. The place was very dreary.'

Western wasn't listening. Other people's problems didn't interest him. 'Convenient for him, wasn't it?' he muttered. 'Lucky chap, getting rid of her so quickly. And getting some money. Well done, Julia. Follow this through.'

'You think it wasn't an accident?' she asked him.

'It doesn't matter what I think. What we want is some kind of proof. You've done good work, but it's not enough.' His tone was sharp. 'We can show him up as a liar, but not a criminal. So far, he can't be accused of breaking any law. And that's what I want. Evidence, proof. Something I can nail him to the cross with.'

He stood up abruptly. Julia said quietly, 'Lord Western, there's something I've got to ask you.'

The eyes narrowed suspiciously. 'I don't pay you to ask me

questions. I'm in a hurry.' She didn't move.

'Why did you pull Ben Harris off the investigation ten years ago?'

He was on his way to the door. 'Because he wasn't getting anywhere. He was wasting my time.'

'He was looking into two suspected murders of men who were business rivals of King. You stopped him. Why?'

Western opened the door and called his secretary. 'I wish you'd trust me, Lord Western,' Julia said. 'If there is something, I ought to know about it. Otherwise how can I protect you?'

Suddenly, unexpectedly, he shut the door. He turned round and looked at her. For a slight man he had enormous physical presence.

'It's a nice thought, my dear. You find me the right kind of dirt on Harold King, and I'll protect myself.' His secretary knocked and he opened the door. 'Bridget, I'm going. Ring down for the car.' Then he was gone.

'You take the private lift, Miss Hamilton,' the secretary said briskly. 'Lord Western won't be leaving for a few minutes. Excuse me.' She stood aside and Julia walked past her.

Ben had gone to his office; she went to hers on the floor below Western's eyrie and sat down to think through that interview. She stared unseeing out of the massive windows with its fine views. Western was out to get Harold King for personal reasons. He had begun a fresh crusade after ten years of neutrality, and there was only one explanation. He had been threatened once, and submitted. Now he was threatened again, and no deal with his enemy was possible.

That was what this was all about. Not a question of morals, but of two jungle predators, circling each other looking for the jugular.

Suddenly she felt tired, and low spirited. She wanted to call Ben, but she hesitated. No strings. That was the agreement. They were lovers and colleagues, but they were professionals first. He wasn't the keeper of her conscience, and she had no right to burden him.

And yet, when he at first refused to work with her, she'd used a moral argument to get her way. 'If King is what you say, you ought to help me stop him.'

So why wasn't that reason good enough to apply to herself? She wasn't the keeper of Western's conscience, either. It was doubtful if he possessed one. She was a journalist, a seeker after truth in the public interest. If she wasn't that, then her job had no integrity.

Her outside line buzzed and she picked up the phone.

'Julia Hamilton.'

'How'd you get on?' It was Ben, and she was flooded with relief.

'Come round for supper and I'll tell you.'

'Wasn't he pleased? What the hell did he expect?'

She smiled at the familiar irritable tone. 'He doesn't pay compliments, you know that. Well done, but it's not enough. He wants a criminal charge, so he can nail King to the cross. He actually said that.'

'He would. Bugger cooking, we'll go out, get a pizza or something. I'll come at around eight. I've got a lot to catch up on.'

'Bye, Ben,' she said. 'Thanks for ringing. I was feeling quite pissed off . . . '

'You're tired,' he said. 'Why don't you go home and put your feet up for a bit?'

In all the years she and Felix had lived together, he had never considered that she might be feeling tired or downcast. She was always on top form, and if she wasn't, he didn't want to know. 'I will,' she said. 'See you at around eight.'

She drove home, and as she went up to the first floor she met the girl who lived in the flat above.

'Hello,' they were neighbours, but like most London flat dwellers, they had never got to know each other.

'Hope you got your flowers,' the girl said, pausing.

'Flowers? I haven't been back for a few days . . . ' Julia shook her head. Flowers . . . not from Felix, surely? Never from Felix.

'I let them in when they buzzed. They said they'd leave them outside your door. I should have taken them in for you. They'll be dead by now.'

'I expect so,' Julia agreed. 'Thanks anyway.'

There was nothing outside her front door. No card notifying non-delivery, either. She sorted through her mail; it was collected by the caretaker every morning and put into the letterboxes. Three circulars and a bill. Flowers from Felix? She must be out of her mind to think such a thing. Maybe the girl upstairs was mistaken. Most likely they weren't for her at all, and they'd simply taken them back. She forgot about it, and went to run a hot bath. She was looking forward to seeing Ben. Bugger cooking. She smiled. No male chauvinist, either.

He didn't stay the night. They ate at a local pizzeria, and he came back for a cup of coffee.

'You don't have to go,' Julia protested.

'Yes I do.' He slipped his arm around her. 'You're whacked out. Ask me tomorrow. Anyway, I've got to go home and feed the cat.'

'I didn't know you had a cat?'

'Had it for years. Found it in the street, poor little sod. It's company. My daily looks after it if I'm away, but she doesn't come in on a Wednesday.' It was so unexpected it was touching. Julia asked him, 'What's it called?'

He grinned at her. He seemed embarrassed at admitting the cat's existence. 'Pussy,' he said. 'I couldn't think of anything else. Good night, love. Sleep well.'

'You too.' Julia kissed him at the front door.

As she locked it for the night, she remembered the flowers. She'd forgotten about them. Felix's note with his telephone number was in her drawer. She saw no reason to call him. Maybe one day, just to be friendly, but not yet. She slept very deeply that night, and dreamed that Ben had given her a cat as a present.

'Daddy?' Gloria King came up to her father's chair, and, bending down, she kissed him on the cheek. He had escaped the weekend guests and was sitting in the library with his eyes closed. He liked to relax when they went to the country. He had bought a big estate in Gloucestershire, which he ran as a farm and a commercial shoot, and he'd built a golf course, well out of sight of his house. He believed that everything should pay for itself, and his four thousand acres were not excluded. 'I didn't wake you, did I?'

He looked at her tenderly, reached out and pulled her onto the arm of the chair. He loved having her near him. The ash blond hair and blue eyes, the physical make-up of her body, woke a folk memory of his own people and his roots. He came from the land, from a line of men and women who were built on a scale to work it. Big bones, heavy muscles, coarse hands and feet for hard labour, like the slow-moving beasts they drove before the plough. But he had been born with brains; God knew what genetic freak was responsible for putting such an extraordinary intelligence in his peasant-boy head. But he knew it was there from an early age. And he concealed it. He read and studied in secret, fearful of his father's scorn. He got a sound beating when he was caught reading one of his school books. It had been torn away from him with a curse. There was work to be done outside, while he idled. His mother understood him. She was proud that he could read and was eager to go to the local school, though it meant trudging for miles there and back. She didn't dare stand up to his father, but she encouraged and protected him from his three older brothers when they bullied him. He loved his mother. Gloria reminded him of her. When he hung expensive jewellery on his daughter, gave her a Porsche for her birthday, spoiled her with the world's luxuries, he felt his mother shared in it. Too late for her, for his family. They were all dead. His brothers killed in the East, his parents lost in the blood tide of invasion. Nothing left of his past.

He had made his own future, and he owed nothing to anyone.

'No, darling,' he said, 'I was just being lazy.'

'You shouldn't work so hard,' she murmured, leaning against him, one arm round his shoulders. He had a warm, comforting smell, a mixture of aftershave and cigar smoke. When she was a little girl she used to insist that she would marry him when she grew up. It made him roar with laughter. He used to swing her up in the air and say, 'Shall I get rid of Mummy, then?' She always said yes, with great vehemence.

'Who's going to pay the bills if I don't work?'

'Don't tease. I'm serious. You come in here to sleep because you're tired. You shouldn't have to.'

'I come in here to get away from your mother and her bird-brained friends,' he retorted. 'So many women are so stupid. And men. I listen to them sitting round my dinner table talking cock, and I can't believe it sometimes.'

'Why do you let her do it?' his daughter said angrily. 'You come home to relax and she has dinner parties and lunch parties and there's never any time for you to put your feet up.'

'She enjoys it,' he explained. 'She likes being social. And sometimes it's useful. What did you think of that fellow Leo Derwent? Was he interesting?' He'd watched Gloria talking to the Junior Minister for Trade and Industry during dinner. He might enter into Gloria's conspiracy against her mother, but he told his wife who to include in her guest list, and the rising politician was one of them.

There were murmurs about his addiction to tying up his girlfriends and beating them. Low murmurs, but they'd come to King's ear through Joe, who knew what he called the Service industry inside out.

Leo Derwent liked S and M. So King suggested that Joe might make some amenable ladies available, and two of them were among the guests that weekend. One of them had already made a mark with the minister, and just to camouflage the ploy, King told Marilyn to seat him next to Gloria at dinner. And, to whet the appetite, the sultry lady was placed opposite.

'He was banging on and on about the *Sunday Herald*,' his daughter said. 'He says Western is running a campaign to discredit him because he's against a Federal Europe. He was quite paranoid about it; he says they've run through articles criticizing his handling of various issues where he showed bias against Brussels. Now he says they've started some Insight-type feature and he told me he'd met the woman heading it when he went to the Westerns' house about five years ago.' Harold King sat up, moving his daughter's encircling arm away.

'Did he?'

'Yes, he talked about it all through dinner. Ego. Ego – they're all the same.'

'Politicians' disease,' he remarked. 'Big heads and little minds. What did he say about this feature? It's called "Exposure". There's been a lot of hype about it in the *Herald*, but they haven't run a story yet.'

'Well, he thinks they'll have a go at him.'

'He's not that important,' King muttered. 'He says a woman's heading up this feature – they haven't come out with any names.'

'Julia Hamilton – she's one of their stars. He said she was a tough bitch when he met her.' Her father got up, heaving himself out of the deep chair.

'Hamilton? She's a news reporter . . . How the hell would he know that?'

Gloria had a flawless memory. She stored everything she thought would be of interest to her father.

'Because he was having a drink at the House with some political journalist filling in for Warburton. Said he used to be her boyfriend but they'd split up. She'd got this high-powered job. Creepy said the ex had had a few drinks, and was throwing hints about her having a go at some VIP. He's sure it's him!' She laughed at the folly and conceit of the man. Like her father, she had scant respect for human beings in general, and cold contempt for human frailty.

'Julia Hamilton,' her father said. 'We saw her at Mario's when we had dinner last month. Redhead.' His face was set and he was frowning.

'I remember. She was giving you hate looks. I mentioned it.'

'You did,' he agreed. 'You did. Go back to the party, darling. Say I've had to take a business call and I'll be with you as soon as I can. Be nice to Leo Derwent. He could be useful to me.'

'He was getting stuck into that girl Freda who came with Ted Ellis. I don't think he'll want to talk to me. I'll try.'

Freda was the bait sent down by Joe. A very high-class, educated call girl who brought a touch of genius to her act of sexual humiliation. The junior minister was hooked. King found himself a cigar and sucked hard on it, bringing the end to a glowing red.

Julia Hamilton. Heading a team of investigative journalists. He knew the *Herald* promotion by heart. *Watch out for 'Exposure'. Watchdog of the nation.* Joe had found nothing in her flat but scrap paper with some jotted timetable for a flight to Germany. And the contact number for the boyfriend. The ex, who'd talked to Leo Derwent.

It was time he asked him a few questions. He got Joe on his car phone. Joe listened, not interrupting. Then he said, 'Yes, don't worry, leave it with me. Is it urgent? I need a few days to set it up. Oh, OK, no problem. How are my toms doing?'

They were hand picked, and they had clear instructions: aim for the one guy and don't mess with anybody else.

'Freda's taken his fancy,' King snapped. 'She knows not to fuck him in my house?'

'Jesus, no, she wouldn't do a thing like that – I told her . . . ' Joe sounded shocked at the idea. King liked a varied sex life himself, but his home was sacred. Must be the generation, he thought. And the foreign background. He changed the subject hastily. 'I'll meet up with our boyo. I'll try it the easy way first time.' King cleared the line.

'Julia Hamilton.' He said it out loud. Something was in the wind, and he scented it like an animal. He went out of his library to mix with his guests. He made a show of being loud and self-important, dropping names and puffing on a huge cigar. He played the vulgarian and the power figure with the skill of an actor. He dominated them all.

In his modest sitting room in Nessenberg, the President of the town's Veterans' Association was finishing his confidential report on the English visitors and their examination of the Control Commission's 1949 file to his contact in Stuttgart. Munich had a core of pro-Nazis and was under close police surveillance. His contact had been changed to Stuttgart. He went through it, checking everything, and then sealed it. It would go by Express Special Delivery on Monday morning. Stuttgart would route it through from there. He didn't know its final destination, and he didn't permit himself to wonder. He had done his duty to their benefactor. That was enough.

5

'There's no death certificate. Nobody called Koenig died in the borough during that year or the following two years. They checked, just to make sure.' Julia shook her head. 'I don't know what to make of it.'

Harris played with his glasses, turning them round so that the lenses caught the light. 'Any joy from medical records?'

'Not yet; one local practice had no records, everything was cleared out when they rebuilt the surgery – just our luck if she was a patient there – they're working on two other practices that were operating at the time. We know,' she went on, 'we know she had an accident because there were witnesses. But there's only *his* word that she died afterwards. So what happened to her?'

'Wait for the medical check,' he suggested. He sat forward suddenly. 'Accident victims go to the local hospital. Get someone over to the Putney Royal and the Hammersmith. They may have chucked out stuff forty years ago, but it's worth a try.'

'Thanks, Ben. I'll put someone on it now. And I bought you a present.'

'Present? What for?'

'To stop you breaking your glasses,' Julia said. 'Here, put them in this.' It was a dark leather sleeve; he knew by the feel of it that it was expensive.

He fitted his glasses inside and put them in his breast pocket.

'I'm not used to presents. What do I say?'

'Nothing,' Julia smiled at him. 'Stop looking grumpy because you're embarrassed.'

'I'm pleased,' he said. 'Really. Thanks. I've got to get back to my office. Meet me afterwards?'

'We can start at the pub,' she suggested. 'Then you can take me home and introduce me to your cat.'

She met Felix going down in the lift; they hadn't encountered each other since he'd left the flat. 'Hi,' he said as she got in. 'Nice to see you.' He looked cool and friendly, without a hint of awkwardness. Julia felt herself stiffen at the sight of him.

'Nice to see you, too,' she said. 'How's it going?'

'It's going well. Matter of fact, I'm off to meet some tout who says he's got inside info on a front-bencher. Something juicy.'

Julia said coldly, 'You know Warburton doesn't deal in that kind of thing.'

'I know – he's a stuffy old fart, that's why. I'm going along to see what this creep's got to offer. I'll have to put him down to expenses.'

He laughed, and as the lift doors opened, he pushed out ahead, calling over his shoulder, 'Bye, Julia – see you!'

Julia followed slowly, watching him stride down towards the car park. There had been no spark left. He had become a stranger, a man she couldn't relate to; a reminder, she admitted, of a period in her life when she'd allowed sexual dependence to sway her judgement.

It wasn't Felix's fault; she was older and should have put an end to the relationship before it deteriorated.

Now a very different man had come into her life. They were drawn closer by work and respect for each other's talents. And making love to Ben was a mutual experience, not a male dominance that satisfied a baser instinct in her nature. Perhaps she'd had a need to submit to Felix because of the imbalance in their ages and their finances. She hadn't considered that before, and it surprised her. Working on the enigma of Harold King, complemented by the acute mind and experience of Ben Harris, she had become more intuitive, more self-aware. She walked to the pub where they usually met after work, and she was looking forward to seeing him. The anticipation made her happy; it was an odd feeling, to be happy because you were about to meet a man who'd only left you a few hours ago. To want to see his pet cat that he brought in off the street. And to spend the night with him and eat breakfast with him in the morning. She pushed her way through the bar, and he was waiting for her.

Felix thought he'd never seen such a sleaze-bag in his life. The expensive trendy clothes didn't deceive him, or the phony Irish-American accent.

He took an instant dislike to the man with his smooth talk, and the over-chummy manner. 'I'm Joe,' he had introduced himself. 'Joe Patrick. Pleased to meet you. What'll you have?'

'Beer,' Felix said, looking round. He wasn't familiar with the Soho pub his caller had suggested. It was wallpapered with old boxing posters and photographs of fighters posing with some tubby little jerk he supposed was the publican.

'Ever been here before?' Joe Patrick asked him.

'No,' Felix said. He sipped his beer. Joe Patrick had a straight whiskey without ice. 'Who put you on to me?' Felix asked him.

'Journalist friend of mine. I was telling him the story and he said you were the guy to talk to; so I called. I think you'll find it interesting.'

'What's it going to cost me?' Felix finished the beer. 'My boss doesn't print your kind of information, so it's got to come out of my own pocket.' Like fuck, Joe smiled to himself. He had formed his own judgement of Mr Felix dick-head Sutton. He'd been the journalist's fancy boy till she threw him out. Big-headed, macho pig with his brains in his crotch. Looked as if he'd boxed or played rugger, with that broken nose. Joe put his head on one side. 'Is that straight? You'd be paying yourself?' Felix nodded. 'Well . . . ' Joe pretended to hesitate. Then he gave Felix a broad smile, displaying the fine white teeth that had been grafted on to his own stumps. 'I'll make a special deal with you. We might be useful to each other. Fifty quid, cash.'

'Let's hear the story first.'

Joe raised a manicured hand with a big gold ring on the middle finger. 'Fifty quid on account and five hundred if you print it. That's fair, isn't it?'

'Fair enough,' Felix nodded. He took the hand held out to him in token of a pact agreed between men of their word.

'What's the dirt, then?'

'Over here,' Joe suggested, leading the way to a small table. 'We can talk here. I'll start with the name.'

Felix looked up quickly. A leading member of the Commons, no less. Subscribing to a paedophile mailing service. Videos, porno photographs, some of the children were three and four years old. 'Very, very nasty stuff,' Joe murmured in mock disapproval. His journalist friend – he was a freelance, and his market was strictly tabloid – he'd heard it from a contact in the Vice Squad. They were watching the man after his name had been found on a list kept by a well-known Dutch supplier. Some of the dirt had been confiscated in the post. Then the word came down. Kill it; he'll be given a private warning, but there's heavy pressure not to show him up, or there'll be repercussions that'll hit the other side on the front benches. The copper thought there might be some money in it, if a suitable market could be found.

'If he works for the tabloids,' Felix interrupted, 'why not go to them? They'd love a Scotland Yard cover-up sex-and-scandal story on a politician.'

'They wouldn't touch it,' Joe insisted. 'Same pressure. It's a powder keg, this one. These pricks are in some very high places. So I thought of you. Your paper's doing "Exposure", aren't you – I've read all the advance hype and it seemed just the sort of thing you'd latch on to. You're not scared off by the heavies . . . What'd you think?'

Felix said flatly, ' "Exposure" wouldn't touch it.'

'You sure about that?' The blue eyes focused on him, gutter bright with cunning.

'I know who's in charge of it,' Felix retorted. 'She wouldn't touch it with a barge pole. And I'm the wrong guy. I cover the political scene. I've nothing to do with this new feature.'

'How do you know they wouldn't be interested if you haven't asked?' Joe persisted. 'Why don't you give it a buzz and see what she says. It's a *lady*, is it?' He made the noun sound like a sneer.

'A very clever lady,' Felix snapped. 'She's already got someone in her sights, and it's a much bigger fish than some dirty old pervert.'

'Oh? You sure about that?' Felix was irritated by the repeated question. 'Course I'm bloody sure. I'm her boyfriend, for Christ's sake!'

Joe noted the present tense. Pride still touchy . . .

'I've got a bloody good idea who it is, too,' Felix insisted.

'You could be wrong,' Joe mused. 'The kid fancier's in line for a job at the next reshuffle . . . ' He let the sentence die.

'I told you, it's not a politician! She's going to do some exposé on the Honours List. Shits like Harold King getting a peerage. If that crook gets a seat in the Lords, I'll give up on this lousy country. Here, I brought some cash with me. Fifty quid, but there won't be any more. No story for us. Sorry.'

Joe took the packet of notes. 'Pity. Next time maybe. I'll keep you in mind.'

'Yeah,' Felix said, 'do that. Thanks for the beer.'

He elbowed his way out. Joe, out of a lifetime's habit, counted the tenners and then put them in his inside pocket. He'd got the information like squeezing milk out of a full tit. The boss was right. Joe didn't know how he knew things before they happened, but it wasn't the first time. He was right. This cow Hamilton was out to make trouble for him.

The contact in Stuttgart was not a veteran. He had been ten when the war ended, and, luckily for him, his family were still together, their home intact. He owned a small engineering business which was thriving.

His father had been invalided out of the German army after the defeat of France. A civilian sniper's bullet had left him in a wheelchair.

He had brought up his three children to believe that only treachery from within had deprived Germany of victory. His eldest son left university with an engineering degree and a secret commitment to the outlawed neo-Nazi movement. He was a fund-raiser and supporter of a political renaissance that was in the open now, encouraged by resentment of the influx of Turkish migrant workers, busy organizing violent opposition to the thousands of refugees from Romania and the Balkans. Jobs were short and times were hard for Germans after the euphoria of unification. Restructuring the shattered economy left by the Communists was crippling, despite the strength of the Mark and the industry of the people. Resentments grew and the movement fed on such feelings.

The engineer from Stuttgart was one of a chain of contacts throughout Germany, with links in France, and Italy, and Spain. Fascism was not dead, and it had many sympathizers prepared to help its cause.

One of those causes was the protection of ex-German soldiers who had found a haven abroad after defeat. The report had come in from Nessenberg.

He read through it, bitter at the interference from the old enemy, still hunting patriots after forty years.

He knew where to send it, but, like the shopkeeper in Nessenberg, its ultimate destination was unknown to him, except that it was tied to generous donations to the movement from abroad. The report was packaged and sent off by airmail to an address in Dublin.

It arrived by special messenger at King's house in Mayfair. It was marked PRIVATE, PERSONAL AND CONFIDENTIAL. No-one but King was allowed to open anything labelled in that way.

Gloria put it in his desk drawer in the study. It would have to wait till her father got back from his latest trip to New York.

He talked his plans over with her; she understood the complexity of his financial dealings, and she was a good sounding-board. Sometimes her sharp instincts had an idea to contribute.

She treasured that intimacy, not least because her mother had always been excluded. She was too stupid, Gloria thought triumphantly. And one day she knew Daddy would take her onto the board of his conglomerates and she'd be like his son. She had wanted to be a boy since puberty; rejecting the female image in favour of father imitation, Gloria didn't like men. At school she discovered the pleasures of sexual activity with other girls. She was not very motivated; the lesbian affairs were short lived and very discreet. Her father didn't know about them, because she chose her lovers from her circle of friends. They were usually married, and dissatisfied.

She'd gone up to Oxford where she got a two/one in economics and modern languages, and then spent two years at the Harvard Business School where she graduated with Honours. Everything was geared to her succeeding her father; she wasn't brilliant, but she was intuitive and she worked relentlessly to succeed. For five years she had been investment manager in the London office of a firm of merchant bankers in American ownership. She was disappointed he hadn't taken her to New York with him. Lately they had started making business trips together. This time he had refused her, explaining that it meant a series of confidential meetings with bankers and money brokers where she couldn't be present. She'd be bored out of her mind with nothing to do all day. Unlike her mother, Gloria wasn't interested in shopping.

'I'm never bored with you,' she wheedled, but she couldn't move him.

'You would be this time, sweetheart. I'll bring you something special back. Tiffany's? How about that?'

'I'd rather come,' she persisted. 'I'll miss you. Two whole weeks. Call me, won't you?'

'I always do,' he had protested. He would bring her something spectacular from Tiffany's, and an equally expensive present for his wife, just to keep both women at each other's throats. He was pleased with Marilyn at the moment. She was looking more beautiful as a result of some discreet surgery, and she was getting a lot of coverage in the social columns. It was all crap, but it was good ground work for the coveted peerage.

He flew by Concorde to New York. It was a heavy schedule. He was going to get the crucial financial structuring he needed to launch his attack on William Western.

It took the research team four days to track down the records, but they found them in the basement of Hammersmith Hospital. In April 1950 a Mrs Phyllis Koenig had been admitted with severe head injuries following a fall. She was in a coma. The case notes said she had been transferred to a private nursing home after regaining consciousness and severely limited speech and movement. The impairment was permanent and the prognosis poor, as she had a blood clot on the brain which was impeding the blood supply. The nursing home had long closed but it was in the Sussex area, near Midhurst.

They began another search for the death certificate going forward for five years from the time of the accident, and found it in 1954. The unfortunate woman had lived until then, little more than a vegetable if the hospital prognosis was correct, and had died in the nursing home from a cerebral haemorrhage.

Julia went over the details and rang Ben through. She couldn't keep the excitement out of her voice. 'We're getting somewhere,' she told him. 'Phyllis Koenig didn't die in 1950, she was brain damaged and she ended up in a nursing home in Sussex. She died there four years later.'

'Why Sussex?' Ben said. 'Was King keeping her hidden?'

'Looks like it. We'll have a copy of a will by this afternoon. You know, I really think we're on the right track!'

'It's about time,' he said. 'Take my advice J, don't wind up the boss till you've got something more. He'll only lean on you.'

'Like he did before,' she agreed. 'I haven't forgotten the lesson, teacher. Same place tonight – what time?'

The pub round the corner from their office building was their staging post. They met there, had a drink and then went home, sometimes to her flat, sometimes to Ben's. Julia had made great friends with the cat. It liked sitting on her knee, digging claws into her skirt and purring.

Their affair was common knowledge now; the clientele at the pub were mostly *Herald* men and women, and they were used to seeing Ben Harris and Julia Hamilton closeted in a corner. Nobody bothered to comment any more. They were an item, like other couples working on the newspaper.

Ben said, eight-thirty, and she promised to call if she learned anything significant from the will.

As soon as he saw her he quickened; he knew that expression and what it meant. Bright eyes, a slight colour and an air of expectancy. He knew her moods and her foibles and he couldn't fault anything. He sat beside her. She'd ordered him a whisky.

'Come on, what've you got?'

She opened her bag. 'This,' she said. It was a photocopy of the last will and testament of Phyllis Koenig, née Lowe. Dated 29 March 1950. Ben read it and said, 'Christ,' under his breath at one point, and carried on reading to the end. Then he looked up.

'She cut him out,' he said. 'She left everything to her niece. The house in Fulham, the stocks, shares, everything. Over a hundred and fifty thousand pounds of estate. That was a fortune in the fifties!'

'We've traced the niece,' Julia said. 'She lives in Sussex, that must be why Phyllis was in that nursing home. I talked to her on the phone this afternoon, and she's agreed to see me tomorrow morning. Ben, I *know* we're on to something now. All the dead ends, all the damned blind alleys, but at last we're seeing light!'

Ben said, 'Phyllis must have sussed him out when she made that will. She knew she'd made a bloody big mistake by then. And a couple of weeks later she has a fall that nearly kills her. My guess is she probably told King she'd looked after him, just to keep him sweet. So he decided to collect before she changed her mind.'

'We'd never prove it,' Julia said.

'No, but it's got his stamp on it. Nobody proved who murdered Hayman in the Bahamas, or drove Lewis off the road. But I know King was behind it.'

On the way back to her flat Ben said suddenly, 'We had a bargain, remember?'

'Now Ben, you're not going to start that—'

'I'm just reminding you, that's all. When I think we're getting too close, you back off this thing.'

'*When* we get close,' she agreed. 'But we're not close enough yet.'

Next morning Julia drove to Midhurst. The address was just outside the charming town, with its narrow streets and antique shops. It was a mid-Victorian house just off the road. Her appointment was for eleven o'clock and she was ten minutes early.

When she rang the bell, it was opened by a small, plump woman in her sixties. She had bright blue eyes and short, crisp grey hair.

'Mrs Adams?'

'Miss Hamilton? Come in. You're very punctual – no trouble with traffic? Midhurst can be a nightmare with all these awful lorries blocking up the roads. I've got some coffee ready for us.'

She was brisk and confident in manner. Very on the ball, as Julia had expected. The sitting room was pleasant, comfortable and chintzy. A black labrador lay in front of the fire which was lit; it raised its head briefly and then went back to sleep.

'Poor old Daisy,' she said. 'She's fifteen now, and nearly blind. Can't bear to think of losing her. Do sit down. Milk and sugar?'

'Just milk, please,' Julia answered.

'Now,' Jean Adams said, 'before I tell you about my aunt, I'd like to ask you exactly what kind of feature on that dreadful man you've got in mind.'

'I'm not sure,' Julia admitted. 'I'm trying to find out the truth about him. He's built up a legend and backed it with every lie under the sun. So he must have something to hide, Mrs Adams, and I want to find out what it is. All that nonsense about your aunt dying of cancer – I suppose you read that biography.'

'I did,' she said. 'Pack of lies. As I expected.'

Julia said quietly, 'But you did nothing to disprove it.'

'No.' The answer was sharp. 'To what end, Miss Hamilton? To show up my poor aunt as a woman who took to drink because she'd fallen victim to a wicked man young enough to be her son? That she died brain damaged and bedridden. No thank you. And anyway he was too powerful, too rich. I couldn't have fought him. He'd have dragged us through the courts and ruined us before I got a proper hearing. I let Aunt Phyl rest in peace. I still feel the same. That's why I want to know what you're planning to do before I tell you anything.'

'I hope to expose Harold King for what I believe he really is. His relationship with your aunt is the tip of an iceberg. It only confirms what a lot of people suspect about him but can't prove: that he's very bad news and he's becoming more and more powerful. You called him wicked, didn't you?'

'Oh he was,' Jean Adams agreed. 'Poor Aunt Phyl knew it. That's what destroyed her. She told me he was a war criminal. More coffee?'

The pieces were fitting in, one by one.

'Aunt Phyl was rather a rebel, I knew that even when I was a child. Unconventional – wouldn't marry and settle down. And she was well off too. She lived – well I suppose it was a raffish life in those days – wouldn't raise an eyebrow now. She liked the men, and they liked her. She was terribly smart and good-looking. Great fun. She joined the Red Cross in the war, worked in London all through the bombing and the V1s and those frightful rockets. Then she simply couldn't settle down. It was too dull, she said, after all the excitement. So she joined UNRRA and went off to Europe to work with the refugees and DPs, displaced persons. You know, Miss Hamilton, it changed her.'

'I'm not surprised,' Julia said. 'It must have been horrific.'

'Yes, it was. So much suffering, such terrible devastation. She wrote long letters describing it. She was a very good correspondent, and we'd always been close. I admired her; I thought she was so dashing and exciting.' Jean Adams gave a rueful smile. 'I wished I'd been able to join in the war and do something useful, but I was just too young. Aunt Phyl was really affected by what she saw in those camps. She threw her heart into working for the people and trying to help. She came back to England in 1947 and took me out to lunch in London. I was working there as a secretary, and I'd just got engaged to Bob, my husband. I remember her saying, "I feel I'm doing something worth while for the first time in my life, Jean. Not just having fun. I'm helping people who've lost everything, families, homes, hope—" Then she laughed at herself, embarrassed, I suppose. "If I'm not careful, I'll be a reformed character, and that won't do." She was a tremendous person. Have you ever hated anybody?'

'No, no. I don't think so.'

'You're lucky. It's a terrible feeling. I've hated Hans Koenig for forty years because of what he did to my aunt. I never think of him as Harold King. She wrote to me about him. I was getting married and she couldn't get time off for the wedding. She told me she'd found this wonderful young man, so sensitive and intelligent – quite alone, all his family lost, he'd been a slave on a farm in East Germany and the traumas had marked him for life. He didn't even know his real name. And then the letters changed.' She looked away from Julia, into some grim memory of her own.

'She wrote she was in love,' Jean Adams said. 'Really in love for the first time in her life. The age difference didn't matter; he needed her so much and he was so grateful and loving – they were so happy together. I remember reading it and thinking, Good God, this isn't Aunt Phyl – it reads like a bad novelette. But I was too wrapped up in my own wedding to worry about it. My mother didn't take any notice. "Oh, it's just one of Phyl's fancies. She'll get bored with him, like all the others." I think Mother was a bit jealous of her; she wasn't the one with the looks and personality. Then my aunt came back to England and asked us to Fulham to meet him. They were married. I don't know what I expected. Some romantic Slav with soulful eyes, I suppose. But he wasn't like that. He was arrogant. Yes, arrogant and smug. Very physical. I couldn't help seeing what she found attractive in him. And she was besotted, behaving like a silly girl half her age. He didn't like me or Bob, and it was mutual. Bob said to me afterwards, "I think your poor aunt's in for trouble." I thought so too. I only saw her a few times after that, and she'd gone rapidly downhill. She'd always liked a drink, but it was never a problem. She was actually tight at lunch-time when she came down here one Sunday. Bringing him with her, of course. There was a horrible atmosphere. I'll never forget it. He was so rude to her, so hostile. She looked miserable.' She paused. Julia sensed that even after all these years, it distressed her.

'When did you see her again?' she asked.

'About ten days before her accident. She rang me up and asked me to come to London. She wanted to talk to me urgently. I thought she sounded very strange. We had lunch together, and she told me this extraordinary story.' She paused, and then went on.

'Koenig,' she said, clearing her throat slightly, 'Koenig never drank. Nothing. Not even beer. He hated Aunt Phyl drinking anything, even in the very early days when she took him to live with her in Germany. She did tell me that, and said it was rather sweet, but she didn't see why she couldn't have a gin and tonic at the end of a long day . . . Of course, as she got more and more miserable and he was nastier to her, bullying her for money, she took to the bottle in a big way.

'It drove him mad, apparently. He used to hit her sometimes – never in the face where it showed, but on the body. He'd punched her black and blue several times. Then one night he'd been out for a walk – she never knew where he went, but he'd disappear off for hours at a time – he came back and she was tight. And then he did something extraordinary, quite out of character. He poured himself a big gin. She couldn't believe it. He stood over her, and he said, "Now, you drunken old cow, I'll show you what you are. I'm going to lie in the bed snoring and stinking of gin like you do. I'm going to be too drunk to fuck you, you old bag, and you won't like that." Apparently it was the most dreadful scene; she began to cry in the restaurant when she was telling me, word for word. The insults, so personal, so terribly cruel. And he did it. He got blind drunk that night. She said she was so frightened she sobered up completely. He was like a madman. And he told her the truth about himself.

'He wasn't Polish or a refugee. He'd been in the German army and fought in the Western Desert. He told her he'd murdered a group of British prisoners of war. He boasted he'd shot them down in cold blood after they'd surrendered!'

Julia drew in her breath. 'He said that! My God – he admitted murder?'

'Yes,' Jean Adams insisted. 'That's what she told me. He boasted of it. He thought he'd killed them all, but one of them survived. He found that out afterwards. She said he yelled at her – "Bad shooting." He was afraid he'd be charged with war crimes after the war. So he threw away his uniform, joined the refugees and invented the whole story. My aunt was trembling. I remember very well. I did say to her he might have been making it up, if he was so drunk and out of control . . . but she wouldn't hear of it.' She paused for a moment. Then she said in a low voice, 'She also told me he raped her that night.'

Julia didn't say anything. She waited until Jean Adams spoke again.

'The next morning he denied it all, of course. He said alcohol drove him crazy, made him imagine things. He begged her to forgive him. She said he was crying.' She looked at Julia. 'Poor thing, she said she wanted to believe him, she really did. But she couldn't. She looked completely broken. I can see her now, sitting there, saying she wished she was dead. "He's not going to get my money," she said. "I'm seeing my solicitor this afternoon, he's drawn up a new will." Ten days later she had the accident. But a copy of the will had come to me in the post. I was amazed to see she'd left me everything. She'd given me the means of getting rid of him. Bob and I faced him when she had to leave the hospital. Her solicitor backed us up. We told him we were applying for guardianship and we showed him the copy of her will. He'd get five hundred pounds from us if he cleared out of the house and undertook never to see her or contact us again. He didn't argue. He just shrugged. "I can't fight you," that's what he said. "I'm only a poor foreigner." He signed an undertaking and Bob gave him the money. He said he'd go back to Germany. We believed him. We sold the house and moved my aunt down to Sussex. We took care of her till she died.'

She got up, putting the coffee cups on the tray. They didn't speak for a while. At the door Jean Adams said, 'Some years afterwards Harold King was being written up and photographed and we realized he was the same man. It was too late then. He was a millionaire and a public figure. We had a family and a lot to lose. My husband was a cautious man. He said it was best left alone. I agreed with him because of my aunt. But I've regretted it over the years. I'll just put these things in the kitchen.' Julia followed her out.

A young labrador, black like the old bitch by the fireside, bounded up to meet them. 'Daisy's granddaughter,' she explained, bidding the puppy firmly to get down. 'Bob died two years ago and I just can't bear to be without one of this family. My son has the daughter and they gave me Poppit for Christmas. She's a handful to train but she's great fun. I wish I could offer you lunch, but I'm going out with a friend. We belong to a bridge club, and we always treat ourselves to lunch first. She's a widow too.'

'Thanks anyway, Mrs Adams, but I've got to get back to my office. Would you be prepared to sign an affidavit, setting down exactly what you've told me?'

Jean Adams hesitated. 'I'll have to speak to my solicitor first,' she said. 'I'll let you know what he says.'

'Do you have the original undertaking King gave you in exchange for the five hundred pounds?'

'The firm would have it; Bob never kept documents at home in case of a fire or a burglary. I'm sure it's still there somewhere.'

A cautious man, as she said. She came to the door with Julia.

'What a smart car,' she remarked. 'Young women have so many opportunities these days.'

'I can't thank you enough,' Julia said quietly. She held out her hand and the older woman took it in a firm grasp. 'I'm so very sorry about what happened to your aunt. I hope it hasn't upset you too much – talking about it.'

'It just makes me angry,' Jean Adams answered. 'I really would like to see that swine gets his just deserts. I hope you do it!'

'I'll do my very best, I promise you. Let me know what your solicitor says.'

'I will. Goodbye.' She turned and closed the door and Julia went down the short path to the road and into her car. She felt oppressed, as if the other woman had laid some burden on her. The burden of evil that had gone unpunished. It was a strange, outmoded phrase, dredged up from somwhere in her memory, but it was very apt.

Whatever she had promised Ben Harris, she insisted, she wasn't backing out of this one.

There was nothing Joe could do till the boss got back from America. He had the information for him and there didn't seem to be any urgency. The *Herald* feature hadn't come out with anything yet. It was still a case of 'Watch this space'. He took himself and one of his coloured girls to the races in France. He had plenty of money, they stayed in good hotels, ate well, and he had a run of good luck with the horses. He felt generous and he gave her some spending money. He was sorry he hadn't brought the other girl; he liked threesomes, but it might have been awkward, where they were staying. He met up with some Irish who were over for the meeting and they had a great time. He picked up the tabs and played the big man, and kept the girl out of sight. He knew his countrymen. They were good at downing the jars, but they were prudes at heart.

When he came back he put a call through to King's personal secretary. Face like a copper's boot and no tits. King never mixed business with pleasure. She had some surprising news for him.

'Mr King flew back two days ago,' she said. 'He's been trying to contact you, Mr Patrick.'

Joe swore softly. 'He wasn't expected till the end of the week,' he said. 'Anything wrong?'

'Not that I know of,' the voice was cool. She didn't like Joe Patrick. She thought he was common and cheeky. Once he'd tried to chat her up. She knew he was mocking her. 'You'd better call him. He's in his car on the way to lunch at BZW.'

Joe was scared. He hesitated, thinking how best to explain his absence – without leaving a contact number. That was his mistake. King wanted him and couldn't find him. He wouldn't like that. He said, 'Shit,' several times, and then nerved himself to dial the car phone.

King always called his home when he was away. He was in a good mood, because the negotiations with Field Bank were going well, and the funding for a frontal assault on Western International looked viable without too big a borrowing commitment. It was early days, but his confidence was soaring. He smelt blood, and his instincts had never failed him. He spoke to his wife first; she was nearest when the telephone rang. She chattered about her committee meeting for the East London hospices and how they had asked the Princess of Wales' office to suggest a date for a big charity function.

The Princess, always eager to help the suffering, proposed an earlier date than they hoped, and her presence would ensure substantial funds.

King let her run on – he was in a good mood – and then cut in and asked if Gloria was there. Gloria was on her way out to dinner, but, hearing her father was on the line, hurried back. She didn't care if she was late.

'How's my girl?'

'Missing you, Daddy. How's it going?'

'It's going fine. Hard bargaining, but I'm getting there. Anything I should know?'

Gloria remembered the special delivery. 'There's a package for you. It came last week.'

'Oh – what kind of package?'

'It looks like documents,' Gloria answered. 'It's marked private, personal and confidential. I put it in your desk. Do you want me to send it over? Shall I open it for you?'

'No – no!' The change of tone alarmed her. He was shouting at her. 'It's been there since last week? For Christ's sake you stupid little . . . ' Gloria gasped as he spat the filthy epithet at her. 'Why didn't you call me at once?'

'Daddy, I didn't know . . . ' Tears were welling up.

'You get it over here by DHL. Tonight, so I have it in the morning – you do it, you hear me?'

'Yes,' she was crying now. 'Yes, I'll do it right away. Oh Daddy, I'm so sorry. It wasn't my fault . . . ' But the line was dead.

Her mother had left the room when she took the phone. She couldn't bear the cosy telephone calls between father and daughter. Now she came back and saw Gloria in tears.

She smiled. 'What's the matter, darling? Lovers' quarrel?'

Gloria swung on her. Hatred flared up openly between them when King was safely absent. 'Shut up! Shut up, you cow!'

Marilyn King kept that maddening little smile on her face. Her daughter looked so ugly when she cried, her skin was blotched and she blundered about like a wounded animal, making her way to the door.

'You'll be late for dinner!' her mother called out.

'I'm not going to fucking dinner!' Gloria shouted, and slammed the door of King's study behind her. She found the package, the cause of that dreadful burst of anger and abuse. It wasn't her fault. Anything marked private was never opened, that's all she knew. It was just a rule. She couldn't even remember seeing anything marked up like that before. She started writing out a label and began telephoning.

What could be in it, to make him erupt like that? Something to do with his business in New York. The delay must have compromised him in some way. But how could she *know*? She wailed aloud as she made the arrangements, at exorbitant cost, to get it on the next plane by special courier to New York and then to his hotel.

It reached Harold King just before a working breakfast with the finance director and deputy chairman of Field Bank.

Harold King didn't open it. He knew where it came from, and he couldn't risk losing his concentration by looking at the contents before an important meeting. It had waited a week, bearing its warning message. It would have to wait another two hours.

The meeting was long and difficult. His American financiers wanted more collateral than he had on offer, and he had failed to convince them that it wasn't necessary. No deal had been in sight when they parted with a further meeting scheduled for the next morning. He was short by too many millions to launch his bid successfully. Unless he could come up with guarantees against the money he needed to back his bid, Field Bank was not prepared to bank roll him.

King kept his nerve. He blustered, cajoled, joked and tried to overbear, but it didn't work. Then he switched roles. He became quietly confident. He had, he said as they were leaving, ample resources which he could call upon if they insisted, but he maintained they were not necessary. He would discuss it further with them in the morning.

The resources were ample, but they were not his to pledge.

They consisted of the Pension Fund of his thousands of employees in all corporate businesses throughout England and Canada.

When he shut the door on them, he was calm. Crises had this effect on him. He had seen his solution, and he was weighing up the risks. If he was successful, the money would never be called in and he would never be found out. He had gambled before, and won. He would win this, the biggest gamble of his business career.

Then he opened the package and started to read the report. The meeting took place the next morning. He was smiling and almost cherubic with good humour. He had thought the position over, and although he deplored the lack of confidence evident in their attitude, he understood the reasoning behind it. He was a man of responsibility himself, and he appreciated the Bank's commitment to its investors. He would therefore pledge the extra money from his personal resources. Details would be made available to them when the agreement was in a draft stage. He concluded the meeting with handshakes and warm expressions of goodwill all round. He cancelled the other meetings. They could take place later.

More urgent business needed his attention.

He packed up and flew home to England almost a week ahead of schedule.

King worked on the flight. He had sent his assistant and his two secretaries on a later flight, so they could clear up and reschedule the meetings with other financial institutions for a month's time. He had promised Field Bank, but he wasn't going to deliver till he'd exhausted one or two other possibilities. Where the moral tone wasn't quite so high. He took his paperwork with him and settled down in First Class, angrily waving away the proffered champagne. But, throughout the flight, the issues blurred. The report written in German overlaid the columns of figures and financial predictions. He was after Western, but Western was after him. Ben Harris and Julia Hamilton had taken up the old trail in Nessenberg, so long gone cold, thanks to his friends and his connections. And the few words spoken to the girl clerk in the Bauhaus as they left the dusty old files in their dusty basement-room . . . those words shrilled in his head like a warning siren.

Thank you. We found some useful information.

What information? What had they found that hadn't been excised from the records? King locked his papers away in his briefcase and pulled an eye-shade over his eyes. He wasn't sleeping, but blackness helped him concentrate. Something had prompted Western's clever newshound to say that. Perhaps it was the woman who had spotted something he had missed. 'A fresh eye,' he muttered. She'd retraced Harris's path and deviated from it in some way. They'd left the Nessenberghof and gone to Munich.

Why Munich? The proprietor of the hotel had answered his contact's questions in all innocence, even showing him the hotel register confirming the names. And added the information that they were going to Munich and had booked into the Bernerhof. The grandest hotel in the city.

Munich. It tormented him. They'd found something that sent them to Munich. He pulled off the eye-shade and reached for the report again.

So painstakingly assembled, every spoken word, however trivial, had been noted down. Thank God for Teutonic efficiency and attention to detail.

Before checking out and going off to indulge themselves – it must be indulgence to stay at the Bernerhof – the couple had asked about the best way to get to Hintzbach. A funny choice, it struck her, there was nothing of interest there for English tourists. But they set off, and left the Nessenberghof afterwards. They didn't seem to be lovers. They had separate rooms. No, King thought savagely, they weren't lovers, they were journalists on an assignment. And Harold King, alias Hans Koenig, was that assignment. It all tied in. The schedule of flights to Germany written on a scrap of paper, which Joe Patrick's break-in had discovered, and now this. Western had been stopped in his tracks following the same line ten years ago. Now it was reopened.

He landed at Heathrow and drove straight home. He didn't wake his wife or look for Gloria. He went to his study and dialled Joe Patrick's number. He'd given the bastard a job to do and heard nothing from him. He wanted answers. He didn't get them that night, or for the following two days.

Nobody knew where Joe Patrick had gone. He had left no contact number. All King needed was confirmation of the evidence from Germany. He had looked to the Irishman to prove it. Then he could decide what to do.

The old lever on Western might not work a second time. A drastic solution might be needed. A permanent solution.

Joe Patrick knew how to take a bollocking. He didn't try to excuse himself while King was in full flow. He shrank into himself as if the furious invective were a rain of blows.

He'd seen the boss lose his temper before. There was no stemming it. You just had to wait till it blew itself out like a hurricane. He marvelled at the scope of insults; King might have a foreign accent, but he had native vocabulary when it came to swearing. Joe had no pride or resentment; he had the good henchman's mentality. He'd fouled up by not being in reach when he was needed. At last, when King stopped abusing him, he ventured to speak. He knew better than to make excuses.

'I'm sorry. I won't fuck up like that again.'

'You do,' King exploded for the last time, 'and you're fired!' His tone lowered. He spoke normally. 'Did you get hold of Hamilton's boyfriend?'

'Yeah, no problem. I needled him a bit and he spilled. He's a dick-head. Hamilton's the boss of "Exposure", the *Herald*'s super snoop, checking on you. He thinks it's tied up with the Honours List. I don't think he knows any more.'

' "Exposure",' King repeated. 'That adds up. They say it will launch its first feature in November.' He was almost talking to himself. Then he looked up sharply. He'd chewed the balls off Joe. Most human beings responded to being kicked, but that type needed assault and battery from time to time, to stop them getting lazy.

He said, 'I want her followed. And Harris. I want to know everything they do, where they go, who they see. I want to know when they crap! Understand me? Reports come to you on a daily basis, and you pass them to me the same day. Take my advice, Joseph,' he said the full name with heavy emphasis, 'don't go to the races while this is on!'

He gave him a cold glare.

'Get out of here.'

'She won't sign an affidavit,' Julia said.

'Did you call her back?' Ben asked.

She shook her head. 'No. I'll have to go and see her again. And this time I want you to come with me. She might respond better to a man. But she's quite a determined lady, and she's not going to change her mind in a hurry.'

Ben slipped an arm round her. They were in Julia's flat; she was wondering whether she could persuade him to move in permanently.

'Listen, you tracked her down, you've opened up the real can of worms on that bastard. What we want to follow up is the war crime angle. If we can prove that – we'll get him! I'll go and see her alone, if you like. We don't want to get heavy with a widow.'

'No,' she agreed, 'you're right. If Jean Adams thinks we're trying to push her, she'll dig in and nothing will shift her. I know the type. You go, Ben. It's her solicitor's advice. He's too scared to let her sign an affidavit in case King slaps a load of writs on her. It makes me furious!'

'Which he would,' Ben countered, 'if he knew. Come on, calm down.' He smiled and said gently, 'Fiery lady, aren't you?'

And then unpremeditated, he said it for the first time. 'Maybe that's why I love you.' Before she could say anything, he leaned over and kissed her. It was a long kiss, tender and then passionate. He let her go and said, 'I mean it, I love you. I hope it doesn't spoil anything.'

Julia touched his lips with the tips of her fingers. 'I never thought you'd say it,' she whispered, and then kissed him in return.

As she felt his hands moving on her breasts, she withdrew a little.

'Don't love me,' she said. 'Not yet. Talk to me. Let me talk to you. That's what I love about *you*, Ben. There's so much more to us than just sex.'

'Like what?' he murmured, still holding her, but now his hands were still.

'Like sharing things, talking them over. Our work, our stupid jokes – I even love your cat!' She laughed at herself. 'Why don't you bring Pussy to live here – I think she'd like it.'

'I think she would too,' he said. 'But not yet, my darling. I caught you at the end of a relationship. I want to be sure you're ready for a real one with me. No rebounds, no second thoughts till you've had time to know me and make up your mind. There's the age gap, too.'

'It's the right way round this time,' she insisted. 'You're your own man, Ben. There's no competition between us. You said it early on; we make a very good team.'

'Then let's keep it that way for now,' he suggested. 'Let's stay lovers and colleagues and friends, till we see how it works out. And if it does,' he looked at her, 'I'll want you to move in with me.'

* * *

Jean Adams put the telephone down. She stood beside it, biting at her lower lip. 'Don't touch it,' her solicitor had begged. He was a family friend of many years, and his alarm had communicated itself to her. 'Don't get involved with the Press, my dear Jean, they'll promise anything. And then let you down without a moment's hesitation. If you sign an affidavit, they'll use it. You'll be dragged into their campaign against Harold King, and God knows where that would end for you.' He'd been sympathetic, but adamant. He owed it to Bob to protect her, as Bob would have done if he'd been alive. He'd told her to forget the past a long time ago, and that advice held good today. More than ever.

Let the lady journalist do her own dirty work. She had the might of William Western to fight her battles. Jean had nobody. He went further. He found the undertaking signed by King in return for money in the office safe, among Bob Adams' papers, and suggested that he should destroy it. 'Tell them what you've done,' he said. 'Better still, if they try to pressure you, call me in on it. I'll get rid of them.'

Jean Adams had agreed, and telephoned Julia with her decision. The call she had just taken was from a man, a colleague of Julia Hamilton. He sounded pleasant enough, very reasonable. Could he come and see her just once, just to fill in some more details? He accepted her decision not to sign anything, and sounded as if he meant what he said, but he would really appreciate a meeting. Jean had said rather sharply, 'With my solicitor present, Mr Harris?' And he had said, 'Of course. All the better.' So she found herself agreeing to an appointment. She sighed. Perhaps she'd been foolish to let him talk her into it. Certainly their old friend would think so. But then, it was up to her, wasn't it? She had a mind of her own, after all. She wasn't going to look like a silly vacillating old woman and ring this man Harris up and say she'd changed her mind again. Let him come down. It might be very interesting. She believed in being decisive. Decision made, why waste time? She dialled the solicitor's office and left a firm message with his secretary.

She was seeing a journalist from the *Sunday Herald* on Wednesday afternoon at two-thirty at her house and she would like him to be there. Then she went out into her garden to tackle the rose bushes.

Joe Patrick didn't deal with sleaze when the client was Harold King. You couldn't rely on the small fry, the ones that were just legal. Only just. He employed the most reputable firm of private detectives in the country, with branches in all the major cities. They had wide-ranging facilities, from business and industrial surveillance to simple domestic.

They charged top rates, but they were absolutely reliable and honest. No operatives of theirs had ever tried to use his information for his own advantage. A twenty-four-hour watch was mounted on Julia Hamilton and Ben Harris. Ben was followed when he drove down to Midhurst to see Jean Adams.

Julia had described her very well, he thought, shaking hands and accepting an offer of a cup of coffee. An independent, outspoken lady, the type that used to be called the backbone of England, before the national spine began to crumble . . . He put the cynicism away. He didn't think like that so much now. Julia had made him optimistic.

The bottle was half full, instead of half empty. She was always slipping into his mind when they were apart.

The solicitor was there. He was tall, with spectacles and untidy tweedy clothes. But no fool. The eyes were wary.

'Now,' Jean Adams said briskly, 'I presume you've come to try and change my mind, Mr Harris.'

Ben said quietly, 'No, Mrs Adams. I wouldn't presume such a thing. I only want to fill in the details a little more and to ask you one or two questions, which might help us. Without involving you.' He glanced at the solicitor as he said it. He got no response. The old boy was deeply suspicious. He switched back to Jean Adams.

'I'd like to say we understand your decision and we sympathize with it. King has managed to frighten and bully his way out of trouble from a lot of people. Important people with resources. That's why we undertake not to use the affidavit if you decided to sign it.'

'In which case,' the solicitor interrupted, 'why ask for it if you wouldn't use it? There doesn't seem much point.'

Ben had anticipated that question. 'Documents can be shown to members of your profession, sir, in confidence. It can influence their judgment and the advice they give their clients. That was the only contingency we had in mind. And the affidavit would be lodged with you, naturally. Mrs Adams could withdraw it or refuse to produce it if she wished.'

Jean spoke up quickly. 'You didn't tell me that, Dick. That sounds quite reasonable.'

'It sounds very reasonable,' he answered, 'except that a court can order you to produce evidence once its existence is established. Mr Harris, I've advised Jean not to get involved with your newspaper investigation of Harold King. I'm here to make certain you don't persuade her otherwise.' He gave Ben a look of frank dislike.

Ben hesitated; he wasn't getting anywhere. He didn't want to play his only ace so quickly, but he hadn't any choice.

'Mrs Adams,' he said, 'I don't like to say this, but did it occur to you that King might have tried to murder your aunt?'

'Oh come on – I must protest!'

Ben ignored the solicitor's interruption. He was watching Jean Adams. Her face had flushed, and then the colour drained, leaving her very white.

'No,' she said. 'Please, Dick, be quiet for a minute—' One hand rose to silence her adviser. 'No, it certainly didn't. It was an accident. She was blind drunk, according to the hospital when the ambulance brought her in. Good heavens—' She pushed back a wisp of hair. 'Good heavens,' she said again.

'You couldn't have proved anything even if she had died,' Ben went on. 'Her drinking was his alibi. But just think about it. He'd lost his head and told her the truth about himself. He was in her hands. I'll go further. I started looking into Harold King ten years ago. I am convinced that the murder of a business opponent in the Caribbean and the so-called fatal accident of another business opponent in this country were orchestrated by him to protect him from a takeover. Your aunt told you he'd admitted murdering unarmed British prisoners. He ill-treated your aunt. He hated her. Do you really think he would have risked being exposed? Look at the timing – ten days after she saw you, she had a near-fatal fall. King wouldn't stop at murder. I'll tell you what I want, Mrs Adams. I don't want to drag your family through the mud. I don't want to cause you any worry or distress. I want to find out what happened to those prisoners in the Western Desert. That's what I want to hang on Harold King. And you are the only person alive who knows he admitted it.' He stood up. Neither of them said anything. He saw the solicitor move close to her chair. She looked pale and very old.

'Thanks for seeing me,' Ben said. 'I'm sorry if I've given you a shock. I'll see myself out.'

He was in the hall when the solicitor caught up with him. 'What you've done is disgraceful,' he said. 'You've no proof, and, even if it was true – nothing can be done about it!'

'Please, Dick,' Jean Adams came out, 'you mustn't abuse Mr Harris.' She came up and opened the front door for him. 'I'm going to think about it,' she said. Ben Harris took her hand. It was trembling slightly. 'I owe it to my aunt if he really did that. Aunt Phyl believed him about the prisoners. I'll be in touch, Mr Harris. Goodbye.'

Ben walked down the short path, past the rose bushes, already trimmed back before their winter pruning, and the watcher in the dark blue Volvo parked on the opposite side of the road, lowered his road map and logged him out on his tape recorder.

'Ben,' Julia said gently, 'you did the right thing. We need that affidavit. It may never be used – you said it yourself.'

'I know,' he admitted. 'But she looked so bloody shaken – I felt a real shit, J. I suppose I haven't been at the sharp end of the job for so long I've gone soft. You sit in an office and send other people out to suck blood. I didn't feel good about it.'

Julia kissed him. 'I know, but you still did the right thing. We both think King tried to kill that poor woman. And if we can follow this lead through and come up with a war crime like shooting British prisoners – we've got him, Ben. Under the new law he can be prosecuted!'

Ben said slowly, 'There's no guarantee she'll do it, even now. Her legal chap will bust a gut trying to talk her out of it. But I just felt she'd come to a decision when I left. I think what I said tipped the balance. Anyway, she said she'd call us, so we'll have to wait and see. Thanks, love.'

'For nothing,' Julia said softly. 'Stray cats and old ladies – big, tough Ben Harris – you're rather a lovely man . . . I'm going to take you out to supper and then I'm going to bring you back here and spoil you absolutely rotten!'

'Daddy,' Gloria King said, 'what's the matter?'

He was slumped in front of the TV in his study, a cigar burning itself out in the ashtray. The programme was a mindless sitcom that she knew he would usually have switched off immediately. He looked tired and preoccupied. She came and perched on his chair and slipped her arm round him. 'Are you still angry about that parcel?' she asked. 'I'm so sorry, I tried to tell you . . . ' Her eyes had filled with tears. Whenever he was distant with her, she felt like a miserable, guilty child, desperate to be forgiven.

King looked up at her. He took her hand and held it.

'Don't be silly, darling girl,' he muttered. 'Fuck the parcel. Fuck everything.' She sighed, flooded with relief.

'Then what's wrong?' she persisted. 'You're not yourself ever since you came back from New York. Is it the business? Isn't it going well?'

'Not as well as I hoped,' he admitted. 'I've got to find a lot more money than I reckoned, but I'll do it. It just needs a bit of fixing.'

He glared at the flickering screen, the muttered inanities and recorded laughter in the background. Joe Patrick was doing his job. He got the agency's reports faxed through, and faxed the copy direct to King's private-and-confidential number.

Ben Harris had gone down to Midhurst to see a Mrs Jean Adams. King felt as if his heart had stopped. The shock was so intense he couldn't feel it beat for some seconds. Jean Adams. The image of her swam in front of him, forty years out of date. Small, sharp tongued, an enemy. Phyl's favourite niece. It must be the same. Midhurst in Sussex where Phyl had spent her last years, his secret locked in the damaged brain. It must be the same Jean Adams. He relived in those few moments the confrontation when she came to see him, her dull husband in tow, and bought him off with a few hundred pounds. He was poor, when he should have been rich. But he was safe and free of Phyllis – the albatross he'd hung round his own neck. Jean Adams. He hadn't thought of her for years. She'd slipped out of his memory, as if she were dead like her aunt. But she wasn't. She was alive, and Ben Harris, back from his trip to Germany with Julia Hamilton, had gone down to see her.

His enemies had been ferreting around for years, trying to discredit him. Without success. His business deals were shrouded in layers of deceit, impossible to penetrate. He was a genius at covering his tracks with nominees, subsidiary companies and offshore operations. His criminal activities were protected by their own nature. Laundered money for drugs in the States, illegal arms supplied to all sides in Eastern Europe . . . He'd contacts among the secret world of the Mafia which were as interested in anonymity as he was. He had nothing to fear there, and he had made a huge fortune, most of which was banked and invested overseas. He glanced up at his daughter.

She said, 'What is it, then? You're not ill, are you Daddy?'

He saw panic in her eyes. He smiled. 'Ill? Don't be silly. I'm like an ox – you know that. No, it's nothing, just a little hiccup. I'll sort it out. I'll tell you about it one day. And I've been thinking – how would you like to give up that job with Hart Investments and come and work for me?'

She blushed. 'Oh, Daddy! You mean it?'

'Why not,' he went on. 'It's about time. You're a big girl and you've got your business degree and five years with Harts – I've always had this in mind, Gloria. I want you working with me. One day, when I'm too old, you can take over. What do you say? Are you ready for the deep end?'

She hugged him, her face radiant. 'I'm ready if you say so,' she said. 'But you'll never be too old. Never.'

'Sweetheart,' he said, 'I'm not immortal.'

Gloria King spoke quietly. 'You are to me.'

He sat on after she had left him. She was so excited, so happy that her face glowed. She'd need a husband, King decided. Clever, but not too clever. A man to support her, but never able to dominate. Father children. He liked that idea. The dynasty principle appealed to him. Pity if it was a Life Peerage because he couldn't pass it on . . . but never mind. Power was what matttered; titles without power and money were a mockery. Gloria would learn from him. Her mind was as quick as her body was clumsy. He'd teach her everything, and little by little confide some of his secrets to her. She wouldn't be troubled by scruples. She'd always appreciated that there were no rules in business except the cardinal one: don't get found out. He dreamed, planning the future for a little while. Then abruptly his heart quickened as he faced reality again.

His past was his one weakness. He never thought about it. He never thought backwards, unless there was a reason. Regret, nostalgia – these were a form of indulgence he despised. What was done was done and necessity was the only rationale. He had set out to survive because that was the only purpose in life. He'd seen other men die and there was nothing heroic about it. Just waste. Natural waste of the lesser breeds, the victims who would always fall before the strong. He was strong and he was clever. He had used Phyllis Lowe – he sneered mentally as he remembered her – sentimental, oversexed, enthralled to middle-aged passion. A natural victim.

A self-pitying drunk who'd brought her fate on herself. She'd goaded him into an act of madness, and paid the penalty. Not the full penalty as he'd intended. He'd always meant to abandon her in due time. But once he'd lost control that night, he knew he'd lost control of her. So he acted. But the blow hadn't been hard enough. It hadn't killed her. It had locked up his secret in her twilight mind and she'd died with it unspoken.

She'd left her whole estate to the niece, Jean Adams. The niece had been glad to pay him off, so she knew nothing sinister. And he had genuinely forgotten her existence in the years when he rose in the public domain, and became a symbol of ruthless power. He didn't fear exposure by the wife of a small-time stockbroker, if she was even still alive. He feared the German records in Nessenberg, and early on he had made a trip over to see the right people and closed off that avenue into a cul-de-sac. He had sympathizers with his story, men he could talk to as a comrade, men with secrets of their own. He thought he had blocked any possible investigation. And he had the power to silence his enemy and rival William Western when he attempted it, because Western had his own secret to protect.

But battle was imminent, and Western had decided on one last throw against him. Harris had gone back to Germany with Julia Hamilton, Western's brilliant protégée, and, this time, they had found a lead. And the lead had led to Jean Adams. And back from her to his dead wife.

He got up, heaving himself out of the deep chair. They could expose the truth about Phyllis's death, but it wouldn't be enough to damage him. He could explain the lies in his biography by the need to protect the poor alcoholic woman's reputation. It wasn't enough for Western to deal him a real blow.

He dialled the number, and Joe Patrick answered. 'I want Adams' phone bugged.'

'It'll be done tomorrow,' Joe answered. 'The agency won't do it, but I have another source. How about Hamilton's place? Harris shacks up with her there. I can fix that, too.'

'You do that,' King said. 'And I want reports on the hour if anything comes up. You may have to pay Mrs Adams a visit.'

'Just say the word,' Joe murmured. King hung up. There was nothing more he could do. Shut off now, slam the mental door. He had other things to think about. His financing of the take-over, his plans for his daughter.

Recognizing his own power induced a surge of confidence. It assured him he was invulnerable. Nobody would ever get near enough to the truth and live to tell the world about it. He could make sure of that.

6

Julia was in her office. Ben Harris had rung in to say his daughter, Lucy, had rung up out of the blue. She was in some kind of trouble. He was meeting her in Birmingham and wouldn't be in till the morning.

There had been no word from Jean Adams since his visit two days ago. Beyond Julia's window, the London skyline shimmered in late-autumn sunshine.

They were getting closer, some of the smoke screen was lifting here and there, showing glimpses of darker things than she had ever imagined.

Harold King was concealed in the heart of it; a charlatan, a liar, and, by his own admission in a drunken frenzy, a man who had shot down unarmed men and gloried in it. And probably attempted to murder his wife. This, Julia recognized, was not the push-button killing of rivals like Hayman and Lewis by men hired for the job. King had reddened his own hands.

She pictured him in the exclusive restaurant, a crude bully, play-acting the part he had adopted as a public face. The man of power, the vulgarian, the genius who overrode opposition like the murderous Juggernaut of ancient India, crushing whatever lay in its path.

That gave him a superhuman image, a larger-than-life perspective that perpetuated the legend. Behind it was someone very different. Someone cold and cunning, with the killer's immunity from conscience. A man with one weakness. He could never drink alcohol; it loosed the demons and took control of his tongue. His well-known abstinence was a discordant note. It was not compatible with King, the self-proclaimed bon viveur who loved the high style. It was part of Hans Koenig, who knew that never again in his life must he touch a drink.

The office was air-conditioned. But Julia shivered as if a draught had suddenly found its way into that controlled atmosphere and chilled her. She would miss Ben that evening. He had sounded worried on the telephone. His daughter was in trouble and she'd surfaced after years of minimum contact. Julia had said, of course he must go and try to sort it out. Lucky girl, to be able to call on him and have him come running. It made her think of her own parents. She didn't feel like spending the evening with friends, though a call would have brought invitations to dinner by most people she knew. She was well known, a social catch. And she wasn't encumbered by Felix any longer. He hadn't been popular with her friends. She hadn't seen him or heard of him, and he had slipped into the background of her mind. She was sure he had replaced her very quickly, and that he was getting on with his own life in his own way. She buzzed through to her secretary.

'Call my parents will you, Jenny – thanks.'

Her father was put through. He sounded delighted when she asked if she might come down and spend the evening. No, Julia insisted, her mother was not going to spend the time in the kitchen – they would all go out to dinner. Would he book somewhere really nice – she didn't know the restaurants in the area. Her mother took over the conversation. How lovely – she sounded so pleased Julia kicked herself for not making time for them more often. Yes, it would be a treat to go out instead of cooking, but only if Julia stayed the night. She wouldn't feel happy if she had to drive all the way back in the dark.

So many dreadful things happened to women these days – supposing the car broke down – Julia didn't argue. It was protective and warm hearted; it didn't irritate her any more as it used to when she was less assured. It would be fun to sleep in her old room. She could start very early in the morning and be in her office in plenty of time. She wouldn't be home when Ben rang, but she could record a message on her answering machine giving him the Surrey number. She felt very happy and the sombre mood had disappeared. She didn't think about Harold King as she let herself into her flat, and changed the message on her answerphone so Ben could get in touch with her.

The hired surveillance reported her leaving the flat at six o'clock. Then they started tailing her BMW as it drove out of London. It was the chance for Joe's other contacts to take over.

They had already called on Jean Adams.

It was quite early in the morning and she had not taken her dogs out for their walk when the telephone engineers rang to report a fault on the line. Jean was in the kitchen eating a frugal breakfast and reading *The Times*. She found the *Telegraph* too solidly right wing; the idea of *The Times*' impartiality was a legacy from her youth and she believed it firmly.

'There's no fault on my line,' she protested. 'I've made two calls out this morning.'

'It's incoming calls, madam,' the man said. 'That's where the problem is. I'd like to send someone round to check the connection. Will you be there in half an hour?'

She decided to postpone the walk till later. She had nothing much to do that morning anyway. Except make the telephone call to her solicitor with her decision. The walk with the dogs had been a planned diversion. She'd slept so badly and worried the problem to and fro before making up her mind. Let the telephone engineer come and put the wretched fault right. 'Yes,' she said, 'I'll be here. I must say your service has improved. I used to wait for up to two days if anything went wrong. Privatization, I suppose.'

'Glad you're satisfied, madam. Half an hour and our engineer will be with you.'

He sounded a pleasant man, Jean thought. They'd been so surly in the old days. At least the Government had done *something* right. She made a fresh pot of tea and finished reading *The Times*. The telephone engineer arrived exactly half an hour later. It took him ten minutes to check the phone in her sitting room and the bedroom extension. He was a dour young man who didn't invite conversation. He came downstairs and said, 'It's all fixed.'

'What was the matter?' she asked him. She didn't like his manner. He gave her the impression he'd been called out for nothing.

'Loose wire, no fault in the connections. You won't have any more trouble.'

'I wasn't aware I had any in the first place,' Jean Adams said sharply.

She wasn't going to put up with surliness. She walked into the hall and let him out. She didn't thank him for coming. She lifted her downstairs phone. It was working perfectly. The bug was voice activated, and the calls were recorded and transmitted by remote control to a central number which in turn logged them and recorded them. Jean Adams took the elderly Daisy for a short trot up and down the street and then put her back in the house. The boisterous puppy needed a good hour's exercise and she set off by car for the open countryside.

It was a lovely autumn morning, crisp and sunny. She came back invigorated and calm. At twelve-fifteen she telephoned her solicitor and told him she would come in the next afternoon and sign the affidavit. He hadn't wanted to prepare it, poor man. He'd pleaded and argued, and used delaying tactics which had cost her a lot of worry and lost sleep, but she had always known in her heart that she was going to hold out against him.

At her age there wasn't much future to consider. Let that loathsome creature do his worst, and damn the consequences!

During the day there were other phone calls. Social calls, a query about a bill from the electricity board, and the call to the office of Barrat & Thompson, Solicitors and Commissioners for Oaths. Joe Patrick played the tape to Harold King on a portable machine no bigger than a cigarette packet.

They sat in Joe's office. It was a plush room, furnished in an aggressive, modern style which he felt demonstrated his prosperity. He had an expensive and very graphic female nude, complete with pubic hair, hanging on the wall opposite his plate-glass desk. King sat sprawled in a big leather Swedish chair that swivelled when he moved. One of Joe's girls had brought them a tray, with whiskey for Joe and mineral water for King. The air was thick with cigar smoke. King listened without movement or change of expression. The deadpan look meant he was at his most dangerous.

The voice of Jean Adams was clear and crisp.

'I know you're going to argue with me, Dick, but I know it's the right thing to do. I'm going to sign the affidavit. I want you to put in it everything I told you, and I'll come in tomorrow.'

The man called Dick was pleading with her.

'Jean – what good will it do? You've no proof King tried to kill your aunt – you've let the matter lie since 1950 – why bring it up now?'

Her voice cut in on him. 'And what about those prisoners he said he murdered—' Joe Patrick risked a quick look at Harold King. His florid skin was greying as the blood drained from the surface. Joe kept his eyes averted after that.

'My dear, it's only hearsay . . . don't you see that your aunt's alcoholism made everything she said suspect? You didn't really believe her yourself.'

'I didn't want to,' the tone rose in self-accusation. 'Bob talked me round. Just like you're trying to – you men all want a quiet life!' She gave a brisk little laugh. 'Dick dear, let's not talk about it any more. I failed to have the courage of my convictions once. I've got a chance to put that right. I'll be in your office at two-thirty tomorrow. And why don't you and Betty come round and have supper with me in the evening?'

'We'd love to,' the voice was resigned. 'All right, Jean. See you at two-thirty.'

There was a heavy silence as Joe switched the recorder off. He waited for King to speak. At last, clearing his throat of nervous phlegm, he said, 'There were other calls, but this was the one I thought you'd want to hear.'

Harold King drew on his cigar. He was in shock. He could feel it. His body was cold, and a chill sweat was breaking out under his clothes. His strong heart pumped furiously in response. He tipped ash off the end of his cigar, on to Joe's geometric carpet. The ashtray was at his elbow, but he didn't see it.

'She's talking cock,' he said. He looked at Joe and there was such a threat in that look that Joe Patrick blinked and cleared his throat again.

'Absolute cock,' King repeated, emphasizing each word. His accent came out as a guttural snarl.

'Yeah,' Joe agreed quickly. 'Cock,' he echoed.

Never explain, was one of King's maxims when dealing with underlings. But instinct counselled otherwise this time. The Irishman was cunning as a rat. 'Her aunt was a piss artist.' He drew on the cigar again, calming himself. There was no reason to explain who the aunt was.

'She had DTs. She had hallucinations . . .'

'Yeah,' Joe nodded. 'Sure. Me own grandmother was like that – shoutin' the odds about being robbed and poison put in her food . . . ' Like King, stress brought out his native brogue. King shut him up with a gesture.

'It's cock, but that wouldn't stop the *Sunday Herald* making use of it,' he said. 'I've got big deals going. I can't afford hassle. Fix it, Joe. No affidavit.' He levered himself out of the chair which swung awkwardly under his heavy body.

Joe Patrick was on his feet. He said in a soft voice, full of the lilt of his native tongue, 'I'd best take care of it meself. Leave it with me.'

King didn't speak. He just nodded and the eye contact confirmed what had been agreed. Joe's girl helped him on with his coat and opened the door for him after she'd called up his car on the phone. She was good-looking, he thought, appraising her. He didn't go for colour, but she was beautiful in her way.

He had recovered his nerve. His body heat had regulated, and the heart was steady. Joe would make sure there was no signed affidavit lodged where Julia Hamilton and 'Exposure' could make use of it. He trusted Joe. He was imaginative. He'd make it convincing. He sat back in his car, and slowly he relaxed. And began to think it through. Germany was where the leak had sprung, in spite of his precautions. Break the Jean Adams connection and there was nothing but hearsay from the past. There was an old business saying he liked to quote: when you want to break up a syndicate, cut the heads off one at a time. Jean Adams would be the first.

Ben Harris faced his daughter. He'd forgotten how pretty she was. She had her mother's blue eyes and blond hair. It was a pretty face, but it was drawn with worry and there were dark shadows under her eyes.

'I can't tell Mum,' she said. 'She'd freak.'

She picked up her cup of coffee and sipped from it. She was a stranger to him, although there were traces of the child he used to bounce on his knee at bedtime. A grown young woman with a problem she couldn't share with her mother and her step-father. So, after years of neglect, she had asked him for help.

'He's the problem,' she said. 'He's a real pain about this sort of thing. He'd say it was disgracing the family.'

Ben didn't answer. He had never met or spoken to the man his wife had married. He had never even been curious about him. He had assumed that he was a good father to his stepchildren. Apparently not in this instance.

'It's none of his business,' Ben said at last. 'It's your choice.'

'Yes,' his daughter said quickly, 'that's what I feel. I want to keep it, Dad. It's not Pete's fault. I was the one that slipped up.' Pete, he had elicited, was the married boyfriend who wasn't ever going to break up his home. He already had three children. 'Trouble is – ' She bit her lip, hesitating for a moment. 'Trouble is, I haven't got much money . . . '

Ben helped her out. It pained him to see her embarrassment with him. He was her father, after all.

'You mean you haven't got any,' he prompted.

'I'm in my last year at college,' she said. 'I've got ninety quid in the bank. My grant pays the rent and Mum makes me an allowance . . . ' She trailed off again. Her eyes filled with tears. 'I feel awful coming to you like this,' she said. 'I took Mum's part when you broke up and it just sort of drifted after that.' Ben reached across the café table and put his hand on hers.

'Lucy love, you don't need to apologize. I was a lousy father. And your mother was right to pack it in. I'd like to make it up to you. You want this baby, go ahead and have it. I'll see you right for money, that's no problem. But you'll have to tell her.'

'I know,' she said. 'She will freak, though.'

'She'll get used to it. She was crazy about you two – she'll love it; you'll see.' She leaned back and sighed. She took out a pink tissue which he suspected was torn off a lavatory roll, and blew her nose.

'You're a real star, Dad. I'll get a good degree and I'll get a job. I won't be a burden to you, I promise.'

'Don't be bloody silly,' Ben told her. 'It's my grandchild, too, you know. How does your friend Pete fit in – is he going to be around?' She shook her head. He felt a jolt of anger. 'No. He's called it off. I don't blame him. He's got enough to pay for with three kids already. I'm on my own and that's better really. I'm not scared, it was just I didn't see how I was going to cope and I did want to finish college. You are a star. I mean it.'

'No problem,' Ben smiled at her. She was an independent free-living product of her age, but her vulnerability touched him as much as her courage. He wished he'd been part of her growing up. Her question took him by surprise.

'What about you? How's your life going?'

'It's OK. I've got a top job and I earn a hell of a salary. No complaints.'

'Girlfriend?' his daughter asked. 'I thought you'd have got married by now.'

'My track record wasn't very good,' he said. 'And I didn't meet anyone – ' He looked at her. 'But that's changed. There's someone very special now. I don't know how it'll work out, and we're not rushing into a commitment. I'd like you to meet her one day.'

'I'd like it too,' she answered. 'We'll come and visit, me and my illegit.' He realized what an attractive smile she had. The clouds had lifted with the rapidity of youth and optimism. Thanks to him.

He'd planned on staying the night in Birmingham and seeing some old newspaper colleagues if he could contact them. He changed his plans.

'Let's get the bill,' he said to his daughter. 'I'd like to come and see some of your work. And then I'll take you out to dinner. How's that?'

'I've got my portfolio in the flat,' she said eagerly. She was studying textile design. 'And dinner would be great. I *am* eating for two,' and she began to giggle. They left the café, and, after a few yards walking on the pavement looking for a taxi, Ben's daughter slipped her arm through his.

Joe Patrick was silent and bad-tempered after King left. He was always nervous, keyed up before a serious job. And there was so little time to prepare. He cursed Harold King, and raised a threatening fist to his hapless girl when she interrupted to ask him something. She fled, and he sank into contemplation. He roused himself and phoned Julia Hamilton's number. He mustn't neglect other tasks, just because King had tossed hot shit in his lap. Hamilton's flat hadn't been bugged. The agency said she'd driven off with what looked like a little overnight case and headed out of London. She was logged in on the M25 by seven o'clock that evening. The phone rang four times and then the answerphone cut in. He listened. It wasn't a normal message.

'Ben darling. I've gone down to my parents for the night. Please call me.' The number was a code and four figures. 'I hope it went all right. Love – J.' The place was empty. He could send his electronic man along with the lock picker he'd used when he broke in before. They'd fix the phones up and have time to put simple bugs in the rooms. She wouldn't be able to sneeze without Joe having it on tape.

He decided to eat something. He came out and yelled and the girls came out looking apprehensive. His temper was always unpredictable. One or both of them could get a punching if they weren't extra careful.

'Get me somethin' to eat,' he snapped. They knew his preferences. He liked simple stuff when he was alone and not showing off in restaurants. Eggs, burgers, chips – the junk food of his youth when such fare was a treat.

He poured himself a measure of whiskey. Irish whiskey, that slipped warm down the gullet and heated his cold belly. But not too much. Just one to set him up. 'Fix it, Joe. No affidavit.' A beating wouldn't be enough. He'd read King's mind and knew what was expected. No contract worthy of hire could be bought at such short notice. It wasn't a job for a greedy heavy, who might foul up and get caught. It called for an expert. Himself, as he'd offered. He ate in the kitchen, washed his food down with a cup of strong tea. Then he looked at his girls. The apprehension in their pretty faces stirred him. He liked to feel a woman's fear. And that gave him his plan of action. He glanced at his Rolex, a present to himself.

It was nine-thirty. He'd be in Midhurst before eleven.

'I'm goin' out,' he said. 'You two tar babies wait up for me, see? I'll be ready for some fun when I get back . . . ' He got up and went to each girl and pinched their cheeks. They'd never heard the term tar babies till he used it. It was Dublin slang for coloured girls, exported from the slave states of America. They hated it, as Joe Patrick knew. He lingered by the older girl, Tina; she was his favourite of the two. 'You be ready for me. I'll want something special tonight.'

'You'll have it, Joe baby,' she promised. She poked out her tongue at him provocatively. When he'd gone she closed her mouth and looked at her friend. 'One day I'm going to bite it clean off—' she hissed.

'Like fuck,' the other girl said. 'He'd kill you. What's up? Where's he off to?'

'Some poor bugger's going to get done over,' was the answer. 'Joe always gets a hard on afterwards. Come on, let's watch telly.'

* * *

Jean Adams ate her supper on a tray by the fire. She let the puppy in to sit with the old labrador bitch, who raised a sleepy head and sniffed, before going to sleep again. It was warm and peaceful and she enjoyed the TV. She loved police series, and never missed her favourite programme. Then there was the news, and if she wasn't too tired, she watched *Newsnight*. Then bed, with the old lady in her basket upstairs by the radiator in her room, and the puppy snug in the kitchen with paper laid out on the floor in case of accidents. She was still young and not always able to last the night. Jean was content. She had made her decision and lifted the burden of that old guilt from her mind. She would sleep with a clear conscience. At eleven-thirty she let the dogs out into the rear garden for a last pee, and then locked up.

Slumped down in his seat in the car parked opposite, Joe Patrick saw the square of light in the upstairs window go out. He waited.

At ten minutes past twelve he broke into the house through the kitchen window.

'You're looking bright eyed and bushy tailed,' Julia's father remarked. She had come back into the sitting room after a long telephone call. She had taken it upstairs. He and her mother had exchanged looks. She had arrived with flowers for her mother and a bottle of special malt whisky for him. She looked relaxed and happier than they could remember and they felt it wasn't connected with her new career. Her mother couldn't resist the question.

'Who was that, darling?'

Julia smiled. Why not say something? She knew they'd be pleased, especially her mother who was convinced that fulfilment lay in a comfortable marriage like her own. 'He's called Ben Harris,' she said. 'We're working together. You'll be glad to know that Felix and I broke up.'

'Thank God for that,' her father exclaimed. 'I thought he was rather a lout – terribly pleased with himself. I didn't say anything at the time—'

'Dad darling, you didn't have to – I could see it on your

face. He was all right. I think he needed someone nearer his own age who wasn't always competing with him.'

'And winning,' her mother interposed. She was shrewd, as Julia knew. Her wisdom came from long experience of life and people.

'And winning,' Julia admitted. 'Ben's quite different. He's older, he's got a big job, and we're very good together. I think you'll like him. I hope so, anyway, because I do.' She looked at them and smiled. Her mother said, 'He's not married, is he?'

'No, Mum,' Julia said gently. 'He's divorced. A long time ago. He's in Birmingham meeting his daughter. She's got some problem she wants sorting out. I'll bring him down one day.'

'Do, we'd love to meet him.'

They'd gone to a hotel for dinner, and come back in happy mood. They had recovered ground lost through lack of contact over the years, and to her relief the subject of her brother and sister-in-law and their children had only been touched upon, instead of dominating the conversation as before. Julia had been irritated and vaguely jealous; it wasn't an incentive to see more of them when they had so obviously closed the circle. Now, ever since that visit for Sunday lunch when she was upset by Felix's absence, the gap had opened, and she was inside a circle of their own. Just her father, her mother and herself. Ben would like them, she was sure of that.

He'd talked to her about his daughter, Lucy; his attitude surprised her. She hadn't seen him as paternal. He sounded pleased about the pregnancy, proud of his daughter's decision to keep her child and resist the easy option. Proud of her work, which he said was very original. And then, before she had time to feel a twinge of jealousy, he asked about her, told her he missed her. And said he loved her, rather abruptly, before hanging up.

Typical Ben. Soft words were still drawn out of him like teeth. She went to bed earlier than usual, because her father looked tired. He was close to seventy; she often forgot that. Loving someone else had sharpened her perceptions, made her think of other people more.

She woke, made herself some breakfast, and slipped out without disturbing them. She left a little note on the kitchen table.

See you both very soon. It was lovely. And signed it with her childhood pet name, Juliette. She drove through empty roads, listening vaguely to taped music. It was a lovely day, and the autumn colours blazed from the trees in the early-morning sunlight. She switched on the news as she came into London, and met the early traffic. It was the usual; signs of a slight economic upturn. A report of bomb explosions in Belfast, Palestinian riots on the Israeli West Bank; a statement on the rise in petty crime in London.

And the murder of an elderly widow in Midhurst.

Ben was waiting for Julia in her office.

'Ben?' She came up to him smiling, surprised to see him so early. 'Did you drive down last night? I thought you were staying—'

'Jean Adams is dead,' he said. Julia stared at him in horror. 'There was a break-in and she was murdered last night. I got the latest update. Here.'

Julia sat down. She blanched as she read.

Jean Adams had been found dead in the early hours of the morning. She had been sexually assaulted, and bludgeoned to death. Neighbours were alerted by one of her dogs howling and barking and called the police. The animal had been kicked and had to be destroyed. Robbery was the motive because jewellery and money had been taken and the room ransacked.

'I can't believe it,' Julia said. 'Ben, I can't believe it's true!' He pulled a chair close to hers. She looked terribly white and shaken.

'I can,' he said.

She went on, her voice uneven, 'What sort of man would *do* a thing like that? She was near seventy—'

He lit a cigarette. 'It's happened before. They break in to rob, the woman wakes up and they get turned on because she's terrified. Then they kill her to stop her identifying them. Makes you think about the death penalty. Come on, have some coffee.'

'I don't want any,' she said. 'Have the police got any clues?'

'They're going through the place,' he said. 'I had a word with the local crime boys. It's the first murder of its kind down there and they're pretty fired up about it. I said we knew her and they promised to call in if they find anything. J, I don't want to sound callous, but I don't think she signed that affidavit.'

Julia looked at him. 'No, I realize that. I suppose we could ring the solicitor to make sure. Later on. God, I hope they catch that brute—'

'He won't have a nice time down at the station if they do,' Ben remarked. She was upset, and he didn't labour the point about the affidavit. He was sure Jean Adams had told him she was signing it that day. It was a very long shot to imagine she'd advanced the timing. But he had to take it. He, not Julia, would call the solicitor's office. He would be better able to cope with the response.

He went downstairs and, after an hour, he made the call. At first the receptionist said her boss was out, then suddenly he came on the line. His voice was shaking with rage and emotion. 'You ring up at a time like this about your bloody affidavit! No, she didn't sign it! You're the scum of the earth, all you media people!' And the line cleared as he banged down the telephone.

It was a busy morning and a hectic afternoon for Ben Harris. He cut his lunch-time drink and sandwich with Julia. The murder wasn't top priority, such cases were no longer headline news. There had been too many of them. Political crisis, disasters, a plane crash in Northern France killing a group of British students – the stories came pouring in and the widow lying in the mortuary in Midhurst rated a few column inches on the inside page. Then Harris's phone rang in mid afternoon. It had been quieter for the last hour, and he swore. He loved pressure, it brought out the best in him, but it frazzled his nerves and primed his temper with a very short fuse.

It was the Detective Chief Inspector from Midhurst in charge of the Jean Adams murder. He talked to Harris for a few minutes. Ben said briefly, 'Thanks – thanks very much. No, we won't print anything. Not without your say-so. Keep me posted.'

One of the fingerprinting team had chanced on something. Faint marks on the telephone upstairs in the bedroom. Similar marks on the instrument downstairs. They'd taken them apart and found that Jean Adams' phones had been bugged.

Ben put a call through to the penthouse office. Julia was out at a meeting. He didn't leave a message. He sat on in his office with the whirl and bustle of his news room eddying outside, and thought it through. Then he made another call. He asked to see William Western as a matter of urgency.

'Take her off this,' Harris said again.

Western made a bridge with his fingertips. 'No,' he said.

Ben leaned towards him. Western was sitting behind his desk and he had kept Ben standing. It hadn't put him at a disadvantage. He came close to the desk and leaned towards the slight man in his big chair and said, 'King is on to what you're doing. He knows we're after him. He had that woman's phones bugged and she was bloody murdered before she could sign that affidavit. That's no coincidence. That's King. You pull Julia off this and I'll see it to the limit for you.'

'No,' Western said. 'You're not as good as she is. You tried before and you got nowhere.'

Ben glared at him. 'I was looking into two murders and you made me drop it. Let's get the facts right.'

'The facts,' William Western cut in, 'are what I say they are. You and Julia are a team. Neither of you drops out. If King is behind this, and it's only supposition on your part – don't shout, Harris – just listen – then it means two things. Somehow, somewhere, you've leaked information. So look into that first. If you're right and the telephone bugging is tied into this murder, then King must think he's safe. He's broken the only link you've got with the accident to his wife and the story about a war crime. So what you do now is put it about that the story's dead. No proof. And check your own telephones. Or hadn't you thought of that?' He raised his eyebrows at Ben Harris, almost taunting him. Harris stepped back.

'I've thought of it,' he said. 'I'm giving you formal notice that I'm resigning. As of now.' Western unhooked his fingers.

'And leave your friend Miss Hamilton to carry on alone? I don't think you'll do that.'

'I'll get her to resign with me,' Harris snarled at him. His fists were clenched at his sides; he looked explosive with anger. Western said coolly, 'I don't think you'll do that either. Or you wouldn't have come to me first. Stop behaving like a bloody fool. She won't give up, and you know it.'

'She will,' Ben insisted. 'She promised; she didn't tell you but it was the condition I worked with her.'

'She won't keep it,' he dismissed it. 'She doesn't quit. If you're worried about her, then do what I've told you. Give out that you've killed the story. Keep your mouths shut and get on with it.' He shifted in his chair, making himself comfortable. 'I'll run a line on the new "Exposure" feature hinting at a completely different target.'

'Thanks,' Ben Harris said furiously. 'You'll have my letter by tomorrow morning.'

'I hope not,' Western murmured. 'I shall be sorry to lose you. Miss Gilbey—' he spoke into the desk mike. 'Show Mr Harris out and tell Parsons to come in, will you?'

'Ben, for God's sake what's going on?'

'Just do as I say, will you? Don't make any phone calls from the flat. Meet me at eight o'clock in the bar at Mario's.'

He didn't wait for her to argue. He hung up. When his line buzzed back immediately, he switched it through to his secretary.

He must make Julia listen. Western's sneer rang in his head. 'Leave your friend Miss Hamilton to carry on alone? I don't think you'll do that.' He was right, he'd called Ben's bluff. He was a ruthless unscrupulous bastard, only one remove from the man he was trying to destroy.

Western wouldn't sanction murder, but he'd sit back and let someone else take the risk. He wasn't going to risk Julia. Ben went home and checked his telephones, listening for the slightest sound that might indicate they had been tampered with. He heard nothing, but that wasn't any guarantee. The systems were so sophisticated now they were virtually impossible to detect without taking the instruments apart.

How had King latched on to Jean Adams? The question sent

him pacing up and down. How did he find out at this early stage that he was under investigation at all? Had Julia talked to anyone? He knew he hadn't. It must have come from someone she knew, some chance remark, some off-the-record hint.

He showered and changed into a dark suit. He'd chosen Mario's because the Fleet Street crowd didn't congregate there as they did in the pub, or some of the trattoria he and Julia patronized. No eavesdropping. Mario's was safe behind the price barrier.

He arrived early and took his seat on a twin sofa up against one panelled wall. A large Edwin Douglas oil of two spaniels gazed down benevolently from above. He couldn't relax; he fidgeted, swallowed his drink, looked at his watch. Julia was late. It was unlike her. She was a punctuality freak; it amused him, because he was quite casual about being on time. When she came through the door, he started up quickly. She looked different; he'd never seen her dressed up before. They led easy-going lives outside the office. He saw the glitter of the sequinned top and the bright paste earrings as she walked towards him.

'You're late,' he said. 'I was worried.'

Julia sat down beside him. She said quietly, 'I'm sorry – I had a late call from Western, after you phoned me. He told me what had happened.'

Ben hadn't expected to be pre-empted.

'I should have guessed he'd try to talk you round. I'll get you a drink. Usual?' He summoned the barman.

'Vodka on the rocks, please, Rudi. Another Scotch for me.' Then he took her hand and looked at her.

'They'd bugged the telephones in her house,' he said quietly. 'They must have heard her talking to the solicitor. She was murdered to stop her signing that affidavit.'

'That's what Western told me,' Julia answered. 'He also said you'd gone into his office and freaked out about me. You shouldn't have done that, Ben. Not without talking to me first.'

'I tried to call you,' he protested. 'You were in a meeting. Julia, listen to me.' He so seldom used her full name that she hesitated. He was so serious that she bit back her reproach.

She had left William Western's office feeling very angry. She didn't belong to Ben Harris. He had no right to interfere in her career.

'I did freak, and I was wrong. I should have waited and talked to you first. But thinking about what happened to Jean Adams got to me – someone breaking in, assaulting her to make it look good, and then beating her round the head . . . It could have been you. It could *be* you, unless you keep to our deal, and drop this whole dirty mess. Please—' He stopped her interruption. 'Hear me out. You're a fine journalist; you've got talent and insight and integrity. You'll go to the top of the profession without "Exposure". That's just the carrot Western offered you to get you to do his dirty work for him. I told him I'm going to resign. I want you to resign with me. I'll pass what we know about King on to certain sources; I've got good friends who might follow it up.'

'Without proof?' Julia asked him. 'No, Ben, that doesn't add up, and you know it. As for the carrot, it wasn't "Exposure". It was your job he promised me. In due time. I know how you feel and I know what I promised, but I can't do it. I just can't give up and back away from this.' She picked up her glass. She said simply, 'You can't either. If you do, it's because you're trying to force my hand, and I won't let you. I'm going on till I find something that will bring that man into the dock.'

Ben didn't say anything. Couples came in and took their places, the bar was filling up. One or two men glanced at Julia.

At last he said, 'You realize Western's manipulating you?'

'Yes, I know he is. But so are you.'

'It's not quite the same,' he said it bitterly and his face set.

Julia spoke quickly. 'I know that, too. But, Ben, I'm not a child that has to be protected. I can see what's going on. I can make my own decisions, and I've made this one. I'm not giving up. After what happened to Jean Adams, I *can't*! I brought her into this. I'm responsible. So are you. You went down there and talked her into changing her mind. If it wasn't for us she'd be alive today. That's all there is to say about it.'

Ben said, 'I asked about the affidavit. She didn't sign it. The old man blew his top at me. He said, people like you are the scum of the earth.'

'People like us,' Julia answered, 'are the ones who will put a stop to the Harold Kings of this world. One day, I'd like to be able to point that out to him.'

Her fingers entwined in his, and gripped them.

'I love you, Ben, but I've got to live with myself, and I couldn't if I ran away from this. I won't try to influence you. If you want to chuck it in because of Western, then I don't blame you. But don't do it to pressure me. I'm committed, and I can't change that. Please, don't let's fight about it. Let's be together.'

'If I didn't love you,' Ben said, 'I'd still feel the same. Let's put the decision on the back burner just for tonight. Let's try and work out what went wrong. How did he *know* we were on his tail? Who could have known about it, and let the word slip?'

Julia picked at the sequins on the edge of her tunic. 'I never said a word to anyone – our researchers only had two names, Phyllis Lowe and Hans Koenig. There was nothing to connect with Harold King. Oh, damn, look what I've done—'

She'd pulled a thread and a few bright beads scattered on the seat.

'That's pretty, that outfit,' Ben said. 'Can't you knot it?'

'Yes, it's all right. I wore it the first time I came here – to see him for real.'

'Did you,' Ben said it slowly. 'You brought Sutton along, didn't you?' She looked at him sharply. 'Yes; yes, of course I did. Oh God.'

'You said something to him,' he suggested.

'He said it to me,' she countered. 'You're after King, or something like that. I'd blown a fuse over the way he shouted at the *maître d*.'

'And what did you say?' Ben asked her. She bit her lip, remembering the conversation. Felix had been aggressive, goading her.

'Oh God,' she repeated. 'I said I was looking at the Honours List, and he might be on it. But that's all, Ben, that's all – he didn't even pick it up. We were having a row and I left without him. You came round with the file that night. It couldn't be Felix . . . could it?'

'Only one way to find out. We'll have to ask him. Or I will, if you like. We've got to know. We've got to plug the leak, if it was him.'

'We?' Julia asked the question quietly.

'Oh for Christ's sake, yes – *we*.' He banged his glass down on the table. 'How the hell else can I look after you?'

The barman saw the pretty redhead lean over and kiss Mr Harris on the lips. He thought it was quite funny. He'd never seen Harris with a woman before, and he'd have bet a week's wages no-one would kiss him in public. He couldn't wait to tell them downstairs.

'Pussy's happy,' Julia murmured. The cat was curled up between them on the bed. She reached down and stroked the smooth fur. It purred like a small engine revving up. 'So am I,' Ben said.

He'd driven her back to her flat after dinner. He wouldn't let her stay longer than to pack some clothes. Tomorrow he would get an electronic engineer to come and check the phones. She had remembered the messenger who had failed to deliver the flowers, dismissing it as probably irrelevant, but Harris decided that once inside the building, they'd picked the lock and fixed the phones. A long time ago, he thought, monitoring them every step of the way. It made him cold to think of Julia staying there alone. It was a strange love making between them that night. There'd been a moment when their relationship had almost broken up and they both knew it. Julia's pride and independence had been threatened; for Harris, backing down in front of William Western might have been too bitter a pill to swallow.

And then, miraculously, they sailed past the rocks. Ben had compromised and so had she. She agreed to move in to live with him and not to stay alone, or put herself at risk. They were a team again, and all the stronger for the crisis. Their love was deeper, and more significant when they went to bed; more of a fusion than a frenzied climax. They recognized it without putting it into words, and slept in each other's arms till the early morning.

With Julia at his side, Ben Harris went up to see William Western. When they came in together his eyes narrowed for a moment. A double resignation? He'd lost his gamble with their lives? He thought not.

So he said it, before either one could speak. Always keep control, never let the initiative slip away.

'A double resignation? Of course not. Say what you've come for. I've got a busy morning, but always time for my star girl and a fiery Welshman. God help us poor English, dealing with the Celtic temperament!' He had swept their prepared speech aside in his usual way, answering his own questions.

Ben said, 'We're not resigning, Lord Western. Julia wants to stick with it, and I'm not going to let her go it alone. As you predicted.' He glared at him.

Western smiled back indulgently. 'That's all then? Good, good. I'll run a red herring with "Exposure" – think who we can give a few sleepless nights to, will you, Julia? Some politician with a skeleton rattling about – it might be quite amusing.' Then his voice sharpened and there was no smile left. 'And you clear up this security mess. Then get on with the job. I want results and I want them quickly. See yourselves out, and tell Miss Gilbey I want her.' He picked up his internal telephone and dismissed them.

Outside Julia turned to Ben. The secretary had given them a superior smile and hurried into Western's office.

'I hate him as much as you do,' she said. 'We're not doing it for him. Thank you for being so brave.'

'Brave? What the hell's brave about backing down?'

'Everything,' she murmured. 'For someone like you.'

'Hello,' Felix said. 'Warburton said you wanted to see me.'

Ben looked at him; it wasn't a friendly look. 'Sit down,' he suggested. Felix lounged in one of the chairs, crossed his legs and gazed at him enquiringly. He wasn't friendly either. This was his replacement; mentally he sneered at the age difference, the heavy spectacles and the hint of grey in the hair. 'Julia's got a problem,' Ben announced. 'That's what I want to talk to you about.'

'Oh? Why didn't she tell me herself?'

'She's busy,' Ben snapped. 'So I'm asking for her.' He said, 'She's told you about her job with "Exposure"?'

'She mentioned something, yeah. She was very excited about it. Why?'

'What exactly did she tell you?'

Felix uncrossed one long leg and sat up straight. It was defensive body language, as Ben recognized. 'What I said; it was a big career jump, big money, bags of opportunity. You haven't told me why you're asking.'

'Because there's a problem, as I said. It could be a serious problem for her. If you'll think back and answer the questions, I'll be able to put you in the picture. Did she ever mention Harold King?'

Felix frowned. 'Sort of, yes. It was pretty obvious she had him in her sights. She hated his guts.'

'Like a lot of people,' Ben said slowly. 'Now this is important. Did you ever talk about it? Ever mention to anyone that Julia was targeting King?'

'No,' Felix protested. 'Why should I? We broke up on account of that bastard. We'd gone to Mario's, and he was shouting his head off – Julia got all steamed up and next day gave me the shove.'

'Just think,' Ben insisted. 'Did anyone ask you what she was doing?'

Felix said, 'Come on, what's the score? I know King's a rough player – he's not suing Julia, is he?'

'No,' Ben answered. He decided to tell part of the truth. Felix wasn't going to make an effort otherwise.

'But her phone's been tapped and bugs were found in the rooms.'

'Jesus—' Felix stared at him. 'Why? Who did it?'

'We think it's King. She *is* investigating him, and that really is confidential. You said he was a rough player . . . that's an understatement. There's been a leak and we've got to trace it to protect her. She thinks it's you, because you're the only one she talked to; nobody's blaming you, Sutton, but it would help if you could remember if you passed anything on and who to.'

Felix scowled in concentration. 'Wait on,' he said. 'I did get a call from some tout with a story to tell . . . It wasn't any good to me, and it cost me fifty quid . . . ' He hesitated, and then said quickly, 'That's right, it was a real sleaze-bag, peddling dirt. He had a juicy titbit about – ' Harris stared as he mentioned the name, 'Porno stuff with kids. A paedophile ring. I told him I couldn't use that sort of thing, and he suggested "Exposure" . . . I remember I said that she wouldn't touch it.' *She*. Ben didn't interrupt him.

'He started arguing; he was that type, cocky little know-all. He got up my nose and I think I said she was after bigger fish.' He stopped.

'Go on,' Ben said. 'He was needling you for information. So what else?'

'I *think* I mentioned King. I think I did. Yeah, the Honours List. That's what Julia said at Mario's. She might do a feature on the Honours List and scumbags like King getting on it . . . '

Ben leaned back. 'I'd say he was a plant,' he said. 'You weren't to know. Anyone else apart from him?'

Felix shrugged. 'No. He never tried again.'

Ben asked, 'He didn't leave a contact number? You couldn't find him again?'

'I could try the pub; it was the Jug and Bottle off Dean Street. He gave me a name . . . Patrick. Joe Patrick.'

The hostility had faded between them.

Felix said, 'You're with Julia now, I hear say.'

'We work together, and we're together,' Ben admitted. 'Look, will you help sort this out for her?'

'Sure. What do I have to do?'

'Go back to that pub, see if you can contact this Joe Patrick.'

'And if I do, what then? Say it wasn't true, put him off the scent? I tell you, he was very sharp. He wouldn't swallow it.'

Ben said slowly, 'He might, if you play it the right way. And I think I know how. We've got to convince King that he's safe. It won't be that difficult because our one star witness was murdered the other day. I don't have to spell it out for you, do I?'

'No,' Felix got up; he moved very lightly for a big man. 'Julia's really in trouble – phew! I opened my big mouth . . . '

'Meet me in the pub at seven,' Ben told him. 'I'll have the line worked out for you. Don't blame yourself, Sutton, just put it right. Get her off the hook.'

'Don't worry, will do,' he said. 'See you at seven.' He held out his hand. Ben took it. 'She's a great girl,' Felix repeated. 'You're lucky.'

Joe Patrick was in a sunny mood. King had sent him a present. It was a confirmation of a transfer of fifty thousand pounds to his account in Switzerland. Joe was a rich man. He was secure for life, and so long as King used him for jobs like Jean Adams, his fortune would continue to grow.

He'd brought back the old woman's few trinkets and the stolen cash. The money was safe, the jewellery, such as it was, couldn't be disposed of to a fence. There were a couple of rings, a string of pearls, and a chain bracelet set with tiny coloured stones. Nothing worth a toss in terms of real jewellery. He prised the small diamonds and a sapphire out of the rings, tested the pearls between his teeth – they were smooth, not gritty, so they were only costume, and inspected the bracelet. It was hallmarked, but the stones were little more than chips.

He gave the bracelet to his favourite Tina. 'Somethin' for you next time,' he said to her friend Tracey. Tina grimaced when he had gone.

'Mean sod,' she murmured. 'Looks like Woolworth's. Wonder where he got it—' Her companion shrugged. She was fond of her friend Tina; they'd grown up together in the black ghetto of Brixton. 'Out of a cracker – last year's,' she giggled. They had a laugh together, and in spite of the rough times, they lived well. They expected to take a beating now and then; both had gone on the game in their early teens, victims of a pimp who ran a string of girls. Joe had picked them out of a cheap nightclub doubling as a brothel. He'd bought them from the pimp. They belonged to him till he got fed up and sold them on to someone else. It was a life of luxury compared to what they'd known. Tracey didn't hate him the way Tina did. 'Try it on,' she said. 'It's pretty. I like it.'

Tina slipped it onto her wrist, fiddling with the clasp. 'I'd give it to you only he'd knock my teeth out,' she said. 'Fuck, I can't get it off—' She wrenched at the delicate chain.

'I'll do it, I'll do it,' her friend said. 'You'll break it—' She peered at the clasp. 'It's got a catch on it,' she said. 'Stop it falling off. It could be gold – that's done it.'

Tina held it up, the little stones glittered. 'Could be.'

'Junk doesn't have a catch like that,' Tracey insisted. 'Might be worth a few quid one day.'

'Might be,' Tina agreed. 'Wonder where he got it . . . '

Felix went up to the bar and ordered a pint of lager. The pictures of the boxers posing with their fists up were faded and dirty, the signatures illegible. There wasn't a recent champion among them, and Felix knew them all from his days as an amateur. 'I'm looking for Joe Patrick,' he said to the barman.

'He's not here,' the answer was prompt and the look that went with it was wary.

'Know where I can get in touch with him?' Felix persisted.

'I can tell him if he comes in,' the offer was grudging.

'I met him here,' Felix went on. 'We did some business together. Can you tell him to call me – Felix Sutton, *Sunday Herald*?'

The man put down the glass he was rinsing out. Joe Patrick was a big man. He mightn't thank him if he lost out on a deal. 'You hang on a minute. I'll see what the boss says.'

The boss, the same pudgy figure posing with the fighters like a fat midget, was in his back room watching TV. He picked up the phone and called Patrick's number.

Felix stayed by the bar, leaning on one elbow and drinking the cold beer while he waited. It seemed to take a long time.

The barman was back, serving customers; an obvious tart was eyeing Felix and getting ready to pick him up, when the proprietor appeared, the barman pointed out Felix and he came up to him.

'Joe's coming round,' he said. 'Take a seat and order what you want. On the house.'

'Thanks,' Felix said. 'I'll have another pint.' He went to a table and sat down. The surface was wet and smelt of slopped beer.

The tart came up behind him. She was young and very pretty with a skirt that just skimmed her upper thighs. The man looked round and jerked a thumb at her. He didn't say anything. She pulled a face and retreated.

Felix grinned at her. She grinned back. He wouldn't have minded, he thought, but he wasn't going to pay for it.

'Hi there,' Patrick pulled out a chair. He was swathed in a cashmere coat, and he smelt of strong cologne. Felix felt as if a rat had sat down beside him. 'You wanted to see me?' The bright teeth flashed at him, tribute to modern dentistry.

'Yeah,' Felix said. 'What are you drinking?'

'Scotch,' Joe said. 'What can I do for you?'

'You remember that story you offered me?' He lowered his voice.

Joe said softly, 'The porno stuff – kids?'

'That's right. I may have a market for it.'

'You said you couldn't use it,' Joe pointed out.

'I can't. It's not my stuff. But I talked to my girlfriend – my ex, she is now,' he shrugged, 'and "Exposure" would be interested. She asked me to contact you. They'd pay good money.'

Joe tossed down half the whisky.

'You said they'd be running something else. I don't want to fuck about with this – it's a hot story.'

'Which nobody else will buy,' Felix pointed out.

Joe squinted at the Scotch, then put the glass down. 'What happens if they don't use it? I'd want money up front. There's my pal on the tabloid and his pal in the Vice – they'd want money up front from me.'

'They'd get it. I told you, there's good money.'

'What made your bird change her mind then?' Joe countered. 'You said she wouldn't touch it with a barge pole. Your very words.'

'She's under pressure from her boss. Western owns the paper. He's my boss, too. Difficult bugger. She had a big feature lined up for the first issue in November, House of Lords and Harold King. Dynamite stuff. But it's dead. They can't run it, and Western's kicking her backside. They had some witness who died on them. So I mentioned your proposition to her and she jumped at it. Western wants a big scandal to kick off with now they've killed the King story. I'd say you can name your price.' He looked hard at Joe Patrick.

'So what's in it for you?' Joe asked in his soft voice, losing the phoney American twang.

'I might get her back,' Felix said. 'And I'd want a cut; nothing big, just luck money, as they call it in Ireland.'

Joe grinned. 'So they do,' he agreed. 'Are you the go-between then?'

'No,' Felix said. 'She does her own negotiating; she'd send someone else to talk figures. You mentioned five hundred.'

'That was to you,' Joe smiled at him. 'For a big feature it'd be in the thousands. You said I could name me price. I tell you what—'

He drained the last of the whisky. He pushed the glass away and Felix knew the meeting was over.

'Tell you what,' Joe was on his feet. 'I'll talk to my pals. Then I'll get back to you. I know they had someone else in mind.'

He held out his hand; Felix made himself shake it, and gave a powerful squeeze that caused Joe Patrick to wince. He enjoyed that.

'You'll be in touch, then, but make it quick. She's pushed for a story . . . '

'You'll hear real soon,' Joe Patrick promised.

Felix left the pub. It was cold outside with a thin drizzle falling. The girl he'd seen in the pub was walking down the pavement, slowly, looking for kerb crawlers.

She came up to him and smiled. 'Hello, handsome. Want some fun?'

'Not tonight,' Felix said. 'Thanks anyway. Buy yourself a cup of coffee. It's bloody cold.' He gave her five pounds, and then swung off towards Tottenham Court Road. He wouldn't hear from Joe Patrick again. There was no story to sell. There never had been. Ben Harris was right.

* * *

Harold King flew to New York by Concorde. He had decided to take Gloria with him. Her gratitude and excitement touched him. She reached for his hand as the plane took off, its ascent was very steep, and he squeezed it affectionately. She was scared of landing, too. The cloud had lifted, and he was in buoyant mood. 'Exposure' had dropped the investigation, because, as Joe repeated, they had a witness who'd died on them . . .

Joe had been grinning like an ape when he reported his meeting with Felix Sutton. He'd cut the main head off the Hydra by getting rid of Jean Adams. Without her, they had nothing but hearsay. He could dispose of Hamilton and her friend Harris when he took over the *Herald*. Neither would ever work in newspapers again by the time he had finished with them.

He was confident, pleased with Joe, but, as always, he left nothing as a hostage to fortune.

'What do you do about Sutton now?' he demanded. Joe had seemed surprised at the question. 'Call him, tell him no sale.'

'You bloody fool,' it pleased King to bully him. Too much praise might go to his head. 'You drop it like that, he'll see it's a put-up. You're stupid, but maybe he's not. You give him another story. A real one.'

'What story?' Joe protested. 'I don't have anything.'

On a mischievous impulse, King solved the problem for him.

'We've set up Leo Derwent. Get the dirt from Freda and give it to Sutton. Derwent likes publicity.' He had laughed and Joe sniggered loyally with him. They had tapes and hidden camera records of Mr Leo Derwent's sexual preferences, supplied by the call girl introduced to him for that purpose. Harold King set off for America with his daughter, light in heart and full of manic energy. He had decided to short-circuit his financial difficulties by taking the massive Pension Funds and using them as his personal security. He wouldn't waste time, he'd conclude negotiations with Field Bank and introduce Gloria into the deal. They might as well accept that she would be side by side with him from now on. It gave him a satisfying sense of continuity to show off his heir.

He had told her about using the funds; it was a test of her business ethics and she hadn't failed him. 'Why not? You need the money – who's going to know?' She was his girl and he was proud of her.

During the four-hour flight to New York they worked on the figures together. He enjoyed teaching her, initiating her into the way he manipulated money. She would never have his originality or lateral brainpower in creative accounting, but all she need do was keep to his guide-lines. The businesses would run themselves.

When he reached the Waldorf he sent several faxes, including one to Joe Patrick at his Export Import number.

'Retain Harper and Drew until further notice.' Surveillance on Julia Hamilton and Ben Harris was to continue.

No hostages to fortune. Once he laid hands on those Pension Funds he had put his whole business empire on the line.

It was Ben's idea that they rent their flats. They couldn't remove the telephone bugs without blowing Sutton's cover story. And neither place was as secure as Ben wanted. Julia didn't argue with him; she was chilled at the idea that her flat had been penetrated and her movements watched. The thought of Jean Adams haunted her with guilt. And the guilt overcame her fear for her own safety. Ben was right. They needed a place in a high-security block of flats, where nobody would be let in without authorization. The cost would be borne by Western. Ben insisted on that and Western didn't quibble. They found what they wanted in Chelsea Green, a charming backwater off the King's Road, where a purpose-built luxury block had a fourth-floor flat for sale. A substantial price, paid confidentially, secured its withdrawal from the market. They moved in together with the ginger cat. Ben had wrung a further concession from Western. Money was available for Julia to redecorate and refurnish it to her own taste. It had amused him to watch Harris turning the screw on him and let him get away with it.

He would turn a very tight screw of his own when they were safe in the plush little fortress he had provided.

Felix Sutton had come up with a story about the Junior Minister, Leo Derwent, courtesy of the man they suspected of being in the pay of Harold King. Sutton passed it on as genuine, and, as a result, tended to view Harris's conspiracy theory with some doubt. Ben didn't waver.

Joe Patrick had been a plant, and he was simply lending himself credibility and keeping contact with someone in touch with Julia.

'Are you going to run this muck on Derwent?' he asked her.

'I don't want to, but we've got to fill the November slot with something. I'll talk to Western about it.'

Ben had seen the photographs and listened to some of the tapes. Felix had thought they were extremely funny and guffawed at the absurdity of the dialogue between the principals in the fantasy games.

Harris decided his sense of humour was the result of a twenty-year age gap. He saw nothing amusing in human degradation.

Western would have no scruples; if it was a strong story, he would authorize it. Julia made an appointment to see him. She took the evidence supplied to Sutton with her.

He was in brisk, cheerful spirits when she came into his office. 'How is your nice new flat?' he greeted her immediately. 'Everything fixed up by now? Good; you want to talk about the November feature – we'll get that over with first. Sit down, Julia. What have you got in that briefcase?' The words came out in a torrent; it was a subtle form of bullying because it deprived the subject of a chance to speak. How well she knew the technique – it always infuriated her.

'I did send you a note of thanks,' she said. 'We're secure and that's the main thing. I've got the material for November in here. It's not very pretty, I'm afraid, but you had better see it and decide whether we should go ahead.' She opened the case and gave him a sealed envelope. He opened it, skimmed through the pictures, his face completely impassive as if he were looking at someone else's holiday snaps.

'Nasty,' he said looking up at her. 'I don't need to listen to those—' He put the tapes back in the envelope and replaced the sheaf of photographs with them. 'Derwent was your first assignment, remember? He was a nasty little specimen even then. Before we use it, we'll have to clear it with the lawyers first. I doubt he'll decide to sue.' He smiled.

'I had another angle,' Julia suggested. 'There is a point, Lord Western, that could be argued on moral grounds. Whatever Leo Derwent does in private has no relevance to the performance of his public duties.'

'Unless it lays him open to blackmail,' he countered. 'Which these activities certainly do.'

'Exactly,' Julia said. 'So who took them and why? Who was going to use them to blackmail Derwent? Why don't we chase up that angle and get Derwent to co-operate in exchange for keeping his name out of it? Ben thinks this is a typical entrapment of a politician someone wants to put in their pocket. I believe he's right. Now they're throwing Leo Derwent to the lions. Maybe he wouldn't give in to blackmail?'

'Very clever.' Western beamed at her. 'We fill the slot and we have the little brute in *our* pocket. Good, strong stuff. Blackmail attempt on prominent political figure, etc., etc. It'll have every hare running in Westminster worrying in case they've been found out. But you're not going to do it, Julia. You've got a damned good staff, give it to John Stevens. *You and Harris* have one target and you're not wasting your time on anything else. Harold King. A war criminal. That's what I want to hear about from you – not dirt like this.' He swept the envelope aside. 'What's your next line?'

She had to face him.

'I don't know,' she said. 'We have an allegation without dates or locations beyond the Western Desert. No charges were ever brought, there's no record in the official histories of the campaign of any prisoner being murdered. It was a clean war out there.'

'There's no such thing,' Western snapped at her. 'Minor atrocities happened everywhere on both sides. I know, I fought in it.'

Julia looked up at him. 'You did? In the Western Desert?'

'Briefly, yes, till I was captured. I'd been wounded and I was repatriated.' He dismissed the subject. 'I'm not going to do your job for you. And I have to remind you that one more slip like the last, when a leak cost that poor Adams woman her life, and there won't *be* a job. For either of you. You've got a month, Julia. I want Harold King in the December issue of "Exposure". Good morning.'

Julia stood up. She said, 'I can't guarantee it by December, Lord Western. But I'll prove him guilty. For Jean Adams, not for any other reason.' Then she left the office.

Western sat quietly; he was a very still man when he was thinking. He knew Harold King was in America. And he knew why. He was gathering his forces for a frontal attack on Western International. Western had contacts in the banking world in Canada and the US. He had friends and he rewarded them for safeguarding his interests. The buzz about Harold King was growing. And he knew that if the scale being mentioned was right, he would lose the battle. December. It wasn't a date plucked out of the air. It would take King time to set up such a huge financial operation, and there was talk of him marshalling private funds. He was throwing everything into the bid. And the opening moves would start early in the New Year. He pressed the red button on his desk. It signalled to his secretary that he was not to be disturbed.

He rested his head in his hands and let his mind roam backwards. Back to heat and sandstorms and the danger of death in the desert.

A clean war, that young woman had insisted, with the assurance of the unborn at the time. Nothing in the official history.

Nothing in the laudatory biographies of the two great commanders, Montgomery and Rommel. A gentleman's war, some idiot had described it.

There had been books written by men who had fought in the Western Desert and distinguished themselves in battle, and viewed it through a romantic haze. Brave men, knights of the desert. He hadn't been one of them.

He had the scars on his body to prove it. They were on his back.

* * *

'I'm going to see Leo Derwent myself,' Julia announced.

'Good idea,' Ben agreed.

'I want to find out if we're right and King is mixed up in this. Then Stevens can take over. You know, I almost walked out this morning when he said that about Jean Adams!'

'He was needling you,' Ben said. 'He doesn't give a bugger about her or anyone but himself. Don't let it get to you. That's what he wants. He was sticking the spur in to get you fired up. Bastard,' he added, pouring wine for them both. She had been right to leave King out of it. She was learning how to deal with William Western.

'Do we have a copy of *Who's Who*?' she asked suddenly. Ben's books had come with his sparse furniture. There were a lot of them.

'I've got it, and Debrett's and all the other references. Over there, top shelf,' he told her.

She got up. 'I want to look up Western.'

She was edgy that evening; the interview had upset her. That barb about the unfortunate Jean Adams had drawn blood. He knew how much she agonized over it.

'Here it is,' she said. 'Look, served with the East Anglian Regiment in North African campaign, 1942, wounded, taken prisoner and repatriated 1943.'

'So?' he asked her. 'What's your drift?'

'The way he talked this morning. "Minor atrocities happened everywhere on both sides . . . " I wonder, Ben.' She was frowning; she snapped the heavy book shut and put it back. 'You said you were sure King had some lever on him, and that's why he pulled you out of the first investigation.'

'There was no other reason,' Ben said. 'He was out for King's blood, just as he is now, and then he backed off. No warning, no explanation, he called me in, told me to drop it and forget the whole thing, and gave me the News Editor's job.'

'Could it have been something he did in the war? Give me the timetable again. When did he kill the project?'

Ben shrugged. 'About ten years ago. Year before he got his peerage. I was sure it was tied in with that. Whatever King threatened him with, he backed down. But why the war? It's a hell of a long time ago—'

'I know, but a lot of things happened then; like King shooting unarmed prisoners. It was the way Western talked . . . he wasn't shocked by the idea, he just wanted to prove it so he could finish off King.'

'J, darling,' Ben reminded her, 'you're not investigating Western. He's a cold-blooded bastard, nothing would shock his conscience, he doesn't have one. You're letting this morning get under your skin. Forget it for a few days, make an appointment to see Leo Derwent, and I'll see if I can come up with anything. I'll ask my pals in the War Office. They helped out before. Your feathers are all ruffled – come here.'

After a while she looked at him.

'What would I do without you? I don't deserve you, Ben. I come home and rant on all evening, and I haven't even started to make dinner.'

'Dinner,' he said firmly, 'can wait.'

7

Leo Derwent was on edge. He'd taken the personal call from Julia Hamilton and when he put the telephone down he was uneasy.

She was doing 'Exposure' and there were rumours flying about the subject of the opening feature in November. The boast made to Gloria King during that dinner party was suddenly an awful threat.

She wanted a private interview, stressing the word private.

He had proposed a meeting in his office in the House. When she came in he appeared to be relaxed and well briefed about her career since they last met.

Very much the junior minister entertaining a member of the quality press, but sweat was beading under his armpits and on the palms of his hands while he went through the small talk. His secretary brought a tray of coffee. 'Well,' he said at last, 'I know you're a busy lady, and my time is limited. What can I do for you, Miss Hamilton?'

Julia opened her shoulder bag and took out an envelope.

'These have come into our possession,' she said quietly. 'I thought you ought to see them.' She watched him as he opened the envelope and saw the first of the photographs. Blood rushed into his face and then drained till he was a ghastly white. He opened his mouth as if to speak. He put the photographs face down on his desk and looked at Julia.

'Where did you get these? What is this?'

He sounded as if he were choking.

'They were sold to my newspaper,' she said. 'With some tape-recording sessions between you and the woman in the pictures.'

'What do you want?' he was staring at her. 'You're not going to print these . . . I'll sue, I'll fight you to the highest court . . . ' The words were brave, but the man was stricken.

Julia said, 'Nobody's going to print such things in any newspaper. I haven't come here to expose you or threaten you, Mr Derwent. I've come because I don't like blackmail, and I believe that's what has happened to you. I want to run a feature, but you won't be mentioned. I want to scare off the kind of people who took these photographs and set you up. I'm being absolutely honest. You've got nothing to fear from us. I want your help.'

He shook his head. 'I'm ruined,' he said, 'completely ruined. If you don't run this story, they'll go to someone else—'

'We bought the negatives,' she countered. 'It was targeted at my feature, and I want to know why. Tell me honestly, was anyone trying to blackmail you? Why did you call their bluff?'

'With these? My God. I'd have given my last penny to buy them back. No. Nobody approached me. Oh my God,' he said again. 'I need a drink. Excuse me.'

He got up and opened a cupboard. Bottles and glasses were assembled for entertaining. He poured a large neat vodka and came back to the desk.

'What a mess,' he said. 'What a bloody awful mess.'

Julia asked him, 'Have you any idea who set you up? Do you have any enemies?'

He swallowed the vodka. 'I've made enemies – who doesn't in politics?'

'Did anyone know about this affair? Does this woman have other clients? Where did you find her?'

Leo Derwent scowled. 'I didn't pick her up, if that's what you mean. I met her at a dinner party.' His frown deepened. 'She wasn't a tart, she was just another guest. We hit it off, and we liked the same sort of games. I never paid her – just a present or some flowers . . . '

'She wasn't a guest,' Julia said. 'She was a plant. Who gave the party?'

He didn't answer for a moment. Then he said, 'Harold King. I was down at his house for the weekend. She came with another man.'

'And gave you a very heavy signal?' Julia suggested. He nodded.

'She came on very strong. Christ. I never thought for a minute . . . '

'Why should you?' Julia interrupted. 'You met her at a friend's house. Would you describe King as a friend?'

'I know him. I've been down there once or twice. I thought he was aiming me at that daughter . . . She was always sat next to me, chatting me up. I thought it was rather funny. Christ,' he muttered again. 'You think it was King?'

'Who else?' Julia asked. 'He wanted to get something on you and he fixed you up. Your girlfriend was in on it. She must have set the camera and the tape and handed the stuff over.'

'Then why didn't he use it?' Derwent demanded. 'Why pass it on to you? He wouldn't give Western the drop off his nose.'

'Something more important was at stake. So he sacrificed you.'

'What do you want me to do?'

He had recovered his nerve. He looked mean and seething with rage. King had made a bad enemy, Julia decided. A cornered fox that would fly at his throat when he got the chance.

'I want you to do nothing,' she said quietly. 'Behave as if this hadn't happened. See King, be friendly, ask the daughter out to lunch if you can stomach it.'

He watched her keenly. 'Why?'

'Because we're working on something that will bring Harold King up on a criminal charge. A very serious charge.'

Leo Derwent smiled. 'I love it,' he said. 'What else do I have to do?'

'Tell me anything you hear, anything you pick up. That's why I suggested the daughter. Did she fancy you?'

He shook his head. 'I've heard she fancies girls. Wouldn't surprise me. But I'll try. By Christ, I'll give it my best shot if it'll put that bastard in the shit.'

Then he said quickly. 'What about this feature on blackmail . . . are you going to hint at him? What about security for me?'

Julia stood up. 'I'll make it a general feature. I can cite several examples in a vague enough way to throw anyone off. My boss wants a lot of hares running, not just one. And here's proof of his good faith.'

She handed him the manila envelope.

'Everything's in it,' she said. 'Negatives and tapes. I don't expect you'll be seeing her again.'

'If I did,' he said savagely, 'I'd make it for real.'

'He's the worst kind of creep,' Julia said to Ben that evening. 'I wouldn't trust him an inch if I could help it. But he'll do anything to get back at King after this. And we might pick something up. He promised he'll chat up the daughter . . . He said she was a dyke, but that won't stop him. My God, we do elect some gems of humanity, don't we?'

'You get good and bad in everything. Our own profession isn't exactly lily white. And here's something to take the taste of Leo Derwent out of your mouth. I read it in an hour.'

It was a small, privately printed booklet. *Memories of the Desert War*. The author had served as an officer in the East Anglian Regiment. He had won a DSO for bravery at the battle of Sidi Abbas and had been captured trying to escape back to the British position at Tobruk.

There was a photograph on the cover of a good-looking young man in shorts and shirt, his cap at a rakish angle, posing with three other men.

'Darling,' Julia said gently. 'I've had a long day. I don't think I'm in the mood for war stories.'

Ben said quietly, 'I think you'll be in the mood for this one. There are some good photographs inside. Trust me . . . '

She looked at him and said, 'Ben? You're on to something . . . why didn't you tell me? You've let me rabbit on about bloody Leo Derwent—'

'You needed to get it out of your system, that's why,' he said. 'I'll make supper tonight. You get stuck into that.'

He was putting steak under the grill, when he heard an exclamation.

He came and looked round the door. 'Ben,' she said. 'It's him! In the photograph – look!'

He said, 'I told you it was interesting. Wait till you get to the end.'

Joe Patrick went through the reports from the detective agency. He didn't repeat his earlier mistake; he kept King informed on a daily basis, but they'd lost the telephone taps on Harris and Hamilton, and there was no chance of getting into the new flat they shared together.

The building was very secure, with TV entry-phone system and resident porter. The surveillance reported Julia Hamilton going to the House of Commons, but that was the only break in her normal office routine. She and Harris led a quiet domestic life, rarely going out. When they did it was usually to the same restaurant and the pub close by the *Herald* offices. There was a dearth of activity that King noted and found reassuring. They were at a dead end after Jean Adams. The negotiations in New York were coming to a climax. He had appointed Gloria to the Board of the Pension Fund Management before they left England. Her signature, combined with his, and that of a terrified accountant who never even read what he was required to sign, released the hundred and twenty million investments into King's personal control. When presented to the Chairman and Board of Field Bank, they appeared as private assets.

He stopped off at Miami, and he didn't involve Gloria in these negotiations. She'd come to that part of his business interests later on.

She accepted the exclusion with her usual docility. He noticed how she bullied the staff who accompanied them from London, and demanded service from their hotels with a high-handedness equal to his own. With him she was a submissive and adoring acolyte.

She went to Mimi's Club, courtesy of King's business acquaintance who owned the place, and sunned herself by the pool while he was busy. She found one of the cocktail waitresses attractive, and secured her services by mentioning her need of a personal maid to the manager. The girl understood that if she wanted to keep her job, she had better accommodate Miss King. There'd be a good tip at the end of it. She was used to taking care of the men. It was her first experience of a woman lover. She confided to her friends that for sheer appetite this ugly bitch left the guys at the starting gate. And she was good, too. It made a nice change having a woman. She rather liked it.

King spent two days in conference with the local Mafia representative who owned Mimi's Club and three of the biggest hotels in the resort. He was a majority shareholder in the company controlling a string of escort agencies and massage parlours. He fronted for the Godfathers who controlled the business in the state. King had obliged him by laundering drug money through one of his own subsidiaries in Liechtenstein. It was more of a courtesy call than serious business, but King believed in keeping his contacts sweet against the time to call in favours. With the take-over planned for the early part of the coming year, he was mustering his allies. On the night before they left for England, King entertained him in his own restaurant, and introduced him to Gloria. She was looking very well, tanned from the sun and relaxed after an afternoon spent with the waitress. King was proud of her.

The mafioso was complimentary. When she had left them to their late cigars he said, 'A lovely girl. Not married yet?'

King had shrugged and said, 'She's hard to please. She loves her old Daddy too much to leave him.'

'Yeah, my daughter's the same. But she's got a good husband and four kids. They make my life, those kids. You find the right guy for her; I picked Maria's man, and they're very happy. A man needs grandchildren when he gets to our age.'

King accepted the flattery. He was at least fifteen years older than the American. 'There's no hurry,' he insisted. 'She'll find someone.'

But the idea stuck in his mind. Gloria was a catch. Never mind that she didn't bother much with men. King paid no attention to that. She was a big girl, and shy. He'd warned her about fortune hunters a long time ago. Maybe that had put her off.

He came back to London in a mood of swelling confidence. Everything was going his way. His instincts scented success and ultimate victory. They had never failed him. The biggest gamble of his business life was coming to the final throw, and all the signs told him that luck was on his side.

'Billy,' Evelyn Western said firmly. 'You've got to stop driving yourself. You're awake half the night, and you're so on edge you can't relax even at the weekend.'

'How can I?' he demanded. 'When nothing's happening? Nothing. There's a bloody feature coming out about the vulnerability of politicians to blackmail in their private lives and nothing about King in the pipeline. I told her, I want the slot in December. So far she's done nothing!' he repeated, banging his hand on the table top. The cut-glass goblet jumped. He wiped the drops of wine off the polished surface.

'Ever since that woman's murder they've ground to a halt on the whole thing. And now this.'

He had told Evelyn the news as they changed for dinner. He was so upset by it he cancelled a theatre engagement with friends and said he wanted a quiet evening at home with her. Evelyn didn't hesitate. She made the excuses over the telephone herself, pleading a cold and a temperature. When he was wrought up like this, she humoured him. But she lectured him, too. Yes, she agreed, forcing herself to appear calm. It was very disturbing news about King's alliance with Field Bank. But he'd known King was in the States raising money. 'But not that sort of sum,' he protested. 'Backed by a huge amount from his own private funds. He's gearing up to strike at me, and I won't be able to stop him. The next step is the rumour mongering. We're in financial trouble. I'm losing control . . . Good God, Evie, we've seen the technique used on other people. I know how the rot starts. He's got two financial journalists in his pocket; they'll print anything he tells them to – you just wait. As soon as Christmas is over and the decks are cleared for news, it'll start. I'm sorry, I can't eat any more of this.'

Evelyn said quietly, 'Come on, let's go and have our coffee in the drawing room. I'll pour you a brandy and you settle down. I've got an idea and I'd like to see what you think of it.'

William Western had benefited from his wife's ideas before. She was a very intelligent woman, with a mind untrammelled by the minutiae of his daily business problems. Sometimes she saw things more clearly than he did.

'Good idea,' he said. 'Sorry I've been such a bloody bore this evening. Making you cancel the theatre. I know you were looking forward to it.'

She smiled at him and took his arm for a moment.

'I'd much rather get a good night's sleep without you tossing and turning beside me,' she said gently. 'I don't care about the theatre. We can go later, it'll run for ever after those reviews. All I care about is you getting into a state. It's bad for you, and you know it.'

He led her to the sofa. The butler brought their coffee and Evelyn said, 'A large brandy for his Lordship, please, Arthur.'

The hapless Filipino was still in the house in Hampshire. Still being bullied by his employer, but tolerated so far because Evelyn Western knew a replacement wouldn't fare any better. The English butler had looked after them in London for twelve years. He had worked in Royal Service, and Western was in awe of him. He gave the Westerns' establishment prestige.

When they were alone, Evelyn said, 'Why don't I talk to Julia?'

'What good would that do?' he demanded. '*I've* talked to her and I didn't pull any punches.'

'I'm sure you didn't, but perhaps that's not the right approach. Have you thought of this, Billy – perhaps she doesn't want the job? That poor woman was murdered . . . Julia's not the type to come to you and admit that she's too frightened to continue.'

After a pause he said, 'But she might admit it to you.'

'Yes. She trusts me. She thinks I'm on her side. And I am, of course, so long as it's not a conflict of interests with you. Let me take her out to lunch and have a heart-to-heart with her. I may even be able to reassure her if she is afraid. A little morale booster.' She smiled at him. 'Bluster doesn't always work, you know.'

William Western looked at his wife. Serene and beautiful, a kindly mentor for a young woman who could be in mortal danger.

'You know,' he remarked, 'you're more ruthless than I am.'

'When something threatens you, I certainly am. Leave Julia to me.'

'Did she say why she wanted to meet you?' Ben asked.

'No, she just suggested lunch, and I couldn't exactly say no,' Julia answered. 'She was always very sweet to me, especially when I started on the *Herald*. Ben, I was wondering – do you think I could ask her about Western? She might confide in me.'

He shook his head. For all her flair, Julia was still naïve about some people.

'No,' he said flatly. 'My guess is she's hoping *you're* going to confide in *her*. Sweetheart, I know she's a charming lady and she took you round the dress shops and all the rest of it, but she's his wife and you don't live with a prize shit like Western for forty years without some of it rubbing off. You told me they were hand in glove, so just be careful. Don't get conned and don't tell her anything you wouldn't say to him. Promise?'

'All right,' Julia agreed. 'But you're wrong about her. She's always been a friend to me. Don't be such a cynic.'

'Just remember,' he insisted. 'She's on Western's side, not yours. Don't be too trusting.'

He hoped Julia would listen to him, but he wasn't sure.

They met at the Hyde Park Hotel.

Julia was early and, as usual, Evelyn Western was late. She came in smiling and apologetic. 'My dear – I'm so sorry. I do hope you haven't been waiting long. The traffic was frightful coming through the park. Now, let's have a drink while we look at the menu, shall we?'

She had an ageless beauty; she was as distinguished in appearance as her husband was commonplace. People were watching her admiringly as she led the way into the restaurant.

'I asked for a table by the window,' she said. 'I love this view of the park, don't you? You're looking very pretty as usual. Charming colour that deep yellow. Most imaginative with your red hair.'

Julia warmed to her, she couldn't help it.

'Thanks to you, Lady Western. One of the first dresses you advised me to buy was a buttercup yellow. I wore it till it fell to bits.'

'Good heavens,' Evelyn said. 'So I did. What a long time ago it was. How many years? And look how well you've done.'

'Thanks to Lord Western. He gave me the opportunities.'

'He's always promoted young talent. He recognized yours from the very beginning. He really thinks the world of you, you know.'

'That's very nice,' Julia said. Evelyn Western gave her a confiding look, and said, 'He's much maligned. People don't understand what a remarkable man he is, and deep down how genuine and sincere. I've often said to him his manner is so off-putting. He blusters.' She smiled indulgently. 'I suppose men feel they have to be macho.

'It would be a tragedy if he lost everything he's built up. This wonderful newspaper, all the other businesses. He's given employment to thousands. I don't have to tell you that the pension schemes are the most generous in the communications industry. William cares very much for his people. He'd never show it or say so, but, of course, he does to me.'

She leaned a little forward. 'That's why he needs your help, Julia. That horrible creature King is out to smash my husband and take everything from him. He's raised a huge sum of money, millions and millions in America, to mount an attack on us and get his hands on the *Herald*. It would kill William if he succeeded. And I wouldn't be able to bear it, either.'

'Lady Western,' Julia said slowly. 'I'm trying, I really am.'

'It's very brave of you after what happened to Jean Adams.'

Julia was unprepared for that. Evelyn Western went on, 'My husband talked to me about it. He was worried that you might feel in danger and didn't like to say so. But you *must* say if that's what's the matter. He wouldn't blame you – nobody would. I'm sure Ben Harris would take over from you.'

'Ben would love me to give up on this. He's tried to talk me out of it, he even went to your husband . . . but I'm not giving up. I want to see Harold King in jail and I'm going to put him there. He's a murderer. I cut my teeth as a journalist on those terrible child murders in Rhys. I was very green, very inexperienced. But I stuck it out because I wanted whoever did it caught and punished. That's how I feel about King. Don't worry about me, Lady Western. I'm going on and I think I may just have found a clue. Would you do me a favour?'

'Of course,' Evelyn Western said. 'If I possibly can. What is it?'

'I'd like a week's leave. Would you suggest it to your husband? Say I need to have a short break away from the office. If I ask him myself he'll think I'm bottling out, or else he'll want to know why and where and what for. And at this point I can't tell him. Could you do it?'

'I should think so. He knows we're lunching. You can't tell me, I suppose?'

Don't be too trusting, Ben had insisted. *She's on his side, not yours . . .* For a moment Julia was tempted to confide. She looked into the fine blue eyes that were gazing into hers with such intensity.

'I'd rather not,' she said.

'Forgive me for asking,' Evelyn Western said. 'It's just that I'm so anxious about what may happen. Time is the enemy, my dear. We have so little to spare. Don't fail, will you?'

'No,' Julia promised. 'I won't. I promise you.'

'You were wrong,' Julia said. 'She wasn't pumping me.'

Ben shrugged. Evelyn Western hadn't tried to prise information out of Julia.

What she had done was apply the most powerful pressure on her to continue without regard for her own safety. It was all very subtle, playing on Julia's gratitude for her help in the past. Western – a man who cared about his employees. Genuine and sincere. Ben had kept his temper while Julia repeated the conversation. She couldn't see through it. She liked and trusted Evelyn Western. 'He'll give you the leave and pretend he doesn't know it's a put-up job between you. Darling, she'll tell him everything you said. Not that it matters.'

'Nothing matters,' Julia insisted. 'Except that I get to Jersey before Christmas. And everyone thinks I'm on holiday.'

'It would be more convincing if I came with you,' he suggested.

'No. I couldn't stay with my cousins. That's all part of it. It's got to look absolutely genuine. You can't hold my hand all the time.'

She reached out and squeezed his. 'Even though I like it,' she added. 'Let me do it my way, Ben. If I come up with something we'll be on course again. And flying.'

She changed the subject.

'Any news of Lucy?' He was in regular touch with his daughter.

'She called this morning. She's feeling sick, but otherwise she's fine. God, I'll be a grandfather by next April. I'm rather looking forward to it.'

Julia laughed. 'I know you are. You talk about other people conning – you're the biggest fraud of the lot. Grouchy old Harris, hates the world. It was just a big act.'

She kissed him lightly. 'You're a soft touch.'

'If I am,' he said, 'it's thanks to you. What do you want for Christmas?'

Julia pretended to consider. 'Mink coat – no, that's old-fashioned. I don't want to get spat at in the street. Some little number with a few diamonds.' She loved teasing him. Then seriously. 'A weekend at Fordingbridge after Christmas. To make up for the one that rotten Felix promised me. That's what I'd like.'

'That's what you'll have,' he promised. 'But I don't fish.'

'I don't either. We can get lessons. Who's going to look after poor Pussy?'

'I'll ask the porter. If I give him a fiver, he'll feed her while we're away.'

They spent a quietly happy evening, watching television and talking. Before she went to sleep beside him, Julia thought suddenly, this is like marriage, this mix of passion and companionship. I've never been bored since the day I went to the pub and had our first drink together. Angered sometimes, frustrated, confused by him, but never bored. She slid her arm round him and moved closer, then fell asleep.

'He's asked me out to the theatre and dinner,' Gloria said.

Her father looked up suspiciously. 'You're not going? With that creep?'

'He's got seats for the new Branagh production of *Othello*. I'd like to see it. Besides, you told me to chat him up, Daddy.'

'That was then,' King said abruptly. He thought she looked disappointed. 'Do you want to go?'

She hesitated. 'Not if you don't want me to. I'd like to see the play, that's all.'

Immediately King softened. 'Go on then, darling, if you'll enjoy it. You won't have to go to Mummy's charity gala!'

They laughed.

'I wasn't anyway. That sort of thing bores me as much as it does you, Daddy,' Gloria said.

Leo Derwent. She was surprised by the invitation. And intrigued. She had gleaned from her father that he had peculiar sexual tastes. She wondered what they were.

She put on some very expensive jewellery that night. Leo Derwent paid her a nice compliment. 'You're looking great, Gloria. Love the dress.' He thought she looked like a big cabbage doll hung with diamonds. Grotesque. He wished he hadn't booked at such a smart restaurant for dinner afterwards. He was sure to be seen . . .

The play absorbed Gloria. That was a relief to him. She didn't talk through the performance; they had champagne in the interval, and she surprised him by making intelligent comments on the play and its interpretation. Briefly he forgot how unattractive she was. But dinner was laboured. She had no small talk after the subject of the play was exhausted. Mindful of the motive for the evening, Leo prompted her to talk about her trip to the States.

She became animated. 'It was fascinating. I'd gone on trips with my father before, but this was special. You know, he's teaching me everything.'

Leo smiled at her. 'Grooming you for stardom?'

She smiled back, a little colour in her pale cheeks. 'Yes. One day he wants me to take over.'

'Really?' Leo wasn't bored any longer. 'What a challenge – think you can do it?'

She was defensive. 'Why not? He thinks I can. He says I've got the same kind of business brain.'

He said, 'You're too attractive to be that clever.'

She didn't simper. She didn't blush. She stared at him with King's pale eyes and said, 'I'm not attractive to men.'

He wasn't fazed. He laughed at her. 'Come on, Gloria, you know that's not true. You've got a hell of a lot going for you. Why be defensive about it?'

'I've got Daddy's money going for me, I know that,' she said.

'I think you've got it wrong,' he said. He was enjoying playing this odd creature like a fish. More of a barracuda, he suspected. 'Money like yours could be a real turn off for most men. It'd scare them to death. How to cope with a girl who has everything . . . How to live up to a father-in-law like Harold King. Have you ever thought of it like that? Have you had a lot of boyfriends?' Then he played it softly. 'If you don't mind me asking . . . Just say so . . . '

She considered for a moment. Other men had dated her, but seldom more than once or twice. She'd been bored and so had they. Manifestly. This foxy-faced man with his sharp mind was a challenge. He wasn't talking to her as if she was a rich dumbo.

'I'm not attracted *by* men,' she said and stared at him. She wondered how he would field that. He allowed a little smile to appear on his lips. They were thin lips over sharp, narrow teeth that were very white.

'I'd say that was because you've never met a man who knew how to cope with you,' he said. 'You're very like your father. Strong personality, quite a challenge to a man. Do you like girls?'

'Everyone knows *you* like them,' she said. She was rewarded by a change of expression. Just a flash of antagonism. She wondered why.

'Some girls,' he said. He smiled at the bitch, probing the remark for hidden malice. She hadn't answered his question about her own sexual preferences. She had avoided that one. He decided it was time to change direction. He had found out one interesting piece of information. King was grooming her as his successor. Taking her on trips to the States. Letting her in on some of his business activities. He would like to know what those activities were, and pass on the information.

If King had set out to destroy him, he was going to hit back at King where it would hurt him most. By using his daughter, with the help of Julia Hamilton. They ordered a last course, and Gloria chose the richest pudding on the menu. He was careful with his figure. He made do with sorbet, which he didn't even like, just to keep her company. She didn't speak, absorbed in eating. Then she said, 'Don't you like food? I love it.'

'I'm as greedy as the next man, but I have to watch my weight. Fat politicians aren't a good example in our health-conscious society.'

She looked at him in faint contempt. 'Do you care about things like that? I wouldn't.'

'I care about making the right impression,' he said. 'I'm an ambitious bastard. Everyone knows *that*, too. I want to get to the top of the ladder. If it means watching my waistline, so be it.'

Gloria looked at him with interest. 'You want to be Prime Minister?'

'Doesn't every politician? Of course they do. They start the caring bit when they know they're not going to get any further. You know, I wouldn't talk to most people like this. You have a man's mind, that's why. I like girls, but I can't talk to them. They're too stupid. Have some coffee. I'm going to have a brandy. Will you join me?'

Gloria said, 'Yes. I often have a brandy with Daddy after dinner. We sit and talk when my mother's gone to bed.' She gave him a sudden smile. 'She's terribly stupid. Daddy never discusses anything with her.'

'But she's beautiful,' Leo countered. 'You can't have everything.'

'*She's* into the caring bit,' Gloria said, 'in a big way. She's on every charity committee, fund raising and running after royalty. She'll love it when Daddy gets his peerage.'

He sipped the fine brandy and said lightly, 'I didn't know about that. In the New Year's Honours List?' Bile rose in his throat at the thought of it.

'No, maybe the Birthday Honours. He'll get it, he always gets what he wants. He's set his heart on this. I think it's because people like Western got titles and Daddy didn't. He hates being outdone.' She giggled. 'I tease him about it sometimes.'

'And you'll be the Honourable,' Leo remarked. 'The Hon. Gloria King. Sounds very grand.' He smiled. 'It'll suit you. You know, I've really enjoyed this evening. I love the theatre and none of my girlfriends would have appreciated that play we saw tonight. You know why I asked you?' Gloria shook her head. The diamond earrings flashed fire. 'Because when I was down for the weekend you told me you liked the theatre.'

She said casually, 'I like opera, too. I'm very musical.'

'I'm not,' he admitted. 'I prefer ballet. Do you like ballet?'

'No,' she said flatly. 'All those gays prancing about. I love Italian opera. They're doing Verdi at Covent Garden next week.'

He said, 'Then why don't we go, and see if you can convert me?'

'We wouldn't get seats; they've been sold out for weeks. It's Pavarotti.'

Leo Derwent summoned the waiter for his bill. 'If I get tickets, will you come?'

Gloria showed her large even teeth in a mocking smile that was not unfriendly. 'If you get tickets, I'll come. I won't tell Daddy.' She giggled again. 'He tried and he couldn't get any.'

Leo said, 'That's a deal.' He drove her home. He didn't touch her. The idea repelled him anyway, and it would have been a mistake. She wasn't ready for anything like that. Yet. He came to the front door of the house in Green Street and solemnly shook hands.

'Good night, Gloria. It's been fun tonight. I'll call you about the opera.'

'You won't get seats,' Gloria said.

'I always get what I want,' he retorted. 'Like your father. Good night.'

She opened the door and went inside. She didn't thank him. She was reluctant to thank people; her father never did. It was a sign of weakness. He wouldn't get tickets for the Verdi opera. Not when her father had failed.

'Damn,' Julia exclaimed. 'They're away. They've gone to France for ten days. I spoke to the cleaner.' She frowned at Ben Harris. 'I hoped to get over early next week.' Her cousins the Petersons were Jersey residents and she intended inviting herself for a week's stay.

The holiday had to seem bona fide. They could make the contact she needed. There was no help for it; she would have to wait till they returned and then fix a date to visit them.

'Stop worrying,' he advised her. 'Nothing's going to happen in the next two weeks. And besides, you've got Leo Derwent and Gloria King up and running.'

'Yes,' she agreed. 'He's seeing her again this week. God knows what they have in common . . . But he's clever. I have to give him that.'

'And he hates King's guts,' Ben said. 'So we know King's putting a deal together in the States, bringing the lovely Gloria in on the act, and working towards a peerage. Which ties in with his take-over of the *Herald*. He'll be the biggest single publishing and communications boss in the whole of the UK. Nobody in politics will want to get on the wrong side of him. Even the royals wouldn't be safe from someone with that much clout. Jesus. It makes the flesh creep.'

'Which is why every day's delay does matter,' Julia pointed out. 'Why do the bloody Petersons have to go to France, just at this time?'

He shrugged. She was pacing up and down. He hadn't seen her so uptight since Jean Adams was murdered. That was the goad driving her, and nothing he could say relieved her sense of guilt. 'I talked to Lucy today,' he said. Julia didn't connect for a moment.

'Lucy – yes, of course, how is she?'

'Still sick,' he said. 'But she's told her mother. She took the news about the baby better than Lucy expected, but she wasn't too pleased about me coming into the picture. I'd like you to meet Lucy. Why don't we go up to Birmingham this weekend . . . she's always asking about you.'

Julia pushed her hair back; she felt tired and slightly irritable. Frustration was fraying her nerves. She should have been in Jersey instead of going up to the Midlands to meet her lover's pregnant daughter.

'Ben darling,' she said, 'I'd rather wait. I've got this bloody trip on my mind. I'd be a drag on both of you. Why don't you go?'

'And leave you chewing your nails on your own here? No way. We'll do it another time.'

'We could drive down and have lunch with my parents,' she said on an impulse. 'They're always asking about you. I did neglect them for quite a time. I was so wrapped up in my work, and they didn't like Felix. And *they* were wrapped up in my brother and the grandchildren . . . I was jealous of that. But we've grown very close now and I want to see them before Christmas. Next time, we'll go up and see Lucy?'

'OK,' he said. 'Why not? I'd like to see where the genes come from . . . either of them redheaded?'

'No,' Julia smiled at him. 'Daddy's father was. I suppose I get it from him. You're sure you don't mind about Lucy – just till I've got this trip to Jersey over?' She sighed. 'It's so bloody crucial to the whole thing. God, I wish I could go there tomorrow!'

'Well you can't, so relax,' he advised. 'Call your family and make a date. See if they can have us on Sunday. I hate Sundays in London. It's so dead. Everything's asleep.'

'I never knew that,' Julia said. 'Why didn't you say so before? We could have done something different.'

'Because I liked spending my day with you,' he said quietly. 'Our mornings in bed were rather special.'

'Aren't they still?' she asked him.

'Oh no,' he mocked her. 'You turn me off these days. Haven't you noticed?'

'Not really,' Julia said, 'if last night was anything to go on. Why do you always manage to wind me up? Why do I fall for it?'

'Because you're so crazy about me,' he said solemnly. 'Don't chuck that cushion at me . . . go and call your mother.'

Listening to the telephone call, he watched Julia and realized how much she had changed his life. Sundays had been his worst day of the week. There was nothing to do, no work unless some crisis broke, just his own company in the empty flat. Quite often he opened a bottle of whisky and settled down to drink his way through it till he fell asleep. Now he thought of the country on a Sunday morning. As a child he had woken to a world that was green. His father loved birds and for a time he had managed to interest Ben in watching them. They were country people with simple values and hobbies that weren't dependent upon money. They had been blessed with a clever and ambitious son. Sometimes Ben wondered how much of a blessing he had really been to them. A foreign wife, a broken marriage, grandchildren that they seldom saw. They were both dead, and in those few minutes, listening to Julia talking to her mother, Ben Harris admitted how much he regretted the past. It was too late for them, but he had a second chance. A chance with a woman he loved and a chance with his daughter Lucy. His son, Frank, had sent him a friendly message through his sister. He had been the more hostile to Ben of the two children when they divorced. It could all come right, he thought.

Julia hung up and turned to him. She looked happier, less strained.

'They're thrilled,' she said. 'Sunday will be fine. I warn you, Mum's a terrific cook and she believes in feeding everyone to bursting point. One thing . . . ' She hesitated, and then said, 'They're dying to see me settled. I could hear the wedding bells in her voice . . . don't be put off by that, will you?'

He gave nothing away. 'Don't worry, J, I won't. Why don't we go and catch that new Harrison Ford film at the Odeon?'

'Some men,' Julia said sweetly, 'just never grow up. Harrison Ford . . . I'll get my coat.'

'Gloria's going out with that Leo again,' Marilyn King remarked. King looked up and scowled.

'It's becoming a bloody habit. What's he up to? I'll talk to her.'

'Why do you have to interfere, darling? She's never had a steady boyfriend. I think she likes him.' Gloria's mother couldn't imagine any man wanting her daughter, but the slim chance of getting rid of her made her take Gloria's part.

'Balls,' King snapped. 'She wouldn't like a turd like that. Anyway, if I want to talk to her I'll talk to her.' He went back to his newspaper. After a time he looked up, and said, 'Where's she going with him then?'

Marilyn said in her soft voice, 'She didn't say. They went

to the opera last week. Pavarotti. You couldn't get tickets, remember?'

That irritated him. His face reddened. He glared at her.

'I didn't try,' he said. 'You wanted to see it.' Leo Derwent dating his daughter. He shouldn't have let her go out with him in the first instance. He'd put a stop to it right now. He threw the newspaper aside. 'Where is she?' he demanded. His wife knew that tone of voice. 'Upstairs,' she said. 'Getting ready.' Her hopes were dashed. King wouldn't let any man take his daughter. She sighed and resigned herself, as she had done all through her married life. Fortunately, her expectations of happiness were limited to money, clothes and social activities. She had given King what he wanted sexually until he obviously tired of her. She had borne the one child, and been surprised that he had not insisted on more in the hope of a son. He had been content with his daughter and left her to her own devices. They had never included lovers. She wasn't that interested in sex; it had been a means to an end with her as soon as she recognized the market value of her own beauty and appeal. It was a great relief not to go through the charade of pretending to enjoy it. All that thrashing about and moaning, she remembered with distaste. So boring. Life was better than it had ever been, with her circle of smart friends, her charity work and the magical contacts with royalty. When she was Lady King her cup would overflow.

She stopped thinking about Gloria and her short-lived romance.

Harold King didn't knock on his daughter's bedroom door. He banged it open and walked in. Gloria was putting on a smart velvet coat lined with fox.

'I want to talk to you,' he said. She smiled at him placatingly.

'Daddy darling, I'll be late . . . Is it very important?'

'You're meeting that shit Leo, aren't you?'

She looked surprised at his tone. 'Yes, I am.'

King sat on her bed. He looked at her and said, 'Put him off.'

'Daddy – why? What's wrong?'

'What's all this interest in you all of a sudden? He's got some ulterior motive.'

A slight colour crept up into her face.

'He enjoys my company, that's all. There's nothing in it. We like the theatre and the opera. Daddy, there's nothing ulterior about it. There's no sex, if that's what you're worried about. He says I've got a man's mind, and he can talk to me . . . We're just friends—'

'Balls,' King said angrily. 'All he wants with women is to tie them up and cane their bottoms. He's trying to pull something.' He didn't notice that she had flushed bright red. He had never seen her angry with him. 'Call him and say you can't make it.'

'It's the first night of the new Lloyd Webber,' she said. 'I can't just let him down at the last minute.'

'Lloyd Webber? Very cultural . . . ' The sneer wounded her.

'Please, Daddy,' her eyes were filling with tears. 'Please. I'll go tonight and I won't see him again. I'll tell him, I promise.' And then, in the first independent gesture of her adult life, she picked up her evening bag and brushed past him.

'I'll tell him,' she repeated and went out, leaving him there.

Leo had booked a table at Annabel's for dinner after the theatre. He was advancing very slowly and carefully on his prey and he felt she was sufficiently off guard to go to the smartest nightclub in London; perhaps even to dance . . . She was good company, he was forced to admit that. She was sharp, with a cynical cast of mind that he enjoyed. She could even be witty in a mordant way. And she was flattered. She liked the attention he paid her, and she felt safe because there were no sexual overtones. Those, he thought coolly, could come later. Lesbians were said to be better in bed with a man than their heterosexual sisters. More practised in the skills of arousal.

She was ugly and coarse, but she had her father's aura of power about her. He didn't find it attractive, but he found it challenging. And most important of all in his scenario, was to hit Harold King right in the balls. He knew all about Leo's fun and games. He'd seen and heard the evidence . . . He wouldn't find it so amusing if the partner in the play-acting was his own daughter.

Gloria sipped her champagne. She hadn't enjoyed the musical. She couldn't concentrate and relax because of what she had promised her father. And she was hurt. Once or twice during the performance, she had blinked back angry tears. Her father had been brutal. He had dismissed the idea that she might have anything to offer anyone. The implication was clear. No-one, not even someone he despised as much as Leo, would bother with her for herself.

There must be another motive. She had never felt a stirring of sexual interest in her companion. She liked his quick mind, and shared his penchant for the arts. She liked going to good restaurants and first nights. That's all there had been in it until now. Hurt pride was accompanied by a childish desire to have her own way. And by something else. Her father's angry words whispered in her mind. *All he wants with women is to tie them up and cane their bottoms* . . . Curiosity uncurled inside her like a worm. What would it feel like? The worm became a pang of sensuality and on an impulse she pushed her leg against him in the darkness. Leo felt the pressure and pressed back. Christ, he said to himself, pretending to concentrate on the spectacle on stage. She's jumping the gun . . .

In the intimate gloom of Annabel's he turned to her and said, 'You don't seem on form, Gloria. Anything the matter?' She put down her champagne glass. It was empty and he signalled the waiter to refill it.

'You mean I've been boring?' It was so quick and defensive that it caught him off guard.

'God, no, don't be silly. You're never boring. I always enjoy myself so much when I'm with you it makes other women boring. What's the matter? Here . . . drink that up. Tell me . . . '

Unlike King, whose teetotalism was famous, Gloria guzzled her wine as greedily as her food. She looked down and then up at him.

'My father wants me to stop seeing you.'

Leo kept his head. 'I'm sorry to hear that. Did he say why?'

She would never admit the reason. She said stubbornly, 'He didn't say. He doesn't give explanations. He just expects people to do what he says.'

'Even you?' he questioned. 'I thought you were his favourite.'

'Oh I am,' she said quickly. 'He adores me. I adore him. He's wonderful.'

Leo said gently, 'Can't you make him change his mind? I don't want to stop seeing you, Gloria. I mean it.'

'I don't want to stop, either,' she admitted. 'I've had fun. We like the same things . . . '

He said, 'What's he got against me – did he say anything to you?' There was a slight glaze over the very pale blue eyes as they considered him. It shocked him for a moment. He had seen that look in women's eyes before. He waited and moved his knee a little till it brushed against hers under the table. She didn't shift away.

'He said you liked bondage,' she said, and her voice lowered to a breathy whisper. Leo risked everything on his instinct.

'And if I did,' he said equally low, 'would that matter to you? I'd never ask you to do anything. Unless you liked the idea . . . '

'I don't know,' Gloria went on. She was staring ahead of her into the dimly lit reaches of the room, where couples gyrated to a throbbing disco rhythm. 'I don't know,' she repeated. 'I've only done it with girls. I might like it, but I don't know.'

'Well,' Leo said, 'you don't have to make any decisions. I'm happy as we are, if that's what you want . . . ' He placed his hand on hers for a moment. She didn't respond but she didn't pull away. 'Can't you talk your father round?'

'I don't think so,' Gloria said. 'He doesn't expect me to argue.'

'Just do as you're told,' he prompted. 'That's the trouble, they go on thinking you're still a child. My old Dad was the same. I had quite a hassle, even after I was elected . . . he was still telling me what to do.' He laughed, indulgent of parental foibles. 'I don't blame your father, Gloria. I'd be the same if I had a daughter. One thing . . . how are you going to make decisions in business if you're not allowed to make them in your private life?'

'I *can* make my own decisions,' she protested. 'If I do see you – he doesn't have to know.'

'I don't think that's the way to tackle this,' he disagreed. 'I don't want you deceiving your old man because of me. I've too much respect for him. Talk to him, Glory. Don't lie about us. Lies always get found out.' She amazed him by laughing.

'Not if they're clever lies,' she said. 'Don't pretend to be moral, Leo. It doesn't suit you. What did you call me just now?'

'Glory,' he said. 'Sort of pet name. I always give pet names to people I like. Do you mind?'

'Do you have pet names for your girlfriends?' she asked.

Leo smiled. 'No,' he said. 'I told you, only for people I like. Let's have another bottle, shall we? And how about a dance?'

'I hate dancing,' she said flatly. 'I haven't any sense of rhythm.'

'I hated opera,' he pointed out. 'But I tried it and liked it with you. Come on.'

She was clumsy. And she was right, she had no sense of rhythm, which was odd because she was genuinely musical. She had no confidence in her big body, that was the trouble. She looked awkward and uncomfortable.

He pulled her up against him. She went rigid. Then he took her wrists and held them firmly behind her back as they moved. He felt her relax and he tightened the grip. She started to move with him instead of resisting. Over her shoulder he smiled. Then after a few minutes he brought her back to the table.

'Well, that wasn't too bad, was it?' he said. 'You've got a very good sense of rhythm.' She took her place and looked at him.

'It was all right at the end,' she said.

He drove her home and pulled up outside the Green Street house. 'How are we going to play this, Glory? I can't call you at home.'

'I could call you,' she said. 'I don't know. I'll think about it . . . '

'I don't want to cause a row with you and your father.'

'I'm not worried about that,' Gloria answered. 'I don't like going behind his back. He wouldn't take it out on me, but you might be in for trouble.'

'He's not a man to cross, I know that much. But I'll chance it, if you will.'

'I'll think about it,' she repeated.

She opened the car door and got out. She sounded very matter of fact.

'We could meet next week,' he suggested. 'Call me.'

She nodded and turned away. He didn't linger, either. He was used to her abrupt departures. She traded on her graceless manner, copied from her father. As he drove home, Leo had a private bet with himself that, without knowing it, King had given him a key to Gloria. Perversion intrigued her. Imprisoning her arms on the dance floor had turned her on. Oddly enough, he admitted, it had done the same to him. He felt distinctly horny at the thought of that big arrogant bitch lying helpless. He'd read somewhere that women with fixations on Daddy could only get satisfaction from sex by submitting to punishment. It eased the guilt of their subconscious incest. He grinned and switched on the radio. Time would tell.

Julia's mother loved a *post mortem* after a party. Julia's father wanted to go to sleep, but he indulged her. Besides he was interested as much as she was. 'He's obviously in love with her,' May Hamilton said. 'And I liked him.'

'But?' he added, when she paused.

'He's divorced and he's got grown-up children, and he's quite a bit older . . . '

'My dear, you can't have everything. One marriage in three goes down the drain these days. Julia's not likely to find a bachelor unless there's something pretty odd about him. I liked Harris, he's intelligent. You've been hoping she'd settle down with someone for ages, and I think he might just be the one.'

'Yes, I think so too. It's just that with a daughter I hoped for a nice wedding, you know, darling, all the trimmings. Like we had.'

'I know,' he smiled in the dark. His wife was a hopeless romantic. She dreamed of Julia floating down the aisle of the local church in a white dress and a virginal veil, with the grandchildren as page and bridesmaid trotting after her. It wouldn't happen like that.

In his way, he was sorry too. 'Julia's not twenty-one,' he pointed out gently. 'She's lived her life and she's an independent woman. She was always like that, even as a child. Went her own way, did her own thing. You used to fight with her about it, don't forget. You said it was such a relief dealing with Tom, he was so easy-going. Nothing was ever easy with Julia, and it's not going to change. I only hope she does marry this chap. Most of her generation don't bother – they live together and that's it.'

'They're afraid of commitment, that's why,' his wife said. She settled down beside him. 'We weren't,' she added.

'I know, May, we were all perfect . . . Come on, let's hope it turns out for the best. I think it will. I think he'll cope with her. Not many men would be able to; now go to sleep, it's late.'

'It was a lovely day, though,' his wife had the last word. 'I was so pleased they stayed on to supper instead of going after lunch. They must have enjoyed themselves. Why don't we ask them to come and spend Christmas with us? Darling, don't go to sleep . . . Wouldn't that be a nice idea?'

'We're going to your sister,' he mumbled. 'You promised, you can't put her off.'

May didn't answer. Her spirits were high with the anticipation. A big family gathering would be like the days when their two children were young, before there were other in-laws to be considered. She could ask her sister and her husband to join them instead . . . She drifted off happily to sleep.

8

'Janey? Hello there . . . it's me – Julia. How are you?'

'Julia, what a lovely surprise. We're fine, how are you? How's the job? May said you were a big noise on the *Herald* now.'

'Don't take any notice of Mum, she exaggerates,' Julia said. 'Listen, I've got a week's holiday due, and I wondered if you could stand having me to stay. I'm tired, actually I've been working flat out, and a breath of sea air and a few days with you and David would be heaven . . . ' She paused, praying that her cousins weren't going on another trip, or coming to London to shop before Christmas.

Janey sounded delighted. 'What a good idea – darling Julia, we'd be thrilled to have you. When do you want to come?'

Julia sighed with relief; her stomach had knotted with tension as she made the call. As she had said to Ben, this trip was crucial . . . and it had to seem completely unconnected with her work. An innocent holiday with relatives. That's why a hotel wouldn't do. King had used surveillance before, with fatal results for Jean

Adams. She and Ben were sure they were still being followed. 'Would Monday be too soon? I'm desperate for a break.'

'You sound it,' Janey Peterson remarked. 'Monday would be lovely. Let us know what time your flight gets in and we'll meet you. David will be thrilled . . . you're such a favourite of his. Do you want to have a quiet time or shall I organize some jollity? It's up to you.'

'Whatever you like – so long as there aren't any journalists!'

'Nobody in your league over here,' her cousin said. 'I've boasted about you to all my friends for ages . . . now I can show you off. See you on Monday. Bye, Julia. Bye.'

They had retired to live in Jersey when David Peterson's mother died, leaving him her house. They had been there for two years, and Julia had seen them on trips to London. They declared themselves blissfully happy on the lovely island. David Peterson had been a consultant at one of the big teaching hospitals, and had a thriving practice in Harley Street. He had abandoned what he described as the rat race of the National Health and private medicine in England for a similar job in Jersey. His mother was May Hamilton's sister. He was fifteen years older than Julia and his wife Janey was a bouncy forty year old who was mad on tennis and sailing. They were a warm and friendly couple, and Julia had always got on very well with them. She pushed her hair back, making a mental note to get it cut before she left.

The Petersons knew everyone in Jersey. They were hospitable and popular. Their circle was not confined to the multimillionaires who settled there for tax reasons. David's mother had been a long-time resident, and her legacy entitled them to move to the island without the stringent financial conditions applied to the super rich. They could get her the introduction she needed. She called through to Ben at his office.

'I've fixed up to go on Monday,' she said. 'I'm going up to see Western.'

On the other line Ben said, 'Don't be surprised when he makes it easy for you. She'll have told him you're on to something.'

'I don't think so,' Julia bristled in Evelyn's defence. 'She wouldn't do that . . . '

Ben didn't answer. He just said, 'I'm glad you've fixed it, but I wish you'd let me come with you.'

Julia said, 'No, darling. My mother called this morning. She thinks you're great. So do I.' She hung up and dialled through to Western's private number, and arranged to go up and see him in an hour.

'I can't see why you need to take time off,' William Western said. 'All you've done is help Stevens put together a feature on blackmail among MPs that anybody could have written.' He stared at her accusingly.

'The feature's explosive,' Julia protested. 'Everyone says so.'

'I'm the one that matters, and I don't think so,' he snapped. 'If you hadn't hooked Leo Derwent there'd be no excuse at all.'

'He's already given us valuable information,' she countered.

'Nothing I didn't know already,' Western remarked. 'I knew about the deal King's putting together in the States. Whether he's bringing in that ghastly daughter to take over from him is irrelevant to me. So is the Life Peerage. He's out for my head, and so far nothing's been dug up to stop him. Now you come and ask for a holiday . . . my wife said you were tired and needed a break. I said it was bloody nonsense.'

He waited. Evelyn had primed him carefully. 'You're supposed to think it's genuine, Billy. I said I'd persuade you she would benefit from a few days away. *Don't* let her see you know there's a reason behind it. Be nasty. She'll expect that.' Evelyn was his right arm, he thought. Shrewd, invaluable in situations where feminine judgement was so superior to his own. And ruthless, as he said. She liked Julia, that was genuine. But she would sacrifice her without a qualm on his behalf.

Evelyn Western hadn't betrayed her trust, Julia decided. She had kept her word, in spite of Ben's suspicions. 'Lord Western,' she said. 'I do need just a few days to clear my head. Then I promise you,' she emphasized the word. 'I promise you I'll get a breakthrough before Christmas. If I don't – '

she faced him calmly, 'then I'll put my resignation on your desk on the first of January.'

'And I'll accept it,' he said briskly. 'Oh, all right then, take a week, if it's so essential to you. I'd get into trouble with my wife if I didn't say yes. Pity she took such a liking to you. When do you want to go?'

'From Monday?'

She hadn't confided fully in Evelyn, so he tried on his own account. 'Where are you off to? Sunshine, I suppose . . . '

'No, I'm going to stay with some cousins, that's all. Thank you, Lord Western.'

'Don't thank me,' he grumbled, 'thank Evelyn. But I'll hold you to that promise. Before Christmas.'

'I know you will,' Julia answered. 'And I'll deliver.'

She went down in the private elevator to her own floor. Inside her office she sank down in one of the big armchairs.

'What a bastard,' she said aloud. 'If I'm right, he'll eat his words. That'll be some consolation. He said I could name my price, and, by God, I'm going to! And for Ben, too . . . '

Harold King had called a special board meeting in his private penthouse. On occasions like this he used his sitting room instead of the massive boardroom on the floor below. His sitting room was the chosen venue whenever he pushed through something of dubious legality. It overawed his company secretary and his finance director. They sank or swam with Harold King and they wouldn't give him any arguments, whatever he suggested. Gloria was there too. She had been admitted to the Board of his Pension Fund. When that formality had been completed, the real work would begin. The transfer of millions of stocks and bonds held on behalf of King's thousands of employees into an investment company of which he had dual control with his daughter. Then, he could fly back to New York and wind up the financing deal with Field. After that Christmas at Gstaad as usual. He had a house there; Marilyn skied and so did Gloria, who showed nerve and unexpected athleticism on the slopes. He had given up some years earlier. One fall where he pulled thigh muscles and was out of action for weeks had taught him to be his age. He read biographies and travel books in the sunshine and planned for the coming year. He loved Switzerland.

It reminded him of home. Gloria was quiet that morning. He had asked her briefly if she'd given Leo Derwent his marching orders the day after their argument, and she'd nodded rather sheepishly and said, yes, she wouldn't be seeing him any more.

King didn't think about it again. She had never deceived him or disobeyed his wishes. He thought she seemed subdued that morning, when she should have been excited. While they waited for the secretary and the other director, King said suddenly, 'What's wrong with you, sweetheart? You don't seem yourself. Got the curse?'

Gloria hesitated. She was miserable instead of happy. She had lied to him, and she hated it. But she was torn between guilt and a growing obsession. She loved him, he was her world. But seeing Leo wasn't a disloyalty. It didn't change her feelings for her father. It was harmless. Nothing had happened between them. They met once or twice a week, went to the cinema or the theatre. Sometimes they had dinner together in a discreet restaurant where they were unlikely to meet anyone they knew. It was completely harmless because Leo had made no sexual advance. The idea of a sexual encounter with a man had always disgusted her. But what she imagined would happen with him at first tantalized her and then obsessed her. It spoiled her lovemaking with an older woman she had met.

She was restless and dissatisfied, and the lesbian lady soon went looking for another lover. She took in a deep breath. 'Daddy,' she said. 'Daddy, don't be angry, but there's something I want to tell you.'

King had answered his own question. Women were often funny at the menstrual cycle. He wasn't listening properly when she spoke. 'Been running up bills?' he joked with her. 'Your mother was complaining about it yesterday. She says you're always buying clothes . . . "Why not?" I said. "Why shouldn't she? She can have everything she wants and more." ' His secretary buzzed through that the two men were in the outer hall. 'Ah, here they are. Remember, always insist on your employees being punctual to the second. It's good for them. And always make a point of keeping *them* waiting. That's good for them, too. But not this morning. We've got a lot of business to get through.

'Send them in, send them in,' King said. He slipped his arm round Gloria for a moment. 'Naughty girl,' he said. 'Spending so much money. You're going to start earning it now . . . ' Gloria said nothing. The moment had passed. She wouldn't get up the nerve to try again.

The flight to Jersey was bumpy; Julia was never airsick and she loved flying. It was a blustery day with rain clouds gathering above the island, but, as always, the temperature was mild. Janey came hurrying to meet her at the airport.

'Julia darling,' she exclaimed. 'How lovely to see you – David couldn't get here, he had an emergency at the hospital. How was your flight?'

'A bit rough, but it didn't bother me. You're looking great, Janey. I haven't got much luggage. I always look as if I've come to stay for a year when I go away – I tried to cut down on it this time.'

'You can stay as long as you like,' Janey enthused. 'All our friends are dying to meet you.' On the drive down to Trinity she chatted at top speed.

Life was uneventful, the usual round of parties gathering momentum for Christmas, their trip to France had been great fun, but she got a tummy bug which rather spoilt the last few days . . . David was happier than ever, enjoying his work and finding plenty of time for golf or sailing. It had been such a hassle living in England, nothing on earth would persuade them to go back now. Julia let it flow over her, making appropriate comments. The Petersons had a charming house, legacy of his mother, with the lush garden for which Jersey was famous. The rain had started, and they hurried inside. 'Damn,' Janey said. 'It was glorious yesterday, blazing sunshine and quite warm. I hope it's not going to be like this for your visit.'

'I shan't mind,' Julia told her. 'It's such a treat to get away.'

They were sitting with a pre-lunch drink in the comfortable sitting room. It had french windows and a view of the beautiful garden. The rain lashed down against the view.

'You do look a bit tired,' Janey remarked. 'Have a nice rest while you're here. Nothing wrong, is there?'

'No,' Julia smiled at her. 'Nothing. Just a lot of work and pressure. Nothing a few days with you and David won't put right. How are the boys?'

They had two sons in their late teens, one up at Cambridge, the other travelling through Australia before starting medical school. Julia hadn't seen them for over a year. The schoolboy seemed nice enough, the undergraduate was rather arrogant and offhand. He had reminded her of Felix at the time. Felix. She hadn't thought about him since Ben told her how readily he had co-operated in contacting Joe Patrick. She was surprised that Ben, who had always been so scathing about Felix, spoke rather well of him. He wasn't jealous, that was why. Felix was part of her past. She looked up quickly when her cousin said, 'How's the boyfriend?'

'Which one?'

'Oh, my goodness . . . like that, is it? Lucky you.' Janey laughed. 'Felix, I met him with you last time we were over. Who else have you got in tow?'

'Felix and I broke up quite a while ago,' she explained. 'I've met someone else. He's pretty special.'

'I'm glad,' Janey said. 'Felix wasn't for you, darling. David couldn't stand him, I can tell you that now. I thought he was rather a dish, but a bit brash. What's the new one like?'

'Older than me this time,' Julia admitted. 'Very bright indeed. We're living together to see how it works out. He's divorced, but a long time ago. It was a bad experience. We aren't going to rush anything. But he's lovely. You'd like him. So would David.'

'You should have brought him over,' Janey said. 'What's he do?'

'He's on the *Herald*,' Julia answered. 'He was my boss until I got this new job heading up "Exposure". Next time you come to London, we'll fix dinner together.'

After lunch, Julia unpacked and asked Janey if she'd mind if she went for a walk. A large red setter wagged its tail at the word, and Julia offered to take him with her. It had stopped raining. The sun was forcing shafts of light through the retreating clouds, the air smelt sweet and warm after the rain. Janey didn't offer to go with her. She had things to do, because a couple of friends were coming to dinner. Not a party, she assured Julia, not on her first evening, but two very close friends . . .

Julia set off with the sleek dog on a lead. There was a path leading down to the shingle beach and she took it. Once off the road, she unleashed the setter who bounded happily up and down.

He was on the island. His photograph was imprinted on her mind, like a transposed negative. Nearly fifty years ago, young, smiling, confident that he would live out the conflict that was claiming so many lives. And with him was another figure, less well defined but clear enough. She stopped and paused to throw a piece of driftwood for the setter. It raced into the surf to bring it back.

If King's bloodhounds had tracked her to the island then she had very little time to waste before they picked her up.

Tomorrow, she decided. She would go back now, and help Janey in the kitchen and suggest it.

Janey was taken by surprise. 'Richard Watson? Yes, we know him. He's very nice, lived here for years. He was a friend of David's mother. Why do you want to meet him especially?'

'I read a book he wrote,' Julia said. 'Actually it was my boyfriend who read it and passed it on. He said it was very interesting and well written. About his time in the Army and being a prisoner of war. I think it was privately printed . . . it said in a footnote he'd retired to live here. I'd rather like to meet him if you can arrange it.'

Janey said, 'I never knew he wrote anything. He was rather a successful businessman. ICI, I think. I'll ask him to dinner. What a good idea. He'll be flattered at you wanting to meet him. We've told him all about you.'

Julia smiled. 'I hope he won't be disappointed.'

'Don't you believe it,' her cousin said. 'He loves attractive women. I'll call him now.'

Julia finished laying the table. She could hear Janey's voice and then her cheerful laugh. She came in and said, 'It's all fixed. He's asked us to dinner. Tomorrow. He had arranged a small party and he was thrilled at the idea of meeting you. Says he's read all your stuff in the newspaper. He's making it black tie in your honour!'

'How very sweet of him. Thanks, Janey,' she said. 'I brought a silk shirt and a long black skirt, will that do?'

'Of course . . . we're not that smart over here. You'll look terrific. You always do.'

The evening was relaxed. David Peterson made a fuss of Julia, opening a bottle of champagne to celebrate her arrival. The couple who came to dinner in the spacious kitchen were a retired diplomat who was a native Jerseyman and his English wife. They were full of amusing stories about his last posting in Rio de Janeiro. Janey told them about Richard Watson's invitation. They assured Julia that she would like her host and find him an interesting man with a lot of personal charm. 'He's all of that,' David agreed. 'I always thought he and my mother might get together. But they never did. She was very fond of him.'

'He's been a widower for years,' the diplomat's wife said. 'People get set in their ways. Quite a number of ladies have had their eye on Richard but he's never fallen for anyone. I think all those years as a POW had an effect on him. It was an experience that marked a lot of people. My brother for one. But he was with those bloody awful Japanese. Came home and went into the Church. He's a parson in Norfolk. High Anglican, never married. Loves bells and smells. Extraordinary . . . But he seems happy enough.'

'Which is surely all that matters,' David said tartly, Julia noticed. Then she remembered that, unlike the rest of the family, he was a regular churchgoer. The more they talked about Richard Watson, the more intrigued she became. There was nothing in the slight volume of his wartime reminiscences that marked him out as different from thousands of other young middle-class men who became officers in the forties. But forewarned is forearmed. Watson was obviously no elderly waffler who would part with information freely. She would have to tread carefully. Before they went to bed, Ben telephoned her. Janey took the call and said, smiling slyly at Julia, 'I think it's the boyfriend, darling. You can take it upstairs if you like.'

'Thanks,' Julia said. 'I'll do that.'

His voice was reassuring. She felt a pang when she heard it.

'How are you? How's it going?'

'I'm fine. Everything's going better than I hoped. I'm seeing our man tomorrow night. Janey fixed it up for me. They're being so sweet I feel lousy to make use of them like this. I miss you, Ben. I really do.'

'Me too,' he said. 'The flat's like a bloody morgue. Pussy won't settle down either. We're both just too fond of you. Get this interview over and get back as soon as you can. I don't like you being out in the big world on your own. No signs of any followers at the airport?'

'No, but I wouldn't see them if there were,' Julia pointed out. 'If King's still got tabs on us, someone is probably on the island looking for me by now. So long as I connect with Watson before they pick me up, it won't matter. Then I'll think of an excuse and come home. Don't worry about me, darling. Take care, won't you?'

'You too,' Ben said. 'I love you. Call me tomorrow night. Doesn't matter what time.'

When he had rung off, Ben took the cat on his knee and skimmed through the book with the smiling young officer on the cover. He paused at the group photograph in the middle section. There weren't that many privately printed records of one man's war. A few dozen at the most. Memories of men grown old or dead who had fought in a war the world wanted to forget. But if he had chanced upon it, thanks to his War Office friend's suggestion, why shouldn't someone else with an interest in the subject? Someone with powerful resources at the push of a button, who knew what they were looking for . . . He shouldn't have let Julia go there alone. His instincts had been against it, and he'd let her overrule them. He swore at himself for giving way. Just twenty-four hours more. Then he would insist she come home or he would fly out, however much she argued. On that resolution, he was able to sleep.

* * *

Joe Patrick cursed the detective agency contact. They met at a pub in the City and in the seclusion of a corner table, Joe Patrick hissed four-letter insults at him. The man sat stolidly, not answering, showing no emotion, though a line of red crept up his neck from under his collar. Patrick leaned towards him, teeth bared, menacing as a rat at bay. 'Jersey!' he spat at him. 'Fucking Jersey and you lost her at the airport – Jesus H. Christ—'

'We sent a man over on the next flight,' the agency man protested. 'He checked all the hotels and she's not registered. Nobody answering our description has booked in anywhere. He even went round the bloody Bed and Breakfasts, and you know how many of them there are . . . '

'I don't fucking know, and I don't care,' Joe snarled at him. 'What else have you tried?'

'Her office. We asked for an appointment. Her secretary said she was on a week's holiday. No contact number. Said she'd give us a provisional for ten days' time but couldn't confirm till Hamilton got back. Look, stop bollocking me for a minute, will you? Maybe she is on holiday. Staying with friends—'

'Then find the friends,' Joe said. 'Your job is to know where she is and what she's fucking doing twenty-four hours of the day, till I tell you to get off the case. You find her, you hear me? Or no payment. My boss pays for results, not some arsehole who can't get his act together because the cow gets on a plane!' He stood up, buttoned his long cashmere coat. He was white with rage and fear of King's reaction. 'You can put the booze down to expenses,' he said. 'And hope you get paid . . . ' Then he pushed his way out through the evening crowd of drinkers. He was in a vile mood. Fear made him vicious. He needed to take it out on somebody. He unlocked his car and drove back to his flat, seething at the agency, at King, at the stinking luck that lost Hamilton on a stinking pissing little island. He dared not tell King. And he dared not keep him in ignorance either. That would be the most dangerous. King wanted daily reports. He conveyed that the immediate threat from Hamilton was over, but he never let up on his precautions. Belt and braces was King's motto. The bitch had taken a holiday. Just before the launch of the new 'Exposure' feature in November. 'Very likely,' Joe said savagely, cutting through the traffic. Leaving the lover boy behind. The team were still covering him, and he was in his office and flat, without any change in his routine.

Maybe that meant it was a genuine holiday . . . Joe bit his lower lip, trying to reassure himself. If Harris had gone with her, it might well have been an assignment. He could try that on King. He could try anything but it wouldn't stave off his rage. And that rage wasn't confined to a flow of insults and abuse. Joe didn't give a toss about that. Words didn't hurt him, but losing money did. That wounded him. King took a lump out of his retainer when he fouled up anything, and that made Joe Patrick bleed.

He parked his car in the underground garage of the apartment block and took the lift up to the third floor. He opened the front door very quietly. He moved with the stealth of a stalking animal. He'd catch those two bitches out whatever they were doing. They wouldn't expect him to be back so early. They'd be sitting on their black arses taking it easy. He'd give them a nice surprise.

'It is a marvellous place to unwind,' Julia said. 'I slept so well last night.'

She didn't look particularly relaxed in Janey's opinion, but she didn't say so. She was living at a high pitch with that demanding job; it would take more than twenty-four hours of beneficial Jersey air and slow tempo to get through to her. 'I'm so glad,' was what she said. 'The Lejeunes thought you were a star. Madge phoned this morning. They say you must come over for lunch if you stay a bit longer.'

'How nice of them,' Julia said, feeling guilty at the deception. 'I'd love to – but I don't think I can take more than the week.'

They were such nice uncomplicated people. She thought suddenly, walking along the beach with Janey and David and the joyous red setter, that she had forgotten what normal couples were like. The island and the Petersons were light miles away from the brittle, power-hungry circle in which she had moved for so long.

And they weren't dull; their lives were busy and their interests were wide. They travelled, they read voraciously; there wasn't a single new novel they couldn't discuss. They were making plans to come over to London early in the new year and see the latest plays and go to the ballet. David was a fanatic balletomane. They lived comfortable, useful lives, and they based their lives on a set of simple values that had been derided in Julia's media world for so long that she had been in danger of forgetting them herself. When all this is over, she made a private resolution as they walked together, I'm going to think about changing things. I'm going to talk to Ben and see what he thinks. Then, dressing for this all-important dinner, Julia mocked herself. Opting out wasn't a real option for her. It was an indulgence, a fantasy, engendered by envy of her cousins' easy lifestyle. She'd go mad with boredom after a few months. And so would Ben Harris. No cosy domestic routines for them. Babies in prams and gardening at weekends. What a fool to have imagined it.

She looked very elegant in the long, pencil-slim velvet skirt. The cream silk shirt was simple, too, with the simplicity of *haute couture*. Her red hair blazed like a bonfire round her head. Richard Watson liked attractive women. She hoped he wouldn't be disappointed. She checked her watch. She was ready. Seven-thirty, and she was down in the hall waiting for Janey and David. Lateness made her very uptight. It was a bad start to what might be a difficult evening. She needed to be at ease with herself. And it might be an advantge to get there independently.

She knew where Watson's house was; they'd driven over there during the morning as part of a shopping, sight-seeing tour of the island before going out to lunch at Longueville Manor. She could drive there in Janey's car. She went up to the landing and called out. 'Janey? Look would it be all right if I went on ahead of you? I'd rather like to get there dead on time and I don't want to rush you. Could I borrow your car?'

Janey's voice came through the door. 'Wait a minute – ' then the door opened and she looked round. She hadn't finished making-up her face. She was always late, and David wasn't much better. Julia thought he must still be in the shower by the sound coming from the bathroom.

'We won't be more than ten minutes . . . Don't you want to come with us?'

'I'd rather get there on time,' Julia explained. 'It's one of my phobias, I'm afraid. I'd really like to set off now . . . sure you don't mind?'

'No, no not at all. You can find your way, can't you?' Janey raised her brows at her cousin's eccentricity, but she didn't argue. 'My car keys are on the hall table. Don't take David's by mistake, will you . . . he goes absolutely ape if anyone touches that precious new Volvo of his. See you there, then.'

As she went downstairs, Julia heard her shouting to her husband.

'David! Hurry out of there, darling – Julia's gone. Got a thing about being late. Must be the crazy life she leads . . . ' And then, muffled as Julia reached the ground floor, 'No she *hasn't* taken your car . . . '

It was a lovely night, quite crisp with bright stars in the cloudless sky and a fresh breeze blowing in from the sea that made her huddle into her velvet coat as she crossed the courtyard to the garage. The drive took twenty minutes, because she couldn't drive fast on the twisting, narrow roads. Rich immigrants with their Rollers and Bentleys were a joke among the islanders. There were few inland roads wide enough for two cars to pass each other.

The house stood on a rocky promontory overlooking the beach and the sea far below. It was illuminated like a beacon in the darkness, and, as she crossed the driveway, the exterior lights came on automatically. She parked the car and got out. The sharp salty air stung her face. Two steps up to a large white-painted front door. She rang the bell. After what seemed a long pause, she rang a second time. Almost as soon as she took her finger off the brass button, the door opened. A tall man was silhouetted against the inner hall light. She said quickly, 'Mr Watson?'

'Yes, I'm Richard Watson. And you must be Julia Hamilton, David's and Janey's cousin. Do come in out of the cold. Quite a wind's come up tonight.' He stepped aside and closed the door.

'I came ahead of them,' she said. 'I hope you don't mind, am I the first?'

He smiled down at her and held out his hand. 'Yes, you are. How very nice, it will give me a chance to talk to you before anyone else arrives. Let me take your coat. You know, Miss Hamilton, I recognized you from your photograph in the *Herald*. But you're even prettier in the flesh.' He had a gentle hold of her arm, and he guided her through the hall and up a short flight of stairs. The house was very warm.

Julia looked round and turned to him. 'What a fabulous room. Oh, and look at that view!' She walked over to the floor-length plate-glass window that made up almost one wall. He came beside her. Lights from the house swept down the cliff; below them a cluster of houses with a bigger building rising up on the very edge of the dark shoreline, gleamed and shimmered with lights. And, far out, the sweep of a lighthouse beam flashed across the inky sky in warning of the rocks.

When she turned round he was watching her and smiling. He was a handsome man, with deep blue eyes. The hair was thick and grey, and a small well-trimmed moustache was like a relic of the soldier he had been so many years ago. He had the upright, lean figure of a much younger man. 'It is even more spectacular in the early evenings,' he said. 'The sunsets here are unbelievable . . . every colour in the rainbow. It's a shame it's dark, but it's still beautiful. That's St Brelades down below, with the Cour Rouge Hotel. It used to be marvellous, but it's always full of tourists now. What can I get you to drink? Gin, whisky, vodka, or white wine?'

'Vodka,' she said, 'with ice and tonic. That would be lovely.' He poured her drink and came back with a whisky for himself.

'I do hope I haven't been a nuisance getting here dead on eight o'clock. I think the dear Petersons thought I was quite mad, but they weren't nearly ready, and I'm paranoid about being late.'

'I'm delighted,' Richard Watson said. 'It's rather unusual, isn't it? Ladies aren't famous for time-keeping. My late wife never managed it. What a charming dress. It is a thrill to meet you, Miss Hamilton. And may I call you Julia?'

'I was going to suggest it,' she said. His charm was washing over her, soothing and seductive. He must have been a serious knockout with women only a few years ago.

At that moment the doorbell sounded and Richard left the room.

Julia turned back to the window. He was right, daylight would be the time to see it at its best. Sunset, or dawn. But she wouldn't be staying.

A middle-aged couple came into the room, led towards her by their host.

'Julia Hamilton, Bob and Fiona Thomas.' The man had a hearty handshake and a hearty voice. 'You're Janey's and David's famous cousin, aren't you? We've heard all about you, haven't we, Fi?' He also had a hearty laugh. His wife was small, very thin and spoke in a very quiet voice. 'Yes, we have. Aren't they here?' She looked round.

'I was early,' Julia explained. She saw the woman's quick scrutiny of her clothes. Satisfied, she smiled at Julia. 'I expect David was held up at the hospital, he works so hard. They've been telling everyone about your visit. You're quite a celebrity before we've even met you.' Small and thin, with that reedy voice, she was rather a bitch, Julia decided. There was only one way to deal with that. She smiled sweetly at her, and turned to talk to her husband.

'This is my first visit to Jersey,' she said. 'It's such a lovely island. I'm already determined to come again in the spring.' He beamed appreciatively.

'I should hope you will. Come and see us next time. This is all in your honour, you know. Dick was just having us to play bridge and have supper till he heard you were here.'

'I told you,' his wife murmured, 'you're a celebrity . . . It's Janey . . . I can always tell when she's a mile off. One of those wonderful voices that carry.'

'Well, nobody can say that about you, Fi, can they . . . can't hear a bloody word she says half the time.' Bob Thomas guffawed at Julia. She laughed. She said to his wife, 'One thing about Janey, she always says nice things about people, so it doesn't matter if they do hear what she's saying.'

The drinks before dinner lasted half an hour. Watson was generous and knew how to get a party going. Soon they were all mingling, paying special attention to Julia as the only stranger in their midst. Even the waspish Fiona Thomas came up and tried to make amends. 'You're right about Janey,' she whispered. 'She is kind to everyone. I didn't mean to say she had a loud voice. It's just that Bob shouts all the time and I feel nobody ever listens to me.'

Julia softened. 'I'm sure they do.'

Richard Watson came up and led Julia aside. 'I hope Fiona's been behaving herself,' he said quietly. 'I saw you being nice to her. She can be a bit sharp, but she's had rather a difficult life. Bob's been a great swordsman in his time, and she had a lot to put up with from pretty women. Dinner's ready. I can see Maria signalling. What would I do without her? The Portuguese are such lovely people. Shall we go in?'

They went into dinner in a glass-fronted room that seemed to be suspended over the cliff. Watson placed her on his right. The table was elegant, with candles and silver, the food compared favourably with the best London restaurants. Julia began to enjoy herself; the atmosphere was relaxed, so civilized and friendly that her tough, competitive world seemed a moonshot away. It was seductive, but she resisted. It wasn't a social occasion. It was the culmination of a careful plan, undertaken at risk to herself if it misfired.

'The definition of age,' Richard Watson was saying, 'is a desire to talk about the past. I find myself doing it more and more. I spent a few nights in London with my nephew . . . the solicitor. You met him, Janey, he came over for a sailing holiday last summer—'

'Yes, I remember him, charming young man,' Janey said brightly.

Richard Watson grinned. 'Not particularly, he's rather bumptious and pleased with himself, but at least he's kin, so I keep in touch. He took me out to dinner at his smart club – excellent food, much better than restaurants – I found myself talking about the time I spent as a prisoner of war. I don't think I'd thought about it, let alone talked about it, for years! But there I was in full flood, banging on about being captured and spending three years in a camp in Germany. I suddenly realized he was bored stiff, poor chap. So I cut it short and changed the subject. I felt what a boring old fool I'd become.'

'That's the trouble,' Bob Thomas snorted. 'The young think they know it all.'

Richard Watson said gently, 'Didn't we? I know I never listened to a word my father said after the age of eighteen. Sad thing was, you know, when I did come back from the POW camp, we couldn't communicate at all. Of course, they were delighted to see me – my mother cried and rushed off to make tea; my old father managed to put his arm round me and then hurried upstairs with my bag. He just didn't know what to say.'

Julia judged the moment had come. 'Did it affect you badly? It must have been awful trying to adjust.'

'It wasn't easy,' he admitted. 'I'd come back home a stranger. To myself as much as to them. I didn't realize what the loss of freedom had done to me. I couldn't make my mind up about anything. I'd lost the habit of taking decisions. If someone had told me what socks to put on in the mornings, I'd have done it.'

'How long did that last?' Julia leaned close, engaging his full attention.

'Couple of years. I tried several jobs, couldn't settle to anything. It was quite a common manifestation of POW fatigue. Then I was taken on by ICI as a trainee, and I got interested. Absorbed, actually. And it all started to come right after that.'

Julia took a breath. *Now.*

'I read your book,' she said. 'I have a friend who's mad on the last war and he gave it to me to read. I really enjoyed it. Did you map it out while you were in the prison camp?'

'Yes,' Richard Watson said, 'I did. It was so desperately boring and miserable, and so damned cold in the winter . . . We were always hungry, too. Most of the chaps spent their time talking about escape or playing chess, or bridge. I worked on my insignificant wartime memoires. I can't believe you found them interesting, but I must admit I'm flattered.'

He smiled at her.

Bob Thomas boomed out, 'Book? What's all this, Dick – been keeping secrets from us?'

'It was years ago – long before I came over here,' Richard Watson protested. 'I had some copies privately printed. I didn't know there were any circulating anywhere. I just wanted to get it off my chest, I suppose.'

'Hidden talents,' Bob Thomas had their attention. 'Better watch out, Julia, or you'll have a rival in Dick here . . . I'd like to read it some time. I bet you've a copy of the great work stashed away. The Army was the best time of my life. I often regretted not making a career of it. Too young to get into the actual war, but I enjoyed my National Service.'

He looked around for approbation.

Julia said quietly, 'Did you feel like that, Richard? Your book didn't read like that.'

He turned to look at her, and then, suddenly, he turned away.

'I hated the Army,' he said. 'I hated everything about it. And I wasn't a good soldier. The idea of killing someone absolutely appalled me. I had no blood lust.'

'Did you ever kill anyone?'

He hesitated for a moment. Then he said, 'No. But I did save a man's life.'

'One of ours?' David Peterson spoke up.

'No. It was a German.'

Julia said quickly, 'How? How did you save him?'

'I stopped my sergeant from murdering him,' he said.

'Good God—' Bob Thomas was leaning across the table. 'Go on, tell us about it.'

His wife said, 'How riveting,' but nobody noticed.

'It was in the Western Desert. We were on the run from Rommel's Afrika Corps – before Monty took over – and we'd got separated from our unit. We were trying to get back to Tripoli. There were seven of us. My captain, Tim Phillips, me, the sergeant and four privates. The desert was crawling with desert patrols, mopping up after the battle. We picked up this German on the way. He had a slight leg wound, and he'd no weapon. I'd say he'd deserted. We took him prisoner because it was safer than leaving him, and have him warn one of his own patrols we were in the area . . . I knew the sergeant wanted to shoot him. He was that sort of man.

We struggled on, hoping to get clear before nightfall, but the German lagged behind, he'd lost quite a lot of blood, and he was a miserable specimen anyway, couldn't have been more than eighteen, if that . . .

The sergeant started chivvying him along with a bayonet, but he couldn't keep up. We saw a dust cloud in the distance. That meant a German armoured patrol was coming our way. We clambered down into the wadi and dragged the boy down with us. My captain took out his revolver and held it to his head. He told the German he'd blow his brains out if he made a sound.'

Richard Watson filled up his glass with wine. 'He didn't mean it. His hand was shaking like a leaf and he was scared stiff. I was watching our sergeant. He had his bayonet at the ready. He said, "We can't risk a shot, sir. And he's slowing us down. You put that away and I'll finish him off with this!" '

Julia said, 'You mean he was going to bayonet him?'

'Oh yes, wouldn't have hesitated. None of the others said anything. He'd had Tim Phillips under his thumb from the start. He actually started to holster his revolver, so I had to do something before the boy was killed.'

'And what did you do?' she asked him.

He shrugged. 'Nothing heroic, I'm afraid. I just announced loud and clear that I wouldn't be a party to murder. Meaning they would have to kill me, too, to stop me reporting what had happened.'

'God,' David Peterson said. 'That was brave.'

'No it wasn't,' Richard Watson insisted. 'But it stopped them. So we went on and left the wretched German behind.' He offered Julia more wine. She refused.

'Did he understand? Did he know what was going on?'

'Oh, he knew all right. He was shaking with terror. I was

sure he understood more English than he let on. He didn't say anything. But he looked at me as we left him. It was very odd, that look. I couldn't make it out. Our sergeant came up to me and said, "You made a mistake there, *Sir.*" ' Watson mimicked the heavy sarcasm in that one word. ' "You should have let me kill the little bastard. Mark my words, he'll send a bloody patrol after us." Which,' he said slowly, 'is exactly what happened. We were captured within the hour.'

'What an extraordinary story,' Bob Thomas said.

Richard Watson looked round at them. He sighed. 'It didn't end there, I'm afraid. Phillips and I were put in a truck and taken back to a POW compound at their base. Preferential treatment for officers. The Germans were like that. The other five were marched off to join a column of British prisoners going to the rear. They came under crossfire; the sergeant was the only one to survive his wounds. The other four poor lads were killed. I only found out about it when the war was over because Phillips kept in touch and he made enquiries about his men.' He paused and Julia saw the muscles tighten in his jaw. 'He had some crack-brained theory that they'd been gunned down deliberately. The crossfire story came from the sergeant, but Phillips said he couldn't find any official record of a skirmish between our patrols and theirs anywhere in the area. He'd got a real bee in his bonnet, but nothing came of it. You know, I've often wondered whether those poor devils would still be alive if I hadn't interfered.'

'You can't possibly blame yourself,' Bob Thomas insisted. 'You did absolutely the right thing. More than a Hun officer would have done for one of ours, I'd say. Though it was quite a clean war—'

'Who would have shot them?' Julia said. 'Wouldn't the sergeant have reported an atrocity like that?' She had to clear her throat and swallow, it was suddenly so dry.

'Well, he didn't,' Watson answered. 'It was just talk, and Phillips tracked him down, but he stuck to his story . . . You're right, Bob, it was a clean war in the Desert. There weren't any war crimes . . . most likely due to Rommel. He was a Prussian of the old school. Well – ' He smiled at them. 'Sorry to have bored you with all this. Comes of getting old, I'm afraid. Now, let's have some coffee. Janey, would you look after Julia and Fiona for me, and we promise not to sit on here too long.'

Janey led the way upstairs. 'How weird,' she said. 'What an awful story. But he was right to save that poor German. He couldn't help it if they got killed in a battle afterwards, could he?'

'No,' Fiona Thomas whispered. 'But I think he blames himself deep down.'

It was long past midnight when Julia was able to leave at last. And get to a telephone. Ben, she thought. Oh Ben, you're not going to believe this. My God. I can hardly believe it myself . . . As they gathered round the front door to say goodbye, she managed to draw Richard Watson aside. 'What happened to Phillips? Is he still around?'

'No, he died back in eighty-one. Cancer. His wife wrote to me.'

'And the sergeant? Was he the one in the photograph in your book?'

'Yes, same man. Whenever people go on about German atrocities, I think of him. He'd have bayoneted that boy to death and enjoyed doing it.'

'And is he alive?' Julia asked, trying to sound casual.

'I've no idea,' his tone was suddenly abrupt. He turned away from her and kissed Fiona Thomas good night. It was a very firm dismissal of the subject.

He was smiling, his charming self again, when he said goodbye to Julia.

'Thank you for a wonderful party,' she said. 'And I really did enjoy your book.'

'I'm flattered,' he said, but the eyes were wary in spite of the smile. 'It was just an exercise in self-indulgence.'

Julia stood her ground. 'But you never mentioned this amazing incident – '

'Perhaps I didn't feel it reflected much credit on anyone,' he said coldly. 'And Phillips was very much alive. I'm not an investigative journalist, you see. I didn't want to inflict hurt.

It has been a pleasure to meet you. I hope you'll come to see us all again.'

'I hope so, too,' she said and shook his hand. 'Thank you again.'

At ten-thirty next morning Ben made the call as they'd arranged. Julia went through the charade for Janey's benefit, saying guiltily, 'That was the office – I've got to go back early. I'm so sorry to cut it short like this. I've had such a lovely time.'

'Oh damn,' Janey exclaimed. 'I'd planned a big drinks party so all our friends could meet you. It was going to be a surprise before you left. Damn . . . ' she said again. 'David will be so sorry he hasn't seen more of you.' Then, because she was good natured, and she saw Julia looking embarrassed, 'Oh, never mind, I'm just being selfish, that's all. Of course you've got to go. Sorry I made a fuss. Come in the spring and we'll do it all again. And don't tell your bloody office where you're going!'

'Janey,' Julia said, and put her arms around her, 'you're sweet to put up with me, messing you around like this. I will come in the spring, and you and David have promised to come to London before that and I'll fix a gala evening with the parents and my new man. That's a promise. Now I'd better call the airport. I really *am* sorry.'

And she truly meant it. But, if she could have grown wings, she'd had flown home to Ben Harris at that very moment.

9

'Come on,' the WPC said. 'Tell me what happened. Who did her over?'

The girl had covered her face with her hands. She was sobbing. Mandy Kent had been in the Force for ten years. She was inured to violence and the hideous results of domestic rows. She prided herself on her emotional detachment. It was essential if she was to do the job properly. 'How did you ever get her into a taxi in that state? Too scared to call an ambulance, weren't you?'

Most battered women refused to lodge a complaint and the bastards got away with it. A badly beaten prostitute was no exception.

She had never seen a girl so smashed up as Tina's friend Tracey lying unconscious in the ward next door. She knew them both; she'd worked on the Vice Squad and she knew the tarts and the pimps in the square mile where drugs, hookers and every kind of sexual malpractice was on offer at a price.

She hadn't seen Tina or her girlfriend on the streets for a long time. She went on, speaking in her calm way.

'She's got fractured ribs, a broken jaw, a smashed right arm – trying to defend herself, wasn't she? – and the doctor thinks whoever did it kicked her so hard her spleen's ruptured. She could die, Tina. So who did it?'

Slowly, Tina touched her own face, it was so bruised her lip was puffy.

'She can't die . . . she can't . . . ' she mumbled. 'We've been together since we were kids. We were in the same fucking council home . . . ' Mandy Kent said firmly, 'If her spleen's ruptured, she could. Next time it could be you, lying in there.'

She waited, instinct sensed a change in the weeping girl. It was said very low. 'Joe Patrick. Joe Patrick beat her up.'

Mandy Kent stood up. 'I'll get us some coffee,' she said. She came back with two plastic cups from the dispenser in the corridor and gave one to Tina.

'I put sugar in,' she said. 'You're in shock. Sugar's good for you. Tell me about this Joe Patrick. Is he your pimp?'

'No,' Tina shook her head. Sipping the hot sweet coffee hurt her mouth. 'He doesn't run girls. Doesn't need to. He's a businessman. We picked him up a year ago in the Caribbean Club. He likes coloureds. He's got a hang up about it. We live with him. I dress up like a secretary sometimes. It's not the first time he's laid into us, you expect that. But this time he came in looking for someone to take it out on. He just wanted to punch the shit out of one of us.'

She finished the coffee and winced.

'Why did he pick on Tracey and not you? She talk back?'

'Christ no. Tracey never did, she was too scared of him. She was wearing a bracelet he'd given me. A fucking bracelet, just borrowing 'cos she liked it . . . He went ape. He was like a crazy, yelling and swearing. He just laid into her. I tried to stop him but he gave me a backhander and put the boot in and I just lay there and watched . . . I thought she was dead. Then he went out. Slammed the door and went out.'

'And you got her out to the street and into a cab,' Mandy Kent prompted.

'I said it was a hit and run,' Tina muttered. 'I had to get her to hospital.'

'And just because she was wearing your bracelet,' Mandy repeated. 'Why, Tina? Was it valuable?'

'No, he never gave us good stuff. Just bits of junk.'

She wiped her face with the back of her hand.

'I've told you,' she said. 'But I'm not doing more than that. I'm not giving evidence. You charge him, I'll deny I ever said anything. If I grassed on him he'd kill me. Or get someone else to do it.'

Mandy Kent had not expected anything else. Girls like Tina and the helpless assault victim Tracey would always be beyond the law's protection. They lived by the rules of the criminal underclass, where the grass was deemed worse than a murderer, and the only law that mattered was survival. 'Maybe Tracey will charge him,' she suggested. 'If she regains consciousness. If she dies it'll be murder. You won't be able to run away from that, Tina.'

Tina said slowly, 'She won't grass on him either. I want to go home now. I'll come and see her tomorrow.'

'You're not going back there, are you? I wouldn't, if I were you.'

'I'll go to a friend,' Tina said. 'Just for a day or two. Give the bastard time to calm down. See how Trace is . . . Thanks for the coffee.'

'If he kicked you, you should let the doctor in Casualty take a look.'

'I'm all right. Just a bit sore. It's not the first time he's done it.'

'I'll get the squad car to take you where you want to go. Keep in touch, Tina. I'm on your side.'

'Like fuck,' Tina said without rancour. 'Nobody's on my side except me.'

Mandy Kent saw her into the squad car. She felt suddenly tired and angry. They'd run the name Joe Patrick through the central computer. Businessman he might be, but the attack had the hallmark of the petty criminal and former pimp.

Not that she had any hope of bringing him into a court.

Neither girl would press charges or give evidence for fear of reprisals. She couldn't blame them but the frustration of seeing a bastard like that get away with it made her seethe. She went back up to the ward. The doctor on duty came out to meet her.

'Any luck?' she asked him.

'No, still unconscious. Lucky for her the spleen's OK. She'll be a terrible mess, though. We've wired up the jaw, but she'll need plastic surgery. No joy with her friend?'

'She told me who did it, but she won't go into court or swear an affidavit. So there's nothing we can do. Makes me really sick.'

'Did she say why he did it? What had the poor little devil done to get a hiding like that?'

'Borrowed the other girl's bracelet. Can you believe it? He was just a thug looking for an excuse to beat up on someone . . . I know the type. Anywhere I can have a look at her belongings? I might as well see what she got herself half-killed for.'

'Go and see Sister,' he suggested. 'Her office's through there. She'll have the stuff till it's documented and locked away. Good night.'

'Good night,' Mandy said.

'Oh yes,' the sister in charge was as familiar with the type of incident as the WPC asking to look at the patient's belongings. 'Yes, I've got everything here, in my desk drawer. You have to be so careful, or some of these people will claim things have been stolen. I'll get out what there is.'

There was little enough. A chain with a lucky charm, three costume rings with blood dried on them like a dirty-brown film, and a thin chain bracelet with little stones that glittered in the light of the anglepoise lamp.

Mandy Kent picked it up. The sister said, 'I haven't seen one of those for years.'

'Oh, what's special about it?'

'It's a DEAREST bracelet,' she explained. 'My father gave one to my mother for their silver wedding. Not as nice as this, though. Hers came from Bravingtons, I think. This has some nice little stones. They spell dearest. Diamond, emerald, amethyst, ruby, emerald, sapphire . . . what's the last one . . . tourmaline. That's right. They were quite fashionable a long time ago. This *is* a nice one, even though the stones are very small.' She had taken it from Mandy Kent and weighed it in her hand. 'I've got my mother's, come to think of it. She died last year.'

'Sorry,' Mandy Kent said. 'If it's not junk, it might be worth running it through the computer for Stolen Goods. I might just get that bastard on receiving. I don't think it belonged to *his* mother. I'll sign for it, if that's all right.'

'I just hope,' the sister said, 'you can find something to charge the brute with.'

Mandy Kent looked at her. She put the envelope with the bracelet sealed inside it in her inner pocket. She put on her hat, and said, 'So do I.'

Ben Harris was waiting at the airport. She saw him outside the arrivals and waved. He hurried to meet her and, for a moment, undemonstrative in public as he was, he took her in his arms and held her for a long embrace.

'Good to see you, darling,' he said. 'God it's been a long few days.'

'Me too,' Julia assured him. 'I've missed you every minute, but,' and drawing back she looked up at him in triumph, 'but we've cracked it. We've got Western in our pockets and we'll have Harold King for war crimes.'

Arms round each other, they made their way to the car park. They were only driving on to the motorway towards central London when Joe Patrick got the call to say Julia had been picked up landing from Jersey and they were on her tail.

At last he could face Harold King. He didn't have to mention that they'd lost her on the island. His spirits had been dour and his mood uneasy when he came home and found his birds had left. There was a mess of vomit and blood on his smart carpet, and no-one around to clean it up.

He had gone over the top with that silly black cow. Seeing her with the bracelet he'd given Tina sparked off the blind rage which was seeking an outlet because he was so scared of King. He'd done her over good and proper and given Tina a fistful for trying to interfere.

But they'd be back. He wasn't worried. They knew what would happen to them if they complained or talked to the police. If they never showed their faces again, he didn't care. Plenty more girls where they came from. Might be good to have a change. He made his appointment and set off in his Mercedes to give Harold King a carefully worded report.

'She went on a holiday,' he said. 'Spent a few days in Jersey, flew back this morning.'

Harold King stared at him. He seemed to change colour, but Joe Patrick dismissed it as imagination. He had been so shit worried, he was still nervous, that was the trouble. 'Jersey,' King said. 'I see. Doing what?'

'Taking a break,' Joe insisted. He decided to invent. 'Staying with friends. Harris didn't go with her.'

'Friends,' King repeated. He got up and walked round his desk to stare at the London skyline with his back to Joe. 'Jersey. Staying with friends.'

'Yeah,' he heard the Irishman say, his voice light-hearted. 'She's a busted flush, like you said. And they're using our plant for the November feature.' He laughed. 'They paid me good money to prove it.'

King didn't turn round. 'Who did she see in Jersey?'

Joe said, 'Nobody. It was just a few days off.'

'She never went out, she didn't meet anybody?' The voice was deceptively calm.

'No. Just got on the plane and came back. She's gone into the office with lover boy. He was there to meet her.'

Harold King swivelled round. 'Those stupid fuckers lost her, didn't they? She slipped them and went to the island and nobody knows what she did or who she saw till they picked her up at Heathrow this morning. Isn't that how it happened, Joe? They lost her!'

Joe bluffed. 'Jesus, they never told me,' he raised his voice in self-defence. 'They gave me the info, just as I've given it to you, Boss. Lookit – ' he dropped into Dublin slang in his agitation, 'lookit, if they've screwed up and tried lyin' their way out—'

'Get out,' King said suddenly. 'Get out. You're finished.'

Joe stood up. He said in a whine of self-justification, 'It's not my fault . . . Anything you've asked, I've done for ye . . . Anythin'. I've risked my bloody neck for ye. You don't mean it; you won't throw me out.'

'You've done nothing for me that wouldn't put you away for the rest of your dirty little life, if that's what you're talking about. Or are you trying to threaten me, Joe? Trying to blackmail me?' To Joe's terror he burst into a roar of laughter. 'You piece of piss, you try anything like that with me, and you'll be scraped from the pavement. I've got friends who'd like to do me a favour. You know them, Joe. You know how long you'd last if I said one bloody word to them, don't you?'

Joe Patrick bit his lower lip. It was a throw-back to his boyhood when he was going to get a strapping from the orphanage principal.

'I'll go,' he said. 'And I'll be no trouble to ye. No trouble at all. Ye may change your mind. You may need me again. I don't hold no grudge. You've been fair with me.'

'Get out,' King said. 'And keep your mouth shut if you want to stay alive.' Then he turned back to the window again. He didn't hear Joe Patrick close the door.

Joe's firm of private detectives had lost Julia Hamilton when she went to Jersey. But islands were small places, places where gossip spread faster than a bushfire. While the London legmen wasted their time on the hotels and public venues, the fact that the well-known surgeon, David Peterson, had a famous Fleet Street journalist staying with him, was all over the island in a few hours. And the guests at Richard Watson's dinner party had been regaling their friends with stories about Julia Hamilton. King's own contact was a radio reporter on the local station. It was his business to pick up news items, local gossip however slight. For ten years he kept a watching brief for Harold King's publications with particular emphasis on a retired ICI executive called Richard Watson. He had reported direct to King. King had been prepared for Joe Patrick's lies. He knew where Hamilton had been. To see the man who saved the life of an eighteen-year-old German soldier in the

Western Desert, fifty years ago. She had found Watson, as he had done, through some unlucky chance. Because she hadn't dropped the investigation. Joe Patrick had been deliberately misled. And misled King in turn.

This was not a problem to be solved by a cheap killer like the Irishman, a rapist and murderer of an old woman alone in her house. This needed sophistication and brains to bring it to solution. He paused, thinking about Joe Patrick. The Irish were a treacherous and vengeful breed. He couldn't leave Patrick like a loose cannon with a grievance. Belt and braces, he said to himself. Patrick would have to go.

He'd deal with him later. He was due in New York at the end of the week. Gloria was flying out with him. He'd make the arrangements then, for that red-haired bitch.

And then he could deal William Western his death blow. And pay back the debt he had thought paid in full. Until ten years ago.

Gloria shifted against him. They had fallen asleep, exhausted, and when he woke he sent Gloria to the kitchen to make coffee. She had obeyed meekly. She liked being ordered about, waiting on him was part of their foreplay.

She said, 'Leo – what am I going to tell them?'

'I don't know,' he answered. 'What have you said before when you were out all night?'

'I never stayed away all night, I always came home.' She looked at him over the coffee cup. 'They never knew I'd been with anyone. I just said I was out with friends.'

He flicked her cheek with his finger. 'Girlfriends,' he mocked. 'But it's better with me, isn't it?'

'You know it is.' She lay back against the tumbled pillows. 'I always hated the idea of doing it with a man. But not with you. I love it with you. Daddy would kill me . . . '

'How about Mummy?'

'She wouldn't care,' Gloria said. 'She's dying to get rid of me, so she can have Daddy to herself. She'd love it if I had a boyfriend . . . or I got married and was out of the way. I never will,' she added.

Leo didn't say anything. Marriage. The thought had never occurred to him. All that money, all that power at his disposal. She liked to talk in a little-girl voice sometimes. She simpered at him. 'Shall I get you more coffee? Anything else you want?'

Leo said, 'I want you. Come here . . . '

'Darling,' Ben Harris said. 'We can't prove it's King.'

'Western can,' Julia insisted. 'I'm going to face him with it.'

'Now?' he asked her. She looked at him.

'Now,' she said. 'Are you coming with me, Ben? I don't understand why you're hesitating? I thought you'd be thrilled, over the moon . . . What's wrong? What is it?'

'Sit down for a minute,' he said. 'Look, of course I'm excited. You brought it off, you did a marvellous job. All your instincts were right. But, we've no proof!'

She stared at him. 'We have!' she exploded. 'And it's on the top floor of this building – I'm going upstairs and see him now!'

'If you do,' Ben said quietly, 'he'll take you off the job. Just as he did with me. And for the same reason.'

'He can't,' she retorted. 'You didn't know the truth. I do. He can't stop me now.'

'He can and he will. Exposing Harold King means exposing him. He'll never let it happen. You haven't thought this through,' he went on. 'Don't fool yourself. Western is no pussy cat. He'll protect himself by any means he can. Think of this – if you're right, then he knew King shot down those prisoners. Why didn't he say anything when you told him? Why did he lie and let you go on looking for proof when *he* was the proof . . . the only witness? J, for Christ's sake, there's something missing in the whole scenario. I don't know what it is, and you don't either. You can't run bull headed into a situation like this. Western was ready to stick a bayonet into an unarmed prisoner. You're going to face him with that. OK. And he knew what happened when he and the others were captured and separated from their officers. He said they were killed in crossfire and he was lucky to survive. So he covered up the whole bloody massacre. Why?'

'That's what I'm going to ask him,' Julia said angrily.

'Wait a minute. Let's take it step by step. We're *supposing* King came on Richard Watson, just like we did, when he was trying to find some dirt on Western, heard the same story and blackmailed him. So what's changed?' he asked her. 'Something has, or Western wouldn't be out to get Harold King now. He'd lie down and let him walk over him, take everything. But he decided to fight back. He brought you and me in on it. He's encouraged and backed us every inch of the way. Didn't he say he'd fire you if you didn't have a result and put King in the December issue of "Exposure"?'

'He's gambling,' Julia said. 'Gambling that I can pin the war crime on King without involving him. It's simple; he's got everything to lose to King and he's not going to let it happen.'

'And have King show him up? No, it doesn't add up.'

'Well,' Julia said and got to her feet. 'There's only one way to find out. And that's ask him. Which I'm going to do right now.'

'Lord Western is in Rio de Janeiro on business,' the secretary said, conveying disapproval of the way Miss Hamilton had marched into her office without an appointment.

'I am in contact with him every day, so perhaps you'd like me to give him a message?'

'No, no thanks,' Julia said. 'When is he due back?'

'I couldn't say. He didn't indicate a date to me. Before Christmas, I expect.' She favoured Julia with a condescending smile. 'I expect too,' Julia snapped and turned away.

Rio de Janeiro. No return date. She felt like bursting into tears. She hadn't realized how wrought up she had become. Fighting Ben Harris hadn't helped. The anticlimax, the frustration, just when she had put the last piece into the jigsaw puzzle . . . only Ben said she hadn't . . .

She went into her office, gave instructions that she wasn't taking any calls and tried to calm herself. Think it through. But she had, surely to God she'd got the answers at last. Harold King had murdered the British prisoners, in reprisal for Western's plan to kill him. Western had escaped, somehow, wounded, but not dead. Lied about it to cover his own conduct. Been discovered and blackmailed by the German who'd killed his companions. She raised her head suddenly. No. No, that wasn't right, that didn't hold up . . . She got up from her desk, began to pace the office. He wouldn't have feared exposure by the man who stood to be accused of cold-blooded murder . . . Neither one could risk a collision with the other if that was the scenario.

'Oh God,' she said aloud. 'God! Ben was right . . . there is something missing . . . But where do I look for it? Where do I start?'

'Don't lie to me, Gloria. Don't even try and lie to me.'

He wasn't shouting at her. He was so calm that she was wrong-footed and she stumbled over her explanation. 'You came in at six this morning,' King said. 'I was up and I heard you. I saw you sneaking up the stairs into your room. You were with that little creep, weren't you?' He came close to her and Gloria shrank back. He gripped her by the upper arm and put his strength into it. She cried out.

'Don't, Daddy. You're hurting me—'

'Tell me,' he said and squeezed harder. 'You spent the night with Leo Derwent, didn't you?'

She burst into tears of pain. 'Yes . . . Yes, I did.'

He let go of her. 'You slept with that creep?' he asked her. His voice hadn't been raised. Gloria clasped her arm and wept. 'Why shouldn't I? You have women—' He slapped her across the face.

'Sit down,' he commanded and she collapsed onto her bed. He watched her for a moment. He loved her; she was the only person in the world he cared about and she had betrayed him and lied to him. She heard him sigh heavily, and ventured to look at him.

'He's the first,' she mumbled. 'The first man . . . I like him. He likes me.'

King came and sat down beside her. She cringed a little and then he put his arm around her. 'Don't cry,' he said. 'I shouldn't have hit you.' Gloria melted; pain for him joined her pain for herself. 'I deserved it. I shouldn't have said that to you. I shouldn't have lied.'

'He's using you,' he said.

She stiffened. 'Don't say that! Don't say that to me. You think I'm ugly, nobody would ever want me . . . just because I'm not like my mother. And what is she? What is she to you, Daddy? All tits and no brains! That's what you say about women. I've heard you . . . Leo *does* like me and we get on together.'

She knew that her father was wrong about her and Leo. Maybe for the only time in his life, but he was wrong about Leo. She said in a very low voice, her head leaning against King's shoulder, 'Don't spoil this for me, Daddy. I'll always love you the best. But don't spoil this for me. Please?' King held her and didn't answer. Leo Derwent. Gloria wanted him. Shared his tastes in sex . . . He shied away from that. He couldn't contemplate it. He ran up a mental shutter on what his daughter did with a man like that.

'You're not ugly, sweetheart,' he said. 'You're my girl. We're doing everything together. We're going to New York. He's not *good* enough for you . . . He's a nothing. For Christ's sake, Gloria, you're my daughter. You could have any man you wanted!'

She said, 'I want to go to the States with you, Daddy, you know I do. How long will we be gone?'

He was too shrewd not to see the significance of that question. She had never queried the length of a trip before. 'About ten days,' he said. 'Then we go to Gstaad for Christmas.' He stood up. Her swollen tear-stained face reproached him. 'Come here and kiss me,' he said. 'We never fight. We're not going to fight now. Let's put this thing on ice, shall we? You see him if you want to.'

Her arms went up and clasped him tightly round the neck. 'Oh Daddy, thank you! He doesn't mean anything to me really . . . I hated deceiving you. I really hated it . . . '

But you did, he thought, embracing her. He meant that much to you. Again the unthinkable came to mind. Like to like. He swallowed bile at the idea.

'Go wash your face,' he said kindly. 'And have lunch with your old father today to show him he's forgiven.'

'I'd love to,' Gloria said, and kissed him warmly on the cheek. King went to his own room. His wife was at her dressing table, starting the long ritual of making-up for the day's engagements. She looked briefly at him. He'd left their room in a fury to confront his daughter. She thought she had heard Gloria cry out. 'Is she all right?'

'Yes. I talked with her. I got too heavy but it's OK now.'

'Did she say where she was?' she asked him. He glared at her. 'Leave it, Marilyn. We'll sort it out between us.' He went off to his dressing room. He'd sort it out. He wasn't having Gloria thrown away on any third-rate little ass licker like Leo Derwent. If she wanted that kind of sex, she could get it with someone in a bigger league. He realized, as he lowered himself into his steaming bath, that he had to accept that his daughter was a woman with her own sexual needs. His girl had grown up. But Leo Derwent wouldn't be difficult to send running. So long as Gloria didn't know he was responsible.

'They've gone to the States,' Leo said. He met Julia in his office at the House of Commons.

'For how long?'

'Ten days. Then they're taking off for Gstaad for Christmas.' He glanced at Julia. 'She wants me to fly out there so we can meet.'

'You have made an impression, haven't you?'

Julia disliked him so much she found it difficult to look him in the eye.

He was aware of her feelings and he wasn't bothered. 'Yes, I have,' he agreed. 'We're growing very close.' He grinned. 'Daddy's not been too pleased about it, but she's talked him round.'

Julia watched him sharply. Something was up, she could sense a smugness that made her uneasy. 'The purpose of the trip to New York?' she reminded him. She wasn't sitting there with him to listen to him boasting about his prowess with King's daughter. No doubt they made a lovely couple.

'To tie up the big financial deal. Then he fires the first shots at Western International when he gets back in January. She was very excited. She tells me everything. I don't even have to ask.'

'Did she tell you any details?'

'Oh, yes. First there'll be some well-placed rumours in the financial press. Rumours about Western and some pending financial crisis due to over-expansion in South America. He's got big interests over there, hasn't he? And he's bought a Portuguese-language publishing company with two newspapers in Brazil. All authentic stuff. But what won't be authentic will be the implications that he's mortgaged his UK interests to support the new ventures. And once that sort of thing starts, one or two bent journalists letting hints drop . . . there'll be a run on the shares. People are so panicky, so are the institutions. They were caught with their pants down by Maxwell, and they're not taking any chances. So King starts heavy buying. With the money he's got, Western won't be able to fight him off. So – ' He grinned his foxy grin at Julia. 'You'll be out of a job. Unless you can dig up this dirt you told me about and stop him in time. How's your end going?'

'We're very close,' she admitted.

His eyes gleamed. 'That bastard,' he said softly. 'The way he set me up. Any other way I can help?'

'Not unless you can get him drunk,' Julia said bitterly.

'He's teetotal, lifelong, everyone knows that,' Leo said. 'Why, why do you say that?'

'Because he got drunk once,' Julia answered. 'Everyone who knew what he said has died since. Except me,' she added.

He stared at her. 'You're not serious?'

'I'm very serious. I mentioned a criminal charge the first time we met, didn't I?'

He nodded.

'It's murder,' Julia said quietly. 'The murder of unarmed British prisoners in 1942 in the Western Desert. So you see what we're dealing with. I'd be a bit careful with that daughter if I were you. Get ready to back off. If he wasn't happy about you in the first place, he's not going to change his mind, whatever he tells her.'

'Thanks,' he said briefly. 'You shouldn't be giving me advice like that.'

'I've got enough on my conscience,' Julia told him. 'There isn't room for you.' She got up. 'I'd better go. You'll be seeing her when she gets back from the States?'

'The same evening,' Leo answered. 'I've planned a cosy reunion. If this is true . . . what you've said . . . shouldn't you have a minder?'

'He thinks I've given up,' she said. 'And my flat is as secure as Fort Knox. Don't worry about me.'

'I'll be in touch as soon as I've seen her.'

'I'll go then,' Julia said. On an impulse she started to walk towards St James's Park. It was a crisp winter afternoon, with a pre-Christmas buzz in the air. The shops were festive and people were walking with the purposeful stride of the shopper. Christmas. Her mother wanted her to come down and bring Ben with her. She couldn't think of Christmas. She couldn't think of presents and turkey and family gatherings while Harold King walked the earth as a free man. William Western was in Brazil. She was expected to launch the attack on King in December. She had the whole format in her mind. Every headline, every paragraph was already written and burned in her brain. But she could do nothing without the vital piece of evidence that identified Harold King as the German prisoner whose life had been saved by Richard Watson. And who had exacted a terrible revenge upon his former captors. The only man who could provide that proof was William Western. It was too cold to sit in the park by the lake so Julia walked towards Whitehall. The roofs and central turret of the old Palace gleamed through the frosty air above the line of trees, like some Oriental backdrop. There had been no record of a German massacre of prisoners in the annals of that Desert War. Not even a rumour circulating. Just the drunken confession of Hans Koenig to his wife, and the suspicions of a dead officer called Phillips who was unhappy about the fate of his men. William Western, the only survivor, wounded and repatriated, had insisted that they had been caught in crossfire during a skirmish between British and German patrols.

Julia paused by the splendid Guards memorial. The clock in the Palace across Horseguards chimed the hour. Three o'clock. It had a sweet if ghostly chime in the still air. Traffic heading up Birdcage Walk towards Parliament Square seemed strangely muted to her as she stood there. She looked at the massive bronze figures on the stone plinth. Dead men from both wars. Dead men in the desert sands. A dead woman, outraged in her bed and brutally beaten. Harold King with his neo-Nazi connections to protect him, controlling Western's media empire as well as his own, taking his seat in crimson and ermine in the House of Lords. She said it out loud. 'I don't care what Ben says. I'm going down to Hollowood and see Evelyn Western. Tonight.'

'Good to see you, Harry. You're looking well. How's business?'

'No complaints,' Harold King said. He spooned up pasta and muttered between mouthfuls. 'Mario, this is the best . . . Mmm . . . What a sauce . . . ' The New York garment manufacturer smiled in gratification at the compliment. 'My favourite restaurant. So good I bought a piece of it. Pity you don't drink wine, Harry. You miss out on a great Chianti.'

King said, 'My only regret. I don't have the stomach. I have all the other vices, so why should I be greedy?'

He looked at the man sitting opposite to him, napkin tucked into his collar, washing the rich Italian food down with draughts of red wine and sopping up the creamy sauce with hunks of bread. He was very fat, with a bulging belly and heavy chins. King had left Gloria to amuse herself that evening and asked his Mafia contact if they could share a meal together. And maybe a few problems.

They didn't talk about the problems till they had finished eating.

Over tiny cups of espresso, the host fortifying himself with a glass of oily strega, he asked Harold King about those problems.

'I've got media trouble,' King said. The coffee was so strong it made his heart race.

'What kind of media?' the Italian asked him. 'The media's

shit. They've been on my back this last year, so I know how it feels. What's the problem?'

'It's a smart-ass woman,' King said. 'Making a big name for herself. She's digging dirt on me, Mario. And she's good. I don't know where it might end up.' He left the mafioso to work out that conclusion for himself. Money had passed between them on its way from Colombia via the Cayman Islands and then to its destination in a Swiss account.

Drug money, with a sweet percentage from vice in New York City.

'In London?' he asked King.

'London,' King agreed. 'I need an outside contract.'

'So what happened to that Mick who worked for you? Can't he find someone?'

King said, 'This won't be an ordinary hit – she's big news. I can't trust a local to do it. I want a contract man that hits and is out of the country in a couple of hours. This bitch is well protected and she's got brains. If she's killed our media will go ape. Could you help out with someone?'

'You'd have to pay,' Mario said. He picked his teeth with one of the sharpened quills provided by the management. 'Prices are high if you want the best. How soon?'

King said, 'Sooner than soon. Now.'

'You want an accident, a sex crime, or just a straight hit?'

'I don't give a damn, just so long as she's dead,' he answered. 'Your man can choose. I don't want to know any details. And don't worry about money. I can match *any* price that's needed.'

The Italian leaned towards him and laid a fat, ringed hand on King's arm. 'You just give me the name and address, Harry. Then forget about it. OK? Leave it with me. Some more coffee?'

'I'll be getting back. My daughter's at the hotel. I'm grateful, Mario. You're a friend. And thanks for the dinner.'

'Next time,' the Italian raised his hand and a waiter came hurrying, 'next time, bring your little girl with you. We'll have a family party.'

* * *

'How was your evening?' King asked her.

Gloria smiled at him. 'It was fine. I read through that draft cost accounting and it's just as good as you said. You're so clever, Daddy. Just brilliant the way you make figures work out the way you want.'

'It's not so difficult, it's a trick, sweetheart,' he said. 'You'll learn it. Never be afraid of figures, get to know and love them and they'll be your friends.'

He laughed. He was in a good mood, ebullient and confident. Mario would solve his problem before it could become *his* problem, too. Everything was tied up, just the formalities to be gone through, like a big corporate dinner being given by Field Bank in his honour. He thought, I'll take Gloria to Tiffany's tomorrow. Buy her a memento. Something she can wear at the dinner. He looked at her fondly.

It might be his imagination, but she was looking more attractive. She took a lot of trouble with make-up, hair and clothes. There was a satisfied glow about her that made her seem more mature, as if an overgrown girl had developed into a confident woman. He didn't want to think of the reason.

He said, 'How would you like a necklace – something special? I want you to knock the eyes out of them all at the Field Bank dinner. I want them to know who you are and that one day they'll be dealing with you! Tiffany's tomorrow – shall we go there together?'

Gloria had spent half an hour on the telephone to Leo Derwent. She had arranged to pay for the call herself. There was no need to irritate her father. He was mean about private telephone calls.

'Daddy, that would be wonderful. But you don't have to buy me anything. I brought plenty of jewellery with me. You told me to, remember?' Then she added, unable to resist the dig at her old adversary, 'You'll have to buy something for Mummy, too, or she'll be jealous.'

'Not this time,' he said. 'I'm going to bed now. Good night, darling.'

She came and kissed him. 'Good night. Sleep well.'

She didn't go to bed for some time. She sat on in her

suite and thought about Leo Derwent. They had talked about what she was doing in New York; he was always so interested in the business side of her life and so encouraging. Just like one man to another.

She wanted to know about him, too, what was happening at his ministry, in the House. Most of that long call was devoted to a mutual résumé of their professional lives.

And then he changed the conversation. There was no smut, just innuendo, coded references to the relationship they shared. Hints of ecstasies in store when she returned. He had warned her fiercely once, when she began to say explicit things, that telephones could be bugged. It added spice to the hidden meanings to clothe them in words that couldn't be understood by an outsider. It heightened their mutual titillation.

She was so restless thinking of him that she flung herself into a bath to try and soothe the urges. Only another five days and she would be home and able to see him. I'm not in love, she told herself. I don't love him, I love Daddy. It's just that he makes me feel so good about myself. He knows how I feel and what I like. I never thought a man could get me going like he does. And I can drive him wild. The thought crept into her mind. We make a good team. And now Daddy's being nice about it . . . She drifted happily away.

Ben said, yes, put his daughter through, and as soon as he heard Lucy's voice he knew there was something wrong. She was crying as she spoke.

'I'm losing it . . . Daddy, I've been bleeding since ten o'clock this morning—'

Ben Harris interrupted. 'Are you in hospital? Lucy, for God's sake, where are you?'

'I'm at home,' she wept. 'I went to the surgery, and they said to go to bed and rest, and it'd probably stop. But it hasn't . . . it's getting worse, and I've got pains. I've just called again and they said my doctor's out on an emergency but one of the others will be here as soon as they can. Oh God, I'm so scared.'

'Have you called your mother?'

'She's away,' Lucy wailed. 'They've gone up to *his* mother

on the Borders. Dad, I don't know what to do . . . If I lose my baby . . . ' She burst into hysterical sobs.

Ben Harris forced himself to be calm. 'Lucy, Lucy darling, listen. Calm down, please. Get hold of yourself. Listen. I'll fly up there. Give me the doctor's number. If they send you to hospital, I'll go direct there. And don't worry, try not to . . . These things happen, it'll settle down, I promise you.'

'I've even felt it move,' she wept. 'Oh hurry up, won't you? Please hurry.'

'I'm on my way to the airport. I'll charter a plane if I have to. Hang on, and don't worry. I *know* you're going to be all right.' Then he slammed the phone down. He dialled Julia's direct line . . . No answer. The call was automatically transferred to her secretary.

'Miss Hamilton's gone home,' the girl said. 'She called through on her mobile to say she wouldn't be in till tomorrow morning. Can I get a message to her, Mr Harris?'

He looked at his watch. Nearly five. He had to get to Heathrow. If there wasn't a shuttle till late evening, then he'd charter . . . He couldn't waste any more time. 'Call through for me, and say I've had to go north, my daughter's been taken ill. I don't know when I'll get back. I'll contact her. Thanks, Jenny.'

A call to the internal airline established that there was a seven o'clock shuttle flight to Birmingham; he was lucky – there was a single seat available. Ten minutes later he was speeding out of London on the M4.

'My dear Julia,' Evelyn Western said firmly, 'I can't possibly see you this evening. I'm going out to dinner.'

'Then I'll wait till you get back,' Julia said. 'I'm on my way now.'

'I insist that you tell me why this is so urgent,' Evelyn said. 'I'm sure you wouldn't force yourself on me like this if William was here.'

'No,' Julia admitted. 'I wouldn't have to; Lady Western, I don't like behaving like this, but I haven't any choice. You asked me to help your husband. That's why I've got to see you and talk to you. I'll be there in the next hour.' She disconnected. Evelyn Western had tried being charming, and then coldly disapproving when the charm didn't work. If the door was slammed in her face, she'd sit outside and shame her into seeing her. But that wouldn't happen. Evelyn Western was a strong and determined woman who loved her husband and would do anything to protect him. She would see Julia and when Julia had finished, William Western would cut short his South American trip. She drove faster than usual; she felt exhilarated, strung up with the prospect of the battle to be fought and the truth at the end of it. Old lies, old cruelties had enmeshed her like a web. The time had come to tear the strands apart and free herself. She slowed at the turning to Hollowood and started down the long gravel drive to the entrance. She could see lights shining in front of the house through the trees.

Ben Harris caught the shuttle to Birmingham. A last-minute call on his mobile had established that Lucy was taken by ambulance to Reidhaven Hospital. The airport teemed with travellers; businessmen, families with children, the skiing contingent with their equipment, passengers from every part of the globe in transit, departing or arriving. The bars and cafés and duty-free shops were full, the lounges had their usual complement of exhausted sleepers curled up on the seats; babies cried, toddlers wandered off, and package tours assembled round their co-ordinators. Life rushed to and fro. Death came in on the Pan Am flight from New York, arriving at six forty-eight at Terminal 3.

He had sixteen murders to his credit. He was thirty-three years old, a married man with two young children. He lived at Queens in New York with his wife and his mother-in-law who was an invalid. He was a respectable businessman who travelled for a firm of software manufacturers. He lived modestly, and he had never had a criminal record. He had learned his skills from a Vietnam veteran when he was very young, and had been persuaded by his uncle to branch out in private business. He carried out his first contract on a debt defaulter in New Jersey, shooting him at point-blank range through the head as he got into his car to go to work. That murder earned him a retainer and led to other contracts. He was called Mike, because he had an Irish mother. He had been a good son, who stayed clear of trouble in a rough neighbourhood, did his schoolwork diligently, and went on to be a good husband and father. And kind to his wife's crippled mother. Killing made no impression on him. Taking a human life didn't excite him, or trouble his imagination afterwards. It was a job and it was very well paid, depending upon the complexity of the target and the risk involved. He could command the top price after the car bomb that killed a Head of Family in Los Angeles. Right outside his massively guarded house. Mike was a rich man with a long business-life ahead of him. He didn't drink or smoke, and he worked out three times a week to keep himself in top condition.

He had taken the job in London. The sex of his victim didn't concern him. Nor did the method he chose; details were left to his discretion unless otherwise specified. Some contracts had to be accidents, others the result of violent crime, robbery or sex murders. Some, like the target in Los Angeles, were plain executions, designed to scare off opposition. He had never lost an hour's sleep over what he did.

He had the name, address – private and business – and a description of the woman he was going to murder. How he did it had been left up to him. He preferred to choose his own method. It didn't tie him down. He liked exercising his own judgement and ingenuity. He prided himself on his professionalism. He took the Underground from the Airport and booked into a small hotel in the Bayswater Road. He had made several trips to London. He liked the city, and planned to bring his family over one year for a holiday. His two boys would love the changing of the Guard outside Buckingham Palace.

He had been given no contacts for this job. He always worked alone. He booked into the hotel, and went out to get something to eat. By Underground again to Sloane Square, and then on foot to the apartment block in Chelsea Green.

As he expected, it was a secure block, but to someone familiar with the fortress mentality of wealthy Americans, with closed-circuit TV, armed guards and trained dogs, it presented him with little problem. He walked the perimeter, noting the position of the outside fire-escape visible at the rear of the building. It was four storeys high. Her flat number indicated the top floor. That was no problem, either. He'd carried out a killing twenty-two floors up and walked out of the building unchallenged. He checked the entry system by pressing a number at random. They would have internal TV screens to monitor the caller at the front; he always wore a soft fedora type hat, the brim shaded his face.

A man's voice answered. 'Hello?'

Mike emphasized his Mid-West accent. 'Sam? It's me . . . Pete.'

The voice was sharp. 'There's no Sam here. You've got the wrong flat.'

'Sorry – shit, I buzzed the wrong bell. Sorry . . .' he said again, but the irritated man in the apartment didn't answer. Then he buzzed Julia Hamilton's number. There were no names, only numbers on the index beside the panel of buttons. He waited. No answer. He buzzed again. Nothing. She was out. He checked his watch. Nine forty. Not working that late. On a date, at a movie with the live-in boyfriend. His brief was one killing, not two. He'd have to wait till he could catch her alone. He went back to his hotel and watched TV for a couple of hours. He called his wife before he went to bed. He'd had a good flight, he said, he was missing her and the kids already, but he'd get her some of that English cashmere she liked and a souvenir for the boys.

'Love you,' he said. 'I'll be home in a couple of days, if I get the business done quick.' He fell asleep and didn't even dream.

Evelyn Western was watching by the library window as the headlights of Julia's car beamed up the drive. She had cancelled her dinner engagement with neighbours. She had put through a call to her husband in Rio de Janeiro as soon as Julia rang off. He had been in a meeting in the city centre. She left an urgent message and the hotel promised to contact him and get him to call her immediately. This was no ordinary visit by Julia Hamilton. Her attitude was forceful, even aggressive, and Evelyn was instantly on her guard. Whatever she had discovered, it must be to Billy's disadvantage. There was no friendliness, let alone her customary deference to a much older woman who was her employer's wife. Then, to her relief, the call came through from Brazil. She didn't waste time.

'I've had Julia on the line,' she said. 'She's got hold of something. I'm afraid it doesn't sound good. She's insisted on coming here, I couldn't stop her. Darling, I'm *not* being alarmist. If it's what I think, you'd better be ready to fly back. Yes, yes of course I'll call you when she's gone. All right, don't worry. I'll cope. Take care of yourself . . . ' *I'll cope*. Her own promise mocked her.

She had always coped, ever since they were married and living on her meagre earnings as a librarian, while William started out in business. She had coped with his struggles, his adversities and his success. She was his rock, his closest ally. And his lover. That had not died in all the years they'd been together. They were indivisible. That girl was coming down with some revelation that could damage William. Yes, Evelyn Western decided, mustering her courage and her will, I'll cope. As she saw the car lights sweep to the front of the house, she stepped back from the window. She rang for the Filipino.

'Miss Hamilton has just arrived,' she said. 'Show her straight in here, please, and don't worry about offering drinks, we'll help ourselves. I don't want to be disturbed. Thank you, Felipe. No,' she added in answer, 'she won't be staying the night. So far as I know.' She was placed strategically in the big armchair reserved for William Western. The light was behind her, turning the soft white hair into a silver halo. She got up slowly and came towards Julia. She seemed taller than ever.

'Come and sit down, Julia,' she said quietly. 'You sounded so agitated on the telephone you quite alarmed me. I'm sure you'd like a drink . . . Sherry?'

'No thank you, Lady Western.' Julia sat on the sofa facing her. She sensed the cool antagonism and it distressed her. She liked, and admired, the older woman and she had trusted her, in spite of Ben's reservations. The message about his daughter was on the answerphone when she went back briefly to her flat. Poor Ben. Poor girl. Then she banished everything out of her mind but what had to be said to Evelyn Western. I won't be put off, she insisted, watching Evelyn take her seat again and carefully arrange her long skirt as she prepared for a tiresome and unnecessary intrusion into her evening. Jean Adams died because of the job they gave me. I'm not going to pull any punches.

'I cancelled my dinner engagement,' the cool voice said. 'It was very awkward for me. I had to make up a story. I hate telling lies and letting people down.'

'I'm sorry,' Julia said. 'But it just can't wait.'

'What can't wait? You said it concerned my husband. Surely it's not so earth shattering it couldn't wait until tomorrow?'

The sarcasm suddenly infuriated Julia. She blushed with anger. 'Lady Western,' she kept her voice level, 'at the beginning of this year I came down here at your husband's invitation and he offered me an assignment. My own feature. "Exposure". It was a top job, the chance of a lifetime to get to the top of my profession. You were in the room, we opened champagne together. I'm sure you remember.'

Evelyn Western nodded. 'I do. I remember it very well.'

'But the bottom line on that job offer, and the editorship to follow – he even threw that in – was to expose Harold King and bring him down.'

'Yes,' the voice was calm. 'Yes, that's absolutely right.'

'So I took it on,' Julia said. 'I persuaded Ben Harris to join me and we started to investigate together. Because of what we discovered, a woman called Jean Adams was murdered.'

'I remember. William told me about it.' The beautiful blue eyes were cold and blank as they considered Julia.

'Did he tell you what happened to her and why?' Julia asked slowly. 'She was an elderly widow, living alone. She was also the niece of King's first wife. King confessed to shooting British prisoners of war; he told his wife when he was blind drunk, and he tried to murder her afterwards. But she'd already told

Jean Adams. Perhaps you don't know all this? Perhaps Lord Western didn't bother you with details?'

Evelyn Western didn't answer. She sat absolutely still with her hands clasped in her lap. Julia went on. She was standing now, moving in agitation in that silent room with the silent woman sitting in her big chair, watching her.

'We found Jean Adams and we persuaded her to give an affidavit. We didn't know it, but we were being tagged and her phone was tapped. The night before she was due to sign that document, an intruder broke into her house. He raped her, Lady Western . . . she must have been close on seventy, then he beat her to death. He stole a few things to make it look like robbery.'

'How dreadful,' Evelyn Western said. 'I didn't know that.'

'Well, your husband did. You asked me out to lunch and said you quite understood if I wanted to back out after what had happened to that poor woman. Your very words, weren't they?'

'If you say so. Yes, I did say that. I didn't want to pressure you.'

'Oh please,' Julia gestured in dismissal. 'Please stop trying to make a fool of me. You pleaded with me to save Western International and not give up on Harold King. The irony is, you didn't need to soften me up. I have to live with what happened to Jean Adams and the only way I can do it is bring King into the dock. I've just come back from Jersey. I went there to see Richard Watson.'

There was no movement, no betrayal, just a tightening of the slim hands in Evelyn Western's lap.

'Watson told me the story of the young German your husband wanted to bayonet in cold blood. That's what King discovered and blackmailed him with ten years ago . . . just when he was coming up for a peerage. It would have ruined him. So he backed off. He told Ben Harris to drop his investigation because he didn't want the world to know he was no better than a murderer himself.'

Suddenly Evelyn Western rose to her feet. 'Don't you dare say that! Don't you dare accuse my husband!'

'That German was Harold King,' Julia went on. 'He went berserk and shot those poor devils because he knew your bloody husband had been going to murder him . . . Jean Adams died for nothing because your husband was *there* . . . he knew what had happened. He just hoped I'd prove it without getting him involved. You should have bought off Richard Watson. I bet you tried . . . ' She stopped; she realized she was trembling. 'I should be saying this to him instead of you. But he's in Brazil building up his empire.'

Slowly, Evelyn Western turned away from her. She moved to a drinks table the other side of the room. She poured a small measure of brandy. She came back, sipped it, and looked at Julia with her vivid blue eyes.

'You fool,' she said. 'Full of righteous indignation. Setting yourself up as judge and jury, and finding William guilty. Now you listen to me. You're right about the blackmail. King contacted Watson . . . that miserable man . . . God knows how, but he did. He had a tape of Watson's story. Watson's version, making himself out such a hero. I even sent someone to see him, but it was useless. He was so high principled, you see. If a newspaper broke that story he felt honour bound to corroborate it and destroy my husband. So King escaped, and went from strength to strength till he's now in the position to drive us into the ground and take everything. You've been very clever, Julia, and so far you've got it right. Except that the German taken prisoner was *not* Harold King. He was a garage mechanic living in Strasbourg. He died of a heart attack last year.'

She finished her drink. 'You were so anxious to accuse William, weren't you? If he knew King was guilty of shooting prisoners he would have been able to destroy him without help from you! So much for your theory.' She sat down again, crossed one leg over the other and examined her foot in its black patent slipper. 'Of course we have proof of the mechanic's identity and a signed affidavit that he was the soldier taken prisoner at the time and date stated. He denied any suggestion that William was prepared to kill him. I'm sure my husband will let you have sight of it.'

'I believe Richard Watson,' Julia said slowly. 'I'm sorry,

but I do. Your husband gambled with other people's lives and held back a piece of vital evidence to protect his own reputation. Nothing alters that. The other officer with Watson was convinced there'd been an atrocity. But he's dead, too. Like your mechanic.'

'You can believe what you like,' Evelyn Western said. 'You stand there, making judgements. What do you know about war? How dare you presume to judge . . . you weren't even born! William was right. Captain Phillips was right. Their first duty was to their men, to get them back to their own lines and out of a bloody running battle. Watson had his precious principles but they cost the lives of all those men because that German was left alive. He did exactly what they said he would. He told his patrol where to find them. Nobody murdered the prisoners. They were caught in crossfire when a British armoured car opened up on the column. William was so badly wounded – shot three times in the back. They repatriated him because he was likely to be paralysed.' She looked at Julia. 'I trusted you,' she said. 'So did William. Now I'd like you to go, please. Just go.' She turned her head away.

'I'm going,' Julia said quietly. 'But I'm not giving up. From now on, I'm working for myself. Good night, Lady Western.'

WPC Mandy Kent was going off duty. She and her husband planned to have supper with friends and go down to the pub for a karaoke evening afterwards. Her husband had a nice voice and he wasn't shy about getting up in public. Mandy would have died with embarrassment, but she was rather proud of Dave when he performed.

'Mandy?' She turned; her sergeant was bearing down on her.

'I'm just off,' she said defensively.

'DCI wants to see you. Won't take a minute.'

'Oh shit,' she said, not quite under her breath. It must be trouble. She couldn't think where she'd slipped up.

'Don't worry, it's a pat on the back.'

She looked up in surprise. 'You're joking?' The sergeant grinned at her. She was popular with her colleagues. A good policewoman who didn't trade on her sex or try to be butch to prove a point. She came into the DCI's office. 'Sir? You wanted to see me?'

'Yes. Sit down, will you.' He looked down, referring to something on his desk. Then he said, 'Couple of weeks ago you were involved in an assault, hospital case, a girl called Tracey Mervyn. She wouldn't press charges, and the friend wouldn't either. Usual story. The boyfriend had beaten her up.'

Mandy said, 'Yes, sir, I remember. It was a vicious assault. They were two prostitutes, coloured girls, well known in our area. I made one more effort to talk them into making charges, but it was no good. Anything happened?' Maybe the bastard had found them, or even worse, the silly cow had gone back and he'd done her over again. It often happened.

'You sent a bracelet into Stolen Property on the off chance, didn't you?'

She nodded, remembering the odd name the hospital sister had given it. 'Yes sir. The stones spelt out DEAREST. It's popular for anniversaries, stuff like that.'

'Well, for your information, it spells out murder,' he said. 'Our computer picked it up. An identical bracelet was listed among the jewellery stolen from a woman in Midhurst who was raped and beaten to death by the intruder. It's been positively identified by the local jeweller who made it specially to order. That was smart thinking on your part. I'll pass that on to the right quarters.'

'Thank you, sir. If I can do anything more . . . '

He shook his head. 'It's out of our hands,' he said. 'It's CID's baby now.'

Evelyn Western sat up waiting for the call from Rio de Janeiro. He was in the middle of delicate negotiations with a Brazilian bank. Western had decided to finance a fight back and the best way of doing that was to issue shares in the new Brazilian publishing and newspaper companies that he had just acquired. He could raise cash, and cash was what he would need as soon as King began his frontal assault on Western International. Evelyn felt very tired as she waited. Emotional scenes exhausted her; she hated Julia Hamilton for what she had said and done. She felt her age and she couldn't afford to when William was threatened and needed her. She had weighed up the situation and decided that he mustn't interrupt what he was doing. She had faced out that damned girl and the next move would have to come from her. She was sure it would be a letter resigning. She thought of her parting words, *I'm not giving up. From now on, I'm working for myself* . . . Not easy without the resources of her job. She might reflect upon that threat and see just how impossible it would be . . . But she was proud and determined. The qualities Evelyn and William had both admired in Julia made her a dangerous maverick, capable of pulling the roof down in her pursuit of what she deemed to be justice and truth. She started when the telephone rang. She must have dozed in the big chair. She heard his voice and said quickly, 'It's all right, Billy. I've seen her. Yes, I was right; she came out with that bloody man Watson's story . . . It was very unpleasant but I didn't let her get away with anything . . . She had some crazy idea that King was the German prisoner and you knew he'd murdered your men . . . Darling, please . . . I told her the truth and gave her a piece of my mind at the same time. There's no need for you to come home, I was just panicking when I said that . . . No, absolutely not. I was so angry, so furious at her attitude. No, I'm not upsetting myself, I feel better already because I've said it. How's it going out there? Oh good, good . . . that's what's important. Yes, I will, I'll go to bed now. Don't fuss about me, Billy. I'm a tough old bird . . . I'll call you tomorrow if there's any more news. And, whatever happens, I think it's time we stood our ground and stopped that Watson telling lies about you once and for all . . . Yes, darling, good night . . . '

William Western heard the line clear. He had left the meeting and made his call in a private office. Don't come home, his wife insisted. He knew her tenacity and her courage; he also knew that she was too old to suffer sleepless nights and emotional turmoil. He thought of Julia Hamilton. His temper boiled over suddenly. 'Bitch . . . ' he snarled it aloud. Bullying Evelyn . . . He knew her home telephone number; he had a photographic memory for figures and never needed an address book. He asked the switchboard to put the call in and said he'd wait. He grabbed the phone at the first buzz. He heard Julia's voice, sleepy since it was the middle of the night, say, 'Hello? Ben?'

'It's Western,' he shouted. 'I've just spoken to my wife. You're fired, Hamilton, and you can tell Ben Harris he's fired too. You give in your keys and your car first thing tomorrow morning. You be out of that office by ten o'clock!'

'I will be,' Julia said. 'But don't think that's going to stop me, or shut me up.'

His line went clear.

Ben Harris sat by the bed and held his daughter's hand. He thought how very young and vulnerable she looked; her face was white and drawn, with deep shadows under the eyes. The nurse had briefed him before he went in.

'I'm afraid she's lost the baby,' she said. 'At this stage in the pregnancy it's very traumatic. She's been sedated but she's not asleep. She'll be so glad you've come.'

Ben came to the bed and said softly, 'Lucy? Lucy, it's Dad . . . '

She opened her eyes and tried to smile at him. A hand came out and he took it quickly. Tears seeped down her face.

'I lost him,' she whispered. *Him.* It struck Ben like a blow. 'It was a little boy. They didn't want to tell me, but I had to know. Oh, Daddy . . . '

There was nothing he could say to comfort her. Instinct warned that this was no time to take refuge in male reticence. He cradled her in his arms as she wept, and kissed her. 'Let it out,' he said. 'Grieve, darling . . . Cry all you want . . . I'm here and I'm staying.'

At last she fell asleep, exhausted, dulled by the sedative. He sat on, holding her hand. The ward sister came and beckoned him away. He followed her unwillingly.

'It's better you leave her to sleep now, Mr Harris,' she said. 'Get some sleep yourself. We'll see to the disposal of the foetus, there's nothing to worry about.'

'Disposal?' Ben squared up to her. 'What's that supposed to mean . . .?'

'It needn't concern you,' her tone was soothing. 'We have facilities here. It's less distressing for the mother.'

'My daughter knows it was a boy,' he said. 'It's not a still-born puppy, it's her child and my grandson. You do nothing, Sister, you understand me. The baby's going to be buried properly. I know that's what Lucy would want. And I'll make the arrangements, thank you.'

He swung away from her and walked towards the lift. He felt a sense of grief and loss, coupled with outrage at what might have happened. Lucy would need a focus for her grief, not a heap of ash in a hospital incinerator. Five months of expectation, of hope and joy, had ended that night in pain and disappointment, leaving a terrible vacuum.

She'd need time to recuperate and come to terms. Time to realize that life went on, and that her very youth was her strength. He would make certain she had that time. He had booked into a hotel near the hospital. He felt drained and sick and he needed Julia badly. It was late, past mid-night, but he dialled her number.

There was no reply. She must have gone out with a friend. He'd leave it till the morning. He woke very early; his first call was to the hospital. Yes, his daughter was sleeping, she had passed a quiet night. There were no complications, but the doctor would be in to see her later that morning. 'I'll be there,' Ben said, and hung up.

When he called Julia it was the time they normally had breakfast before leaving for the office. She answered so quickly he knew she was waiting for his call.

'Ben . . .? Oh Ben, what's happened?'

'She lost the baby,' he said.

'Oh darling, I'm so sorry . . . Is she all right?'

'She's fine,' he said. 'Physically. But the worst is ahead of her. It was a boy.'

'I'm so sorry,' Julia said again. 'Where are you? Can I send her some flowers?'

'No, I don't think so. I want to get her out of hospital as soon as possible. Darling, I may have to stay with her for a few days, see what she wants to do. Her mother's away, and I don't want Lucy staying on her own after this. I may bring her down with me. I'll let the office know.'

'Don't worry,' Julia took a quick decision. This was no time to tell him the bad news. He sounded so low. 'Don't worry. I'll do it for you. I'll ring tonight, what's the best time?'

'Around eight, I think. She might even be discharged today, I don't know. But try me here at eight. Thanks, darling. I just wish you were here with me . . . No, I didn't mean that, you know what I mean . . . How are you?'

'Missing you,' Julia evaded any question about their last disagreement.

'You didn't go and see Western did you?'

'No,' she said. 'He's in Brazil.'

'Good. Do nothing till I get back. I love you.'

Julia said gently, 'I love you too. I'll talk to you this evening.'

He was outside the apartment block when she came out. He was standing with a street map open in his hands, studying, and watching the entrance. The description had been accurate, even without the photograph, copied from the inset picture that appeared in the newspaper under her byline. Red hair, real fiery colour, medium height, good figure, legs, pretty face. Tense expression, purposeful way of walking. Black BMW on residents' parking space. He took a note of the car registration number and jotted it down on his street map. She unlocked it, got in, drove off. He checked his watch. Then he crammed the map into his pocket and set out to find a cab and take a look at her office. He needed all possible venues checked out and weighed up, before he decided where to hit her. On balance the apartment block looked the best, he liked the outside fire-escape as a way out afterwards, but an underground car park at her office might be a better option. He had done several jobs in that kind of environment. He dismissed the cab and took out the map again as he studied the entrance to the big glass-and-aluminium building. Outside lifts were a pain. He glanced up at the ant-like figures speeding up the walls of the building. He came to the entrance and the doors hissed back automatically.

A security guard approached him. 'I'm looking for the car park,' he said.

'Left and round the corner, you'll see a sign. Can I help?'

Mike grinned disarmingly at the suspicious look. He knew the type. Ex cops, ex Army, dick-heads in uniform. 'No thanks,' he said. He walked out without any explanation.

The car park was on two floors with an underground area. There was a man in a cubicle behind an automatic barrier. As he waited, map in hand again, on the opposite side of the street, two cars came in, halted, pushed a card into the machine beside the cubicle, and the barrier lifted. He noticed that the man, also in uniform, leaned out and scrutinized the drivers and saluted them as they drove past him. He didn't like the idea of the garage. It was impossible to slip in from the street, and although there would be an internal entrance in the building, a stranger wouldn't get past the security guard at the entrance without some identification. He wasn't in the business of being recognized by anyone. He gave up on the office. He hailed another cab – he never hired a car on a job, that left traces like licence and insurance certificates, phoney or not, he avoided paper. He spent the rest of the day shopping for his wife's cashmere sweater, bought two because the rate for the dollar was so favourable, and spent a couple of hours choosing toys for his sons in the toy department at Harrods. At five o'clock he called Julia's number from a public call-box. No answer. He called again at six. Nothing. He called on the hour until 11 p.m. without success. He gave up. She was not home, and his one chance of gaining entry diminished the later at night it became. Tomorrow he would go through the routine again.

'Sorry to burst in on you like this,' Julia said. 'But I just needed to come home and talk to someone.'

'We're so glad you did,' her father said. 'After all, what are families for?'

'Not all families,' Julia said. 'I'm lucky.'

'But why?' May Hamilton asked. 'Why did he sack you? And fancy having to clear your desk and give the car up, just like that, in one morning!'

'In one hour,' Julia corrected. 'I'll be going back to discuss the termination of my contract, of course . . . They'll have to pay me off because there's no reason for my dismissal. But it was quite an experience. My staff didn't know what had hit them. Jenny, my secretary, burst into tears. I was very moved.'

'I thought they only behaved like that in America,' her mother exclaimed angrily.

'Not any more,' Hugh Hamilton said. 'It's another of their customs we've adopted. Disgusting way to treat people. You stick out for a damned good payout, Juliette. If you need a good lawyer, I'll ask around.'

Julia said gently, 'Don't worry, Daddy. I know lawyers if I need one.'

'You could sue,' her mother suggested. She was up in arms over the way her daughter had been dismissed. She had a fiery sense of injustice; Julia didn't realize how much of her own sense of fairness she owed to her mother.

'Mum, I'm not getting into all that hassle. Western won't cheat me, he'll pay proper severance money and that'll be the end of it. Now, why don't we have a cup of tea? I've talked it all out, and now I want to hear about what you've been doing.'

She hadn't explained the real reason to them; it was too complicated. A policy disagreement was the reason she gave for losing her job. They seemed to accept that. Neither of them had any experience of high-powered journalism and the despotism of the great Press lords. Luckily for them, Julia thought. And Ben has to be told some time. Maybe tonight, if his daughter's out of hospital. He doesn't have to hurry back. They can clear his bloody desk and send his things round to the flat . . . typical Western to punish him as well. But he needn't sleep easy because he's got rid of me. I meant every word I said. I'll show the world what Harold King really is, and now I don't have to protect William Chancellor Western or cover up for him.

* * *

'They want you to go round ahead of them and soften the toms up. They know you, it might help.'

Mandy Kent said, yes, both girls did know her, but she didn't hold out much hope they'd be co-operative. She'd go and catch them at home half an hour before the CID arrived. They were staying with another girl and her boyfriend in Brixton Road. It was a heavily coloured area and they felt safer there. Mandy changed out of uniform; it made her less threatening. Tracey, with her broken jaw and multiple injuries from that beating, and Tina her friend, were the only witnesses who could tie in their ex-boyfriend with that bracelet.

She found the place on the busy Brixton Road, a run-down wreck of a mid-Victorian house, cracked walls, windows on the ground floor boarded up, a few curtains hanging drunkenly on the first-floor windows. There was no bell, only an old-fashioned cast-iron knocker. Mandy banged on the front door, and after a long wait and a second series of knocks, a young woman with a baby on her hip opened the door. Mandy said in a friendly way, 'I've come to see Tina and Tracey – are they in, love?'

'Upstairs, dear,' the girl said. The baby smiled enchantingly at Mandy who smiled back and touched the smooth fat cheek.

'Sweet kid,' she said. 'How old?'

'Fourteen months. Always laughin' . . . never cries.' The girl had a West Indian lilt in her voice. 'First floor,' she told Mandy, and stood aside to let her pass.

The bruising and swelling had gone down on Tracey's face. Her jaw was mending, but still painful. She looked haggard and miserable. Tina was always the stronger personality of the two; she had more self-confidence.

'I thought I'd drop in and see how you were getting on,' Mandy said. Both girls were expressionless.

'Taken up social work, then?' Tina asked.

Mandy didn't rise. 'No. Just a routine follow up. In my own time. How's it going, Tracey?'

'All right,' it was a mumble. 'I'm mending.'

'That bastard know where you are?'

'No,' Tina answered. 'And he's not going to find out. Soon as she gets the nod from the doctor we're going up to Liverpool. My friend's got a friend there.' She looked at the policewoman with suspicion. 'What do you want? And don't give me any "friendly" crap. You're a copper. So why are you bothering us?' She stood with both hands on her hips. She wasn't afraid of the cow. She and Tracey were both clean. No men, no drugs, nothing since it happened. She glared at the symbol of white authority. People like her had been pushing her around since she was a skinny teenager, put into care because she was working the pubs for a few quid to feed and clothe herself after both parents walked out and disappeared, taking her little brother and leaving her behind. Mandy didn't answer. Or react. Then she opened her bag and took out a packet of cigarettes.

'Mind if I light up? Want one?' She proffered the packet.

'No,' Tina snapped. 'Why don't you just leave us alone?'

Mandy Kent made a police decision. Nothing would be gained by being nice. No hearts and minds to be won with either of them.

'Because I can't,' she said. 'There're other police officers on their way here. They want to ask you some questions. Serious questions. You won't talk back to them, Tina. Or you'll find yourself down at the station in real trouble.'

Dealing with criminals for the last ten years had hardened Mandy Kent. It had made her the match for any of them when it came to being tough. Tina's dark skin paled. The girl, Tracey, made a frightened sound.

'What trouble?' Tina wasn't cowed yet. 'We've done nothing, we're not in any trouble.'

Mandy Kent said, 'That bracelet, the one that caused the row and got you both beaten up . . . It was stolen. Did you know that?'

'No,' Tina sat down suddenly. Theft. They could hang anything they liked on her. She didn't know where it came from, only that Joe gave it to her.

'It was a present. He gave it to me. I told you.'

'I know you did,' Mandy agreed. 'We ran the description through on a computer and it came up. Stolen property. Part of a robbery in Midhurst. And you didn't know?'

She saw Tracey turn in anguish and Tina got up and slipped an arm round her protectively. She had suspected, and she was sure now, that in their own time, the girls were lovers.

'We knew nothing,' Tina said fiercely, thinking of Tracey, not herself. 'He just gave it to me one day. Said, "Here's a present for you." I'd given him a good time the night before. We both had. He was feeling really generous . . . We never stole anything.'

'If you didn't,' Mandy suggested, 'maybe he did?'

Tina's scorn was genuine. 'Him? Steal a crappy thing like that? He was in the money . . . big money. He didn't need to thieve.'

'Well, he got it from somewhere, didn't he?'

Tina shrugged, still holding on to her friend. 'Must have. Look, what's this all about? You're trying to scare us—'

'I'm not,' the answer was very calmly spoken, and the look was hard. Tina had seen its kind before and she bit back an insult. 'You wouldn't give evidence against this man Joe Patrick, would you? You let him half kill your girlfriend but you were too chicken to charge him. Not that I blame you. You were right to be scared, Tina. Shit scared of what he'd do to you. But if you and Tracey want to get back at him and be in the clear yourselves, now's your chance.'

Tina sneered. 'On thieving a bracelet . . .?'

'On thieving a bracelet,' Mandy agreed. 'A bracelet that belonged to a sixty-eight-year-old widow who was burgled, raped and beaten to death.' She pushed back her coat sleeve and checked her watch. 'It's murder, Tina. The CID will be here any minute. I hope you two have good memories. They'll be asking you a lot of questions.'

She got up and turned her back on them. She drew back the flimsy curtain on its sagging wire and looked down into the street below. The squad car came into view, its blue light flashing, the thin wail of the siren came through the badly warped window frame. Joe Patrick. They'd learnt a lot about him since that first check – a one-time pimp, a petty crook who had gone on to bigger and better things in the criminal world, posing as a businessman. But, elusive as an eel, never convicted for lack of evidence. He might live to regret losing his temper with his girlfriends. But she had done her part. The rest was the responsibility of the Murder Squad. She turned back to them. The girls were sitting side by side, staring at her. They could hear the loud rattle of the iron door knocker from below.

'I'll be off now,' she said, and walked out of the door as the first steps echoed on the bare stairs up to the landing.

'You can't stay here on your own,' Ben insisted. His daughter looked up at him. She was pale and hollow eyed, but in control.

'Biddy's here,' she said. 'She'll look after me.' The student she shared with had been kind and anxious to help, but she couldn't stay away from her classes to keep Lucy company.

'I know,' Ben agreed gently. 'And she's a sweet kid, but she can't be here in the day. Listen, Lucy, you're going to feel shaky for a week or so. The impact hasn't sunk in yet. You're still in shock. Let me take care of you. Just for a little while. Please.'

She had made a good recovery, and the medical staff felt she would benefit from living in her own environment. The sad little funeral was over, and Ben refused to go down to London and leave her to grief and loneliness. Her mother had been contacted; Ben felt she was secretly relieved at the resolution of Lucy's problem, but he didn't say so. His ex-wife was openly relieved when he assured her that it wasn't necessary to interrupt her stay with her parents-in-law. He would remain with Lucy and look after her. He had spoken to her husband for the first time.

His mother was in her eighties, and far from well . . . He didn't really feel they ought to hurry back if he, Ben, was coping with the situation. He was very sorry to hear what had happened, of course, and please give his best to Lucy. Thank God she was all right, that was the main thing . . .

It's my responsibility, Ben decided, and prepared to do tactful battle with his daughter for her own good. He'd let that responsibility slip all those years ago when he made the job his first priority. He was not going to fail his child a second time.

Julia was out of London, taking time off to be with her parents in Surrey. He didn't have to worry about her, and it eased his mind to think of her staying with them. She had sounded unworried about being away from the office; it was out of character but he didn't question it. She knew what she was doing; he had never tried to direct her life except when he felt she was in danger, and it had the opposite effect. And he was relieved she wasn't on her own. He didn't feel pressured. He didn't have to hurry Lucy into going back with him. Speaking to Julia he poured out his anxieties for his daughter, and even admitted to a pang of personal grief for the stillborn child. So Julia didn't burden him with the news that they were both out of a job. That could wait. He needed time to sort out his personal difficulties, and, she realized, expunge a sense of guilt for that marriage break-up all those years ago. She realized it made her love him even more.

'Darling,' she told him, 'Lucy can stay with us. We've an extra bedroom, and we might even take her away for a few days. Do you good as well.' And when he protested that he actually had to go back to the office before too long, she said disarmingly that he could worry about that when he was back in London.

'All right, Dad.' Lucy had surprised him by giving in sooner than he expected. 'All right, I'll come south with you. I can't stand seeing you doing the cooking and washing-up another minute . . . ' She'd managed a smile at him when she said it. 'If you're sure there's room . . . and your girlfriend doesn't mind. I don't want to get in your space—'

'She wants you,' he said firmly. 'She's been asking to meet you for God knows how long. And you'll like each other. I guarantee it. How about we go tomorrow?'

'Day after?' Lucy asked him. 'I want to sort things out and get myself organized. I want to go and see my Principal and make sure they'll keep my place open.'

'Day after tomorrow would be fine,' Ben said. 'I'll ring Julia tonight and tell her. Thanks, sweetheart. I would have missed you like crazy . . . '

'I must go home,' Julia said. 'I've been dodging the issue long enough. It's been lovely unburdening everything but it's really time to go and sort myself out. And see a lawyer. Before I go and talk to my ex-employer's contract department.'

'You do that, darling,' May Hamilton said. 'Don't you let them cheat you out of a penny that's due to you!'

Julia laughed. 'Don't worry, Mum. I'm not your daughter for nothing. I won't! And thanks for being so supportive. You and Dad have been angels.'

'Nonsense,' both parents insisted. 'And you and Ben are coming for Christmas, don't forget. And if his daughter's still with you, bring her too. We'd love it.'

Julia drove back to London in a glow of gratitude and thankfulness for both of them

When her telephone rang at six o'clock, she put down the ginger cat who had dug herself into her lap, delighted to have company, and rushed to answer. It might be Ben . . .

'Hello, Julia Hamilton . . . ' It buzzed in her ear before the words were out. Wrong number or misdial, she thought, and picked up Pussy who was sulking at having been put down. The porter had fed her daily as instructed, but she missed her human friends and relieved her feelings by scratching vigorously at the upholstered sofa.

She lifted her back on to her lap and stroked the silky fur. Funny how fond she had grown of Ben's cat. It gave her a feeling of calm and domesticity to fuss over her. Dogs were her parents' passion, but they lived in the country. London flats were no places for dogs. Maybe one day, if she and Ben moved . . .

She caught herself in surprise. Jumping the gun, as her father would say. Going far into the future. It wasn't like her to think impractically. Three days removed from the mainstream in sleepy Surrey and she'd gone soft. It made her smile. Those musings were for much later in her life. When she had finished what she had set out to do. *Harold King*.

No doubt Evelyn Western was telling the truth. There *was* an affidavit signed by a dead German mechanic exonerating William Western of the intention to murder an unarmed prisoner . . . Whether it was genuine was something else. But who was to disprove it? Very clever, she thought bitterly. They'd got a fail-safe, by bribery or God knew how. Then why hadn't they felt secure enough to see off King's first blackmail and shut Richard Watson's mouth? She sat up sharply.

Of course they couldn't, because the stooge in Strasbourg was still alive! Western couldn't risk a confrontation or have his witness brought into court. Now, with its signatory beyond cross-examination, that affidavit would hold up in court. Harold King was going for the jugular, and William Western had weighed the risk and decided to strike first. He'd fired her in a fit of fury, frustrated that she had opened the closet on his skeleton and failed to incriminate King. Maybe he regretted it. But she didn't. She had been careful with her salary; she had enough saved to go ahead alone.

And to look after Ben if he'd been less provident. There'd be offers pouring in for both of them. They could name their price anywhere in the media world. That was no cause for worry.

The telephone shrilled again. 'Julia? Hi, it's me, Felix.'

'Felix? Well, hello. How are you?' She hadn't thought of him for so long, his voice was quite a shock. Antagonism rose in her; the same cocky, casual tones grated on her, reminding her of a relationship that shamed and irritated her.

'I'm fine. I've been trying to get you for a couple of days, but you forgot to switch on your machine.'

'I didn't forget,' she said tersely. 'It's an invitation to break in if you're away. I was staying with my parents.'

'Good on you,' he chuckled down the line. 'You weren't the loving daughter when I knew you.'

'What do you want?' Julia asked.

He had a skin like a rhino. He said, 'I heard on the office grapevine that you'd been given the shove. Sorry to hear it.'

'Thanks,' she said. 'I'm not worried. I'm relieved.'

'All that lovely money—' She had a mental picture of him grinning in disbelief, and just stopped herself ringing off. 'What happened? You were the old man's blue-eyed baby . . .? Fall out with him?'

'Felix, why do you want to know? Why should you care? It's not your province. There's no mileage in it for you.'

'God, you do think I'm a shit,' he protested. 'I was just sorry to hear it, that's all. I was even going to ask if you and Ben would like to meet me for a drink.'

'Ben's not here,' she said. She felt guilty because she'd been so hostile. He was brash and tactless and she'd over-reacted. 'He's up in Birmingham, family business.'

'Didn't know he had a family,' Felix said. 'Why don't you come out then?'

'I don't think so,' Julia said. 'I've got a lot to sort out—'

'Oh come on,' Felix urged. 'Just for old times. I might even buy you dinner if you stop biting my head off. Look, I'll come and pick you up in half an hour. I'm in a pub now. It's that lovely lad Joe Patrick's water hole. Full of gorgeous tarts. See you. Bye!'

She didn't want to go. But it was typical of Felix to steam-roller when he wanted something. A drink with him wouldn't hurt. Joe Patrick . . . King's contact man. The photographs and tapes supplied to ruin Leo Derwent. Yes, she'd meet Felix. It might clear her own mind to talk to someone who wasn't so closely involved. She bribed the cat with a dish of milk, changed out of her leggings and sloppy sweater into trousers and a top, and brushed vigorously at the fiery untamed hair.

Then she recorded a message for Ben in case he phoned while she was out. 'Gone for a drink with Felix. I hope you're jealous. Back around nine. I'll call you then. Love, darling.'

Felix, inevitably, was twenty minutes late. When he buzzed from the street, she said, 'I'll come down,' and hurried out, double locking the front door. The man with the street map idling by the corner, turned his head and watched her leave.

10

'He just said he was going out?' Detective Chief Inspector Roy Bingham was being calm and patient. The girl who'd been beaten up was cowed and compliant. The other dyke was a much tougher proposition. Intelligent and wary, still trying to protect the girlfriend and herself at the expense of bringing a murderer to justice. Roy Bingham considered both of them to be the scum of the earth, but he went on with careful questioning, leading, not bullying. Everything was going down on tape and his detective sergeant and a CID woman police officer were present. They'd given the two women coffee and ordered sandwiches. He went on, 'He was going out. That's all he said?'

'That's right,' Tina agreed sullenly. ' "I'm going out." ' She remembered the glib insult that went with it. 'You two tar babies wait up for me . . . I'll want something special tonight . . . ' And Tracey's apprehensive whisper as he left them . . . 'What's up? Where's he off to . . . ' And her answer,

'Some poor bugger's going to get done over . . . Joe always gets a hard on afterwards . . . ' The widow at Midhurst had been done over good and proper. And raped.

'And when he came back,' Roy Bingham prompted, 'then what happened?'

Tina glared at him. 'I told you. We went into our double act . . . you want to know the dirty details?'

'No,' he said. 'I'm not interested. What I'm asking is did he say where he'd been, give any indication what he was doing while he was out?'

'Nothing,' Tracey muttered. 'He never did.'

'And you never asked?' That was the detective sergeant, taking the lead for a moment.

She looked at him. 'You must be joking. He'd have knocked the shit out of us. He didn't like questions.'

'He often beat you up, then?' He was concentrating on the weaker one, leaving his boss to wear down Tina.

'Not often,' Tracey admitted. 'If he felt like it.'

'Didn't you resent it?'

She shrugged slightly. 'He was good to us in other ways. He fancied Tina more than me. That's what got up his nose, her lending me the bracelet . . . '

'And when did he give you the bracelet?' It was the boss, taking it up with Tina.

'I told you. Next day. We'd given him a good time.'

'When you were with him the night before, did you notice any marks . . . bruising, skinned knuckles . . . anything at all?'

'No,' Tracey turned her head. 'If he did a job he always wore gloves. He never marked himself.'

Tina glared at her in warning, but it was too late.

'What do you mean by a job?'

Roy Bingham sensed a breakthrough. He abandoned Tina. He moved his chair a little closer to Tracey. It seemed to her as if they had all moved in on her, crowding her. She stared from one to the other and round to the policewoman sitting in silent witness of the scene.

'When he did someone over. He used a knife on the girls. He never cut us. He only used his fists.'

'And his feet,' Roy reminded her. 'He kicked you, didn't he? Kicked you in the ribs so hard he fractured three of them. Kicked you in the back. The old lady who owned that bracelet was kicked too. And punched. I've got some photographs. I'd like to show you what was done to her.'

'I don't want to see,' Tracey said, and started to cry.

Tina got up and came over to her. 'You bastards!' she snarled. 'Leave her alone . . . '

'If you'll sign a statement,' the sergeant suggested. 'You can both go home.'

'Yeah?' Tina turned on him. 'And wait for a visit from his mates when he finds out we've been talking to you . . . Get lost. We're not signing anything.'

The Detective Chief Inspector got up. He addressed the tape recorder. 'Termination of interview at seventeen twenty hours, Thursday 9 December.' He snapped the machine off. His tone changed. 'Right,' he said, 'let's separate these two. Joan, take Osborne to another interview room. Mervyn stays here.' He barked at Tina, 'Come on, Osborne. Move your ass.'

'I'm not going,' she said loudly. 'I'm not leaving Tracey. I won't and you can't make me!'

Her voice rose. He heard the panic in it and he mocked her.

'You want to bet? Joan call up another WPC and get this one out of here. I want a few quiet words with her friend.'

Tina stood rigid. She heard the mutter from the policewoman into her mike, 'Send someone up to Interview Room Five, will you? We've got a recalcitrant.'

They'd manhandle her out and Tracey would be left to fend off that ugly white bastard on her own. She was still weak and shaky from the ordeal. Her jaw was set, but it was a mess and it would have to be re-broken and done again. Then surgery on her nose and cheekbones. She slept badly and panicked if Tina went out for long. She was scared to be alone. Joe Patrick hadn't killed her, but he'd marked her inside and outside for life.

Tracey clinched it. 'Tina,' she wailed. 'Tina . . . don't leave me . . . '

Roy Bingham knew he had won when the body language

changed. Tina slumped as the fight went out of her.

She said, 'All right, all right. I'll make a statement. Just don't get heavy, will you?'

Bingham nodded to the policewoman who cancelled her request. He switched on the tape recorder and started the interview again.

'Interview recommenced at seventeen twenty-eight, 9 December. Detective Sergeant Fitch and Detective Constable Joan Lewis present, interviewees, Tina Osborne and Tracey Mervyn, conducted by DCI Roy Bingham. Now, Tina, let's get the story right from the beginning, shall we? The bracelet identified as the property of Mrs Jean Adams, who was murdered in the course of a robbery at her home address . . . '

The monotonous tone went on, repeating the details. Then the real questions began.

'You can positively identify this bracelet as the one given you by Joe Patrick on the twenty-seventh of September?'

Tina said, 'Yes.'

'And the night before, Joe Patrick left you both in his apartment at approximately what time?'

'Around nine,' Tina said. There was no turning back.

'Did he say where he was going?'

She hesitated. Then she took a breath. 'He said he was going on a job.'

Bingham stared at her. 'He said that? He said he was going on a job?'

She was lying and he knew it. He spoke to the other girl. 'Did he say that to you, too?'

'No, he didn't.'

Tina interrupted. 'He said it to me. She didn't hear him.'

Bingham nodded. 'I see.' He switched off the recorder. 'You've decided to nail him, have you?'

Tina looked at him. 'That's what you want, isn't it?'

He didn't answer for a moment. He took out a packet of cigarettes and lit one. He'd tried and failed to give up smoking. He couldn't afford frazzled nerves in his job.

'Right then,' he said briskly. 'Let's have some more coffee and get down to business.'

They dropped Tina and Tracey back in an unmarked police car. The flat was empty. The friend and her man spent a lot of time out picking up punters and pushing drugs. Tracey looked at her. 'You've done it now,' she muttered.

'We'll be all right,' Tina told her. 'We'll be moved out of here tomorrow and we'll have protection. I'm glad I did it, Trace. After what that piece of dirt did to you, I'm glad. I always said I'd pay him back one day. Come on, let's get to bed. We'll be fine. So long as we've got each other.'

Felix took Julia to a wine bar in Jermyn Street. It was discreet and expensive. They settled into a corner banquette. 'This is like old times,' he said.

'Except that I'd be paying,' Julia cut that approach off at the start. 'You must be doing well if you come to places like this.'

Unabashed, Felix grinned. 'I told you I like the good life. And I am doing well as it happens. I'm the Warbler's assistant now. You wouldn't believe how many important politicians I know.'

Julia said, 'Go on, impress me then.'

It was silly to rise to him; nothing would change Felix. He had always rather enjoyed needling her. She might as well relax and enjoy her drink. He named several MPs, including one ambitious Cabinet Minister. 'I get asked to lunch and taken aside for off-the-record chats . . . It's fascinating. They all talk such a load of cobblers really, doesn't matter which side they're on.' He drank his gin and tonic and ordered another. 'What are you going to do now?' In sheer mischief he added, 'Some people'd change sides. Trot along to King and offer to work for him. Bringing a few titbits about the noble Lord along with you . . . '

Julia said angrily, 'Don't be so bloody stupid, Felix. As if I would!'

'I only said some people, not you,' he pointed out. 'You've got too many principles, that's your trouble.'

'And you've got none,' she countered.

'Never pretended I had,' he said. 'Have another vodka and let's stop scoring off each other. What *are* you going to do?

You'll have to drop the King investigation for a start.'

'I'm not going to,' she said.

He glanced sideways at her. 'That's a bit rash,' he said. 'Without back-up. What does Harris think?'

'I haven't told him, he's had to go to look after his daughter . . . He's got enough to worry about. But he'll go along with me. Felix, can I try a few things on you? Would you mind? It might help me to see my way clearer.'

'Mind? I'm flattered. Go on, try me.'

Julia didn't notice the time. At the end Felix said, 'That's quite a story. A riddle inside an enigma. If Western's wife was telling the truth, you're back to square one. An unsubstantiated allegation that King shot British prisoners, somewhere in the Western Desert. Did you believe her?'

'I believed *her*, but not what she was saying,' Julia answered slowly. 'I know that four men were killed and Western was wounded, and I know Harold King was responsible. But how do I prove it? What have I missed?'

'God knows,' he shrugged. 'Unless you can get King drunk!'

She stared at him. 'Felix . . . Felix,' Julia said slowly. 'Can you drop me home?'

'Why don't I buy you dinner?' he suggested. 'Pizza on the Park's great . . . What's the matter? You look funny.'

'Nothing's the matter,' she said. She picked up her bag. 'I won't eat, thanks anyway. Can you drop me back?'

'Yeah. I'm not doing anything else. I'll get the bill. You're a Liberal Democrat, by the way. Goes on expenses.'

They came out into the crisp winter night and Julia shivered. Not with cold but with a growing sense of excitement. Felix, flippant as always, had said something more momentous than he would ever realize. She saw a cruising taxi, its orange light gleaming up front, and on an impulse she turned to Felix.

'Don't worry, I'll take this cab. Thanks for the drinks. Thanks for letting me talk it out.'

'OK.' Felix didn't mind not driving out of his way back to Chelsea Green. There'd been a dishy little redhead in Joe Patrick's favourite pub who'd been eyeing him earlier. She might still be hanging around there. Being with Julia had turned his thoughts to more than pizza. 'Sorry I couldn't help,' he said.

'I think you have.' To his surprise Julia reached up and kissed him lightly on the cheek. The cab had drawn into the kerb, and she got inside. Felix stood looking after her for a moment. Definitely the little redhead, he decided. She wasn't Julia, but she'd do.

He dialled the number from a call-box. He listened to Julia's message for Ben Harris.

'Gone for a drink with Felix. I hope you're jealous. Back around nine. I'll call you then. Love, darling.'

The time was just past seven. He went into a pâtisserie in the shopping centre nearby and had some cakes and two cups of coffee. He never drank on a job, but he loved sweet pastries. Then he went back to Chelsea Green and slumped down in the darkness of a doorway. It was just across the street from the apartment block. The entrance was well lit, part of the security system. That suited him well. One or two pedestrians passed by, but didn't bother to look twice at the figure huddled in a doorway for shelter. London was full of homeless drifters, begging by day and sleeping rough. He had seen a number of them for himself. He wore dark clothes and trainers; the overcoat made him look respectable, as did the fur hat, ear flaps pulled down. The footwear was light and made running easy. If he had to run. He didn't expect to; he expected to walk away from the job and simply disappear into the London murk. Then the first flight home in the morning. He had an open-ended ticket. The killing wouldn't be discovered till he was well *en route* across the skies. A single man and then a couple, followed later by another, came to the apartment block and went inside, but he didn't move. Then he saw what he was hoping for. Three young kids, teenagers, converged on the front door. He had noticed girls and boys coming and going while he was on watch during the day. He moved very quickly, up from his seat on the step and across the street, catching up with them just as the front door opened. One of the girls had a key; as she pulled it out of the lock, he pushed in past her. He said, 'Thanks,' over his shoulder, and he was past the TV camera in the entrance hall as they followed. He heard them laughing and talking behind him as he hurried to the stairs and began taking the first flight two steps at a time. They'd been too busy to notice him. He'd counted on that. Kids, he thought dispassionately. His would have been just as careless. Hamilton's apartment was on the fourth floor. Top of the building. He slowed his pace and listened for sounds coming from above.

He paused, watching the red eye of the elevator. It stopped on the third floor. He heard teenage voices floating down the stairwell, and stayed out of sight. Then he climbed the last two flights of stairs. An arrow pointed right for two flat numbers. Another arrow indicated one number only, Hamilton's number, on the left. Through glass doors and round a corner. It made an isolated little cul-de-sac on that top floor. The front door of the flat was at the end of a short passage, 403, in gilt bronze figures on a heavy mahogany door. He moved without sound on the thick pile carpet. He noticed the TV eye sunk in the wall above head height. Anyone ringing the bell would be instantly viewed on a double screen inside. One screen for the street entrance, another for the passageway outside the flat. He stood and listened. She had said around nine. It was near that time now. He went back down the passageway. From his observation from outside the building in daylight, he knew the fire-escape must be close by. And there it was. Clearly marked with a red arrow and the warning, 'This Exit must be kept clear at all times.' It was a simple push-lever model, easy for a young or old escapee to open. He shifted it with one hand and stood for a moment on the narrow iron plaform outside. Heights didn't worry him. The wind was biting up there and he shrugged deeper into his coat. Then he went back inside. He pushed the glass door and let it swing back. It made a definite click as it came to rest. He'd hear that. And he could watch through a crack in the door to the fire-escape and see Hamilton come in. If she was alone, the hit was on. If she wasn't . . . He never carried out more than one contract at a time. He didn't believe in two for the price of one. He'd seen her meet a man outside. If she brought him back to her apartment then he would slip downstairs and go to his hotel and try the next day. He was calm; postponement wouldn't bother him. He had no nerves, just a dislike of any kind of risk, however minimal. He stepped back onto the narrow fire-escape, the door just an inch ajar, and looked up at the stars in the clear dark skies above him. And waited.

Julia paid off the cab, opened the front door and took the lift up to the fourth floor. It was later than she had intended, long past nine o'clock. She let the glass door swing back behind her and hurried to her door.

She didn't even glance near the fire-exit. Pussy came into the hallway and mewed. She stroked her and went quickly to the telephone to see if Ben had tired of waiting and phoned her. The machine winked at her. She pressed 'play' and heard his voice. 'I'm taking Lucy out for supper. It'll cheer her up. I'll ring if we're not too late. Otherwise tomorrow morning. Then home on Friday. No more drinks with other men for you . . . Bye, sweetheart.' 'Damn,' Julia said out loud. Damn . . . just when she needed to talk to him. She wasn't hungry; her stomach was tight with tension. She poured herself a drink and ran a hot bath. She opened a new tin of food and gave the cat an extra feed to make up for being absent. Ben said she was getting fat. Julia was always giving her titbits. He'd said to her once, half teasing, 'God knows what you'll be like with a child . . . you'll spoil it to death.' She stripped off her clothes, took the drink into the bathroom and sank into the hot water. A riddle inside an enigma. And it seemed that now there was only one way to prise open that enigma, and solve the riddle. King couldn't control himself with alcohol.

Which was why, since the fatal night with his wife Phyllis Lowe, he had never touched even a glass of wine in forty years. *Get him drunk*. Felix had tossed in the flippant suggestion. She was going back now, her memory in full recall. The bath water chilled without her noticing, the drink was unfinished on the side. He'd told Phyllis that he had murdered the prisoners. In the wild confession that spilled out under the influence of alcohol he had put himself in thrall to her. There were people who lost all control, who couldn't tolerate even one drink. Not alcoholics, but people suffering from a kind of mental allergy. The inhibitions common to normal behaviour were suspended. They were at the mercy of a drug that robbed them of self-will. They were rare cases, very rare, but they existed. Harold King was such a man. The evil was in him; the alcohol made him proclaim it without fear of the consequences. She got out, dried herself, changed into pyjamas. She tipped the unfinished vodka down the sink and heated some hot milk. It might help her to sleep. Ben hadn't called. It was midnight, he wouldn't ring now. She got into bed, the cat curled up by her feet, and lay awake, thinking. How? How to trick King into breaking that embargo . . . And then, suddenly, the answer came to her.

He had come into the passage; he was getting too cold outside. He checked his watch. Ten to twelve. He went to the glass door round the corner and opened it, watching the lift panel to see if anyone was coming up. The red eye didn't change to green. The block was very quiet. He went to the top of the stairs, and leant over the stairwell, listening. Sound travelled upwards. There was nothing. No voices, no movement. He stayed where he was, making sure that no-one was coming in late. Nobody did.

At twenty-five minutes past twelve, he went back round the corner, through the glass door and came up to the entrance to apartment 403. He wore tight leather gloves. He muffled his mouth with his left hand and struck a heavy blow on the mahogany panel. Then another. And another. And he shouted.

'Fire! Fire! The block's on fire! Everybody out!'

Julia was half asleep when she heard the hammering on her door. She woke fully and sprang up. She heard the voice yelling, 'Fire . . . Fire . . . '

Fire! She felt a rush of terror. Four floors up . . . Oh God . . . She paused to grab the coat she'd tossed on a chair. The cat . . . Where was the cat? She couldn't leave it. She was still on the foot of the bed. She grabbed her, breathless with fear, and ran barefoot to her front door. She wrenched the safety chain out of its socket and fumbled with the latch. He heard the movement from inside the flat and he drew himself up; a knife with a thin blade was in his right hand. As Julia opened the door he crouched to spring.

She saw the figure, saw in one second that it was poised to attack her. She gave a piercing scream of terror, and blindly, instinctively, she threw the cat at him. The cat was wild with fear – Julia's fear, communicated in that rush for safety.

It half sprang of its own accord, hissing, teeth bared and claws extended. It struck him full on and it clung to his face, ripping and snarling before he wrenched it off him. He had dropped the knife, and, in the same few seconds, Julia slammed her door shut.

She didn't think; she was so shocked she could hardly breathe. She had slipped and fallen to her knees. She managed to crawl to the door, and it took both hands to slide the heavy chain into place. She began to shake, and she felt for a moment that she was going to be sick. He was out there. Outside the door waiting. He couldn't get in. He couldn't . . . She couldn't hear anything. No sound. Just that terrible menacing silence with the man who had tricked her into coming out, still there . . .

She found the keys on the hall table, and, trembling, fitted them into the interior locks and turned them both. The locks and the chain. Nobody could break that door down without a sledgehammer. She stumbled to the sitting room. Her legs were giving way. She calmed herself, or believed she did. There was no fire. There was an alarm system throughout the building, smoke detectors, signals relayed to every flat . . . There was no danger, except in the passageway outside. The police . . . She lifted the telephone and dialled.

His face was bleeding. It was on fire from the deep scratches, and blood stung his lip. He didn't waste time. He picked up his knife. He'd failed, and he wasn't going to push his luck. He turned and sprinted down the passage, through the glass door and raced down the stairs, into the entrance hall and out of the front door into the street.

He was gone before Julia had finished locking herself in from the inside. He wiped his face, the handkerchief was stained.

Jesus Christ. A cat . . . He made for the Underground. A

few taxis cruised the streets; one of them might recall picking up a man in the area around the time of the attack. He had asked for a key, explaining that he might be late picking up his luggage. He had paid his bill, and they had left his suitcase behind the reception desk.

He had stayed there on two previous trips to London, one of them connected to his genuine business, and he was known and trusted by the proprietor. A nice, quiet American businessman, a prompt payer and no trouble. A lot of foreigners tried to slip women in past reception. Nothing like that about him.

He looked at himself in the hallway mirror. His nose was swollen and oozing blood from the cat bites. His cheeks were ripped by scratches. He was scarred and thereby recognizable . . . He opened the case and took out his wash bag. He always carried a small first-aid pack. Plasters, antiseptic ointment, paracetamol. He covered the deep scratch and bite mark across his nose with a plaster, pulled up his coat collar and drew the earflaps over his burning cheeks.

It was safe to hail a taxi and, after a little while, he spotted one in the Bayswater Road. Suitcase in hand and keeping his face in shadow, he said Heathrow and jumped inside . . . He tossed a double fare to the driver and hurried into Terminal 3. He spent the night in the departure lounage, the cap pulled down over his face.

He boarded the eight o'clock flight to New York, refused breakfast and said he wanted to sleep. He hunched himself in his pillow and dozed.

It was around 10 a.m. New York time when they landed. He collected his car from the Terminal car park, and drove home. A cat. Nobody would believe it. He could hardly believe it himself. He had reason to, when the bites on his face turned septic a few hours later.

'Now,' the WPC said, 'is there anyone you can stay with tonight?'

Julia was drinking hot sweet tea. She had made her statement to the police who arrived after the emergency call. The building had been searched, the caretaker roused from his bed, and the immediate neighbours woken and asked if they had seen or heard anything. Nobody had. They suggested it was more likely to be a burglar who'd been prepared to turn very nasty once inside, and Julia found herself agreeing. They would dismiss any suggestion of a more sinister motive as hysteria on her part. She was much calmer now; the woman police officer was good at her job, quiet and reassuring.

'You don't want to be here on your own,' she said. 'You've had a nasty experience. And a lucky escape, if you look at it. We'll be going soon, now the building's been searched. An officer from the Crime Squad will be down to see you tomorrow morning and we'll test for fingerprints. Isn't there a woman friend you could call on? We'll drive you wherever, don't worry about that.'

'I'm all right,' Julia insisted. She wouldn't call Ben. She wouldn't panic him in the middle of the night. And she wouldn't call anyone else. She had to keep the incident quiet.

'I could try a man friend,' she said. 'He's just a friend, but we were having a drink earlier this evening. He might come round.'

'Good idea. I'll get the number for you.'

Julia didn't mean to do it, but when Felix arrived she burst into tears. He was round at the flat within twenty minutes. He looked tousled and dishevelled. He had only just sent the redhead home in a cab an hour before the telephone call. He had been sleeping the sleep of the just, as he liked to say, labouring the joke. The just after . . .

The police left them. Julia sat and cried and tried to tell him what had happened. He put a brotherly arm round her and let her go over it again and again, reliving the few nightmare seconds when the man loomed up at her, arm upraised.

'He had a knife, I'm sure of it,' she whispered. 'I'm sure I saw something in his hand . . . '

'Did you tell the police?'

'I tried to, but I could see they thought I'd probably imagined it. Oh God, it was so terrifying . . . The worst thing is, they can't find Pussy!'

'That,' Felix said, 'is the least of your worries. It's

probably hiding somewhere, terrified out of its life. You really think he was going to kill you?'

'Yes,' she said slowly. 'I'm sure of it. That was no burglar. He'd planned it all, waiting till the middle of the night, shouting "Fire" to panic me into opening my door. It's Jean Adams all over again.' She shuddered. 'It could be the same man . . . '

'Look,' he said. 'You put this on the back burner for tonight. Do you have a sleeping pill? No – OK. Then go to bed and try to sleep. I'll doss down here on the sofa and we'll call Harris first thing in the morning. My guess is he'll move you out of here. I haven't got room, or you could stay at my place. It's just a bachelor pad.'

Julia looked at him. 'Thanks,' she said. 'Thanks, Felix. Thanks for coming over. I didn't know what to do, or where to turn . . . '

'No problem,' he grinned at her. 'What's an ex-boyfriend for, when you nearly get yourself murdered? Now, off to bed. And don't worry about the cat, you silly female, it'll be found tomorrow.'

Joe Patrick was not at his address. The office was closed and there was no-one in his luxury flat. He hadn't been seen for nearly a fortnight. Nobody knew where he had gone. Enquiries were circulated among the shady denizens of the half world where Joe Patrick had his early contacts. The word was out. Find Patrick and there was money or favours in kind. No public statement was issued; Jean Adams' killing was still unsolved, and interest had soon died down. Murder, even with such a vicious element in it, was too commonplace. A pre-Christmas child abduction made the tabloid front pages, and filled the TV screens. The search for Joe Patrick was kept under wraps for fear of alerting him. Tina and Tracey were living in a safe house under round-the-clock police protection. But, so far, nobody had come forward with information.

'I'll never forgive myself,' Ben Harris kept saying to her. 'I shouldn't have left you.'

'Darling, don't be silly, I wouldn't let you come home. You

had to look after Lucy . . . I was just shocked. I'm all right now.'

'No you're not,' he said. 'You look a wreck. We're packing up here and you're coming to a hotel with me and Lucy, and that's the end of it. This place belongs to that bastard Western, anyway. He can have it back. I called the office and he's due home tomorrow. I've got an appointment. He won't like what I've got to say to him.'

She let him hold her close. It wasn't time to argue. He was too upset by what had happened to her, too guilty about his absence. The news that he had been sacked didn't give him a moment's concern. His only thought was for her. She knew that he would insist on her giving up. Publicly withdrawing from the campaign against Harold King. Stepping out of the firing line. And she knew that, in spite of nearly losing her life, she wasn't going to do it. But it wasn't time to tell him. Yet. She changed the subject gently. 'Thank God we found Pussy. Do you know, darling, I was so upset about losing her.'

She had been discovered the next day crouched down under the hoover and cleaning materials in the caretaker's broom cupboard. No-one could think how she got there, except that she'd slipped in during the police search when the door was open.

'She saved your life,' Ben said slowly. 'That makes me feel even worse.'

No, Julia decided, changing roles and trying to reassure him, it was not the time to argue about Harold King. She had made up her mind what had to be done, and she had to do it alone. Afterwards, she could explain it to Ben Harris and persuade him that she hadn't any choice.

'I feel bad about it, Harry. Real bad. He's never fouled up on a business contract before.' Mario was apologetic. He had called King in the country on a weekend, just a few days after he got back from his trip.

'These things happen,' King was dismissive. 'I understand.'

'I didn't!' the voice was an angry snarl. 'Just didn't believe it. I sent a guy down to verify. And it was true. Cat attacked him; he's just out of hospital. Yeah . . . blood poisoning. Incredible, eh? Never keep a cat – ' Then, after a pause, 'You want we should send another contract expert to take a look at the proposition, find a bottom-line solution?'

'No need,' King said. 'It's solved itself. Thanks, anyway. There's no fee for your expert, then.' It wasn't a question.

'We pay on results,' was the answer. 'No fee. He can meet his own goddamned medical bills. How's the family? Getting ready for Christmas? We've got my wife's mother, my sister and her kids, my uncle and *their* kids. But it's Christmas. It's goodtto have the family all together. How about you?'

'We go to Switzerland, to my place in Gstaad. Just Marilyn and Gloria and me.'

And Leo Derwent, but he didn't mention that. Gloria had booked Leo into the Regent. He wouldn't be at all surprised if she was paying the bill. A junior minister couldn't afford a week's stay at the Regent around Christmas. If he'd even been able to get a room in the attic. The name of King had secured a vacancy.

'You ski?' Mario was making conversation. King knew he was embarrassed by the failure of his man to get Julia. It didn't matter now. Her departure from the *Sunday Herald* was in every newspaper and rated a mention on BBC and ITV news. Western had fired Harris, too. It was made to sound an amicable parting with a lot of unctuous horseshit from Western himself, saying how sorry he was to lose such a talented young journalist. 'Exposure' would be headed up by a new star in the newspaper's stable . . . The December issue would expose a national scandal, etc., etc. Western had lost his nerve. And Harold King knew it. Hamilton had gone to Jersey, looking for something to incriminate King, and come back with Richard Watson's well-told tale about a sergeant, name of William Western. And nothing else.

He answered the question about skiing. 'Not me, not now. I used to be good, but one accident was enough. I haven't time to lie up with a broken leg.' He laughed. 'Like you, I'm a busy man. Have a good holiday. My best to all the family.'

He hung up. It was a cold, grey day. Western's feature was due out that Sunday. He wasn't worried. Hamilton would get another job, but she wouldn't be taking any story with her. And when Western went down, he'd exercise a little influence with her new employer. She wouldn't hold on to any job for long. If she was lucky, she could write another book . . . if she could find a publisher prepared to make an enemy of Harold King. He chuckled to himself. He went to the window and looked out at the grey landscape, the leafless trees and the mist rising from a lake which he could glimpse from his study window. It was cheerless, bleak. He thought of the crisp snow and sun, the bright skies of Switzerland. The mountain air, the majestic alps rearing their heads into the clouds . . . the scenery spoke to him of his origins. He would never go to Germany now. Switzerland was as near as he would come to his roots. He had no roots, he reminded himself, impatient with the brief twinge of nostalgia. Nostalgia was for the senile. He had years ahead of him. He thought of his daughter and her infatuation. Let it run for the moment. He wouldn't buy Leo Derwent off with money. His price was political office. Soon, King would be powerful enough to obtain it for him. On condition that he gave up Gloria. She'd get over it. She'd go on to a better man, a man worthy to be her consort.

He felt contented, happy. He turned away from the dreary view of an English landscape in December. They'd go to Gstaad early, he decided suddenly. Marilyn could spend his money Christmas shopping there just as well as in London.

'William,' his wife said, 'you can't win.' He had never expected her to say that. If ever his spirits flagged, Evelyn rallied them with her own courage. They were out walking in the chill, damp afternoon, muffled in tweeds and heavy scarves, two elderly people braving the miserable weather to take exercise in their own parkland. Two golden labradors ran on ahead of them. Western didn't like dogs, but they were part of a country gentleman's equipment, like Purdey guns and a keeper. Evelyn made pets of them, so they were not good gun dogs. He didn't care. He used his shoot to impress his guests, not for his own enjoyment.

'I can try,' he said. 'I've got a lot of money. I can fight back.'

'You can't fight on his terms,' she answered. 'Rumours, share fixing, bought financial journalists. You can't win, darling. Not without Julia Hamilton.'

'I can't win with her,' he said. 'After what happened at her flat, I had to buy Harris off with public statements and a hefty contract settlement. It *could* have been a burglar, it could have been something else. Harris was convinced it was a contract killer. Like Jean Adams. It's no good Evie – I tried to get Harold King exposed for what we know he is. A crook, and probably a murderer. But I failed, so all I can do now is fight him in the open and take my chance. It's getting really cold. I think we should go back in.' They turned, calling the dogs who trotted back to them obediently. They walked in silence until the house came into view.

'She wasn't telling the truth, was she, Billy?' The question caught him unprepared.

'What do you mean? Truth about what?'

'Those other men weren't shot down, were they? It was crossfire?'

He stopped and turned her to look at him. A wisp of white hair had escaped her hat and drifted across her cheek. It filled him with tenderness to see it. She was so beautiful he often forgot how old she really was. 'I've never lied to you, Evie. Never.'

'I know you haven't,' she said gently. 'I shouldn't have asked that. I'm sorry.'

He hooked his hand through her arm, and guided her towards the house. 'We'll have tea together by the fire,' he said. 'I'm not going to do any paperwork tonight. We'll have a nice evening, just the two of us.'

He hoped she didn't notice he hadn't answered her question.

'When are you leaving?' Julia asked.

Leo said, 'On the Tuesday after Christmas. She wants me to stay for ten days. She's making it a Christmas present.'

He thought she looked thin and very pale.

'You know it's a crazy idea, don't you?'

'You don't have to do it,' Julia said. 'If you want to play footsie with his daughter and let him get away with trying to ruin you, it's up to you.'

'I never forget a bad turn,' he said.

'How about a good one?'

He glanced up at her sharply.

'I persuaded Western not to run that story,' she reminded him. 'I don't expect you to be grateful, Leo. I don't think it's your style. But this is your one chance to get back at King. Don't think he'll let it run on between you and his daughter; he'll find a way to finish that, too. It's a gamble, that's true, but if it comes off, it's the Old Bailey for him.'

'If it doesn't,' he mused, 'we haven't lost anything.'

No, only my job, and Ben's job, and nearly getting knifed . . . She didn't say it; she hadn't told anyone about the terrifying incident. She said, 'Are you on?'

He played with his watch. 'Yes,' he answered. 'Yes, I'll give it a go. Where can I reach you?'

'I'm going to my parents, in about two hours. Staying for Christmas. I'll contact you at the Regent when you get there.'

'Merry Christmas,' he said.

'Thanks, same to you.'

Julia had parked her car on a meter; a warden was loitering near by, hoping to catch out an overdue shopper. Julia checked the time. She and Ben and Lucy were driving down to Surrey that afternoon. With the cat in a basket. She had gone through the motions, bought presents for everyone, wrapped and tagged them and piled them up in the boot of the car. She was sorry for Lucy; she was subdued and shy with Julia, and she clung a shade too closely to Ben. All she knew was there had been an attempted break-in at Julia's flat, and they were moving to a hotel. Then on to Julia's parents for Christmas. Lucy had shown no desire to go back and spend the holiday with her mother and stepfather. Some mornings she met them at breakfast with red eyes, obviously downcast. Julia tried hard to get close to her, but there was a quiet resistance that she hadn't overcome. She reasoned that Lucy was still mourning, still trying to readjust physically, as well as emotionally, to the loss of her child. Julia was sympathetic and rational about it, but there were times when she felt left out. Ben was protective, dividing himself equally between the two women who needed him. He paid their hotel bill, reacting with a display of male pride that surprised Julia when she offered to pay her share. When they travelled down together the cat howled in protest at being confined in her new basket, and Lucy finally took it on her knee.

'She's so furry,' she said. 'I wish I had a kitten . . . '

Ben said quickly, 'I'll get you one. Cats aren't like dogs; they're very happy in flats. We'll look for one tomorrow.'

Later he said to Julia when they were washing up in the kitchen after dinner, 'That's a good idea. She needs something to look after. Poor kid. You've been wonderful, darling. She thinks the world of you, she told me . . . And your mum and dad have made us both so welcome.' He turned Julia towards him and kissed her. 'I love you so much, J; I want us to put everything behind us now and make a new start. I'm glad we're out of the whole bloody mess. Coming down here, being in a normal family, makes me realize what life's about. Why don't you go and sit down and watch telly with them? I'll finish this.'

'I'd rather be with you,' she said. 'Darling, you've let the drying cloth fall in the sink . . . Here, let me do it. I love you too, but you're not domesticated—'

'I could be,' he protested. 'The new Ben Harris. Wouldn't you like me to be a New Age Man and do the housework?'

She laughed. 'I wouldn't. I'd hate it. I like the old model. Grouchy, tough as old boots, and the best editor in the business!'

They shared the big double guest room, and he made love to her that night, and when they rested in each other's arms, he said suddenly, 'Will you marry me, J?'

She turned to look at him. 'Do you want to get married? We don't have to.'

'I know we don't,' he said. 'But it would stop you having drinks with Felix. I hated that, you know. It really churned me up to think of you with anyone else. Even him. That's when I knew I wanted a full commitment. I'm ready for it, and I won't make the same mistakes as last time. What do you say?'

Julia didn't answer. She held him closer for a moment. It was the wrong time. She couldn't give an answer and do what she was planning. In two days it would be Christmas. The house was decorated, the tree was up and the presents stacked beneath it. Even Pussy had a few parcels. Her parents were so happy, so ready to give to them all. Her brother and sister-in-law and their children were coming over on Boxing Day. It was all planned and it was going to be idyllic. A healing process for Lucy. A family gathering to celebrate the family. She wished with all her heart that he had waited until it was over.

He touched her tenderly. 'What do you say? Can you take me on?'

'Ben,' she said very gently, 'we've just made love and all I want to say is yes and not think it through . . . That wouldn't be fair to either of us. Will you give me a little more time?'

'As long as you need,' he said. 'I'm not about to ask anyone else. Good night, sweetheart.'

He slept very deeply; Julia didn't. She saw the dawn creep through the edges of the curtains. The air ticket was in her notecase. It was dated 28 December, the Swissair flight leaving Gatwick at eleven in the morning.

Joe Patrick was in Dublin. He had lost his sinecure with Harold King, but he had plenty of money stacked away, and he didn't owe anybody except his bookmaker. And that wasn't much. He had decided to go into a different kind of business. He'd run girls, he'd come up through pimping and protection, he'd fixed a few nasty problems himself, like the old biddy at Midhurst, and travelled as King's troubleshooter to the States and the Caribbean. He had dabbled in drugs and he had a keen understanding and love of money. And in this new business, the money would be as big as King's retainer and bonuses. He had felt his way carefully in his native city, throwing hints to known sympathizers. He had baited his hook and the fish had struck.

The IRA could use a front man in London, a man with a business exporting leather goods to Europe. He could launder money through to centres in Amsterdam and Bruges, where they had units whose mission was to strike at military personnel in Germany and on NATO bases. He had a lot of criminal contacts in the city itself who would assist with safe houses and target surveillance. Joe Patrick had a lot to offer, and because he was a man with money, he wasn't expected to come cheap. He had done the deal in Dublin City itself with a man whose name he didn't know and didn't ask. He had a cash deposit in his briefcase when he flew home. Home was London now. He found Ireland too provincial, its rackets too seedy. He liked the high life. He hated Christmas. It reminded him of the grim celebrations in the orphanage that never varied year after year. He came back to his smart flat. No girls to greet him and wash the travel dust off him in the Jacuzzi. He'd find others. He had some correspondence . . . a few bills . . . some Christmas cards. He threw them away. He showered and changed and went out, making first for his favourite pub, and then, if he found a pick-up he fancied, he'd take them on to Soho to his favourite restaurant, and then home. He never went to a tart's place. He was fastidious about clean sheets and general hygiene. He got slightly drunk that night, and had to kick the girl out when he woke in the morning . . . Usually he sent them home with a taxi fare on top of the fee, whatever time of night. But he was in a good mood. He'd enjoyed himself, been welcomed back by cronies anxious to curry favour with him. God never shuts one door but he slams the other. He laughed. Life was looking good . . . It was Christmas Day and he'd bought himself a present. He was sitting with a Scotch in his hand watching a television sitcom about three girls sharing a flat when his front door buzzed. Joe wasn't expecting anybody. He turned the sound down and went into the front hall. He had closed-circuit security TV. Two men showed up on the screen. The bell buzzed again, and then there was the powerful knock.

'Mr Patrick! Open up! Police!'

'It's been such a lovely Christmas,' May Hamilton said. She smiled at her husband in contentment. 'Everyone got on so well, and the children were so funny opening their presents . . . Patsy said "Granny it's like Christmas day come twice!" '

'I know,' Hugh said. 'She's a dear little thing. And did you notice Tom and Julia didn't cross swords once?'

'That's because she's so happy,' his wife said. 'Ben's such a nice man and he's so in love with her . . . That poor child

Lucy . . . it was pathetic to see her fussing over that kitten.'

'Clever thing to give her,' Hugh agreed. 'She's young, she'll get over it. It's been a great success and it's all thanks to you, darling. You worked so hard to make it a happy time for all of us. Thank you.' He reached over and squeezed her hand.

Hugh Hamilton hesitated, but he never kept his thoughts on anything important from his wife. 'Maybe it was my imagination,' he said, 'but I felt Julia wasn't quite herself. She made a big effort, but she was strained . . . not *quite* herself . . . '

May nodded. 'I did notice something,' she admitted. 'I thought I was imagining it, but, since you say so, she wasn't relaxed, not really. I just wonder whether it isn't time for that girl to go home to her own mother?'

'You think she's jealous?'

'I think they're both a bit jealous of each other and they can't admit it. Ben doesn't see it, of course, men never do.'

'Why should they? They only want a quiet life and everyone getting on,' he countered.

'You're probably right. That's what was wrong with her . . . I think that's Ben and Lucy coming in now. I'd better get the lunch.'

'What time will Julia be back then?' Hugh asked.

'Not till tea-time. She's gone to buy shoes and get her hair done. Oh, Ben – there you are. Had a nice walk?' She turned to him, smiling. 'Lunch won't be long, you must be starving . . . ' She hurried out to the kitchen. Ben didn't find the letter Julia had written him till he went up to their bedroom later that afternoon.

Julia had booked into a small pension on the outskirts of Gstaad. It was a modest little chalet, scrupulously clean, the bedroom functional and sparsely furnished.

'You're not for the skiing?' the proprietress asked her, helping carry her one case upstairs.

'No,' Julia said. 'I don't ski. I'm here to see a friend.'

She closed the door and looked round the rather bleak room. She unpacked her clothes. It might happen in the first twenty-four hours. It might take a week. She was prepared. The flight had been uneventful. She felt tired, but too tense to rest, so she went for a walk instead, wrapped in a thick coat and with a fur hat pulled down against a cold, crisp wind that carried flurries of snow with it. Harold King owned a luxury chalet in the smartest residential area. The Regent Hotel was close to the slopes, exclusive and expensive, a playground for the super rich and the parasites of both sexes who lived off them. She thought of Leo Derwent and King's daughter, Gloria. She was so hooked on him that she was paying for him to be near her during the holiday. And Harold King himself, probably adding the last refinement to his plan to seize Western's media outlets and make himself the single most powerful figure in mass communication in the country. Power was his lifeblood.

She had lost her job and her power base. He knew he was safe because Western had sacked her. He wouldn't bother sending any more nocturnal messengers armed with a knife. Soon King would be so powerful he could ruin her professionally by dropping a word. Her career was finished, and Ben's equally destroyed. She had come here to confront him, and she wasn't afraid. She was risking everything on one last challenge. Her future and, above all, her future with Ben Harris. He must have read her letter explaining what she had done and why, even as she ended her walk and sat in a café drinking coffee to warm herself.

He would see it as a betrayal, she realized that. He would be deeply hurt at her deception and very angry. He was a man who nursed anger, goaded by his own self-doubt. He might never forgive her, whatever the outcome. King didn't frighten her, but that did. She sat on for a time, while the lights went on and the town began to vibrate with disco music and the onset of the *après-ski* as the gilded young and the darlings of the gossip columns prepared to enjoy themselves after a day on the slopes. She ate at the pension; the food was heavy and too rich. The atmosphere oppressed her. She had called the hotel and left a message for Leo. He knew where to reach her. But though she waited up till nearly midnight, there was no call.

It came in the morning, while she was having breakfast. There were two couples staying and a single woman, well into middle age, who left for the slopes before the others came down. There was a German husband and wife, keen skiers who made no effort when they found out she wasn't a devotee, and a French boy and girl who seemed to be either quarrelling or fondling each other regardless of an audience. Julia hurried from the dining room into the hall.

'I got your message,' his nasal voice said. A less than Oxbridge accent came out when he talked on the telephone. 'I'm going to try and fix it for tomorrow. I'm having lunch with them today.'

'You think he'll fall for it?'

She heard a snigger. 'He will if golden girl asks him to; and she'll do anything I tell her. She loves it!'

'When will you know?' Julia cut in.

'Give me till this evening,' he suggested. 'We're having some time together and she can go back and work on him. I'm pretty confident he'll say yes. And then we put your theory to the test.' He lowered his voice slightly. 'What do we do if he gets violent?'

'I'm sure you'll deal with it,' Julia said. 'You're a man, after all. When will you know?'

'This evening,' he said. 'They're all going out to dinner – I'm not included. I'll come over to you.'

'All right,' Julia agreed. 'I'll be here.'

Then she hung up. She hated him, but she had to trust him. Not because of his loyalty or his obligation to her, but his malice and desire for revenge. Whatever she felt about him, he was her only ally.

Gloria had gone off skiing, and Marilyn had decided to have a full beauty treatment instead. She had come back to lunch, and she was pleased with the result. She didn't look a day over thirty-eight . . . well, maybe *just* forty and she decided to be nice to her husband. He'd given her a set of crocodile luggage and half a dozen sets of Janet Reger underclothes that were mouthwatering. He was working as usual, and he grunted when she came up and kissed him.

'You smell good,' he remarked.

'I ought to, at a hundred and eighty francs an ounce,' she giggled slightly. 'I've been very naughty. I had everything done this morning. Does it look all right?' She stepped back and posed for him, one hand on a slim hip. She was beautiful. King nodded. He was proud of her, proud of the way even the glitz glamour queens of the resort stared at her. Not to mention their men. But she didn't arouse him any more. He enjoyed her as he would a piece of lovely Dresden china.

'It looks very good,' he said. 'That little shit Leo has asked me to come over this evening.'

'Oh?' Marilyn was wary. She knew how much he hated Gloria's lover. And lover he obviously was. She was so libidinous when he was near, it made Marilyn squirm. And he was playing his part very cleverly. Deferential to King, charming to her, and attentive to Gloria. Marilyn didn't claim to be clever. She had got where she was without brains, but she was acutely streetwise. Leo Derwent was in the game for big stakes. And Harold King knew it.

'Hasn't he asked both of us? That's surprising. He's had a lot of hospitality. It's about time he returned it.'

She sat down and crossed her fine legs, and wiggled her foot. It was a habit he found irritating.

'For Christ's sake stop doing that,' he snarled at her. 'I told you, he wants to see me. He called up while Gloria was here.' He scowled. 'She went on and on at me to go.'

'And you said yes in the end,' Marilyn prompted. 'You always do. She's crazy in love with him, you know.' She couldn't resist needling him, just a little.

'She doesn't know what she's doing,' he said scowling at her now. 'This is the first man she's ever had . . . what do you expect?'

'Well, what did he say? What reason did he give?'

'He said he wanted to discuss something with me. It was very important. I suggested he come here, but he wouldn't do that. And there was Gloria standing beside me, listening and saying, "Oh please, Daddy; please, Daddy, he does want to talk to you." So I said yes, I'd go. If he thinks he's got a proposition with my daughter, he can bloody well think again.'

His wife looked at him. He was jealous of Leo Derwent. He hated the idea of his daughter shacking up with anyone. Personally she couldn't imagine how anyone would want to; she was so big, so brutal, with her clumsy body and mannish ways. Drooling like a lovesick girl over the mean-faced, foxy man. If only King was right and he wanted to marry her . . . what a relief it would be to get her out of the house and leave Marilyn some space . . . She said softly, 'Don't be too hard on them. You could lose Gloria over this. If she's really in love, she'll never forgive you if you scare him off.'

King looked at her with contempt. He understood her motives, and maternal concern wasn't one of them.

'You think I'm a fool? I'm not going to get heavy. I don't want to alienate my daughter. I'll buy him off. And he'll be bought.'

'I'll go and tell Monique we're ready for lunch,' his wife said. She permitted herself a rare oath of disappointment when she was out of his hearing.

'I don't understand,' Hugh Hamilton said. 'What do you mean she's gone?'

It had been a difficult scene that became distressing when Julia's mother burst into tears. Ben had come down with the letter and said brutally, goaded by his own feelings, 'You needn't expect Julia for dinner. Or for anything else, either. She's gone to Switzerland.'

He was torn between anger and pain; he had no time for social niceties. She had deceived them all, planned it well ahead and simply taken off, leaving with lies to her parents and that letter for him. He dismissed what she had written about loving him. He rejected out of hand her plea for understanding of why she had to go without telling him . . .

You would have tried to stop me or come with me and I couldn't have stood the pressure. It's taken all my courage as it is . . .

Courage. He had exploded when he read that. Obstinacy, foolhardiness. And, above all, upside-down priorities. Never mind about her family, never mind about him. She has to go on and try to win . . . Seeing May Hamilton in tears calmed him down. He had apologized. There was no use alarming them. It wasn't fair. They didn't know what had happened at the flat. It wasn't the time to tell them now.

So he lied to them. It was a job offer, he said. She knew he didn't want her to take it, so she went off without telling him. He was hurt and angry, but he had no right to take it out on them. They'd been so kind to him and Lucy. It might be better if they packed up and went back to London. They wouldn't hear of it. May Hamilton recovered quickly; she made light of her tears and said she was just a foolish old woman. 'Please stay and don't upset Lucy.' When did he think Julia would be back? He couldn't answer.

I don't know how long this will take, but I've got to see it through to the end. I wish I could tell you about it, but I will when I get back. Promise me you'll listen.

'I don't know,' Ben had to tell them. 'It may take some days. She didn't give an indication. If you're sure . . . of course we'll stay. It's done Lucy so much good. Thanks.'

The rest of the day and the evening had been a strain of which his daughter was unaware, with forced *bonhomie* on all their parts for her benefit. Ben was glad to excuse himself early. He felt like getting drunk. But he couldn't. He wanted to be alone, but the bed where they'd made love, and she'd sidestepped his idea of marriage, was no place for him to sleep. Marriage, commitment, they weren't for her. He had been building a fantasy world for both of them. No cosy domestic future with a child of their own instead of a cat . . . Her career came first. It had always come first, and he had refused to face that. She was going to confront Harold King. She had said it in those words, and then added something that turned his stomach with jealousy. *I won't be in any danger. There'll be someone with me.* Someone. Not him. Who? Who could she ask to go on such an assignment? Felix Sutton. Sutton had been the one she'd called on after the attempt to kill her. She'd been out drinking with Sutton that same evening. Sutton, the ex-boxer, must be the 'someone' she'd taken with her. *He* was too cautious, too bound up with Lucy . . . He wouldn't be up to the challenge. He was too old.

He slipped downstairs in the small hours and helped himself to Hugh Hamilton's whisky. Then he dialled Felix Sutton's home number. Officially the holiday was over, all newspapers were working, but not necessarily the political staff. The House was in Christmas recess. He swallowed the neat spirit and tipped more into the glass as he let the phone ring. He wanted to yell, Answer . . . Answer, you bastard . . . But there was no reply, and no taped message. Sutton wasn't home.

He went back upstairs and fell asleep on top of the bed without getting into it. When he woke in the morning he realized he couldn't spend another night in the Hamiltons' house. He said to Hugh, 'I'm afraid I raided your Scotch last night. I couldn't sleep. I must buy you a bottle.'

'Don't talk rubbish. I raided it myself.' He lowered his voice slightly so that his wife wouldn't hear him in the adjoining kitchen. 'All this upset, it's so bad for May. I'm sorry to say this, but what Julia's done was very selfish. We thought she'd changed in the last few months. For a long time she thought of nothing but getting on and getting to the top. We hardly saw her . . . I'm going to say something when she does come back. Lying and walking out like that. Especially on you. It's just not good enough. I hope she'll think this damned job is worth it.'

'If she brings it off,' Ben said bitterly, 'I don't think she'll care. I have to tell you, I think this is the end of the road for us, anyway. And I'd better get back to London. I lost my job, too. People forget about you if you're away from the action. I'll go and get Lucy up and organized. See you and May later.'

When they had gone Hugh came and slipped an arm round his wife's shoulders.

'He was so hurt,' she said. 'He looked dreadful, as if he hadn't slept. I just can't understand my own daughter.'

'Well, we're not going to try,' he said firmly. 'All I can say is that she'll regret it. He's a good man and he'd have made her happy. No, darling, you're not cooking lunch. I rang up

Tom and they've asked us over. We can spend the day with our grandchildren. That'll cheer us both up.'

'This is grim,' Leo Derwent remarked, looking round the small residents' lounge. 'Are you the only one here?'

'No,' Julia answered. 'Two couples and one woman. She's English, but she spends all day skiing and goes to bed early, I think she said good morning once. Anyway, I didn't come here to have fun.'

His condescension irritated her. She recognized it as a sign of nervous tension. When she was uptight she snapped for very little reason. Ben teased her about a redheaded temper. She dared not think of Ben. Leo had asked for whisky and soda. She had ordered wine for herself.

'He didn't want to come to me,' Leo said. 'Tried to get me to go over there. But Gloria talked him into it. She thinks I'm going to ask for her hand in marriage.'

He had a sneering laugh that grated on Julia. She stared at him, 'You haven't asked her?'

'No, but I might. Depends how this turns out. And she's shown me how to make his favourite drink. He mixes it himself at home. It has to be just right.' He looked at her; he had pale flint-coloured eyes. 'Grenadine, Perrier and freshly squeezed lemon juice.'

She said slowly, 'And he won't taste anything else?'

He shook his head. 'No. I tried it out. With alcohol and without – he likes so much lemon juice and it's so strong it masks the taste of the vodka. He's coming round at six-thirty. So you'd better arrive at about seven. I can keep him talking and get two drinks into him. He swallows the stuff like water. I've noticed when I've been at the chalet. I must admit,' he said suddenly, 'it could be very interesting when you walk through that door. Aren't you just the teeniest bit nervous?' He mocked her to disguise his own apprehension.

'No, not nervous. Scared witless,' Julia answered. 'And so are you. I've brought the tape for you. Here.'

It was so small it fitted into her purse; a narrow oblong box less than six inches across.

'It's simple; you just set it and it's voice activated. The range is thirty feet minimum. Just put it on a table out of sight. It'll record up to two hours.'

He weighed it in his hand. 'It's small enough.'

'They come much smaller,' Julia pointed out. 'But they're not so accurate and the range is less. We want every word clear.'

'What a dirty business journalism is,' he remarked. 'Almost as dirty as politics.'

'I'm glad you said that instead of me. I'll be there just before seven. But what happens if by any chance he hasn't drunk the stuff?'

'They'll ring through from reception when you arrive,' he answered. 'If anything's gone wrong, I'll tell them I'm busy and will meet you in the bar. Don't worry, I've thought of everything. My head's on the block too, don't forget.'

Julia stood up. She held out her hand. 'It'll be worth the risk. He's an evil man, Leo. It's time someone stopped him. Good luck.'

He shook her hand briefly. He still had that limp clasp she remembered all those years ago when she met him with William Western. Somewhere, buried in a box file, was the unpublished profile she had done on him. It was ironic that they should have come together in any common enterprise. 'Good luck to you too,' he said. 'We're both going to need it.'

Then he was gone, and as he left, the young French couple poked their heads round the door, saw Julia sitting alone, smiled at her briefly, and retreated. It was the last evening she wanted to spend alone.

11

'Daddy,' Gloria said, 'you will be nice to him, won't you?'

Harold King was in a bad mood. He didn't want to leave his own home and drive to the Regent Hotel. It disturbed his evening. The meeting with Leo Derwent hung over his day like a cloud. Gloria's pleading annoyed him. 'She's crazy in love with him,' Marilyn had said. She was certainly behaving as if she was, and that enraged him. He didn't soften when she clung to his arm and smiled up at him.

'Depends what he wants,' he snapped. 'If it's some political cock-up and he thinks he can make use of me . . . I *won't* be nice!'

She looked away from him. 'I'm sure it's not anything like that,' she said defensively. 'He'd never try and take advantage of you.'

'He knows he wouldn't get away with it, that's why.'

Gloria stepped back from him. 'Supposing he wants to talk about me?'

He glared. 'Why should he? What about you?'

'About our relationship,' she said. She felt close to tears. He had a bruising way with other people; she wasn't used to it, and it hurt.

'Your relationship is no business of mine. What are you, for Christ's sake, a child? You're sleeping with him and that's nothing to do with me. You know what I think of him, and I haven't changed my mind. I'm going, and it had better be something important or I'll have his balls!' He swung away from her.

Gloria blinked back tears. She started to get angry. He was being deliberately brutish and difficult. She didn't know for certain why Leo wanted to see him in private, but there had been hints . . . 'If you ever do decide to get married,' he'd mused one day, 'your father would have to agree first.'

She had allowed herself to think of something more permanent than the episodic lovemaking, the evenings spent together at the theatre and the opera, and the days they had to spend apart. When she did spend a full night with him, which was not too often because her father didn't like it, she enjoyed making him breakfast and pandering to his little whims. It satisfied her need to feel enslaved instead of guilty.

She found her mother watching television. King had satellites and could tune in anywhere. Marilyn loved Sky TV. She had never had a serious interest in her life, Gloria thought.

'Has your father gone?' She glanced up and then said, 'You look upset – anything the matter?'

Gloria had never confided in her mother. She had never shared anything with her. They had been incompatible from the start. She had never ever criticized her father to her. Gloria said sharply, 'No – nothing! Do we *have* to watch this crap?'

Marilyn was used to her rudeness. She shrugged. 'You don't. There's a set in the library, there are sets all over the house. But I'm watching this one. And I'm not changing channels.' She heard her daughter slam the door as she went out.

Leo hadn't felt so nervous since he stood up in the House and made his maiden speech. His stomach was churning, and it heaved when reception phoned through to say Mr King was in the lobby.

'Ask someone to bring him up,' he said.

Good manners required him to go down and greet Gloria's father, but he dared not risk a suggestion to go to the bar . . . He was in the corridor when King emerged from the lift, following a page boy.

'Good-evening, Harold,' he said, coming forward. He slipped a few francs to the boy and guided King to his room. 'Sorry I couldn't come down when you arrived, but I was in the middle of a call from London. Official business. They never leave you alone . . . '

King grunted. Call from London . . . Self-important little sod, trying to impress him. He looked round the room aggressively. 'This is nice,' he said. 'Must be costing Gloria a packet.'

'Please sit down.' Leo's freckled skin tinged with pink at the jibe, but he smiled at King and added, 'It's very nice of you to come; I do appreciate it. And I have your special all ready for you.' He turned to the table with the jug of rosy grenadine and lemon juice. Ice cubes bobbed on the surface. He had poured half a bottle of 80 proof vodka into the mixture and stirred it vigorously to distribute the spirit. He had sipped some himself. No taste; just the bitter-sweet mix of lemon and grenadine, that was the advantage of vodka; it was flavourless and didn't smell on the breath. His hand shook slightly as he poured out a glass and then added Perrier. He stirred once more with a long cocktail spoon and handed the drink to Harold King. 'I've been coached by Gloria,' he said. 'I hope that's how you like it?'

King took it and set it down beside him. 'What's this all about, Leo? Why do you want to see me?'

Leo took a deep breath. 'I'll get myself a glass of wine,' he said. He poured some chablis for himself and came and sat down opposite Harold King. He couldn't take his eyes away from that untouched drink. He swigged it down in a few swallows when he was at home. But not this time. He sat and glared at Leo, emanating hostility.

'Well?' He raised his voice.

Leo lifted his glass of wine. 'Your very good health,' he said, and waited.

King didn't respond.

'I asked you to meet me in private because I've got something rather . . . well, personal to talk over with you. See how you feel about it. Is that drink all right?'

'How do I know when I haven't tried it!' King snapped. 'Get to the point, can't you? Stop waffling.' It was Gloria, he knew that now. The little creep was going to sound him out about Gloria. He felt a rush of anger. His pulse rate began to rise.

'I've been seeing Gloria for some time,' Leo began. His throat felt so dry he sipped more wine before he could continue. The ice was melting in that untouched drink by King's elbow.

'I know that,' King interrupted. 'I can't say I'm impressed by her choice, but that's her business.'

'I know you aren't happy about it,' Leo was losing hope. He'd been there long enough and hadn't touched the drink. It wasn't going to work. At any moment he might just lose his temper if Leo got it wrong and walk out. Julia mustn't come up. The whole bloody plan was going wrong. He said, 'She told me how you feel about me. I don't blame you. If I had a daughter like Glory, I'd be protective, too. That's why I wanted to reassure you.'

King looked at him. 'I don't need reassurance from you. I don't know what the hell you're talking about.' He shifted forward in his chair. It was the attitude of someone about to get up.

Leo risked everything. 'I'm in love with her,' he said. 'I've never been in love with anyone before. I've never met a woman like her. She's got everything, brains, poise, personality . . . '

King sat back in his chair. He said in a flat voice, 'She's ugly.' Then he reached out and took the glass and drank very deeply from it as if he was thirsty.

'Not to me, she isn't,' Leo said. He tried not to look, but a second's glance showed King had drunk half of the lethal mixture in one swallow.

'She's not ugly. She's different, she's not a bimbo.'

He got up, he felt excited, all his nervousness had disappeared. He said, 'Let me refresh that for you,' and taking King's glass he refilled it to the brim and handed it to him.

'She's rich,' he said. 'She could give you everything you want, that's what you mean. She's my daughter and you could ride to the top with me behind you. Isn't that what you really mean, you little bastard?'

Leo couldn't be sure he detected a change. He went on, 'I've told you, I love Gloria. She's in love with me. I haven't talked to her about marriage. I wouldn't, till I'd had a chance to discuss it with you.'

King leaned forward. 'Well, you've discussed it,' he said, 'and the answer is no. Not in a million years will I let my girl marry a fucker like you.'

His voice had grown louder, the German accent more pronounced. Leo stayed calm. He said in a pleasant way, 'You don't have to insult me, Harold. I've told you, I understand how you feel. She's your only daughter, you're very close in every way. You don't want to lose her. But you've nothing to fear from me. I'm not the possessive type.'

He got up again, and as he passed the table on the other side of King's chair, he switched on the little tape recorder hidden behind a pile of magazines. He filled his glass with wine and turned to Harold King. 'I'm glad you like my mixture,' he said. 'One more refill?'

And then the phone rang. Leo answered it. He smiled and said, 'Yes, up to my room, please.' He came over with the jug this time. The glass was empty. King had drained it while he was speaking. He looked different, Leo realized; his features were suffused with red, his nose seemed enlarged and his mouth had slackened.

The eyes were bright and glowing with a demonic rage. For a moment Leo's elation waned. He felt afraid. Then there was a knock at the door. King didn't seem to hear it. 'Another,' he snarled at Leo, holding out his glass. 'Fill me up, *dummkopf*! Marry my daughter . . . ' He started to laugh. 'She likes her bottom smacked, that's all you mean to her!'

Leo had gone to open the door. He said quietly, 'Come in,

Julia.' He glanced back at Harold King and nodded to her. 'He's pissed,' he murmured and then stood aside to let her pass. Julia hadn't seen him since that night in the restaurant when he was showing off by bullying the manager. He had looked so powerful, almost bestial then. Now he was *louche*, sprawling, his limbs at an angle, his face red and bloated.

She stared at him. Her heart was beating so hard she felt it in her throat. Leo was right. King was drunk. Drunk and dangerous, his eyes travelling over her, resting on her face. She said, 'Good-evening, Mr King. I'm Julia Hamilton.'

'I know you,' he said. 'I remember that ugly red hair. I won't have anyone with that hair in my building. You stink like foxes. You're Western's bint, aren't you?'

'No,' she said. 'I'm not anyone's bint. I don't sleep with my employer.'

'More bloody fool him, then,' King sneered. 'If you worked for me you'd have to dye that mop.'

'I wouldn't work for you,' Julia answered.

Leo said, 'Why don't you sit down, Julia. Like a glass of wine?'

'Try some of my special mixture,' King heaved himself up from the chair. 'Go on, try it. This little creep that's screwing my daughter made it for me. Trying to curry favour, aren't you? He thinks he can fool me . . . You know I can't be fooled, don't you? Nobody fools me.'

'I'm sure they don't,' Julia said. 'I'll have some wine, please, Leo. Thanks.' As she took the glass he saw her hand was shaking. But she was composed, very cool; he had to admire her for the way she was handling the brute.

'I've always been curious about you, Mr King. I've wanted to interview you. But you don't give interviews to Western journalists, do you?'

'The only thing I give to anyone working for that little shit is a kick up the backside,' he snarled, suddenly aggressive. His eyes raked her up and down, lingering on her legs. She uncrossed them and pulled down her skirt to cover her knees. He said, 'Western fired you, didn't he? Why don't you come and work for me? You've got brains, even if you haven't any tits. Why don't you come and work for me, eh? Why don't you? What did that shit pay you? I'll double it!'

He was swaying on his feet. Julia said, 'Why don't you sit down, Mr King, and we can talk about it.'

He shrugged his big shoulders, his mood changing abruptly. 'Why not?' He repeated it as he lowered himself back into his chair. 'Why not.'

'Would you like to talk to me about yourself?' Julia asked. 'Now that I'm here, there's such a lot I want to know about you.'

King leaned his head back. 'Like what? The story of my life and achievements – I'll send you the book . . . it's very heart-warming.' He broke into laughter, coarse and raucous. 'But that's not what you're after, is it? You've given me a lot of trouble, snooping . . . You're good at it, you know that? Better than any of the other hacks. You were getting close, weren't you? But then it all went wrong. You found out about that little shit Western. So he threw you out. You realize that saved your life?'

Leo bit back an exclamation. Julia was very pale. 'Yes,' she said. 'I expect it did. I met a Mr Richard Watson in Jersey. I asked him a question. We were talking about the last war. I asked him if he'd ever killed anyone.'

Harold King cleared his throat. For a moment she thought he was going to spit on the carpet. 'Not him,' he jeered. 'A real English gentleman, a man of principles . . . an arsehole in my book.'

Julia waited. It was coming close now, the crucial moment. He was drunk, but was he drunk enough?

'In your book, then,' she said quietly, 'people do get killed? If I asked you the same question I asked him, what would you answer?'

'Oh, very clever, aren't you! I'll ask you a question . . . what's so special about dying? Everyone dies in the end. What's it matter when . . . ?'

He pulled himself up in the chair; he turned and looked at Leo. 'You put something in that drink, didn't you?' Leo said nothing. King hunched his shoulders, gathering his body as if he was going to propel himself out of the chair and launch himself on Leo.

Now, Julia decided, before he goes out of control . . .

Her voice cut across the tension. 'You called me a bint, Mr King. That's a wartime expression. It's Arabic, isn't it? You learned it in the Western Desert, didn't you? You were with Rommel's Afrika Corps. What did you do out there, Mr King, that you've taken so much time and trouble to hide for all these years? Murder unarmed British prisoners?'

He had started by laughing, then he talked and talked, the truth flooding out in a tide neither Julia nor Leo could have stemmed. The vile and brutal truth about what he had done. Suddenly he stopped. He glared at them. Then he lurched at Leo, both fists upraised like hammers to strike at him. He was yelling. 'I'm drunk. I'm drunk and you did it . . . you spiked my drink with something . . . I'll kill you . . . ' Leo was quick on his feet; he side-stepped easily and impelled by his own weight, King crashed into the wall and almost fell. Leo had retreated to a safe distance, safe enough for him to gloat and shout back in defiance.

'You bet I did. You've had half a bottle of vodka in that filthy pink muck, and you're pissed out of your skull! And you've opened your big mouth wide . . . '

Hitting the wall had steadied King. He pulled himself upright and leaned against the door. He had told her everything. He'd talked and he couldn't stop himself. He was out of control, just like the night when he confessed to his wife, Phyllis Lowe, and pursued her upstairs to rape and beat her in a fury of rage and lust because he had betrayed himself.

The same with this woman, standing out of reach behind a sofa, that hideous hair flaming in the light. He had been unable to stop the flow of words, the rush of memories. He'd dragged her back with him into the past, back to the heat and sand-filled dust of the North African desert, as if she were a witness born out of her time.

Leo's voice taunted him. 'You tried to ruin me, you rotten bastard. You set me up with your paid whore and sold the evidence to Western . . . But I've been bonking your daughter, and I've got some pretty pictures of my own now!'

'You'll pay for this,' King shouted him down. 'I'll make you pay—'

'You threaten me,' Leo jeered. 'You try anything and I'll have the hotel throw you out! You're finished, bust . . . We've got it all on tape!'

As he said it, Julia reached over and slipped the little tape recorder into her purse. King had blundered about like a maddened bear, and she had heard Leo shout at her, 'Look out, Julia . . . ' and sprang out of his way.

Just as abruptly, his strength seemed exhausted. He was breathing hard, glaring from one to the other of them. He held onto the door.

'You can't touch me,' he said, and he seemed less than drunk. 'You can't threaten me, either of you. I made the whole story up. There's nothing you can do to me . . . I'm too powerful – I'm more powerful than God!' He drew himself upright. Then he wrenched the door open, and stumbled out into the passage.

'Oh my God,' Julia said. She sank down onto the sofa. 'My God,' she repeated, 'I feel completely gutted. I'm shaking all over.'

'Well I'm not,' Leo exulted. 'We got him. Between us we got the bastard. Come on, he's finished. I'll take that tape to the right quarters and he'll be arrested as a war criminal. Christ, I'm going to order a bottle of champagne . . . '

'Not for me,' Julia said. 'After that scene I couldn't celebrate anything.'

Leo stared at her. 'What's wrong with you? You should be dancing on the bloody table. You've got the evidence . . . a full confession. Everything you could have wanted. Let's switch on and run through it. Here, where's it gone?'

He was searching among the magazines on the table, peering down to see if it had fallen to the floor. 'Where is it?' He swung round in alarm.

'I've got it,' Julia said. 'Leo, I'm sorry. I want to listen to it on my own. Then you can have it. We should get copies made as soon as possible. And make sure the original goes to the right people. We'll have to give affidavits swearing to its authenticity and in witness of what happened here. We haven't won yet. When he sobers up, he'll fight.'

'Practical lady, aren't you?' he mocked her. 'Very cool head. What do you have in your veins, anti-freeze? Never mind, you go home and have a listen and I'll come round and pick it up later. Meantime, *I'm* going to celebrate. I've just thought . . . ' He stopped and then he said, 'I wonder if he had his driver tonight? Those roads up to his chalet are pretty tricky . . . Now that *is* a thought.' And he laughed.

Julia stood up. 'I'd rather he stood trial,' she said quietly. 'It's owed to all those people.' She left without saying good night.

'I'm drunk,' King said aloud to himself. 'I'm drunk. I shouldn't be driving.' They'd brought his car to the hotel entrance and he'd managed to steer it out and onto the road. His vision wasn't clear and his reactions were muddled. He pulled in. He could wait, even sleep for a while till the booze wore off. He'd talked about himself. He'd lost control. But his God-like vision of himself insisted that he had nothing to fear. He could crush the pygmies with a gesture. He switched off the engine and wriggled down in the seat to get comfortable. Thoughts, wild and disconnected, danced like goblins in his mind when he closed his eyes so he abandoned the idea of sleeping. He would rest, give his formidable system time to absorb the poison and dispel it. Then he would drive home. He switched on the radio; Swiss popular music assaulted his ears. He pushed the button several times at random till he found the BBC World Service. That was better. Listen to things of importance, events of moment. That was his world, his *métier*, not unimportant crap from an old war that nobody cared about any more. Nothing could touch him; no law could reach him. He could buy immunity from anything. World issues were his concern. He opened the window an inch to let in some fresh air, and settled down to listen and sober up.

Julia went straight up to her room. She put the tape recorder on the table. The voices were clear. The opening gambit of her confrontation with him, 'What did you do out there, Mr King . . . ? Murder unarmed British prisoners . . . ?' How confident she sounded, how calm. No sign of the pounding heart, the feeling of apprehension.

'What do you have in your veins, anti-freeze . . . ?' Leo Derwent had sneered at her. He wanted to savour his personal triumph. If King had dropped dead in the room, he'd have kicked the corpse. By the end, Julia had felt numb. King, voice rising, accent thickening, jeering and insulting them, falling into the trap.

'What did you do out there, Mr King, that you've taken so much time and trouble to hide for all these years?' And he had told her. The voice didn't sound slurred or the sequences confused. It was a strong voice, full of self-confidence and contempt.

'We were on patrol . . . Armoured cars . . . We picked up one of our own men – he'd been taken prisoner and been left behind—' Her own voice interrupting him. 'What do you mean? You were the one they captured!' His brusque denial, 'Me? No, I wouldn't have surrendered. I was a German soldier by Christ! I wouldn't let the enemy piss on me! This was just a boy . . . he'd got a leg wound, no weapons . . . But I didn't like him for putting his hands up. He told us where to find the British. We came on them, two officers, an NCO and four men. They didn't even fight, yellow bastards. They put the officers in a lorry and then I laid into the kid, in front of the rest of them. I kicked his arse and told him he was a disgrace to the Corps. Nobody tried to stop me. I was tough. I scared them. They looked the other way. I got so angry with the kid . . . then he told me. He told me they were going to kill him. He knew a bit of English and he heard them talking. Going to stick him with a bayonet. Like a bloody pig.' The angry voice filled the bedroom. She felt as if she might look up and see him standing there. Then her own tones, still deceptively calm and unemotional. 'So what did you do, Mr King?'

'I said to the boy, don't you worry, forget I kicked you around a bit. I'll sort them out for you. And just you remember, you're a German soldier! You ever forget that and

I'll kill you . . . It was so hot. I remember, I'd got prickly heat in my crotch and under the arms, the itch was driving me crazy. We had some brandy in the scout car. One of us had pinched it off a dead officer. We made the British form up and marched them back towards our base. We went on ahead with our machine-gun trained on them. Any move and that was it . . . Their sergeant was leading them. And you know who he was, don't you? You found out when you went to Jersey, eh? William Western. Lord Western of Bradenham.' His ugly laugh boomed out, 'Peer of the realm, upholder of public morals . . . Wanting my hide just to save himself . . . You heard the story, didn't you?'

'Yes', Julia's answer. 'I heard it. But I thought you were the prisoner they were going to kill.' He wasn't listening to her, caught up in his own flow of words. 'I watched them trudging through the sand, all set for a nice base prison camp and then back to Germany and out of the war, while we had to fight on, and maybe die.' He paused then. The tension had been broken suddenly by Leo Derwent. 'So tell us, Harold, what did you do about it?'

'Do?' King sounded like a lion. 'Do?' It was a roar, and it ended in a sharp German expletive. '*Scheisse!* I'll tell you what I did. I took over the machine-gun and I started to play with it, swinging it from one to the other of them, making them sweat. Like the kid sweated when he was going to be stuck . . . I had fun with them, real fun.' Listening to the disembodied voice, Julia shuddered. 'I called the kid and he came to the back of the scout car and sat with me. I said, "You know English? You tell them . . . you tell them I'm going to teach them to respect the rules of war . . . You tell them that . . . " And he did; I'd given him a few sucks at the bottle, and he was shouting at them. You know what happened? Western turned and ran like a fucking rabbit, left his men and ran to save his own skin. So I gave him the first burst and dropped him. He hadn't got far. Then . . . ' There had been a deliberate pause for dramatic effect. 'Then I shot the rest of them. I just kept my finger on the trigger and went on firing, making them jump about on the ground . . . Raised so much bloody dust it got into my throat . . . Then the stupid kid started to vomit. Perhaps it was the brandy or the corpses. I don't know, but he hung over the side of the car, puking his guts out.' There was a breathless, 'Jesus,' from Leo in the background.

King didn't notice. He went on, 'But I made a mistake. I didn't stop the car and go and check. That shit was hit but he was still alive. One of our patrols came along later and picked him up and took him to hospital. I thought I was safe. I thought I'd killed them all. We were back at base when I heard about it; some talk about British casualties being caught in crossfire and only one survivor. In the very same place on the same day . . . I knew then it could mean trouble for me. When we lost the war I knew it might mean big trouble. So I deserted, got myself in as a refugee . . . Faked the whole story . . . Clever, wasn't I? Poor stateless, homeless victim . . . I was so thin I even looked the part. We hadn't eaten for days on end, grubbing for roots and berries like bloody animals . . . Then the nice lady from UNRRA took pity. All she wanted was my hand up her skirt.' His laughter rasped in Julia's ears. 'Crossfire,' he said. 'He thought that up to hide his own stinking cowardice. Running off, leaving his own men . . . *I* was the crossfire!'

She remembered so vividly, seeing him get to his feet, reaching the climax of his self-imposed performance. His harsh voice rising in exultation. 'I killed them all,' he shouted. 'And you know something? I'm proud of it . . . Proud . . . I'd do it all again if I had the chance!'

Then her own voice broke in, a scream of loathing.

'You bloody murderer! You filthy bloody murderer! You'll go to jail for the rest of your life . . . You had Jean Adams murdered . . .' And then she had broken down in a flood of tears. He had answered with surprising calmness, almost indifference.

'She asked for it. She was stupid. Stupid meddling little bitch . . .' The next sound was a crash as he knocked a side table over and the splinter of glass as it crashed to the floor. She heard her own gasp and Leo's shout of warning, 'Look out,' as he sprang to safety himself. Without warning, Harold King had gone berserk. He had lashed out blindly, and then launched himself at Leo Derwent, hurling himself into the wall. The tape played it all back to her, the shouting, Leo's taunting voice, the megalomania of that last boast as King was leaving.

'There's nothing you can do . . . I'm too powerful . . . I'm more powerful than God . . . '

Julia switched off the machine. She felt sick and exhausted. The last piece of the jigsaw was in place, and the hideous story of cowardice, treachery and evil was complete. She had been duped by William Western. He was a coward who had deserted his comrades and lied about their murder to protect himself. He'd lived with that betrayal, safely buried with the bones of his own men until his enemy and rival Harold King had unearthed an ex-officer with a tender conscience living in retirement in Jersey.

Both were public figures, neither recognized each other after thirty years. That was the irony. Why should King connect a British infantry sergeant with the millionaire newspaper owner, Lord Western? Why should Western identify the mega-rich King with a drunken German sitting behind a machine-gun?

When King went on trial it would all come up. The two would be each other's Nemesis. Leo might drink champagne in triumph, but for Julia there were too many losers to warrant any celebration. King's description would haunt her for a very long time. Perhaps she would never get it out of her mind. 'I just kept my finger on the trigger and went on firing, making them jump about on the ground . . . So much bloody dust . . . ' Jean Adams, his casual dismissal, 'She asked for it . . . Stupid, meddling little bitch.' She had died an obscene death. Poor deluded Phyllis Lowe, in love for the first time. She had ended in a brain-damaged twilight. No, Julia thought, there was nothing to celebrate except that justice would be done to all of them at last. The shrill of the telephone made her jump. It was Leo Derwent. He sounded in high spirits and slightly drunk.

'Julia? Had a listen yet?'

'Yes,' she said. 'You can pick up the tape any time you like now. I'm going to bed. I'll leave it downstairs for you.'

'We won't be needing it,' he said. 'Get over here. The bastard's dead.'

* * *

Gloria had been waiting for her father. She avoided the sitting room where her mother was immersed in some mindless TV quiz show. The vacuity and banality of her mind amazed Gloria and made her furious with contempt. She read the financial papers in the study and tried not to watch the time and wonder what was happening with Leo.

He had been secretive and teasing with her, refusing to be drawn when she asked him what it was he wanted to see King about . . . about her? In a way, yes . . . But why, why wouldn't he elaborate? Then the hints, the sly looks and the hard probing kiss with the injunction to open her mouth and stop talking. She switched on the big set, ranged through the channels and found nothing to interest or distract her. If he did want to marry her, would she want to take such a big step? Leave home, commit herself to another man than her father – leave that stupid woman with a clear sphere of influence . . . ? She havered, clinging onto Harold King, yearning for Leo at the same time. How late he was! Her own dilemma had made her forget that it was past their time for dinner together.

Nine o'clock. What were they discussing? What was happening? She reached for the telephone to call the Regent Hotel when she heard the front door open. Immediately she sprang up and ran out into the hall. He was standing there, still in his heavy overcoat; he was so red in the face, so odd and unlike himself that she hurried up and caught him by the arm.

'Daddy? Daddy, what's the matter – are you ill?'

He didn't answer. He just looked at her with bloodshot eyes, and put his free arm round her, drawing her close.

'What is it? Daddy, for God's sake . . . '

'I'm all right,' he said. He sounded out of breath. 'Just don't ask me any questions. Don't take any notice of me. Leave everything till the morning. You're my girl and I love you.'

He lifted her face up and kissed her on the forehead. He seemed unable to let go. She had never been so frightened as she was then. Not of him, but for him. It gave her unexpected strength. 'I won't ask anything,' she said. 'Just come and sit down. You need a doctor . . . you don't look at all well. Not at all well.'

He let her guide him to the study, take off his coat, minister to him as if he were a big, helpless child. He sank into his favourite chair.

'I'll get Doctor Halperin,' Gloria said and moved to the telephone. He must have had a heart attack. She couldn't think what else it might be. That terrible red, purplish colour, the laboured breathing . . .

'No!' His voice was loud and rough and it stopped her. 'No! I don't need a doctor. Leave that alone.' She put down the telephone. He said slowly, 'My darling girl, I didn't mean to shout at you. I'm not ill, believe me. Just get me a glass of water, will you? That's all, iced water.'

She opened the cabinet where there was a supply of iced Perrier and soft drinks always at hand for him. She poured a glass and hurried back with it.

'Here you are. Do you want anything else . . . anything to eat? It's so late for you . . . ' She had forgotten Leo Derwent. She thought only of her father in her terror that something was wrong and he wouldn't admit it.

'Nothing,' he sounded breathless again. 'Nothing to eat. There's nothing to worry about, silly girl. I'm not sick. I'm never sick, you know that. Just do as I say. Switch on the news, will you, and go out and leave me for a while. Leave me alone till I call you. And give me a kiss. I'm proud of you. Never forget that. Now go on and don't worry about me . . . '

She did as he told her; she switched on the set and gave him the remote control. She bent over and kissed him, and went out, closing the door quietly. Her mother came into the hallway. 'Is he back? What happened? How did it go?'

'He didn't say,' Gloria cut her off. 'He doesn't seem well, but he won't let me call Doctor Halperin. He wants to be left alone for a while. Don't go in. He doesn't want you!'

Marilyn shrugged. 'No need to shout. I know his moods better than anyone. Look, I've told Monique to serve supper. She can't wait all night. I take it he's not eating with us?'

'No,' Gloria snapped. 'I asked him.'

She looked backwards at the closed door. She could just hear the faint murmur of the English television newscaster. Gloria's anxiety always expressed itself in hunger. She devoured potatoes, two omelettes, and stuffed herself with the hot fresh rolls and butter. Her mother said to her at last, 'You're such a pig, Gloria. You shouldn't eat so much.' She gave her a look of malice. 'Perhaps your father and Leo have had a row. Maybe you should go and see if he's all right?'

'He'll call me, he said so. Why don't you go? You never take any care of him. All you think about is yourself!'

Marilyn ignored that. 'I think I'll have some fresh fruit. Oh, Monique, bring me some grapes and some of those nectarines . . . they are ready, aren't they? Good. You want anything more, Gloria . . . Chocolate torte, ice cream?'

'I hate you, Mother,' Gloria said when the maid had gone.

'I know,' the beautiful smooth face was quite impassive. 'You've never said that to me before. Why now, suddenly?'

'I'm going to see how my father is,' Gloria stood up. She turned her back on Marilyn. The door to the study was open. The room was empty. The fire was low. The television set was blank, with the single red eye glowing below the screen.

The envelope with her name on it was propped on top of it where she couldn't fail to see it. Gloria picked it up; she felt a surge of panic standing in the empty room, opening a letter written to her by her father. He had fine handwriting, legacy of a teacher who expected a fine German *Schrift* and got it by the use of a sharpened ruler across his pupils' knuckles. The page was covered in his writing, but it sprawled, as if his hand was unsteady and the pen slipped between his fingers. She read it, mouthing the words.

'My darling Daughter. Something has happened and you have got to be very brave. I employed a man called Joe Patrick. You may have seen him, he came to the house once or twice. He took care of problems for me. When you are Harold King you need people like that. He has been arrested and charged with murder. I heard it on the car radio tonight. It's just been on the TV news. I gave him a special job to do and he bungled it. He will implicate me. I'm not going to stand in a court and let them throw mud at me. My enemies would love it. So many people want to see me brought down. I won't give them that satisfaction. And you wouldn't want me to. I know that. So I write this letter to you, because when it's written I am going out and I won't be coming back. Everything is in order; you will want for nothing, your mother is well provided for. I saw Leo Derwent tonight. He tried to blackmail me with photographs of what you did together. Now you know what he is worth, you will know what to do when he tries to come back. He will, once I am gone. I have left you great power and all the money you can imagine. Use them as I would have done. You are part of me – I shall go on living through you. No-one but you must read this letter. Destroy it. Always remember two things: you are my daughter, and I am your loving Daddy to the end.'

Gloria knelt by the fire, poked at the smouldering logs until a little flame spurted and then fed the letter to it till it blazed up briefly and then fell into ash.

She went on kneeling by the fire, not moving, not even able to weep. The world had come to an end. He had gone and he was never coming back. She was so chill and numb she felt as if she had died with him. She didn't move till she heard the doorbell ringing and then, after an interval, men's voices, and her mother screaming. Slowly she raised herself, smoothed her dress, lifted her head, and went out to take control.

She packed her mother off to bed and summoned the doctor, who gave her an injection. She was interviewed by the police officers in the sitting room. They were sympathetic and very tactful. Harold King's car had been found wrecked on the road to the valley below. He had driven straight into a tree, and died instantly. Privately, they remarked on her extreme composure. She didn't shed a tear. She turned her pale eyes on them and just nodded and said, 'It must have been a heart attack.' And dared them to question that solution.

There would be an inquest, all very unfortunate and distressing for her and her mother, but, of course, the Swiss authorities would make the ordeal as easy for them as possible. She thanked them gravely, and ended the interview by standing up and walking to the door with them. Then she summoned the staff. They gathered round her in the hall, headed by the housekeeper. She was an upright, austere German Swiss who had been with them for ten years. Gloria addressed them.

They looked shocked and subdued; they had felt secure in King's tyranny. Without it they were uneasy. Gloria said, 'You must know by now that my father died in a motor accident tonight. When this is known, the media will come here and we will be under siege. They will turn my father's death into a circus. If any one of you, or any member of your families, is induced to speak to anyone about this, you will be instantly dismissed without a reference. And I will make certain that no-one else in Gstaad ever employs you. My mother is in shock. I won't be taking any calls or receiving any visitors. Without exception. Nobody is to be allowed in. Is that understood?'

The housekeeper took a step forward. 'It's understood, Fräulein Gloria. You can be certain of our loyalty to you and to Frau King. We are all very shocked by this terrible thing that has happened.'

'Thank you,' Gloria said. 'You will be glad to know that it was instantaneous. My father didn't suffer. Good night.'

One by one they filed past her and went through the service door to their own quarters. She put the lights out and locked the doors herself. Then she went upstairs to her own room. She was alone. She would always be alone from now on. The tears began to stream down her face.

Ben had taken Lucy to Euston. On the platform she hugged him. 'Thanks for everything; you've been great to me. Everyone has. And you will come up and see me, won't you?'

'Don't worry,' he assured her. 'I'm not losing you a second time. Give my best to your mother. Call me in a day or two. I'll be at the hotel till I get myself a rented flat.'

Lucy held on to his arm. 'Dad . . . don't lose Julia, will you? She's pretty special. Don't make the same mistake again . . . Like you did with Mum.'

That surprised him. He said, 'What do you mean?'

'Being too proud to make it up. Mum would have gone back if only you'd got in touch. She's happy enough now, but she was miserable for a long time. Don't mind me saying it, will you?'

Ben put his arms around her. 'I don't mind. I'm just sorry I screwed up on all of you. You'd better go, sweetheart – find yourself a decent seat. And don't forget to ring.'

'I won't,' she smiled at him and paused on the step of the carriage to wave. 'Bye, Dad. Don't screw up a second time!'

He turned and walked down the platform and into the body of the station. A muffled announcement about a train departure boomed out over the loudspeakers. He thought it might as well have been Swahili it was so indistinct. As he came out into the street he saw the huge headlines on the *Evening Standard* billboard, HAROLD KING DEAD. He stopped, stared, then rushed to buy the newspaper. More headlines, splashed across the front page. MYSTERY OF TYCOON'S DEATH. FATAL CAR CRASH AT SWISS HOLIDAY RESORT. Ben read it through at speed, only too familiar with the news format. It was unbelievable. King was dead, killed in his car in an unexplained drive from his chalet down twisting roads at night. The information was still sketchy, so speculation was passed on as news. A probable heart attack. His wife and daughter were flying back to England. They were refusing to make any statement. He got into his car and listened to a newsflash. It had a slightly more slanted angle than the newspaper story.

It was reported that the financier and publishing magnate had been seen leaving the Regent Hotel shortly after eight o'clock in a distressed state. Distressed, Harold King . . . It was newspeak for a variety of conditions. He couldn't imagine which one it could be. When he got back to his hotel room there was a message for him.

A Miss Julia Hamilton had called from a Swiss telephone number. What had she done . . . ? She and Felix . . . What part had they played in this incredible development? Or had Fate intervened to settle it for them? He felt sick with jealousy. He banished Lucy's parting words in angry denial. Julia had broken faith with him, turned for support to another man, put her crusade above their relationship . . . He wasn't going to call that number. Or take a call from her if she tried again. He dialled reception and said, 'I'm not accepting any calls from Switzerland,' and the girl said, 'There's a call on the line for you now, Mr Harris. A Mr Sutton . . . Shall I have the switchboard put him through?'

'Yes,' Ben said quickly. 'I'll talk to *him* . . . '

He heard Felix's cheerful voice. 'Are you opening a bottle?'

'Aren't you?' Ben demanded aggressively.

'Bloody amazing, isn't it?' Felix went on blithely. 'Bet Julia's over the moon.'

'You tell me,' Ben snapped at him.

There was a pause, and then Felix said, 'What's that supposed to mean? What's going on? I just rang up to share the glad tidings . . . '

'She's out in Gstaad,' Ben said slowly. 'I thought you were with her . . . '

'Me? I'm in bloody London, in the office . . . Are you off your trolley?'

Ben took a breath and said, 'Not now, but I was . . . Sorry, Felix. What's the word in the office? Was it an accident? What was all that about him being distressed when he left the hotel?'

'About as distressed as a bull elephant,' Felix retorted. 'Rumour going round is he was pissed . . . staggering.'

'He was teetotal . . . never touched booze . . . '

'Well, it sounds like he broke the golden rule last night,' Felix answered. 'Maybe the arrest of that little sleaze-bag Joe Patrick had something to do with it . . . He's been charged with murder – that old widow Julia was so worked up about. All happened within hours, his legman gets picked up, he gets boozed and runs into a tree. Why aren't you at the hot spot? What's Julia doing out there on her own? And why the hell did you think I was with her?'

Ben said, 'Why don't we open that bottle together? If you don't mind drinking with a bloody fool.'

Felix Sutton laughed. 'I'll drink with anyone so long as they're paying. See you around seven.' He hung up.

Joe Patrick had been arrested for Jean Adams' murder. He had been occupied with taking Lucy out to a film and giving her dinner on their last evening together. He hadn't switched on a TV set or opened a newspaper that morning because she was catching an early train. He had missed out on it all till he saw those flaring headlines outside the station.

He switched on the set in time for the twelve thirty news bulletin on ITV. It was the lead item. There were clips of Harold King, comments by media experts and then, staring at him from the screen, William Western.

'A remarkable figure in the world of publishing and communication,' the precise voice intoned, the expression suitably grave. 'We had differences of opinion about a great many issues, but his energy and abilities earned the respect of everyone in the media. His contribution to our industry will be greatly missed.'

'Christ Almighty,' Ben exploded. He snapped the control to 'off', fading that calculating, lying image into darkness.

Then he picked up the telephone and asked for a call to Switzerland.

'I didn't think you'd forgive me,' Julia said. 'I didn't expect you to . . . '

'I didn't think I would, either. When does your flight get in?'

'Six o'clock your time. Ben, I can't wait to get away from here and get home. Are you sure you want to come and meet me? I've got so much to tell you . . . I've got a tape of the whole thing. I wish I felt happy about it, but somehow it's left such a filthy taste . . . I had to do it. I had to follow it through. Please try and understand . . . I tried to explain in my letter.'

'I know,' he said. 'We'll talk about that later. I'm glad about one thing. Jean Adams.'

'That's the best part,' Julia said slowly. 'It helps to make sense of the whole dreadful nightmare. Oh Ben – I do want to talk to you – tell you—'

Ben Harris said, 'We've got a lot to talk over, Julia. I'll see you at six.'

'You came over beautifully, Billy,' Evelyn Western said. 'Just the right balance. Dignified, generous . . . Oh, what a wonderful relief!'

He held her hand under the table. They were lunching at the Connaught; she looked so animated and beautiful, he was proud to show her off.

He felt twenty years younger. He kept smiling all the time. 'Word is,' he told her, 'he committed suicide. There's a lot of rumours flying about . . . he seemed to be drunk when he left the hotel. There was a time lag unaccounted for when he came home and then went out again. And that Irishman being charged with Jean Adams' murder on the very same night . . . I think he realized the game was up, and he killed himself. Well, my darling, here's to him. I only hope hell's hot enough!'

They lifted their glasses of champagne, and drank the toast together. Evelyn Western said gently, 'You've nothing to worry about any more. It's all over.'

William Western looked at her. 'If you wanted a quiet life, Evie, you shouldn't have married me. Hasn't it occurred to you that there's nobody there to pick up the pieces. He only had that daughter. I think the whole thing will be up for grabs. And I'm going to take the first handful.'

'Knowing you,' his wife said calmly, 'you'll take it all.'

'Julia – I thought you were in Switzerland?'

'Felix . . . how are you?'

'Pissed off; Harris asked me round to the hotel for a drink, and never turned up. I had to pay for my own. What the hell happened?'

'He came to the airport to fetch me and forgot,' she said. 'He's here. Do you want to talk to him?'

'No, I don't want to disturb the reunion. Just tell him he owes me.'

'I will,' she promised. 'And, Felix . . . we're getting married. You'll have to come.' She looked across at Ben Harris. 'He says the cat went on hunger strike when I left, that's why he asked me.'

She heard Felix laugh. 'Sooner you than me. But good luck, anyway. You won't be asking for your old job back?'

'I'm quitting journalism. I've got a book to write and a man with a cat to look after. I'll let you know the time and the place.'

Ben Harris came and took the telephone away from her. She reached up to him and said, 'I'm so happy.'

He said before he kissed her, 'So am I.'

It was strange, they admitted, how well she filled her father's chair at the head of the boardroom table. Nothing had been changed in his office except that the portrait of him that used to hang in that same boardroom now hung on the wall opposite his desk, where Gloria King could see it. There were six men sitting there grouped up one end. The finance director, the deputy chairman of a major London Merchant Bank, and a director of Field who had flown in from New York. The company secretary had been Harold King's employee for twenty years. King had trusted him, and bound him to loyalty with share options. There were two other directors present, both seasoned King employees. The principal board meeting would follow in a week's time, followed by an Extraordinary General Meeting of the shareholders. This had been postponed till after the funeral as a mark of respect. The inquest had revealed that Harold King had a high alcohol content in his blood, and the verdict was accidental death. Over two million pounds in Life Assurance had been claimed for his estate.

Gloria sipped from the same carafe of iced water he had used and spoke to them. 'I'm grateful to all of you for your support,' she said. 'It's been a sad and difficult time for my mother and for me. But it's over and my father is at rest. He's left me a daunting legacy, everything he built up and achieved, his plans for the future of one of the biggest and most powerful communications networks in Europe. And he had already involved me in his plans for the future.

'I want you all to know that I am Harold King's daughter, and I shall do what he would have done if he were still alive. We have the money and the means. We will proceed with the bid for Western International and the *Sunday Herald*. That will be announced at the Extraordinary General Meeting.

'Thank you, gentlemen.'

She got up, and one by one they shook hands, and left. She said quietly to the company secretary, 'A word with you, Ken,' and he stayed behind. She said, 'I want a top-class defence lawyer for Joe Patrick. I owe it out of loyalty for work he did for my father. On condition that my father's name is not mentioned during the trial, and anything he may have said in his statement to the police is withdrawn.'

'That can be arranged, Miss King. I know just the QC for the job.'

'Good,' Gloria said bleakly. 'And one more thing. There's a junior minister called Leo Derwent, Department of Trade and Industry. My father didn't trust him. We should bear that in mind when it comes to political editorials.'

He said blandly, 'I'll make sure that message gets across. Anything else?'

'No,' she said. 'Nothing else. You can go now.'

'Good-afternoon, Miss King.'

He paused, but she didn't answer. When a meeting was over, Harold King had never bothered with goodbyes.